Immortali

Anne Lewington

authorHOUSE®

AuthorHouse™ UK Ltd.
1663 Liberty Drive
Bloomington, IN 47403 USA
www.authorhouse.co.uk
Phone: 0800.197.4150

Published by AuthorHouse   02/06/2014

ISBN: 978-1-4918-9330-2 (sc)
ISBN: 978-1-4918-9329-6 (hc)
ISBN: 978-1-4918-9331-9 (e)

Author's Website: www.annelewington.co.uk

Author's Note on the Commedia dell'Arte

That William Shakespeare saw at least one Commedia dell'Arte play is not in doubt.

His ... *lean and slippered Pantaloon*, recruited to represent the sixth age of man in *As You Like It*, is confirmation enough. What is not so widely known is that his comedies owe a great deal to the Commedia scenarios and *Much Ado About Nothing* was a title in regular use by the Italian troupes long before Shakespeare purloined it.

Molière, on the other hand, admits his debt of gratitude to the Italian company in which he learned the actor's craft and where he found inspiration as a playwright, even if he did go on to found the forerunner to the world-famous Comédie Française which put the Théâtre Italien out of business.

Alas, unlike the plays of Shakespeare and of Molière, those performed by the Commedia dell'Arte are lost to us forever and their written scenarios do little to convey the artistry which, for centuries, charmed and captivated rich and poor alike. Hardly a trace of the genius is left because the magic was all in the acting and the actor's skill was improvisation. No lines were learned. Nothing was written down apart from a brief copy of the scenario pinned in the wings. Yet a common misconception that these troupes consisted merely of buffoons and slapstick artists denies their true professionalism, '... *a mastery so skilful as, by a kind of magic, to compel even the most sophisticated members of his audience to submit to the illusion and in spite of themselves to laugh, applaud and acknowledge their admiration*' - Casanova, on seeing a performance of the actor, Antonio Sacchi, in the role of Arlecchino.

So who were they, the Commedia dell'Arte? Where did they come from and when?

The second question is the easier to answer. They came from Italy, in the middle of the sixteenth century, when the Renaissance was at its height. Troupes of travelling players containing stock characters, some of them masked, made their first impact upon the social scene at a time of fervent creativity. It is likely that certain individuals (Arlecchino is recognised as coming from Bergamo, Pantelone from Venice) had already appeared in impromptu regional entertainments but not until the middle of the century did these types come together within a single performance.

As to who they were, opinions differ. Some scholars trace their origins back to the mimes of Ancient Greece and Rome. It has even been suggested that Arlecchino is a direct descendant of the god Hermes (patron of herdsmen, artists and thieves). They are both fleet of foot, wear a similar hat and were rumoured to have fathered many children. But on one thing all are agreed - Arlecchino, the most endearing and enduring of the roles, is '*a child of the Tuscan sun*'. And it is perhaps only in such a place at such a time that he and his companions could have flourished because, while they sought first and foremost to entertain, they also challenged.

The Commedia's art was of the street, concerned with romance, intrigue, jealousy, all the human frailties; a true soap opera in fact. But there was also within the tradition something else, something then quite new to society, an awareness of the growing tension between servant and master, a burgeoning realisation by the common man that he was as good as the next. Beaumarchais borrowed the concept and Mozart turned his brilliant, scandalous play into a masterpiece, *The Marriage of Figaro*. So, if you thought you knew nothing about the Commedia dell'Arte, you were wrong. You just didn't know their name.

Throughout the centuries Commedia plots have been plundered, the names of their characters changed to suit national taste. Arlecchino became Harlequin. The French took Pedrolino to their hearts and renamed him Pierrot. But that's OK because these people are common property, recognisable citizens of the world - Pantelone, the elder, the symbol of authority; sometimes a miser, sometimes a lecher, eternally duped. Pedrolino the dreamer, the nice guy who never gets the girl. Brighella, the cultured sociopath. Arlecchino, the sexy bad boy women love to hate. And Colombina, the feisty, independent-minded heroine striving to keep one step ahead. Do they sound familiar? They should. Peak viewing ratings mark them out.

In my novel, I too have taken liberties with the Commedia dell'Arte. Within a real company, the actors would have kept the same role for much of their lives but gone by their own names off-stage. Mine are known only by their characters' titles and the essence of a Commedia performance, filled with its predictable plot lines and outrageous coincidence, spills over into the narrative so that the novel becomes its own scenario. Like others before me, I have also tweaked the personalities so that they are more in tune with a modern readership.

All I hope is, the world I have recreated for my troupe would be preferable to them than their current ignominious fate. Trapped in two dimensions, they decorate greetings cards. Abandoned by time, their empty costumes are filled now by oblivious revellers on their way to masked balls. No place for the Commedia, not even in the modern pantomime!

Anyway I disclaim responsibility for what happens in this book. All I did was invite some characters I love back on stage to improvise. They did the rest.

I have held and hold souls to be immortal ... A person, whether in or out of body, is never completed. He has the opportunity to experience life in different forms. Even as infinite space is around us, so is infinite potentiality, capacity, reception, malleability, matter.

There is a single general space, a single vast immensity which we may freely call Void; in it are innumerable globes like this on which we live and grow. This space we declare to be infinite ... In it are an infinity of worlds of the same kind as our own.

Giordano Bruno,
Catholic priest and philosopher.

February 17th 1600: burned at the stake in Rome.

1

ried blood. Crushed bone. Brought together in the crucible. Under aspects favourable, three seeds of liquid metal introduced, together with a solvent known only to the alchemist. None but he was witness to the firing. The precious sediment was carried in a silver cask then thrown, again at the most auspicious moment and with the benefit of a gentle breeze, from the highest point above the Olivieri vineyards.

The ritual had been performed some eighteen years before and the vines had prospered.

Now, in this last hot week of August 1599, the mood was one of quiet watchfulness in anticipation of the harvest. A sense of marking-time prevailed like that of a pregnant woman in *her* eighth month; excitement long-gone, she waits, holding on to hope that all will be well.

Fat magenta fruits dusted with healthy bloom were almost at their pinnacle of sweetness. All there was left to do was tend the foliage; remove any threat to the grape from shade or blight. Sulphur-coloured leaves, their work almost done, fluttered momentarily in a warm yet welcome breeze while human workers sweltered. Sometimes these peasants sang, but not today. The only sound was the tolling of the campanile bell.

Even peasant children were subject to languor. A few held baskets for the adults; the rest played games with stones, or sprawled in the dust, making patterns with their toes.

To take in the vista from the ledge where a magus had once cast his magic was to be transfixed; row upon ordered row of vines caressing rolling hills. A pale dirt track wound away. Dark fingers of cypress, some grouped, others lone, must have been placed by the hand of an artist.

1

This was an August afternoon like any other. Hot, slow, tranquil. Yet there was a difference. Tension existed between earth and sky. The glowing land had become the light-giver and deep azure, with indigo threatening, was displeased. In response, sky threw out luminous carmine, crimson, flame. The tapering trees turned black.

Suddenly the vines appeared unstable. Landscape shuddered. Grapes turned livid and looked ready to burst. No breeze stirred the leaves. The air became stifling. Peasants paused, anxious and wondering.

Just beyond the horizon where land challenged sky, some interfering deity, bored with a landscape of vines, took a handful of gems, shook them like dice then bowled them along the buff-coloured road. Bright topaz, ruby, amethyst too, breathed on by the mischief-maker, exploded out of the dust into a living tableau.

Music accompanied the birth: pipes and tabor, lutes, guitar, each offering up their voice.

Earth was charmed. Sky placated. The landscape was restored and the harvest saved from ruin.

～

It was hot. Too hot, even for Giulia with her pale olive skin and nut-brown hair.

She had come to her room to rest and sent her maidservant away. Giulia loosed her own hair, removed the pins, unwound the plaits that customarily restrained and tamed shining locks into a polished frame to compliment dark eyes and set off delicate features. She lay on the bed, smoothed her hair over the stiff white coverlet and sighed. She was hot. Hot and bored.

Boredom might have been banished. She had lines from Ovid to learn and her needlework had been neglected for days; but, when she glanced at the half-finished pattern of white, gold and green lilies, she endured crushing lethargy. Vexed by the heat, she pulled at her clothes. Was there no relief? She thought about going downstairs to the courtyard garden where she could trail her fingers in the fountain's pool; relish the cool kiss of spray. It was tempting, so why remain here, trapped within a hot and sweaty state, resenting discontent yet unable to shake free of it?

No answer came, other than the sense of something impending.

And yet nothing could happen. Her life was ordered, constrained within predictable and respectable regularity. She wanted for nothing; yet she wanted something.

Her gaze settled on the left-hand post at the foot of her bed then moved across to the right. Upward over foliage so lifelike it might have been sprouting from the dark wood, it took in grapes too heavy for any real vine, fat pomegranates and bursting figs. She smiled, knowing where this visual journey would lead – to the very top of the post where crouched her little imp. He was extremely ugly, face all squashed up so that the tip of his nose met his furrowed brow. He had pointed ears and the legs of a frog, drawn up beneath a pot belly. On top of that his knobbly fingers rested, three to each hand. His squinting eyes were narrow; his tongue stuck out of his mouth.

Giulia poked her own tongue out at him, remembering how he used to frighten her. But she had long since ceased to fear him and delighted in the fact that only the one who slept in the bed could see him. She had told no one of the imp's existence and he remained her coveted secret, known only to her and the man whose mischievous artistry had chosen to create him.

Bored with the imp, she rolled over to face the open window. The shutters were thrown back. There was nothing between her and a sky the colour of the Madonna's robes. It occurred to her there was a sound in the air yet in truth she could not really hear it, not yet. Perhaps it was birdsong, or peasants singing as they worked in her father's vineyards. She had heard him say this year the yield would be huge.

She closed her eyes but the sound persisted and grew louder, impressing urgency onto a somnolent young mind fertile for diversion. No, not birdsong, nor peasants singing; but music nevertheless. Could she hear the playing of lutes and pipes of some kind mingled with cheering and cries of excitement? Suddenly a distant drum began to beat.

Giulia opened her eyes. The imp was grinning. She sat up, swung her legs off the bed and ran bare-foot to the open window.

3

2

he sound Giulia had mistaken for birdsong filled the Tuscan air. Workers tending vines let their baskets slip. Children ran from the fields.

At the head of the cavalcade walked a drummer boy whose monotonous note sounded more fit for an execution. Behind him, a pair of garlanded oxen strained to pull a covered wagon up the incline. The driver wore a black gown and red breeches, wisps of hair stuck out from beneath his round black hat; his pointed beard was grizzled. A brown leather mask covered his face to the mouth, its heavy beaked nose and down-turned features making him look careworn. Next to him sat a matronly woman.

Dancing girls skipped alongside, carrying baskets of wild flowers. One child in a violet satin dress much too long for her tripped and grasped the hand of a nubile companion. Some began throwing their flowers. 'Too soon!' the man scolded. 'Tell them not to waste them.'

The woman relayed the information to the girls, adding a warning of her own not to wear themselves out before reaching town. By now though, all attention was fixed on the following cart which was drawn by mules and open to the sky, a moving platform on which two figures cavorted. One was dressed in a baggy white suit and wide-brimmed hat of straw. No mask hid his fresh young features and he was beardless.

His companion was in sharp contrast; his drab brown suit was covered in coloured patches. Peasant children laughed and pointed and, had they known his name, would have called it; but years had passed since the troupe had visited this town. Some of the adults recognised the character and the smiles on the lips of women of a certain age, their labour in

4

the fields forgotten, spoke of more intimate knowledge. Those smiles, although discreet, did not go unnoticed by their menfolk.

This actor wore a mask, not so grotesque as that of the man driving the leading wagon. His full young mouth was visible above his neat brown beard. Twirling his baton, he faked a brief sword attack upon his companion; then rammed the baton under his belt and, to the amazement of all, performed an effortless backwards somersault, catching his black felt hat as it fell. Cheers and clapping greeted his landing, which was sure. Lithe in body and supple, he possessed an air of masculine self-assurance. Sweeping his hat with its hare's foot pinned to the brim before him in a bow, he acknowledged the applause.

❧

Back at the palazzo, Giulia leaned out of her window. Grooms and other male servants were gathering in the courtyard and she could see the new kitchen maid running to the gate, skirts hitched high above her ankles. An angry shriek issued from the window directly below Giulia's, bringing the girl to a sudden halt. Giulia drew back inside at the sound of her mother's voice, unmistakeably shrill. She waited until the scolding ceased then, hearing the window slam shut, looked out again to see the shamefaced servant scurrying back to the kitchens.

The music could be heard clearly now and noise in the street told of a gathering crowd. Giulia hurried to pull on her stockings and shoes then dashed to the elegant table de toilette, a present from her father imported from Paris to mark her seventeenth birthday. 'Who's coming?' she demanded of her maid, who appeared in the doorway.

Rosa laughed as she came towards her. 'It's the troupe Immortali. They're paying us a visit, the first in many years.'

'I've heard of them.' Giulia sat for Rosa to dress her hair. 'Signore Panesse was talking about them at dinner a few weeks ago. He'd seen their performance in Venice and was full of how wonderfully gifted they were – especially the Arlecchino. I thought it funny to see him so animated. He's an old bore.'

'He's a good man, Giulia. And lonely since his beloved wife died.'

'I know.' Giulia wrinkled her nose. 'Anyway, when he was giving an account of their play, my mother made darting eyes at my father and he

5

shut the poor man up by offering him more food. I tried to lead him back onto the subject but my mother dismissed me on account of the lateness of the hour – even though it was early. But now they're here in our dull little town. Just think, Rosa, how exciting it will be to watch them perform!'

Rosa drew breath as she tucked a plaited strand into place. Giulia frowned and twisted to face her. 'Why silence?'

'Mistress, I fear…'

'No! Don't say it!' Giulia rushed to the window.

But the palazzo walls were far too high and the actors would pass by without her seeing them at all. Hope leapt when she caught sight of her father. 'Rosa! Come with me. My father won't refuse, not if you plead for me.' She dragged the maid from the room, down the marble staircase, out through the echoing loggia into the bright fierce heat of the courtyard. Elbowing her way through the throng of servants, she hurled herself into her father's arms. 'Please, oh please,' she begged. 'Please let me see the Immortali!'

Signore Olivieri held the daughter he adored at arm's length while she beguiled him with pleading looks and the voice she knew would get her own way.

He gave in with a smile. 'Very well, child. You can watch from here.'

She faced the gate. 'But I can't see from here!' There were amused glances as she pulled free and pushed to the front. Her father's stern call went unheeded and she reached the grille the moment the leading wagon drew level. Curling her fingers around the bars, she gazed at the curious masked man and jolly woman. The dancing girls were charming.

Once the wagon had creaked past, an open cart replaced it. On it were two actors. One, dressed in white, was seated. The other was standing with his back to Giulia. The actor in white wore a big straw hat and was playing a lute; his tune sounded melancholy. 'Aren't they wonderful?' breathed Giulia as Rosa came puffing up to join her.

'Please Mistress, come and stand with your father.'

But Giulia's attention was fixed on the actor standing. He was facing Signore Panesse's house across the street and the old man was waving from an upstairs window. In his shabby brown suit, this actor might have been taken for a beggar, had it not been for something about him that made the thought ridiculous.

6

The procession had come to a halt and, snatching off his companion's hat, the actor in brown doffed his own then used both to juggle. Letting go of the bars, Giulia brought her hands together in appreciation. Amidst the clamour, that small sound should not have reached his ears. The actor spun round.

Shocked by the sight of his mask, Giulia stopped clapping.

'Come,' whispered Rosa, gripping her mistress's elbow.

Casting aside the straw hat, the actor leapt from the cart. Giulia held her breath, palms pricking with sweat as he came walking towards her. She could hear a slow drumbeat – her heart beat much faster. 'My respects to you, ladies.' He bowed with a flourish.

Giulia felt her maid's grip tighten.

With a sudden movement, the actor darted forward. Giulia gasped, feeling his soft lips brush her knuckles.

'Sir!' exclaimed Rosa.

Giulia laughed with the eyes behind the mask; then a commotion in the courtyard made her look round. 'Go!' she hissed, waving the actor away. 'Hurry, before…'

'Such a beauty should not be kept caged. Tomorrow you will watch my performance. I dedicate it to you.'

As a palazzo guard rushed out of the side gate, the actor sped off, leapt onto the cart and somersaulted across it, disappearing into the crowd. Giulia pressed her face to the bars, trembling young body suffused with emotion. This was the happiest day of her life! She had been chosen. He had called her beautiful. *Touched her!* She longed for another sight of him, but heard only laughter. Wherever he went, she knew there would always be laughter.

With a sigh, she let go of the grille but remained there a moment, watching a tall man walking alone at the end of the procession. He was strumming a guitar, wore a white fitted suit slashed with green and a gathered white cap at an angle. When he whirled round to face her, she stifled a cry – his black mask was hideous and the rasping sound he made on the guitar sent shivers right through her!

Signore Olivieri was waiting in the loggia. He looked displeased, but that did not worry her. Glancing up at her mother's window, Giulia glimpsed the drapes sway.

3

Giulia avoided her father's stern gaze but knew his love for her would not let him be cruel. Besides, as she expected, it was Rosa who took the blame. Once her father began speaking, Giulia paid close attention and was relieved to discover he had not witnessed the actor's kiss but was simply displeased she had placed herself near to the common people. And though he said he did hold Rosa partly responsible, Giulia was not concerned. He always treated the maid with the utmost consideration.

It would be a different matter once it came to the inevitable confrontation with Signora Olivieri. Giulia had not actually seen her mother at the window but guessed she had been watching. Suddenly she sensed, rather than saw, the imperious figure standing at the top of the stairs. She lowered her gaze to delay falling victim to the daggers surely shooting from those piercing dark eyes.

As Signora Olivieri began to descend in a manner calculated to increase the anxiety of those awaiting her, Giulia tried to catch her father's eye. His gaze remained fixed on his wife. Risking a glance up at the stern slender woman with raven hair sleeked back in a filigree cap fringed with pearls, Giulia saw she was wearing her newest gown, its ruched satin sleeves shot with saffron silk, a tight bodice emphasising the tiny waist from which green velvet flowed. People sometimes told Giulia she resembled her mother. She preferred to think she was more like her father.

'My dearest, dear friends!' All eyes fixed on the one who had spoken. Hard on his heels, came the servant, who had not had time to announce him. 'Did you see them? Did you get a glimpse of the Arlecchino? The very same I had the good fortune to see in Venice. How fortuitous!

How simply marvellous they are gracing our humble town with their magical presence.'

Sidling over to Signore Panesse, Giulia smiled up at her mother, confident that artful innocence would conceal the satisfaction she felt in watching those tight lips, which had been on the point of emitting poison, twist forcibly into the semblance of a smile. Signora Olivieri hurriedly descended.

The old man's thin white hair stuck out from his bony pink head. His watery eyes glistened as he continued to sing the actors' praises. He found a more than eager listener in Giulia.

'Good friend,' said her father. 'Do not excite yourself so in this heat.' He brought a chair and helped Panesse to sit.

'Bring a goblet of wine,' called Giulia's mother.

'Forgive me,' panted Panesse, fanning himself with a freckled hand, 'but I have not felt such pleasure in life since my poor...' Giulia watched with distaste his bottom lip wobble. Grasping the goblet offered, he supped noisily; then returned it to the tray with a clatter. 'What would I do without such friends to comfort me?' Signora Olivieri was close enough to have her hand seized. Giulia suppressed her amusement.

'No loving wife.' He squeezed the captive hand. 'No children. No beautiful daughter! No fine strong son to take on the mantle of my business, to inherit the fortune I have amassed.' At this point Signora Olivieri, who had been discreetly attempting to twist free, seemed suddenly compliant.

Panesse let her go, then, facing Giulia, grinned, exposing his rotten teeth. 'How blessed you are to have this lovely creature for a daughter! You, my dear, must think me very foolish. But what did you think of the actors?' He wagged a finger. 'I saw you watching at the gate.'

Giulia gulped, heart thumping. She glanced at Rosa.

'Signore Panesse,' interjected her mother. 'Will you grace our table this evening?'

'Thank you, no, dear lady. I have overtaxed my frail body and must to my bed in preparation for tomorrow. He fixed Giulia with liquid eyes. 'What a treat it will be for you to watch the Immortali!'

Signora Olivieri made a sound in her throat prompting her husband to whisper in Panesse's ear.

'Oh no. How silly of me.' He cast Giulia a sheepish look as he was helped to his feet. 'Never mind, my dear. You can watch them perform the next time they visit, when you are a respectable married lady and I am in my grave.'

Giulia threw pleading glances to her father, Rosa – even to her mother.

'I bid you good evening. God bless you for your care and patience with a man in his dotage. I am so excited, I swear I feel young again.'

'Father?' ventured Giulia.

'Go to your room,' snapped her mother. 'Immediately!'

꙳

Giulia buried her face in her pillow and screamed. Hopes raised, dashed, then raised again! She hated Panesse for his stupidity. And for his great age! What right had he to watch the play, when she could not? She thumped the mattress, rolled onto her back and gazed at the dazzling blue sky. She could still feel the actor's kiss on her knuckles and, pressing her own lips against them, gave in to exquisite sensation.

4

rawn together in front of the church, beneath the gaze of stone saints bathed in torchlight, carts made a stage. Spectators pressed forward, some with children on their shoulders. Closed carriages parked in the square had blinds pulled down, discreetly lifted. Excitement filled the air and the clearest voice was that of a child: 'When will it begin?'

In answer, the man in the mask with the pointed beard mounted the makeshift stage. There came a drum roll and, when he raised his hands, it became clear that, far from being old, he was a fit man in his middle years. 'Good people!' His strong voice filled the square. 'We, the Immortali, have come to entertain you. Not merely entertain. Transport you! To lands and times you can only dream of. We will take you to a world of mirth and magic. And, through our excellent plays, create for you honest hard-working folk a portal through which to escape harsh and dreary lives. For we are the peddlers of dreams. Purveyors of enchantment!'

Cheers mingled with calls for Arlecchino.

'All in good time. All in good time.' He patted the air to suppress their impatience. 'First, allow me to introduce our leading lady.'

A skinny, black-haired woman mounted the church steps and took the stage. Her face was pale, her lips wine-red and, in the torchlight, her white gown was dazzling; although, if any spectator had had the temerity to come close enough to this haughty beauty, they would have noticed her cuffs were yellow and threadbare. She glided across the stage with a fluttering of fingers and the swish of satin, inspiring a murmur of approval and chorus of whistles.

'Ladies! Gentlemen!' The man drew her to face the audience. 'May I present to you, Franceschina? She it is who leads our actors on a merry

11

dance. For she it is whom all men desire. Even myself, on occasions.' Assuming his aged guise, he turned side on to the crowd and extended his neck to an improbable length. 'Sometimes I play the lecher!' He ogled the woman's décolletage. 'Regretfully though,' he glared at the people, 'more often than not, I am cast as the cuckold!'

They laughed.

'I am frequently the miser.' He thrust a hand in his pouch; then wagged a finger at Franceschina. 'I can also be a scolding parent.' He spread his arms out wide. 'For, I am always – and ever will be – Pantelone, father to the actors.' He bowed with a flourish.

Applause erupted into deafening cheers as a lithe, masked figure sprang on stage. 'Move over, old man!' Sweeping Pantelone aside, Arlecchino grasped Franceschina's hand and pressed it to his heart. 'She loves me!'

As she covered her coyness with a fan of fingers, the people's joy spilled over. They whistled and stamped while Arlecchino expressed his love with extravagant gestures. Whether or not his sudden appearance had been planned was impossible to say – and unimportant. All that mattered was, hats were filling.

Franceschina let her suitor take her in his arms and he planted a kiss on her lips then sprang away. 'Fait accompli!' he bellowed. Rubbing his hands, he bent towards the audience. 'Or, to you honest but ignorant folk down there, JOB DONE.'

They cheered at the insult. Franceschina retreated, dabbing her eyes.

'You enjoyed that then, good mother?' Arlecchino crouched in front of a cackling old woman dressed in black. 'Tell me, Madam. How many children have you been blessed with?'

She giggled just like a young girl. 'Nine living. Three dead.' She crossed herself. 'The Good Lord save their souls!'

'Amen to that!'

'And twenty-two grandchildren,' she added, nodding proudly.

'Twenty-two grandchildren? My, my!' Arlecchino sprang up and strutted back and forth. 'What a fine and fruitful – if little over-ripe,' he threw the old woman a wave, 'example we have here of Tuscan womanhood!'

She flapped a gnarled hand at him.

Crouching again, Arlecchino drew out his baton. 'Then, dear lady, I daresay you know what this is for?'

Women shrieked as he made the stick quiver. The old one doubled up with laughter yet managed to pull off her scarf and fling it over the offending baton.

Arlecchino sprang to his feet, stick still quivering. It rose, scarf draped over it. He whooped and cavorted. The crowd went wild until, with an agonised roar, he snatched off the scarf and let the baton hang loose. 'Thank you, dear lady,' he gasped with a stagger. 'I shall treasure this always. Now! Back to the business in hand.'

The crowd erupted.

Once there was quiet, he beckoned to the young man in white. 'Allow me to introduce to you someone I love almost as much as myself. Pedrolino! Brother! Come forward.' Pedrolino limped centre-stage. 'Here, friends, is the only actor, apart from my good self of course, endowed with any great talent. You'll notice he has an affliction. When he was a baby his father broke his leg. Or was it your mother?'

The young man spread his hands, eliciting some sympathetic *ahhs*.

'Pedrolino was treated cruelly as a child. But we are his family now and what he cannot manage with the lower limbs, he more than makes up for with his hands. Now now!' Arlecchino scolded in response to some tittering. 'This gifted chap can tell stories to melt the hardest heart without speaking a single word. But no time for that!' He pushed Pedrolino unceremoniously aside. 'We're wasting good drinking hours. Come, come! All you actors waiting for your moment!'

A short, dumpy man in black gown and wrinkled stockings took his chance.

'Here is our Dottore, a pompous chap. You know him well. Each time you visit a doctor, a lawyer, an official of any kind, there he is with his jargon on the one hand – and his other hand in your pocket. He's followed by our Capitano – a military type. Brave in bluster, cowardly in the fight.' A moustachioed man, dressed in striped doublet of garish colours and wearing a tall hat sporting a feather, mounted the steps. He brandished his sword at the crowd and they booed him.

'We have our young lovers. Ahh!' cooed Arlecchino, accompanying the smitten pair across the platform. 'And dancers and music makers.'

When he clapped, girls skipped on stage and performed a rapid dance to music. Then two burly men stepped up. 'We also employ gentlemen to help those who forget their manners on their way.' There was more booing and hissing.

'Finally!' Music faded as Arlecchino glanced this way and that. 'Last of all. But, by no means… Oh, by NO means, LEAST. I give you, Brighella!' He backed off with exaggerated steps as the man in white with the hideous mask came up to a muted response.

Arlecchino returned centre stage. 'I see some of you know him of old. And do well to show respect! For who knows what goes on behind that cruel mask? Here is one who makes music sweet enough to serenade an angel, whilst planning to stab the blessed creature in the back.'

A man pushing through the crowd passed a scroll to Pantelone. He glanced at it briefly then joined Arlecchino. 'Excellent news! A patron has come forward. Signore Panesse, esteemed merchant of your town, will furnish us with board and lodging at the inn.'

Arlecchino scanned the letter. 'And he will even pay for the wine! God bless you, Signore Panesse. And all your descendents.'

'He has none,' shouted someone. 'He's an old crock.'

'Then may the Good Lord send him some. And quick!'

Once laughter had died down, Pantelone twirled a hand up towards the stone saints. 'Good people, tomorrow night, under the gaze of your heavenly protectors – at this very hour – the Immortali will offer for your delectation the tale of *The Reluctant Bride*. Count yourselves blessed by Muses.' He bent over the audience and wagged a finger. 'Or be forever damned, if you fail to watch our dramatic masterpiece for…' stepping back, he raised both hands to the sky, 'the Immortali are the most illustrious troupe in all the land!'

A loud cheer filled the square. 'Until tomorrow night, my friends.' Doffing his hat, he bowed with an exaggerated flourish then left the stage, followed by the rest.

But the crowd pressed forward, chanting the name of their favourite. Some threw coins.

Arlecchino ran back, somersaulted and landed on his knees. Cheers were deafening. He stood then signalled for quiet, wiping the back of his neck with the old woman's scarf. 'I beg of you, friends. Let me go. Even

14

Arlecchino needs rest. Tomorrow night I am yours, both body and soul. But the inn awaits me now and I must pay homage to Bacchus.' Bowing briefly, he ran from the platform.

Still they called out his name. Many lingered, but were rewarded only with another brief dance performed by the girls who, on cessation of the music, promptly gathered up the coins and scurried off.

5

iulia woke suddenly in the dark. Exhausted by emotion, she had fallen asleep and dreamt of something she could not recall. But the dream had left her with a pleasant feeling. She lit a candle and returned to bed.

When light played across the carved face at the top of the post, she was plunged into shame. Now she remembered her dream. She had been lying naked on the bed and the imp had come to life.

There came a knock on the door. 'Come in,' she called, making her best efforts to gain composure. 'What are you doing here?' she demanded. 'Where's Rosa?'

The new kitchen maid curtsied. 'Begging your pardon, Mistress, but Signora Olivieri sent *me*.'

'I don't want *you*. Go and get Rosa.'

The girl curtsied again but remained.

'Are you stupid?' Giulia glared at the pretty plump face. 'Do as I say!'

'I'm sorry, Mistress. She can't attend you no more.' The girl closed the door then regarded Giulia from beneath thick lashes. 'Signora Olivieri reckons Rosa didn't guard you well enough at the gate and she's decided to take her for her own maidservant. And... and you've got me.'

'What?' Giulia sprang up, then, overcome by a sinking feeling, turned her back on the girl.

'I'm sorry, Mistress. It's not my fault. But if you give me a chance, I'll try...'

'Be quiet,' snapped Giulia. 'Light more candles.'

❧

t the inn every lamp was lit. Sputtering candles adorned the long table which groaned with the best cuts of meat, poultry and fine cheeses. Wine flowed. 'How many did you dedicate the performance to this time?' asked Pedrolino as Arlecchino refilled their vessels. Arlecchino, who had removed his mask but was still in costume, laughed through a mouthful of roast pork.

'One day they'll all turn up together,' remarked Renaldo, the company's Capitano. 'I reckon you cut it fine with that stunner at the gate.'

'He'll be the ruin of all of us,' grunted Pantelone.

Arlecchino gave a snort. 'I am my father's son.'

In response to some sniggering, Pantelone paid closer attention to his meal.

'And speaking of tomorrow's performance,' Arlecchino raised his cup, 'since we have such a generous benefactor... to the venerable Signore Panesse, who is without issue!' Several joined in the toast. 'In homage to this man of quality and obvious good taste, I say we should make some improvements.' There was a communal groan. 'My costume, for instance.' He plucked his sleeve. 'Within our illustrious company, the Arlecchino should veritably glitter!'

'That suit was good enough for me to wear,' muttered Pantelone.

'Exactly my point, venerable parent. But times have changed since you could fit into this moth-eaten remnant. All Arlecchino had to do then was fall on his face. Or receive a good kick up the arse to fill the town square with applause. Think what I have to do now to keep our public entertained – the capers, somersaults, the constant wit and banter...'

'Yes, yes. You are quite the genius. And who is going to pay for your adornment, that's what I should like to know? The good merchant Panesse has furnished us with board and lodging, not visits to the tailor.'

'The word on the street,' came a slow refined voice, 'is that Panesse made his fortune importing spices and trading cloth-of-gold.'

Arlecchino leaned forward to face the masked man down the table. 'Well now. Is that not news both pertinent and welcome? Trust the company's nose Brighella to sniff out what's needed. What say you now, father? A few bales of cloth wouldn't be begrudged by old Panesse. And not merely for my benefit. Sweet Franceschina,' he grasped the hand of the woman sitting next to him and kissed it. 'See how threadbare she has become!'

Pantelone pushed his plate away. 'Do as you wish! If the merchant Panesse is agreeable, why should I object?'

'Yes!' Arlecchino snapped his fingers. 'At last Arlecchino will be clad in colours worthy of his talent. This calls for celebration.' He tried to refill Pedrolino's cup.

'I'm to my bed,' said the young man, covering it.

'Come now, it's early and there's a bunch of pretty serving girls loitering outside.'

Pedrolino laughed. 'It's not me they're waiting for. Besides, the thought of sleeping alone, between clean sheets and on a down mattress, does more to seduce me. I bid you all *good night*.' The rest acknowledged his leaving. Some moved to follow.

'Well I am set in for the night,' remarked Arlecchino. 'I sense rich pickings in this town. What d'you say, Brighella? Are you up for making a night of it with me? Something tells me this place is about to bring a change in our fortunes.'

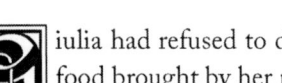

iulia had refused to dine with her parents and left most of the food brought by her new maid, Silvia. As she began to undress, Silvia stepped forward. Giulia waved her away. The maid moved to close the shutters. 'Leave them,' snapped Giulia. The night air was warm and she had no wish to shut out the stars. There were distant noises too, sounds of celebration. She undressed down to her chemise and sat before the mirror. 'You may unpin my hair.'

The pins were removed, hair unplaited. Giulia tossed her head and Silvia took up the silver comb. Lifting a lock, she drew it through. Giulia stole a glance at her new maid's reflection. The girl's blue eyes stayed fixed on her task. She worked painstakingly, removing each tangle with care and her gentle touch was more pleasing than Rosa's. 'I know what happened at the gate today.'

Giulia almost leapt from the stool. 'To what are you referring?'

'The Arlecchino kissed your hand.'

Giulia swung round and the comb snagged in her hair. She let out a yell and Silvia stepped back, apologising. Giulia tugged out the comb and threw it at her. 'Get out!' she screamed. 'No! Come back! I demand to know what you think you are saying.'

Silvia curtsied. 'I'm sorry. I...'

'Just tell me what you meant.'

'I have the honour to be courted by the head groom of Signore Panesse, who was watching from the far side of the street and...'

Giulia held up a hand. If the groom of Signore Panesse had seen, then the rest of the street... she sighed, the worst had already happened. She had lost Rosa and been given instead this impudent girl. She could have wept with rage but said stiffly, 'I will forget what just happened. We will start afresh. I am not pleased to have you in place of Rosa and may speak to Signora Olivieri in the morning but right now I'm too tired. Continue with my hair.'

Silvia picked up the comb. For a while, no words passed between mistress and maid. The only sounds in the room were the guttering of a spent candle and the occasional rustle of Silvia's skirts. Somewhere, in the distance, Giulia heard the strains of a lute. 'What exactly did your suitor see?'

Silvia was eager to tell. '... And Vincenzo told me the Arlecchino paid you the compliment with the utmost respect. If you don't mind me saying, Mistress, I think you should feel honoured.'

Instead of being affronted, Giulia found herself smiling. She was beginning to warm to this girl. 'Where are your family?'

'Oh,' was the awkward response and the pleasing combing ceased.

'You don't have to tell me, not if you don't want to.'

'My mother died six months ago. I... I never knew my father.'

It was Giulia's turn to feel awkward. 'Do you like working here?'

'Oh yes! Especially now, since I've the honour to serve you.'

Giulia searched the girl's reflection. Either she *was* simple and charming, or an expert liar. Their eyes met and Silvia's rosebud mouth widened into the broadest of smiles. 'Enough with my hair!'

Silvia put the comb down. As Giulia stood, her chemise slipped from her shoulder. The girl backed away and curtsied. 'It really isn't necessary to do that quite so much.'

'Sorry.' Silvia stopped herself doing it again. 'What would you like me to do for you now?'

Giulia sat on the bed and arranged her locks. 'Talk to me.'

The maid looked astonished. 'What about?'

'Anything. Tell me about the groom of Signore Panesse. How long have the pair of you had an understanding?'

Silvia blushed but volunteered the information. They had met after the death of her mother. He had offered to find her a position with a family of quality but she had never imagined she would be fortunate enough to end up in such a great house. Throughout the animated account, Giulia watched the girl's eyes. By the time she had finished, she was convinced Silvia was no liar. 'Would you like to have an understanding, with the Arlecchino?'

Giulia was aghast. She should have ordered the impudent girl from the room, had her dismissed. But instead she found herself searching her mind for an answer.

'I should not have said that, Mistress.'

'No you should not.'

'But you would like to see him – in the play?'

'Yes,' replied Giulia. The music of the lute seemed much closer.

'I think it's sad that you can't, especially when he dedicated his performance to you.'

Suddenly Giulia realised her maid was sitting next to her, had joined her on the bed. This was insupportable! So why could she not find it in her heart to chastise her? She felt a light touch on her bare shoulder, fingers slid to her neck. Resisting just a little, Giulia abandoned all propriety and burst into tears in the arms of her maidservant.

6

iulia tossed and turned, convinced she was walking around her room searching for something; then, sensing the yielding softness of her bed, she drifted back to sleep. She dreamt she was in an artist's studio watching an elderly man painting at an easel. She could not see his work; but the sitter, a young man with a mop of curly hair, looked round and smiled at her.

The image of the young man's face fled as she opened her eyes. Immediately she covered them against the brightness. The shutters had been left open. Rosa should have her up and dressed by now. Suddenly she remembered.

Now those small instructive tasks – a reading from the classics, needlework – seemed no longer to be boring. She touched her temple. What had she gained in place of normality? A brazen girl too free with her smiles and opinions, the girl in whose arms she had lain for most of the night while she stroked her hair and kissed her cheek and told her things Rosa had kept from her. But what of the things the maid had whispered when they were together in bed? Were they true? No, they were monstrous. Silvia must be a demon sent by Satan himself to invent such abominations. And, while the servant had been dropping sweet pearls of poison into eager ears, she, the mistress, had allowed delicate fingers to tell their own story. This is how and this is where; and that's what this is for – Giulia felt quite sick.

Suddenly the door burst open and Silvia rushed in with a tray of wine and bread. 'Mistress, get up.' She put down the tray. 'Everything's arranged.'

Giulia stared at the girl, bereft. How could the unspeakable be put into words?

There was nothing in Silvia's manner to suggest she felt the least bit embarrassed. 'Come along.' She sat on the bed and grasped Giulia's hand. 'You're going to see the actors!' Giulia's instinct had been to recoil but, on hearing the news, she let Silvia draw her up. Silvia let go and whirled round in delight. 'Signore Panesse has requested your company this very morning on his visit to the Immortali.'

'But how?' gasped Giulia.

'Well, you know the groom of Signore Panesse..?'

'Yes, I know. You have an understanding.'

'That's right. And, while you've been sleeping, I've been arranging.'

'But my mother... She would never allow...'

'I told you, it's fixed and there's no time to delay. Today you must look beautiful. Begging your pardon, Mistress, you always do. But this morning even more so. He may be there. He will be. I know it! And... well, you want him to fall in love with you. Don't you?' Giulia felt numb and seemed to turn into a lifeless dummy on which the maid hung, then arranged, her finest garment. Silvia talked non-stop, telling her how she must behave when they met the actors, how to seem haughty without being proud. How to stay composed but not appear cold. 'He must think that you're out of his reach, but not unobtainable.'

Once Giulia was dressed, she gazed in wonder at the lavender haze of shot silk in the mirror. Her bodice trimmed with black Spanish lace made a fine undulating tracery against the pale skin of her breasts. Then Silvia turned her expert attentions to Giulia's hair. Those fingers had a deftness that belied their pudginess.

The thought made Giulia blush but, once the maid had finished plaiting and pinning, she could only marvel at such skill and had to admit that Rosa had never managed anything so stunning.

'There,' said Silvia. 'Perfect! No, not quite. Bite your lips. Bite them! Harder so they almost bleed. Red lips make men want to kiss them.' The sound of a carriage and squeak of gates sent her rushing to the window. 'They're here!'

Giulia felt light-headed and could not shake off the feeling she might still be asleep and dreaming. She tried questioning Silvia as to how this had been arranged but all she would say was: *When the uniting of lovers is the object, a way can always be found.*

Signora Olivieri was waiting in the loggia with Signore Panesse. When he set eyes on Giulia, she found it hard not to laugh at him; gaping, he looked like a dead fish from the market.

'Here is my precious jewel!' Signora Olivieri swept forward and did something she had never done before. Taking her daughter's hand, she smiled with what appeared to be a mother's pride then offered her to the dumbfounded old man.

'Oh,' was all he managed, bowing stiffly. For one dreadful moment, Giulia thought he was going to kiss her hand but, to her relief, he turned and led her outside.

'Now, you will take care of my pride and joy?' clucked her mother. 'And Giulia! Under no circumstances are you to get out of the carriage.'

An ebullient Signore Panesse led Giulia to his open carriage. It seemed to her the sun had never shone so brightly, nor the air smelt so sweet. The groom, who was a good few years older than Silvia but quite handsome, was dressed in the black and green livery of the Panesse house. He doffed his fine feathered hat and hastened to open the door. 'Sit here, my dear.' Signore Panesse indicated the seat facing forward. 'Then you will not be looking into the sun.'

When Silvia climbed up, Giulia could have sworn Vincenzo stroked her rump.

Signore Panesse had to be helped aboard.

As they drove through the gate, Giulia could hardly contain her excitement. *Such a beauty should not be kept caged.* No longer. She was free!

❧

In the square a stage had been erected. Two roughly painted screens were resting on the church steps, one depicting a pastoral scene with trees and a fountain, the other a house with a cut-out window. Onlookers were being encouraged to go about their business by the burly men and the actors were assembled in full costume. All except one.

'Where is he then?' Pantelone glanced towards the inn. 'Pedrolino, the pair of you need to work on your routines. Your last performance was sloppy.' The master dismissed Pedrolino's apology with a wave. 'Why am

I asking you? You were to your bed at a reasonable hour. Brighella, I see you can stay up half the night and still…'

'Here he comes!' called Pedrolino. Arlecchino was not in costume and had stopped to exchange pleasantries with a woman selling fruit.

The tip of Pantelone's false beard bristled. 'Get your idle arse over here!'

The woman handed Arlecchino a peach from her basket. He crossed the square and, faking a punch to the young man's chest, slid an arm around his shoulder. 'Pedro! You missed a good night out. This town has more than its share of talent, eh Brighella?' He bit into the fruit and juice ran down his beard.

'May we proceed?' enquired Pantelone. 'And you were told full costume.'

'It's ripped. I've left it with the inn-keeper's wife for mending.' Pantelone threw up his hands. 'Keep your beard on! It'll be ready in time. Besides, I told you it was fucked and, if I'm to be kitted out anew by our generous benefactor… speaking of which…' Arlecchino cast aside the peach and let go of Pedrolino as an elegant carriage turned into the square.

Signore Panesse was calling and waving in a manner befitting an over-excited child. Giulia did not know where to look. Silvia laughed at him openly. Pantelone hastened forward.

Throughout the approach of the carriage, Arlecchino's gaze remained fixed on the beautiful girl dressed in lavender silk whose delicate features were framed by lustrous hair which was braided and dressed in such a way as to make it appear a little less than perfect, making her all the more appealing. And her breasts! That tracery of black defined perfection.

Giulia scanned the troupe. There was no sign of Arlecchino. 'He's not here,' she groaned in a whisper. Two men were carrying a screen across the stage.

Almost before the carriage had come to a halt, Signore Panesse was out of his seat. With the help of his groom, he disembarked, launched himself at Pantelone and embraced him as a brother. There was much bowing and curtsying as the benefactor was led along the line. 'But where is your Arlecchino?'

Giulia held her breath.

'Well, he was here, a moment… Ah! His costume was in need of repair. No doubt he's gone to make sure it will ready for tonight's performance.'

Her hopes were crushed.

'Tonight's performance!' Panesse rubbed his hands. 'I can hardly contain myself.'

'Sir,' said Pantelone. 'Would you do me the honour of taking wine with me?'

'I should be delighted. Oh, just a moment. I have charges.' Vincenzo stepped forward, whispered in the old man's ear and Panesse beamed. 'Yes, yes. My groom can look after the young ladies. And you, my dear,' he nodded to Giulia. 'Have a mind to what your mother told you.' With Pantelone supporting him on the one side, Franceschina on the other, he tottered off towards the inn.

'What *was* it your mother told you?'

Giulia jumped, startled by the sudden appearance of the young man standing next to the carriage. She frowned and averted her gaze; yet he was handsome, there was no denying – with the darkest brown eyes, a neat brown beard and a strong, slightly aquiline nose. His smile was quite charming. 'Are you looking for someone?' he asked, watching her scan the square.

'No,' she said coyly.

'I work for the Immortali.'

'That must be wonderful,' she breathed.

'It is.' A lute began to play; Giulia was shocked to see by the man in the hideous mask sitting on the church steps. This time, his playing was delightful. She sighed. If only…

Silvia giggled as Vincenzo opened the carriage door. To Giulia's astonishment, the maid sprang up then hurled herself into his waiting arms. 'Silvia!' she gasped and, gripping the side of the carriage, watched the pair hurry off to who knows where.

The delicious sensation on the back of Giulia's hand was thrilling and felt familiar. She held her breath, gazing down on rich brown hair curling over a neck so tanned it appeared almost black against a white linen shirt. She could not breathe but did not care. If she died now, she would die happy.

7

iulia's world retreated into something other than real. Every-
thing she wanted was here, offered in those umber eyes once
hidden behind the Arlecchino's mask. He did not speak, nor
did he smile. Still, he told her things she longed to hear. Only the
playing of the lute penetrated her joy and its sweetness wove a web of
pure gold in which she was content to be caught and bound.

'You are so beautiful,' he whispered and rubbed the back of her hand
across his unshaven cheek.

She froze with pleasure. Her face and neck burned. So intense was
the feeling, she thought she might faint.

'You are the one, the only one, to whom I dedicate my performance.
I shall look for your beautiful face in the crowd. Yours will be the only
face I see.'

'I cannot come to your play,' she managed.

'You must!'

'There's nothing I want more. Believe me! But I am forbidden. My
mother...'

He let her go and stepped back. 'So! *That* is what your mother told you.
Do not consort with the actors! Why then has she allowed you to visit us
in the company of an old man who left you unguarded? Look at me!' He
spread his arms wide. 'What is there to fear? Do I look like a monster?'
She shook her head. 'Rather, I am a man fallen under the spell of the most
beautiful girl he has ever seen who is set upon breaking his heart.'

'Don't say that!'

'No. I cannot go on.' He turned away, a hand to his brow. 'They will
have to cancel. Arlecchino is too sick at heart to play the fool the whole
town is waiting for.'

'Oh no!'

He was back at her side and grasping her hand. 'Then come to me. After the play. Please! If you cannot watch Arlecchino on stage, then come to him afterwards. Alone.'

'Alone?' She shook her head. 'That's impossible.'

'Nothing is impossible – not for lovers.'

'Lovers?'

'That's what we are.' His gaze never faltered.

She looked away. Anxious as to who might be watching, she glanced round the square. 'The young man in white, why does he look so sad?'

'Pedrolino?' Arlecchino shrugged. 'Because I am with you, and he is not.'

She looked back into those lambent eyes with their lashes of sable.

'I love you,' he whispered.

Giulia's world exploded, with joy and colours and the scent of flowers and the music of a lute under hot noonday sun in the square of a dull little town where she floated in Arcadia. Then suddenly the real world intruded as Vincenzo and Silvia came hurrying back. Arlecchino moved away, eyes fixed on Giulia's. 'Tonight,' he mouthed and blew her a kiss. She imagined she caught it, on the lips.

Silvia scrambled into the carriage; she looked very flushed.

Arlecchino beckoned to the groom. Arm around his shoulder, he steered him away. All Giulia caught was: *You seem like a resourceful...* and then the word *proposition* before they were out of earshot.

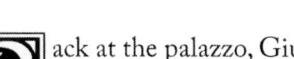

ack at the palazzo, Giulia stepped from the carriage. This time, when Vincenzo helped Silvia down, she definitely saw him stroke the maid's rump.

Signora Olivieri rushed from the loggia. 'Signore Panesse, you must take some refreshment.'

'Thank you, dear lady. I was about to go and...'

'No.' She scrambled into the carriage and veritably dragged him from his seat. 'Here! At our table. I will hear no argument against it.' With the help of Vincenzo he was bundled out.

Giulia whispered to her mother, 'Would you mind terribly if I..?'

'You will dine with us,' came the hissed response.

'Then may I go and refresh?'

'Of course. But don't be long.'

In her room, Giulia gave vent to joy. She threw herself back on the bed and kissed the hand Arlecchino had kissed. 'He loves me!'

'Of course he does.' Silvia sat next to her. 'I told you he would.'

All through lunch Signora Olivieri fussed, flapped and snapped at the servants if they failed to respond quickly enough to her instructions to put more food on Signore Panesse's plate than he was clearly inclined to consume. More curious was her conversation – or rather her constant chatter – which was all of Giulia. How accomplished she was, in music for example. She had the sweetest voice. And her needlework was very neat. Even her understanding of the classics was advanced, for a girl. 'But,' was added firmly, 'as a devoted mother whose first concern has always been the welfare of a cherished daughter...' Giulia stifled a gasp. 'I must have in mind the elevated station of her future husband. I am of the firm belief that too much learning is inclined to make a girl forward with her opinions.' Giulia sipped her wine, wondering if her mother had given thought to Silvia's disposition. 'Finally,' declared Signora Olivieri, 'the dearest hope of my husband and myself is that, one day soon, our daughter will make a good marriage to a man of quality, worthy of her beauty and attributes.'

Giulia found it hard not to voice her objection to being discussed in front of a neighbour. Yet, to all this, Signore Panesse had been simply nodding; on occasions, nodding off. In response to his periodic lack of attention, Signora Olivieri increased the volume making him spring to life momentarily and gaze at her like a mesmerised rabbit. Giulia directed numerous dark looks at her mother. Predictably, they were ignored. More disturbing was the lack of reaction from her father. He was sitting opposite Giulia. Not once, did he meet her gaze.

At last the ordeal was over and Panesse was allowed to go home; but not without more fuss and praise for Giulia, who was forced to see him off. After that, she escaped to the courtyard garden where she planned to relish the memory of her meeting with Arlecchino. In this, she was further frustrated. No sooner had she settled herself on the stone seat, than Rosa came bustling through the gate. Giulia returned her smile; yet her heart ached to be left alone with thoughts of the one who had set it on fire.

'I can't stay long,' whispered Rosa. 'I just wanted to reassure myself that all's well with you.'

Giulia nodded and invited her to sit, feeling guilty it was so.

'You look very pretty.'

Giulia's joy would not be suppressed. 'I have seen the actors! And the Arlecchino was with them. But he wasn't in costume and I didn't recognise him, not until…'

'I heard you visited the square.'

'Oh Rosa, he loves me! He told me so, there and then. I'm so happy.'

'I'm pleased you are happy.'

Giulia frowned. 'No, you're not.'

'I am. But such happiness is fleeting. It can be nothing more. These people…' Rosa grasped her hand. 'Please, Mistress…'

Giulia pulled free, pleased the words were cut short and, for once, glad to hear her mother's shrill voice.

'I must go,' whispered Rosa. 'I am truly sorry to have upset you. Have a care for your sweet young heart, Mistress. I fear it may be broken.'

As Rosa hurried away, Giulia ignored her parting wave. What did Rosa know of love? She was an old maid. Her heart had never burned so; been consumed by longing. Yes, that was it. Rosa must be jealous. She tried to recapture her mood, helped by the scent of jasmine. She could hear her mother yelling at a servant and wondered if she had ever loved her father with the kind of passion she felt for Arlecchino. She dismissed the thought. No one had ever experienced anything to compare!

And now it all came flooding back – the touch of his lips, the exquisite embarrassment she had endured once she realised who he was. The roughness of his unshaven cheek. And most of all his beautiful words, especially the words: *I love you*. She conjured them over and over again. And those dark eyes, full of something mysterious. Was it love? It must be. But something else had burned there, something dangerous. It had not repelled her. On the contrary, she found it thrilling.

She heard the creak of the gate and sighed, thinking it must Rosa returning to lecture her.

Silvia came running. Without waiting to be asked, she sat herself down. She was out of breath. 'Let me guess your thoughts.'

Giulia tried not to smile.

'Tell me, Mistress. Do you have courage?'

'I believe so.'

'And are you in love?'

'Oh yes.'

'So, if you are in love and have courage, what would you do to be with the one you love?'

'Anything. I would do anything.'

'I thought so.' Silvia sprang up and held out a hand. 'Come with me. Your maiden's dreams are about to come true.'

8

he plan was bold and at first Giulia dismissed it, believing such recklessness beyond her. But Silvia persisted. It was not so very reckless – not if they were careful. And, after all, Giulia had said she would do *anything* to be with Arlecchino.

Giulia swung from refusal to reluctance as the maid continued to cajole, tempt and even bully her until she finally extracted a '*Yes. Yes I will do it!*' And once it became a matter not of *if* but *how*, she found herself swept along with the arrangements. Then she could no more have changed her mind than swum the River Arno.

The plan was this. She was to dress in servant's clothes. Just before the end of the Immortali's performance the pair would go down the back stairs to the side gate. Nobody would question them, Silvia assured her. She often slipped out to see Vincenzo and the guard was very understanding. 'But what will he say when he sees there are two of us?'

'I'll tell Franco you're a new girl just started in the kitchens. You must keep your face covered and I'll tell him you are shy. If he teases you, as I'm sure he will – he thinks he's so clever – say nothing. Leave the talking to me.'

A closed coach would be waiting round the corner. Silvia would not say who had made this possible but Giulia guessed the resourceful Vincenzo had a part to play. The coach would take them to a place; a very romantic place insisted Silvia, where Giulia and Arlecchino could be together.

'And you will come with me?'

'Well, yes. But lovers don't need a third party so, when the time is right, I'll make myself invisible, so to say.' And that was as much as Silvia would say. All that was required of Giulia was courage and determination.

Yes, she thought, *I am determined.* Still, excitement turned to fear; then swung back to longing to revert to something like terror. 'What if my mother checks my room while I'm gone?'

'Has she ever done so?'

'Not to my knowledge.' But then Giulia thought about her mother's strange behaviour at lunch. Could it be that she had begun to care for her at last and, on the one occasion she did not want her attention, she would get it? By now though, she was committed. It was nothing short of destiny she meet with Arlecchino.

First she had to endure dinner with her parents. This time, in Signore Panesse's absence, he became the topic of Signora Olivieri's conversation: his excellent good nature – his great wealth. But Giulia's thoughts were elsewhere, in a closed coach on the way to bliss.

At last she escaped. Silvia was waiting. When Giulia saw the clothes she had brought she was filled with a mixture of repugnance and amusement. She made to undress. 'Not yet,' said Silvia. 'Wait until the bell rings for Compline.

Giulia did not ask why; she had given up asking questions. It seemed hours before the bell rang then Giulia pulled off her outer garment and snatched up the dowdy linen dress. It took a while to make it fit but, once the laces were pulled tight, it was not unflattering. Giulia looked at herself in the mirror. 'Will he still love me, in this?'

Silvia gave an odd laugh. 'Of course. Here.' She took a phial from her skirts.

'My mother's scented oil! Silvia, are you mad? It cost a fortune.'

'So? It's more use to you than her. Anyway, I'll put it back before she knows it's missing.' She dabbed perfume behind Giulia's ears then wiped the stopper down between her cleavage. 'Now,' she said, secreting the perfume and draping a homespun cloak over Giulia's trembling shoulders. 'Courage! Think of what's to come.'

They hurried down the servants' staircase. 'Quick,' hissed Silvia and they dashed past the half-open door.

Outside they could hear laughter coming from the square. Just as Silvia had predicted, the guard unlocked the gate but, when Giulia passed through, he spoke. 'I see Vincenzo has a taste for a *ménage a trois* this evening.'

32

Silvia rounded on him. 'I don't know what that means, Franco, but it sounds dirty to me, so you can stop it! This is our new kitchen maid. She's a respectable girl who's caught the eye of the baker's lad. He has a mind to meet her.'

'Well sorry for my coarseness, your ladyship.' The guard swept his hat in a mock bow. 'Who am I to stand in the way of true love?'

'Who indeed?' Silvia giggled and nudged Giulia to do the same.

'Please excuse this, Mistress,' she whispered, linking arms with her outside the palazzo. 'It looks more natural.' Giulia was glad of it, especially when they attracted the attention of some young men. Silvia was fearless in dealing with their lewd comments.

The coach was waiting. As Giulia had expected, it was Vincenzo who climbed down and ushered them inside.

n the square, magic reigned. Torches fixed to stout poles framed the Immortali stage on which the father of the troupe was engaged in conversation with the people's favourite. 'And if I wear this hat,' asked Pantelone, 'you say the object of my affections will find me irresistible?'

'Yes, Master.'

'Yet it is a strange design. These, for example?' He held the hat up by its horns. 'Have I not heard it said..?'

'I assure you, Master, this *is* the very latest fashion. In Rome, all the gentry are wearing them. In fact, so popular have these hats become, a law had to be passed forbidding common folk from sporting them.'

'I see. How fortunate am I then!' To peals of laughter, Pantelone donned the ridiculous headgear. 'How does it look?'

'Like it was made for you.'

'And should the horns stick up, like this? Or hang down, like that?' He twisted the horns so that they drooped.

'In your case, Sir? Down. Most definitely, down.'

More laughter.

'Now, to win the lady's favour, you must play the gallant. Where is your horse?'

33

'I have no horse.'

'What? No horse? How can you expect to win a lady's heart, serenading her on foot? Wait! I have an idea. You have another servant.'

'Pedrolino. But he's a useless servant.'

'Yes I know. Pedrolino!' bellowed Arlecchino.

The young man in white entered from behind a screen, strumming a lute and gazing about him dreamily.

'Pedrolino, your master has found a use for you. At last!' Arlecchino snatched the lute. 'You are to be the back end of a horse.'

Pedrolino expressed wild excitement.

'Bend down and put both arms about my waist. Just a moment!' Arlecchino stuck out his backside and gave a loud fart. 'That's better. Can't have our horse passing out.' The square exploded with mirth.

Wafting the air, Pedrolino grasped him round the waist.

'Climb up, Master,' called Arlecchino. 'Your steed awaits.'

'I am indeed fortunate to have such a servant. How can ever I repay you?'

'That's simple.' Arlecchino thrust his hand out, palm up.

'Ah, yes.' Pantelone cleared his throat as he fumbled in his money pouch. 'Alas. I regret to say, it appears at the moment…'

Arlecchino shook his head and spread his hands to the audience. 'Nothing changes.'

They understood only too well.

'On with my wooing.' Pantelone rubbed his hands then tried to climb onto Pedrolino's back. But the young man's damaged leg slipped from beneath him. He grasped his knee, tried again and Pantelone got his seat. 'But will the lady not see that this is not a real horse?'

'Don't worry,' returned Arlecchino. 'I have it on good authority she is short-sighted.'

'Oh? Why then must I wear this silly hat?' Pantelone snatched it off. 'Would it not look better on you, Arlecchino, since you are the front of a horse and these horns could pass for ears?'

'No no!' Arlecchino pushed it back at him to laughter. 'That hat is definitely *not* for me! I told you, only gentry are permitted to wear them. Now, put it on. Look, she is coming to the window!'

Franceschina appeared at the cut-out square.

'Ah yes,' breathed Pantelone. 'Oh, such beauty!' His beard began to quiver. 'I can hardly contain myself.'

'Please try!' came a plaintive cry from Pedrolino.

'Quick, Sir. The lute.' Arlecchino passed it to his master.

'But I have never learned to play.'

'Never mind. I have it on good authority the lady is quite deaf.'

'That too? My word, I am becoming a trifle anxious in my choice.' While Pantelone studied the strings and strummed discordant notes, Franceschina was replaced by a matronly woman.

'Enough. Enough!' wailed Arlecchino. 'You've softened her up by now. The lady is ready for your entreaties.'

While Pantelone addressed his love in flowery terms, Franceschina and the Capitano sneaked out from behind the screen and tiptoed across the front of the stage, fingers pressed to their lips.

'Wait one moment,' called Pantelone as the back of his horse began to sag. 'I'd swear this lady has got bigger.'

'Do not concern yourself, Master.' Arlecchino hitched up his breeches with Pedrolino clinging to them. 'Now you are closer, she is bound to appear so. It's all to do with an invention of the artists. I believe they call it *perspective*.'

'But wait. I am sure. Yes, I am convinced of it. This lady has grown fatter!'

'Sir,' gasped Arlecchino, hanging onto his breeches, 'that means you have triumphed. 'Have you not heard, love makes women swell? And the more in love they are, the fatter they get. I heard of one in Pisa who exploded!'

'Hurry, Sir,' called Pedrolino, amidst riotous laughter. 'Your horse, I fear, is knackered.' He gave up the struggle and collapsed, dragging Arlecchino, bare-arsed, down on top of him. Pantelone completed the undignified heap, to the unbounded delight of the audience.

iulia found it hard to believe she was on her way to meet a man. Suddenly life seemed to be rushing forward with the speed of the carriage. 'Are we here?' she gasped as it slowed down.

'Not yet,' returned Silvia abruptly. The carriage stopped, the door opened and Vincenzo appeared. Silvia got out. 'Wait here, Mistress. All will become clear.'

'What's happening?' called Giulia as the coach began to move. Lifting the blind, she saw Silvia and Vincenzo entwined. Soon they were left far behind. She called to the driver to stop but he laughed.

She resumed her seat, nervous and tearful and, once the coach came to a halt, sat rigid. The door opened. Fear gripped her. The actor in the hideous mask was inviting her to step outside. Suppressing misgivings, she allowed him to help her down and found herself in a clearing. On a stone table wreathed in vines stood a silver goblet and an unlit candle.

The actor led her to the table. As she took her seat on a rough wooden bench, he lit the candle then poured wine into the goblet from a leather flagon. Unslinging his lute, he backed off and began to play.

Giulia had no idea where she was but the air smelt clean and stars, more in one night than she had ever seen, studded the heavens like the diamonds her mother sometimes wore in her hair. Silvia was right – this was a romantic place.

As she sipped the wine, she felt fear give way to anticipation. Where was Arlecchino? How long would it be before..?

The answer came swiftly in the sound of galloping hooves. She held her breath as he rode in and dismounted. He was still in costume. Passing the reins to the masked actor, he hurried to her side. 'Like this?' he asked, indicating his mask. 'Or, like this?' He removed it.

'Like this,' she whispered. 'Oh yes. Like this.'

9

 love you.'

'I...' Giulia's words were smothered by a rough kiss. Breaking off, Arlecchino stroked her cheek; then he kissed her again, this time his tongue exploring her mouth. When Silvia had told her of this, she had thought it repellent. But it was not and she responded. One kiss melted into another and then another, until he broke away and looked at her strangely, almost as if she had hurt him.

Picking up the goblet, he put it to her lips but allowed her just a drop of wine before draining the vessel himself. He flung it away, pulled the pins from her hair and unravelled her plaits. She shook her locks free and he kissed her neck, burying his face in her cleavage. 'You have the scent of paradise.'

She held his head, relishing the feel of his soft damp hair. He had the scent of a man who had laboured to win a thousand hearts and she adored him for it. When he looked into her eyes, her world turned upside down. 'Come with me,' he whispered and led her from the table.

'Where are we going?'

He slid an arm about her waist. 'To heaven.'

They followed a path to the top of a rise then stopped to look down on an ancient barn bathed in moonlight. He pulled her close, covering her face in kisses. She let him lead her on with music following. The sweet strains of the lute imbued the scene with a mystical quality and she imagined herself and Arlecchino walking together throughout all eternity within a living painting.

He pushed the barn door open to a scraping of hinges. Moonlight poured through a hole in the roof, bathing the floor in silver grey. Giulia watched with increasing desire as he heaped straw onto the pool of light, becoming himself a shimmering apparition within an aura of dust motes. 'Come.' He held out his hand.

She felt her heart pounding as she took a first step, then a scurrying startled her. 'What was that?'

'A mouse. A *rat*.'

She ran to him and he laughed and hugged her. 'Isn't this the most beautiful place?' He slid the cape from her shoulders; then tugged off his jacket and cast it away. 'That's the last time I shall have to wear that thing!'

Cold light adorned his fine torso, the like of which she had only seen in a marble statue. He talked eagerly about his new costume. He had designed it, had insisted on several fittings – stripped naked for the first, to the tailor's dismay. But it had to fit him like a second skin. For a moment, he seemed to have forgotten entirely she was there. Then his eyes fixed her and, forced to lower her gaze, she found herself regarding the line of dark hair running down from his navel.

He reached out and took her by the hand then led her to his bed of straw. He drew her down, easing her back so that she lay looking up at stars through the gap in the rafters. Was this real, this perfect dream? If only they could remain like this…

Arlecchino leaned across her and his face blocked out the stars. His kiss was urgent. He began to unlace her. Feeling his hand slide beneath her shift, she held her breath. He peeled back her bodice to ease down her inner garment. Surprised and a little ashamed to find she enjoyed this, she thrilled to the touch of his tongue encircling her nipples.

Murmuring something she did not catch, he grabbed her hand and pushed it down his breeches.

With a gasp she tried to withdraw her hand. Silvia had not warned her of this! He was nothing like a statue. He made her take hold of his member, forced her fingers up and down as the rod of flesh grew harder. With a groan, he pushed up her skirts. When she tried to stop him, he thrust his fingers into her crotch.

'No!' She closed her legs and wrenched free the hand being forced to caress him. Then she heard the creak of hinges. Over his shoulder, she saw the masked actor enter. 'What's he doing here?' she cried, struggling to cover her naked breasts.

The actor shut the doors and stood facing her, arms folded.

'He's here for my protection.' Arlecchino continued to fondle her. 'Who knows how many lovers you have lurking in the shadows, waiting to slit my throat.'

'I have no other lovers.'

'I know that. Now.'

The masked man gave a coarse laugh.

'Let me go.' She tried to sit up. 'If you don't, I shall tell what you tried to do.'

'Oh yes?' Arlecchino pushed her back down then spoke in a voice she did not recognise. 'And who's going to believe a poor serving girl we picked up on the streets?'

'I'm not a serving girl. Everyone knows…'

'Yes they do.' Arlecchino nuzzled her ear. 'So why have you come to me dressed as one?'

Again she heard the masked man laugh. 'And he won't be the only one asking that question.'

'Please,' she begged. 'You must not do this. I shall scream!'

'Go ahead. Only Brighella will hear you and it will afford him great satisfaction.'

'You told me you loved me.'

'I do. I love all beautiful women, especially those who fight.'

Giulia fought; but her strength was no match for his. He tore her bodice and threw up her skirts, exposing her to the man who stood watching. 'Please. Please don't do this!'

He pinned her. 'Shall I get Brighella to hold you down? He'd like that.' Seeing the actor move from the doors, she burst into tears. 'If you let me do this on my own, you might enjoy it.'

Her wail of despair failed to soften Arlecchino's heart and he prised her legs apart, manoeuvred his naked thighs between hers. The pain was acute when he thrust fingers inside her, yet nothing compared to when he tried to push in his member. She cried out for him to stop as the burning pressure mounted. This was not going to be possible. She would surely die! Blind to her tears, deaf to pleading, he burst through the flesh that barred him.

Giulia screamed, hating herself for giving vent to distress, now that she understood the kind of pleasure derived from her violation. Worst of all, was the evil mask leering down at her.

Arlecchino took his pleasure without consideration. His body, which she had thought so beautiful, ground her like hot granite and the love he had declared was revealed for what it was – the thrusting lust of a brutish animal. With a savage cry, he crushed the breath out of her, as if even her life meant nothing to him. Then he collapsed on top of her.

The evil mask retreated.

Giulia looked up at the sky through tears, hoping to see some stars. It seemed they had all gone out. Arlecchino raised his head and smiled at her.

'I hate you,' she murmured.

'No you don't.' He withdrew with a rush of warm liquid. Wiping himself on her petticoat, he pushed the vile weapon back inside his breeches, sprang to his feet and snatched up his jacket. 'A keepsake.' He threw it at her.

Hurling it back, she tried desperately to cover herself.

'Brighella,' he called, 'the lady is all yours.'

She gasped and shrank away. Both men laughed. Without another word, without so much as a glance, Arlecchino left the barn.

Brighella picked up Giulia's cloak and held it open. 'My lady.'

She glared at him then noticed Arlecchino's jacket lying crumpled in the straw. Now she could see and smell it for what it was – a stinking rag worn by a liar! 'His father will want this,' said Brighella, stooping to retrieve it.

'Leave it!' she said, shuffling over to grasp it. 'He gave it to me.'

'Most certainly.' Brighella inclined his head; then he offered her his hand. 'May I assist you?'

She waved him away and struggled up unaided. Convinced she would not be able to walk, she forced herself to do so. Disgusting fluid trickled down between her legs. She would have stopped to wipe herself, had that hateful man not been watching. When he dropped her cloak onto her shoulders, she raised a hand. 'Don't touch me!'

He went ahead and held the door open.

Outside in the fresh air, Giulia paused. She could hear the sound of galloping hooves growing fainter.

Her walk to the carriage was torture. Twice she stumbled. Twice her escort stepped forward to assist her. She refused all help and struggled on alone. When at last she reached the carriage, she had to let him support her up the steps – but she slammed the door in his face.

Giulia sat staring into blackness. She had been defiled, humiliated. She felt desolate and angry. The trusting child was dead and the woman who had taken her place was a stranger.

10

s the wagon came to a halt, Giulia drew up her hood. Soon, she guessed, the despicable Brighella would hand over the reins to Vincenzo.

When she heard men's voices, it was hard to keep control because to her they seemed laced with a clear note of triumph. The door opened and Silvia entered. Giulia faced the other way. The maid took her seat and touched Giulia's hand. 'Mistress?'

Giulia turned and, throwing back her hood, struck Silvia across the face. With a cry, the maid bent forward, hands shielding her head as Giulia hit her again and again. 'Mistress, please! What have I done?'

'What have you done?' Giulia ceased her attack, then she started to laugh. When she became hysterical, Silvia shook her. A brief squirm and Giulia let herself be gathered in, gave up the struggle to make her servant the villain. 'Oh Silvia,' she wailed. 'He hurt me. He hurt me so badly.'

'Ah.' Silvia sounded relieved. 'Well, sometimes it does hurt, the first time. It never will again and…'

'Again?' Giulia pulled free. 'You don't imagine I would let any man do *that* to me again? Look what he did!' She flung open her cape to reveal the torn dress. 'And…' she clutched her skirts, 'I think… I am bleeding.'

Silvia sighed and put an arm around her shoulder. 'What's this?' she asked, retrieving Arlecchino's jacket, which had fallen on the floor.

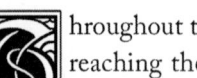

hroughout their walk to the palazzo, Giulia leant on Silvia. On reaching the gate, she kept her face, if not her mood, hidden from Franco, who made some comment about the baker's lad not being quite the gentleman he appeared.

Safely back in her room, she stepped out of the bloodstained dress. 'It's ruined,' she sobbed, knowing she spoke not only of the garment. She sat on a thick pad of folded linen Silvia placed on the bed, then watched her pour water.

'Would you like me to help you, Mistress?'

'No.'

Silvia brought out a clean shift then picked up the dress. 'I'll have to wash and mend this secretly.' She began to roll it.

'No!' shrieked Giulia, wincing as she shuffled off the bed. She snatched the garment, flung it on the floor and took coins from a drawer. 'Buy a new one. Go on! Take it. Take it all!' She threw the coins into the air and they fell with a clatter. 'For that's all you want, you... you servants! To make fools of us all.' She went back to bed and curled up facing the wall. She heard Silvia crying. 'Get out,' she said. 'I can wash myself. Get out and leave me alone.' There was a rustling of skirts. The door opened, then closed. When she looked round, Silvia had gone. So had the coins.

iulia became aware of someone standing at the foot of her bed. She looked up to see Silvia dressed in her cape and clutching a small package. 'How are you feeling?' asked the maid.

'I ache,' growled Giulia. 'And I smell of him. I've washed and washed, yet I cannot rid myself of his stench.'

'I've got something to help, with the aching.' Silvia slipped off her cape.

Giulia sat up.

'I purchased it with the coins. It cost a great deal but I'm assured it's most efficacious in cases of... well, of soreness and of bruising.' She placed the package on the bed and a coin next to it. 'There was one left over.'

Giulia removed the wrapping and peered at the round jar containing white ointment. Now she felt guilty. When the money had disappeared she had thought the worst of Silvia. 'Thank you,' she said. 'I'm sorry I was harsh.'

'That doesn't matter. Mistress, I know that you've been violated and are feeling wretched but at least… well, at least you have the satisfaction of knowing you lost your maidenhood to a man of vigour.'

Giulia gasped. It had happened again! Just when Silvia seemed redeemable she had come out with the most outrageous remark. Then she noticed the maid's expression – there was something she was not telling her. 'What made you say such a thing?'

Silvia shrugged. 'You were wrong about me, Mistress. I don't want your money. I care about you and it makes me sad that you and the Arlecchino couldn't be lovers, like me and Vincenzo.'

'That's all that you meant?'

Silvia nodded.

Giulia inspected the jar. 'Where did you get this? And at such a late hour?'

'Oh, I know where to get lots of things and the hour's no problem when you've got money.'

Giulia offered her the leftover coin. Silvia shook her head. 'Take it.' She pressed it into her palm. 'Put it towards your wedding chest.'

'Thank you,' breathed Silvia, eyes shining. 'This will buy…' She sighed and gazed at Giulia. 'I really do want to help you, Mistress. Let me wait on you, at least. Make you comfortable.'

Giulia allowed her to plump up the pillows, then she lay back and watched Silvia bustle about making things tidy. She began to wish she was like her, almost wished she was her. Yes, with a pang, she wished with all her heart that she could be simple, happy and poor. Silvia poured wine and Giulia took a drink, remembering how happy she had been when Arlecchino had put the silver goblet to her lips beneath a canopy of vines. She burst into tears. Silvia took the goblet. 'There's something I haven't told you. It was worse than I said. He cared so little for me, he allowed another man to watch.'

'Not that horrible actor, in the mask?'

Giulia nodded. 'I was nothing more than one of his performances. How could I have been so stupid?'

'You're not stupid. And you've nothing to blame yourself for. He's a brute!' Silvia put an arm around Giulia; rocked her as she cried. 'Mistress, I know a way to ease your pain, of the body if not the heart.'

'Oh?' Giulia wiped her eyes.

'Here, finish your wine. It will help calm you, then, if you'll allow me…' She picked up the jar. 'I know how to apply this so that you will feel the greatest benefit.'

Giulia frowned but said nothing. She had no wish to appear ungrateful and craved any comfort on offer. Silvia took away the empty goblet and placed the candle on the chest at the foot of the bed. 'Lie back,' she said softly.

Down pillows cradled Giulia's aching head and the effects of the wine made her feel she was floating. Silvia was talking, telling her not to worry but, sensing the hem of her shift being lifted, Giulia tensed and clenched a fist. Silvia reassured her. 'I just want to see what damage he's done.'

So Giulia allowed herself to be exposed and felt her legs eased apart in a way quite unlike the treatment she had suffered at the hands of Arlecchino. Silvia's touch was gentle, her gasp of shock sympathetic. 'You are very swollen. And there is bruising. The maidenhead's torn, of course. That's to the good. Now, if you're ready, I'll apply the ointment. It may sting a bit, at first.'

The ointment did not sting. It soothed. And Silvia spread it so gently, her fingers working its coolness over and in between the tender folds of flesh. Soon a light perfume filled the air, the scent of roses. Giulia sighed and moved a little.

'Am I hurting you?'

'No,' she murmured.

he following morning Giulia woke with no vestige of pain. The imp was wearing his customary grin and she smiled at their shared secret. She lay, legs slightly apart, as they had been when Silvia worked her magic.

Silvia entered the room but was strangely subdued. 'I'll lay out your best burgundy velvet.'

Giulia sat up.

'Signore and Signora Olivieri are awaiting you in the banqueting hall. They have, I believe, some important news. Oh, Mistress!'

'What?' In response to the maid's look of horror, Giulia scrambled out of bed, rushed to the mirror and groaned. All along the left side of her chin was an ugly red graze.

'It must have been his beard,' said Silvia. 'Some men's do bring ladies out in a rash. Don't worry, I'll get flour from the kitchen then fix your hair so that it will hardly show.'

While Silvia went to fetch the flour, Giulia's spirits plummeted. This business with the rash had brought her crashing down and her maid's ministrations had served only as a temporary salve to a much deeper wound; the knowledge that she had been ill-used by a man.

In keeping with her customary skills, Silvia turned the graze into a blush.

'Well then.' Giulia stood to smooth down her skirts. 'I am ready. Though, for the life of me, I cannot imagine why I have to wear *this* at such an hour.'

Giulia's parents were seated at the long table, her mother at its head. Silvia curtsied and made to leave. 'No, stay!' called Signora Olivieri. 'What we have to tell our daughter has implications for you.'

Giulia glanced at her father. His eyes were fixed on the table, his fingers working. 'Why have you sent for me?'

'Sit down, my dear,' said her mother.

'I prefer to stand, thank you.'

Her mother frowned as she studied her face. 'You look flushed.'

'She has a chill,' put in Silvia; then curtsied. 'Begging your pardon, my lady.'

'Oh no!' Signora Olivieri sprang to her feet. 'Not now! We must send for the apothecary at once. He will make potions. And *you*, Silvia, will make sure she takes them.'

'Mother, please. I'm fine.'

Once Signora Olivieri had calmed down, she moved away from her chair. 'I think,' she said, directing a tight-lipped smile at her daughter, 'you might already have an idea as to why we summoned you?'

'No, Mother. I have no idea.'

'As you wish.' She trailed a pale hand in the air and spoke as if being indulgent. 'I must say it does become a girl to feign ignorance of the good opinion she has elicited from a person of standing.'

Giulia frowned.

'Well, I can see no reason to put off the delightful moment any longer. Giulia, you are to be married.'

'Married?' Giulia's jaw dropped.

'Yes.'

'To whom?'

'Why, you silly girl! To the venerable Signore Panesse, of course. Who else?'

11

Back in her room, Giulia rounded on Silvia. 'You knew! You treacherous creature. You knew, yet you said nothing!'

Silvia wrung her hands. 'Oh Mistress, how could I? If I had told you, you would have gone straight to Signora Olivieri and I…'

'You would have been dismissed. See, that *is* all you care about. Yourself!'

'Oh, Mistress. Please.'

'Get out of my sight! I cannot bear to be near you. And to think I let you…' Giulia shuddered, watching Silvia slink towards the door. 'How did you find out? Listening at keyholes, I suppose?'

Silvia faced her. 'Vincenzo heard your father talking to Signore Panesse. And no, he wasn't listening at any keyhole. He was attending his master and hadn't been dismissed.'

Giulia was left to stew in the bitter knowledge that, not only had her mother conspired to marry her off to a decrepit old man, but her father, whom she trusted and adored, had been party to it. And, just now, when she had pleaded to be spared this dreadful fate, he had said nothing; just sat there, head in hands, while her mother stormed about screeching and yelling at her to be grateful.

Once she began to face the grim prospect of becoming Signora Panesse, she was filled with disgust and was soon in such a state she had no choice but to ring for Silvia. 'What am I to do?'

Silvia sat next to her. 'Perhaps it won't be so bad. You had thought one day you would marry?'

'Yes, but not a man old enough to be my grandfather.' She gave a loud sniff. 'Before my recent disappointment, I had hoped to be wooed then wed to a fine young man who would love and cherish me.' Silvia nodded.

'But that's not going to happen. Is it?' Giulia swung away. 'Oh, what will it be like, if it was so awful with a fit young man?'

Silvia patted her hand. 'I don't think you need worry. Signore Panesse is very old.'

'What's that got to do with it?'

'Well, when a man reaches a certain age he's inclined to be, let's say, less vigorous. He'll be looking for companionship. Nothing more.'

'*That's* what you meant!' Giulia sprang to her feet. 'When you told me I had the satisfaction of knowing I'd lost my maidenhood to a man of vigour.' Silvia sighed. 'So, I endured a painful defloration at the hands of a ruffian, only to be married off to a man who cannot perform!'

Silvia laughed. 'Well, you can't have it both ways.'

'It seems I cannot have it *any* way! I am to be handed over against my will, like a carcass of meat, to satisfy the greed of my mother.'

'It does seem very cruel.' Silvia thought. 'Perhaps, if she lets me go with you, that would help lighten your days.'

'Oh yes? I see it now! You and Vincenzo at play all hours of the day and night. Me with my ancient husband, counting the days, the months, the *years* until death comes to rescue me.'

'You're not thinking clearly, Mistress. Remember, Signore Panesse *is* very old. Perhaps your mother isn't being cruel after all. You'll be his only heir.'

'I don't care.' Giulia paced the floor. 'I don't want his wealth. And my mother doesn't need it. I will try again to appeal to my father. He cannot care so little for his daughter that he would see her desperate and unhappy.'

That had to wait. The reason she had been dressed in her finery was not just to receive the news, but so that she could accompany her parents to Mass. Usually the family received the Sacrament in their private chapel. On this occasion of *family rejoicing*, her mother insisted they attend church. Giulia had declared she would have to be dragged there. Her mother had started yelling, her father buried his head in his hands. Only Silvia had remained calm and, having gained permission to sit with her mistress in church, had practically hauled her from the room.

Now she handed her a goblet of wine. Giulia downed half and hurled it at the wall. It bounced off with a clatter, an arc of pink liquid staining the plaster. She let out a long scream and Silvia blocked her ears. 'Do you feel better now?' she asked, removing her fingers.

'Yes. No! I wish I was dead!'

'You mustn't say that. Now come along.' Silvia led her to the mirror. 'I'll make you beautiful. You will walk proudly into church. All eyes will be on you. The women's with envy – the men's with desire. When there's nothing we can do to change things, we must act as if we don't care.'

iulia had caught sight of the Immortali stage the instant the carriage entered the square. Steeling herself to walk past it, she felt Silvia's reassuring touch.

Following her parents up the church steps, Giulia imagined herself a human sacrifice. Once she entered, she was reminded of Silvia's words: *You will walk proudly. All eyes will be on you.* And though her lace mantle provided a welcome shield to a curious congregation, she knew it was true. All eyes *were* upon her.

The priest smiled a greeting as the Olivieris took their place at the front. Giulia sat behind them with Silvia. As she knelt to pray, she breathed in the heady incense. Looking up, she felt her senses carried aloft to where putti played. Here, in this church, she had been baptised, then confirmed; had prayed that true happiness would one day be hers. In what form it would present itself had not been very clear but she had always known she would marry. Had she imagined the face of her future husband? A vision of Arlecchino's induced a cold shudder. That such male beauty could disguise so bestial a spirit! She took another deep breath but, this time, mustiness filled her nostrils. Glancing across the transept, she saw being helped into his seat the wizened figure of her husband-to-be.

Suddenly there was a noise at the back, the shuffling of many footsteps. A murmur ran through the congregation. Heads turned. Silvia looked round a fraction before Giulia and their hands became enmeshed. Signora Olivieri also turned, her face turning ghastly. She immediately faced the front, shoulders rigid.

'How dare he come into church?' gasped Giulia, risking another look. Arlecchino was soberly dressed, as were the other actors; some had children with them. One of the company was conspicuously absent.

Thank God! If the odious Brighella had tried to enter, surely the stones would have tumbled to crush him?

All eyes were on the priest as he raised his hands. 'Welcome, my children. Good people of the congregation, make space for the actors.' There was more murmuring and shuffling as places were found. To Giulia's relief, the actors sat at the back.

Her mind was in turmoil and she took no conscious part in the Mass. When it came time to receive the host, she hurried forward. In her haste, she failed to notice Signore Panesse, until she found herself kneeling beside him. He had not failed to notice her however and cast a watery eye in her direction. Her reaction was to blush, look away; but out of politeness, nod. She heard him mutter something then his turn came to receive the Sacrament. Afterwards a server stepped forward to assist him.

Giulia fixed her eyes on the priest. But he was not looking at her. 'The body of Christ,' he intoned, gazing fondly down on the one who had taken the old man's place. 'God bless you, my son, for bringing such joy to so many.'

'Thank you, Father.' Arlecchino crossed himself as he received the host.

Giulia's heart almost stopped at such sickening hypocrisy. Her turn had come. 'The body of Christ.' The priest placed the host upon her tongue.

She wanted to spit it back, shout loud enough for the congregation to hear, '*You have just given the Blessed Sacrament to a rapist!*' But she remained silent, the host dry upon her tongue. In accusing Arlecchino, she would be damning herself. Brighella was right. The question would be asked in every home, street and tavern. *Why had she gone to meet Arlecchino dressed as a serving girl?* And the answer would spread like the plague, but with only one victim. She was condemned by her own folly. She swallowed the host.

Arlecchino was gone. Giulia made the sign of the cross. Returning to her seat, she tried not to look for him. He was kneeling at the end of a row, head bowed, hair covering his face. He looked up, hands clasped in mock prayer; and she felt his eyes pierce her. Even here in God's house, he could do it! She felt him uncovering her, fondling her breasts, ravishing her all over again and there was not a thing she could do about it.

51

t the inn, lunch was about to be served.

'Ho la!' A glittering masked figure leapt onto the table. Pedrolino whistled. Children laughed and clapped.

Arlecchino twirled. 'Well?' His new costume was fashioned in red, green and yellow lozenges. Gleaming black satin delineated his neck, shoulders and limbs.

'It must have cost a fortune,' said Pantelone, entering.

'It did.' Arlecchino jumped down.

The master's eyes blazed. 'Where is your beard?'

'I shaved it off.'

'Then you will grow it back! Arlecchino has a beard.'

'Not any more. No longer will the public be denied my handsome face.'

'Next you'll be wanting to discard the mask!'

'If you believe that, you don't know your own son.' Arlecchino took off his mask and hat. 'See!' He thrust the hat at his father. 'Brand new. But look!' He flicked the moth-eaten hare's foot pinned to the brim. 'Your very own. I have as much respect as you for the tradition.'

'So why are you always trying to change things?'

'Not change. Improve. If the Immortali are to become the most famous troupe in all Europe…' he persevered through peals of laughter, 'we need to stay one step ahead. Fail to give the public what they want and we won't be the first actors to find ourselves begging on the streets.' Pantelone shook his head. 'Here.' Arlecchino brought a pair of shoes from under the table. 'For you.'

The master beamed at the gift of bejewelled Turkish slippers.

'Now *Pantelone's* costume is complete!'

A shining white figure appeared in the doorway. Gasps of admiration greeted her entry. Arlecchino rushed to take Franceschina's hand. Her gown was pure silver, or so it appeared. 'Well!' said Pantelone admiringly. 'I must say, our patron and the tailor have done you both proud.'

The landlord entered, carrying flagons. 'Honoured guests, the best wine in the house!'

'What's this in aid of?' asked Arlecchino, seating himself at the table. 'My new suit?' He patted the serving girl's behind as she set down a tray of beakers and poured him the first drink.

'Your esteemed patron, Signore Panesse, has asked for our finest wine to be served to his friends.' The landlord handed Pantelone a vessel. 'He wishes you to celebrate with him his forthcoming nuptials.'

'Signore Panesse is to marry?'

'The old goat!' snorted Arlecchino.

Pantelone shot him a glare. 'Who is the fortunate lady?'

'A girl of good standing, from a noble family. That's all I know. Enjoy your wine.' The landlord left the room.

There was much speculation concerning the betrothal.

When the actor who had been absent from church arrived, Pantelone told him, 'Our patron is to marry. We are about to drink his health. To Signore Panesse on his betrothal! Felicitations to you and your intended, whoever she may be.'

'She is the young girl who accompanied him on his visit to the square,' said Brighella.

'What?' exclaimed Franceschina. 'That scrap of a thing in the dress of burgundy velvet who was in church this morning? You knelt beside her, Arlecchino, during the Blessed Sacrament.'

Arlecchino spluttered his wine and Pantelone narrowed his eyes. 'You are not acquainted with this lady?'

He shook his head.

'He's not used to wine of such quality,' offered Pedrolino.

'What a waste,' muttered Arlecchino.

'What did you say?'

'I said, *a toast*. Another toast. To the venerable Signore Panesse.'

'Who is without issue,' joked Renaldo.

'Maybe not for much longer,' sneered Brighella. He bent to whisper in Arlecchino's ear. 'What d'you reckon? Such a tender young beauty might well send the sap rising – even in a dry old stick.'

Arlecchino drained his cup.

12

Giulia spoke to her father but it did her no good. Although he did not seem overjoyed at the betrothal, it was clear he was not inclined to challenge her mother. Now, for the first time, she realised he was weak and deep hurt replaced anger as she endured the double disappointment of being duped by two men who had meant so much to her.

The wedding was to take place within a few weeks. Giulia was getting ready for her first meeting with her husband-to-be since the news had been broken; lunch at his palazzo in the company of her parents. She had been granted leave to take her maid, who would, of course, be dining in the kitchens. For the occasion, she insisted on wearing black brocade and ordered Silvia to apply flour to her complexion so that she would appear deathly. She entered the home of Signore Panesse with a solemn air.

He was attentiveness itself, his manner apologetic. Luncheon was a predictable trial and more than once Giulia came to believe she might strangle her mother. At length, her parents took their leave.

Signore Panesse invited her to look over her future home. Although she tried not to show it, Giulia was impressed. She knew his wealth had been accrued through trading with eastern ports but could not have envisaged such splendour, or imagined the riches he showed her with pride; but not in an arrogant, boasting way. Rather, he expressed a childlike delight in his collection of rare and beautiful things. She had, throughout their tour, avoided looking at him. Now he invited her to sit with him upon a gold damask ottoman at the top of an elegant flight of stairs. 'My dear,' he said. 'I would like now to speak of things I sense are troubling you.' She tensed, refusing still to meet his liquid gaze.

'I ask that you hear me out, then, if it pleases you, say whatever comes into your mind. Will you do this?'

Giulia nodded.

He cleared his throat. 'I am cognizant of the honour you do me in consenting to become my wife. I am aware also of concerns you must have, as to the difference in our ages.' She shifted uncomfortably. 'As you know, my late wife and I, God rest her sainted soul,' a tremor came into his voice, 'were not blessed with the gift of children.'

It was all Giulia could do not to jump up and flee.

'Long ago I accepted this as God's will. My only regret since her passing has been that, on leaving this world, I have no one on whom to bestow my riches.'

She looked at him at last.

'You, my dear Giulia, I have known since you were a baby. Since you were a tiny child, trying to run when you could hardly walk, I have adored you and wished you were my own daughter. Now fortune has favoured me, as you yourself have honoured me, and I have been granted the privilege of taking you for a bride…' he held up his hand, 'but you will become my wife in name only. To me, Giulia, you are – and shall remain – the child I never had and I shall die happy in the knowledge that my estate will pass to someone I care for deeply. Now,' he patted her hand. 'Have you understood?'

'I think so,' she managed, relief spreading through her.

'Good. Is there anything you wish to say, or ask?'

She shook her head.

'Then I have one part of the house left to show you.' He led her towards some double doors and, taking a key from his belt, unlocked then pushed them wide open.

Giulia stepped into the large airy room with its floor of black and white marble. Rose-coloured pillars supported a domed ceiling decorated with scenes from antiquity. The gods of Olympus she recognised from her reading: Neptune with his hair of tumbling foam and trident; the huntress Diana, riding the sky in her chariot, bow slung over her fair naked shoulder. Deities, nymphs and centaurs, all were painted with such skill they could have fooled the bemused onlooker into believing they were real.

There were many fine mirrors, frames inlaid with gems. Tapestries adorned stucco walls and drapes of cloth-of-gold framed tall windows looking out onto a balcony. Most stunning of all was the view from the balcony, which Giulia found herself running to take in. Breeze caressed her face as she breathed in the scent of a bountiful harvest. Fields glowed bronze. Dark spikes of trees graced undulating slopes, the dots of red roofs nestled amongst them. She could hear peasants laughing and two wheeling birds might have been soaring to heaven.

Glancing back, she realised her escort had remained outside the room. 'This, my dear Giulia,' he croaked, 'is your suite of rooms. Your private suite. Here no one, including myself, shall enter – unless invited by your sweet self.'

Giulia laughed; she could not help herself. Nor could she have wished for anywhere more delightful. Returning to the doorway, she noticed a small bronze statue on a plinth. The athletic young man looked poised to take flight. There were wings on his heels and he wore a familiar helmet.

'What is it, my dear?' asked Signore Panesse in response to her frown. You don't like this statue of Hermes? It is very old. And of considerable worth, I am told. But if it fails to please you …'

'No, it's a very fine statue.'

'Yet I see that it does not please you. So it will be removed, together with anything else that does not meet with your approval. And, if there's anything you see within the house you do like, I shall have it brought here. Anything at all.' Light, rapid footsteps were heard on the stairs. 'And here is your cheery maid. I believe I might be right in thinking you would like her to attend you, once we are wed?' His tone dropped to a whisper. 'She and my head groom have an understanding. She comes here often. They think I don't know, but it amuses me to play the blind old fool to lovebirds.'

ack home, Giulia went into the garden. Relieved at being spared the ordeal of sharing Signore Panesse's bed, she felt sad for him. But, if she had to marry a man not of her choosing, she decided he was as good as any. When Rosa joined her, they took a turn about the fountain. 'I know this marriage is not what you dreamed of…'

'It's all right.' Giulia told her what he had said.

'He's a good man.'

'He is. Oh Rosa, I've been so foolish. I want to tell you but…'

'Don't.' Rosa touched her hand. 'There are things better left unsaid. And don't judge yourself too harshly. Love makes fools of us all.'

'Even you?'

'Even me.' Rosa smiled. 'And, if it could not, then …' she glanced round, 'then we'd be no more human than that cherub on the fountain.'

ays turned into weeks and the impossible dream of passionate love with a handsome young man below Giulia's station melted away. In its place came resignation at the prospect of marriage to an elderly one who wanted to give her everything and demanded nothing in return. The words *such a beauty should not be kept caged* caused her sometimes to sigh – for she would be a captive, be it in the most luxurious of cages. However, better a life with kind Signore Panesse than to remain under the roof of a tyrannical mother and a father who had let her down.

One afternoon, she was sorting through her many items of clothing. At the suggestion of her husband-to-be and of course at his expense, she had decided to discard almost all in favour of a new wardrobe. Silvia was folding linen. 'Mistress,' her tone was reticent. 'Your monthly bandages. I notice they haven't been needed.'

'Not yet. Why?'

'Well. I don't want to worry you, but it's now some weeks since you… since he…'

Giulia frowned. 'Out with it!'

'I'm sure everything's fine.'

Giulia stopped what she was doing. 'Are you saying you think I'm with child?'

'It's possible.'

'No, it's not.' Giulia shook her head. 'Not by one… one encounter.' She crossed to the maid. 'And the first time at that!' She looked for reassurance but Silvia offered none. 'But my parents – one child in twenty years of marriage? And what about you and Vincenzo? How many times have you..?'

Silvia blushed. 'Vincenzo is always very careful.'

Giulia's anger flared. The insufferably perfect Vincenzo! She felt hot and flustered, began to pace the room. 'How long will it before… before I know?'

'How late are you now?'

Giulia thought. 'Ten days, or thereabouts.'

'Ten days?' The maid's jaw dropped.

'Tell me, Silvia!' Giulia grabbed her wrist. 'How long before I know?'

'Well, if you don't start to bleed the next time you're due, then… then I fear…'

'I can't wait that long!'

Silvia frowned and thought a moment. 'I know of a woman skilled in such matters. She would be able to tell you. I could try and find her, if you like. But you'd have to pay.'

'I don't care. Find this woman and bring her to me. Now!'

13

aiting for Silvia to return, Giulia was beside herself with panic. She sprang off the bed the moment the maid popped her head round the door.

'I've brought the woman, Mistress.'

'Then bring her in!'

'My lady.' The woman inclined her head as she entered. She was middle-aged and slender; wrinkles could not disguise the fact that she had once been very beautiful. She wore a brown mantle slung over one shoulder, under that a red bodice over a fine chemise trimmed with coloured lace. The fingers of her left hand were decked with rings and her wrists were encircled by gold bangles. Giulia watched the dark eyes of a woman who knew many secrets. 'I believe you are in need of my craft?'

'I want to know if I am with child.'

The woman gave a nod. 'If you will allow me to examine you?'

Giulia sat on the bed and told Silvia to leave.

'One thing,' said the woman once they were alone.

'You want money. There, on the table. Is that enough?'

'It's enough.' She scooped up the coins. 'Lie back with your skirts up, feet together and knees wide apart.' Taken aback by such abruptness, Giulia simply did as she was told. 'Do you have a clean cloth?'

'In the chest, at the foot of the bed.'

The woman eased linen under Giulia's buttocks. Her hands were cold, her touch not gentle. Giulia endured pressure on her abdomen then, feeling fingers open and enter her vagina, stifled an *Ouch!* She held her breath, watching the woman's blank expression.

Withdrawing her fingers, the woman wiped her hands on the cloth. 'Sit up.' Excusing herself, she forced a hand down Giulia's bodice and squeezed each tender breast in turn. Then she stepped back. 'I am finished.'

'Well?'

'You are with child.'

'No!' wailed Giulia.

Silvia came rushing in.

'It will be born at the onset of summer. I cannot be more precise – unless you know the exact occasion…'

'I know,' groaned Giulia.

'In that case, if you wish, I can make a clear prediction as to when you will be brought to bed in labour. Will there be anything else?'

'No,' replied Silvia. 'I'll see you out.'

Giulia could hardly think. Sick to her stomach, she felt numb everywhere else. Suddenly she became aware of the two women arguing. 'What is it?' she asked. 'What are you saying?'

'Nothing,' said Silvia. 'Lie down and rest.'

'If you have any further need of me, my lady, your servant knows where to find me.'

'Wait!' called Giulia. 'Do you mean when I come to term?'

The woman eased round the maid. 'I could not help but notice you were less than delighted by the news.'

'Most certainly.' Giulia swung her legs off the bed.

'In that case, there are things…'

'No!' cried Silvia. 'Come along now, you've been paid.'

'Silence!' said Giulia. 'I'll hear what she has to say.' She nodded to the woman. Silvia wrung her hands.

'There are ways of ensuring you do not come to term.'

Hope leapt. 'What ways?'

'They are known only to those of my craft.'

'And they are all dangerous,' wailed Silvia. 'And against God's law!'

'Shut up!' snapped Giulia. 'Could one of these ways be of help to me?'

'Most assuredly.'

'How soon? How soon could this be done?'

'As soon as your ladyship wishes. The sooner, the better. But I have to assemble certain items and… there's the question of…'

60

'Payment. I have money. As much as you want.'

The woman bowed her head and left, promising to return after nightfall.

ilvia pulled on her cloak and hurried from the palazzo. She was too preoccupied to register, let alone respond to, Franco's customary impudence. Soon it would be dark. Oh why had she suggested consulting the gypsy? It seemed everything she had ever tried to do to help her mistress had only ended in disaster.

On reaching the square, she glanced this way and that then made a dash for the church steps. It took all her strength to push the doors open; their ancient timbers creaked. As she slipped through into hushed sacred space, the last rays of sunlight were filtering through high windows. Candles burned around the feet of saints. Two women knelt in prayer at the altar but the Lady Chapel was empty.

Silvia fell to her knees in front of the statue and the tiered crown of flame fluttered in a breeze made by her skirts. She clasped her hands and muttered her way through two Hail Marys then forced herself to look up at the Holy Mother and her Child. Unable to bear such accusing imagery, she burst into tears.

'You are in torment, my child. I will hear your confession.'

'Yes, Father.' Silvia scrambled to her feet and, wiping her eyes, entered the confessional. 'Forgive me, Father, for I have sinned. It is now five days since my last confession.'

'Proceed.'

Silvia rattled through a list of sins, the most serious being pride. That she considered herself guilty of pride and not lust was down to simple honest logic. Having lost her virginity to her beloved Vincenzo, she was convinced whatever they did together could in no way be sinful. Something that brought joy to people so much in love must be good – and therefore innocent. Besides, one day they would be married.

Having divested herself of her sins and been given the customary number of Hail Marys by way of penance, she broached the subject which troubled her. 'Father, I need your advice.' She heard him grunt. 'I have a friend, a very good friend who… who is in trouble.' She paused, then plunged in. 'My friend is with child. And… and she is so desperately afraid of what will happen that she… she…'

'Your friend is unmarried?'

'Yes, Father.'

'Continue.'

'Well, like I say. My friend is so afraid of the consequences of this unforeseen circumstance that she… she is considering. I mean she might… I fear that she might harm…'

'You are speaking of yourself, my child?'

'No, Father.'

'Confess it! Now! Or I shall hear no more and you must face damnation alone.'

'Oh yes. It's me then, Father. I am the one.'

She heard him sigh. 'Now. At last we can begin on your path to deliverance.'

But what the priest had to say sounded nothing like deliverance. Having lectured Silvia on her wickedness for engaging in a carnal act, he went on to describe in lurid detail what would happen if she so much as attempted to harm her unborn child. The pit of hell into which she would be cast, naked and helpless, was filled with demons skilled in the use of instruments designed to torture in ways pertinent to her crime. And, once he began to explain the exact nature of the torments they would inflict upon her, she felt herself start to swoon.

With the words *damnation, eternal torment, shunned by angels, hated by God, despised by all the blessed saints for such evil mockery of the Mother of God* ringing in her ears, she staggered out of the confessional and stumbled from the church.

Outside on the steps, she took gulps of fresh air. She knew now what she had to do.

14

he sun had set. Giulia was terrified. She knew how painful, or at least she thought she could imagine how painful her forthcoming ordeal would be. She wanted to cry, wanted it to be over and done with. Better still, not to be at all.

She had brought out some linen, filled the bowl from the ewer. She had no idea how else to prepare, not daring to dwell on what the gypsy had in mind. One thing she made sure of was the grinning imp was blindfolded with a shawl.

When a sharp rap made her jump and the door flew open, Giulia nearly fainted. The unsmiling figure of her mother stood framed in the doorway. 'The gypsy has been sent away and paid well for her silence.' Signora Olivieri swept into the room.

Giulia stood, robbed of the ability to think; then she noticed Silvia hovering in the corridor. 'Silvia!' she gasped.

'Get in!' hissed her mother.

The maid scuttled in, puffy-eyed. Giulia tried to think what had happened. Had she been caught with the gypsy? Her mother closed the door.

'I'm sorry, Mistress.' Silvia fell to her knees, hands clasped. 'Please forgive me. I just couldn't let you go through with it and suffer eternal damnation.'

Traitor! thought Giulia.

'Get up,' snapped Signora Olivieri. 'Sit over there and be quiet.'

Giulia stared at her mother – the rage she might have expected was curiously absent.

'Well.' Signora Olivieri drew breath. 'This is an unfortunate state of affairs. Your maid has informed me of your condition. Or rather, I managed at last to make sense of her blubberings.' Silvia whimpered. 'However, in spite of my threats to throw her out on the street, she has refused to name the culprit. She may be stupid, but at least she's loyal. Just as well, under the circumstances.'

'What are you going to do?'

'Do? Why nothing, my dear. What is there to do except bring the wedding forward?'

Giulia gasped then shook her head.

'We'll see to it at once. Your father will speak to Signore Panesse first thing. He will tell him you are now so content – no, keen – to marry that you have requested the wedding take place as soon as possible.'

'You can't!'

'I have no choice.'

'But Signore Panesse said he saw me as a daughter. That he was content for us never to…'

Signora Olivieri gave a shrill laugh. 'You don't seriously think that he meant it?'

'He did. I know he did.'

'Well, if you believe that, then you're more gullible even than *this*,' she waved a disdainful finger over Giulia's abdomen, 'has shown you to be. Signore Panesse is a man and, regardless of age, all men want one thing. You have discovered this to your chagrin. Besides, it will be up to you to make sure he fulfils his conjugal duties. How else will he believe the child is his?'

Again Giulia shook her head. 'I can't. I can't do it!'

'You can. And you will! And, judging from your recent behaviour, you are well qualified.'

'It wasn't like that. I… He…'

Her mother's hand flicked up. 'I do not want to know. I don't care who this worthless creature is, noble or otherwise, on whom you chose to cast away your maidenhood. Besides, it does not matter. Your child will be a Panesse. There's no more to be said.' A satisfied smile crossed her lips. 'Yes, in fact this slip of yours suits us rather well if, as you say, Signore Panesse really had it in mind to leave you a virgin.'

'He did. I know he did.'

'Then, after his death, which cannot be far into the future, you alone would have inherited his fortune.'

'That's right. He said that was his reason for marrying me. To leave it to someone he loved, in place of the child he never had.'

'Hmm.' Her mother turned away as she thought. 'But then, you might have remarried and the fortune would have been lost entirely to our family. This way, the child will inherit and the Olivieris' influence will be assured. Yes.' She turned back, beaming. 'Very clever, my dear. You are to be congratulated! For once, you've done something useful.'

Giulia was speechless.

Signora Olivieri glared at Silvia. 'And *you*, my girl, say nothing of this. I hardly need tell you what will happen if you do. You will not be the only one to lose your livelihood. I shall personally see to it that the groom of Signore Panesse shares your fate.' On her way to the door she swung round. 'One thing though! Spread word throughout the house that the gypsy came here to tell your mistress's fortune but she has decided against it, being so content with her forthcoming nuptials. Yes.' Signora Olivieri beamed again. 'All in all, this has turned out rather well. Look after yourself, Giulia dear. What you carry within you is worth a great deal.'

When she had gone Giulia sat on the bed and stared at the wall. That her mother could be so callous did not surprise her, although her lack of anger was surprising. Curiously, Giulia felt relieved – probably because she no longer had to face what the gypsy had in mind. It did not, however, excuse Silvia's treachery.

Silvia covered her face. 'Forgive me, Mistress. I feared for your life, as well as your immortal soul. Women have bled to death doing what you would have done.'

Giulia was in no mood to comfort her, now facing the appalling prospect of enticing Signore Panesse into bed. Nausea overwhelmed her. She ran to the bowl and vomited.

❧

he following morning she rose at dawn. She had cried a lot and slept badly. Gazing out of the window, she waited for her father to appear. An hour after sunrise she saw him walk to the side gate and pass through into the street.

The door opened behind her. 'Your father has gone to break the good news,' said her mother, joining her at the window.

'I know.'

'He knows nothing of your condition. If he did, anger would get the better of him and he would want to know the name of the culprit. That would spoil our plan.'

'*Our* plan?'

'Well you must admit, your behaviour could have brought disaster upon this house. As it is, things will turn out to our advantage.'

Giulia imagined her father breaking the news to her husband-to-be that very moment. 'Won't Signore Panesse be suspicious at my sudden impatience to become his wife?'

'Why should he be? You are a girl of good character, or so he believes. That you would stoop so low as… well, I can assure you, that will be the last thing on his mind.'

'But he and his late wife had no children.'

'Then it will become clear that she was the one at fault. And he will congratulate himself on being the man he never thought he was. Believe me! He will be delighted.'

'And what about when I come to term? The child will be born too early.'

'Babies are always being born early. Besides, approaching your confinement, you will come back here to live. Nothing could be more natural than for a girl to want to be close to her mother at such a time. And, if the worst happens and the child is born much too soon, we can keep its birth a secret and break the news when it suits.'

'You have it all worked out.'

'Well, someone has to.'

'But what about me? Doesn't it matter at all to you that I shall be utterly miserable?'

Her mother threw her a look that supplied the answer. 'Ah!' she said, glancing out of the window. 'Your father is returning already. He looks pleased. I must go to him.'

As soon as she had gone, Silvia entered. 'How are you this morning?'

Giulia did not answer. She went back to bed.

'Perhaps things will be better than you think. You will have a child.'

'And every time I look into its eyes, what will I see? Those of a man

I fell deeply in love with, the one I thought loved me until he viciously raped me.'

Silvia winced.

'I shall be living a lie. I will have to endure being bedded by a man I find repulsive. And, once my child is born, I will be haunted by the memory of how it was conceived.'

The pair fell silent and remained so for some time.

But dormant within every human being lies courage born of desperation. It was stirring in Giulia now. Anger as powerful as the love she had once felt for Arlecchino surged within her. 'He will not get away with it!'

'Mistress?'

She sat up and looked fiercely at the maid. 'Why should he? This is Arlecchino's child I am carrying. I am not responsible. And I shall not carry the responsibility alone.'

'What do you mean?'

Giulia threw back the covers. 'I shall go and see him. Tell him. Challenge him!'

Silvia was horrified. 'But, Mistress, then everyone will know. And your reputation?'

'I don't care! Really, I don't. Arlecchino must be made to face what he has done and, if I am ruined in the process, so be it. Yes, I shall go now.' She leapt out of bed.

Silvia caught her mistress's mood. 'Perhaps, when you tell him you're with child..?'

Giulia frowned. 'You think he might be pleased?'

Silvia pulled a face.

'No. Neither do I. But how he feels doesn't matter.'

'You are very brave.'

'Brave. Reckless. Insane, perhaps! But I am determined. Help me get dressed.'

'I'll come with you.'

'No. I go alone.'

'But, Mistress…'

'No. I can only say what I have to, if I face him on my own.'

Silvia helped her get ready. 'My heart goes with you, Mistress. This is all my fault.'

'We have both been foolish, Silvia. But there is only *one* at fault. How do I look?'

'Determination itself. But… please, wear a veil.'

'Very well.' Giulia drew up her hood and Silvia draped over it her finest black lace.

'One thing.' Silvia went to the table de toilette and brought from the bottom drawer an item wrapped in linen. 'I kept this. I believe you forgot all about it, but I have a feeling…' she slipped the cover from Arlecchino's jacket. 'Well, I think you're going to need it.'

iulia half-expected to be challenged at the gate, delayed while the guard sought confirmation she was to be allowed out on her own. But her mood had imbued her with authority and, though Franco looked uncertain, he let her through.

Outside, her courage wavered. A man riding a huge draught horse and guiding another almost ran her down. There were piles of stinking rubbish to avoid. Two mangy dogs picking at the rubbish plunged into a snarling vicious fight until a fat woman threw a bucket of foul water over them. Giulia kept going, ignoring the stares, trying not to hear the jibes. The veil may have been hiding her face but her clothes marked her out as not belonging. At last she reached the inn. An old man shovelling horse dung stopped what he was doing. 'Wanna see the keeper?'

'Yes, please,' she replied.

He nodded towards the side of the building and, hitching up her skirts to step over some droppings, she went and knocked on the door. The man joined her. 'Have to be 'arder than that!' he said, banging on the door with the handle of his shovel.

From within came shouting. The door opened suddenly and a brawny man in a grubby apron glared down at Giulia. 'Can I help you?'

She glanced at the old man.

'Bugger off,' the innkeeper told him. 'So, lady. What can I do for you? Surely not after a room?'

'No,' she replied. 'I have come… I wish to see the Arlecchino. I believe he resides here?'

The man raised a bushy eyebrow. 'He does. And you wouldn't be the first young woman come asking after him. I've instructions to send them all packing.'

The old man chuckled.

'He will see me,' she said, pushing past the innkeeper. The place smelt of liquor and stewed meat. In one corner a man was slumped, facedown on a table, snoring. 'Where will I find him?'

'She wants to see the Arlecchino,' explained the landlord to a dumpy woman who came bustling out of the kitchen. 'This is my wife.'

Giulia marched to the staircase. 'Is his room up there?'

'Oi!' The woman came after her. 'You can't go up there!'

Three children appeared on the landing. One, a scruffy boy of nine or so, slid down the banister. Two girls came running down the stairs, shrieking and pulling at each other's clothing. 'Those brats!' muttered the keeper. 'I'll be glad to see the back of them.' The smallest of the girls, who had a head of blond curls, pawed Giulia's cloak.

'If I have to go from room to room,' Giulia told the innkeeper, 'I *will* find him.'

'You after Arlecchino?' asked the boy.

'Yes,' she replied.

'He's up there.' He pointed. 'First room you come to.'

'Thank you.' She began to climb the steps.

'Lady,' said the innkeeper, following with his wife close behind. 'Don't you think..?'

Giulia knocked on the door. There was no answer.

'He's in there!' grinned the boy.

'Is it locked?'

'Doubt it.'

The fresh-faced young actor appeared on the landing. 'Is this anything I can help you with?' he asked, smiling at Giulia.

'No,' she replied, and, lifting the latch, pushed the door open.

15

The room was in darkness but it was easy to make out the bed and its occupants. The man lay facedown. Still, Giulia recognised him. The floor was littered with clothing and flagons. The air stank of stale wine and body odour. Suddenly the girl gave a shriek and sat up, tugging her shift over her ample bosom.

'It's that slut of a kitchen maid,' gasped the innkeeper's wife. 'I've been calling her this past half-hour.'

The girl nudged her bed-mate.

'What?' he grunted and looked round. 'Fucking hell!'

As Pedrolino ushered away the giggling children, Giulia stepped in. 'I want to speak to you,' she said and threw back her veil. 'Alone.'

'Who's she think she is?' demanded the maid.

'Get out,' Arlecchino told the girl.

'What?'

'Get out!' He pushed her out of bed.

'Come on, you!' The innkeeper's wife grabbed the girl and hauled her from the room. Giulia shut the door.

Arlecchino got up. 'May I get dressed?'

'Please do.' In spite of what Giulia had suffered at his hands, she could not help but admire his strong chest with its dusting of hairs, the slim waist and tight hips, the delineated muscles of his agile legs and… and… she cleared her throat and looked away, thinking he looked even more handsome now he had shaved off his beard.

'Well?' he said, pulling on his breeches. 'To what do I owe this honour?'

She faced him. 'I am with child.' Did he flinch? She thought so.

He sat to pull on his shoes.

'Did you hear what..?'

'I heard. So? What's that got to do with me?'

She gave a gasp. 'You know very well.'

The door burst open and Pantelone strode in, chin lathered, cloth draped over his shoulder. 'What's going on here? The house is in uproar.'

'Shut the door,' said Arlecchino.

He did so. 'Madam, who are you? And what is your business with my son?'

'I am the mother of his unborn child.'

Pantelone groaned and, wiping lather from his face, kicked aside an empty flagon as he strode to the window. When he flung open the shutters, Arlecchino shielded his eyes. 'The girl's insane. I don't even know her.'

Giulia gasped at the outrageous lie and pulled his jacket from underneath her cloak. 'Then how did I come by this?'

Arlecchino muttered something.

Pantelone frowned as he took the jacket from her; then he glared at Arlecchino. 'Well?'

'I have no idea. I told you, I lost it.' Pantelone took a step towards his son. 'All right. All right!' Arlecchino held up both hands. 'I do know the girl. But the kid can't be mine.'

'It can only be yours!' shrieked Giulia.

'How many times..?' Pantelone threw the jacket on the bed. 'And the money it's cost me. This inability of yours to keep your dick in your trousers… Pardon me, Madam.'

Giulia acknowledged his apology.

'There you go then!' Arlecchino sprang to his feet. 'She's just like the rest. Here to extort…'

'Do you take me for a complete fool? Does she look like she needs money?' Pantelone studied Giulia's appearance then frowned at Arlecchino. 'Who is this girl?'

Arlecchino shrugged, then sat down.

'Please… *Please* tell me she's not who I think she is.'

Arlecchino heaved a sigh.

Pantelone pushed his fingers through his greying hair. 'You really have done it this time!' There came a knock on the door. 'What is it?'

71

'I have a letter,' came a voice, 'brought to the inn.'

Pantelone opened the door. 'You may as well come in, Pedrolino.' Snatching the sealed parchment, he tore it open and read it. 'What more can befall us?'

'What?' asked Arlecchino.

Pantelone clipped the letter. 'Our esteemed patron is withdrawing his support. From tomorrow night, at sunset, we are out on our ear! Here, read it yourself.'

He flung it at Arlecchino and Arlecchino read out loud, '*Owing to my forthcoming nuptials being brought forward, I regret to say…*'

Pantelone glanced at Giulia. 'Signore Panesse doesn't know..?'

She shook her head. 'When is the wedding set to take place?' she enquired.

'You don't know?'

'In seven days' time,' read Arlecchino.

Giulia felt herself sway and Pedrolino rushed to assist her. Pantelone brought a stool.

'That's it!' exclaimed Arlecchino. 'If she's to be married next week, I am in the clear. She can marry the old man and pass the kid off as his.'

Giulia burst into tears.

'You really are the very worst of scoundrels!' bellowed Pantelone. 'Have you no finer feelings? How, by all the gods, did I sire such a son?'

Arlecchino threw down the parchment. 'You have no room to talk. Now old bones ache and it takes a bit longer to get it up, you've conveniently forgotten past habits. All I said was, she can marry the man to whom she's betrothed. Is that such a bad idea?'

Pantelone cleared his throat. 'I have to say,' he said softly to Giulia, 'he does have a point – about you marrying Signore Panesse.'

'That's what my mother wants.'

'It would seem to be a solution.'

She shook her head.

'Well then. Do you wish to marry my son?'

'No!' howled Arlecchino, springing to his feet.

She glared at him. 'I just want *him* to accept responsibility for what he has done.'

Again Pantelone cleared his throat. 'Forgive me for saying, but Arlecchino was not the only one present when the act, which has had this regrettable outcome, occurred.'

Giulia glared again at Arlecchino. 'No, indeed, he was not,' she replied and derived great satisfaction from his look of panic.

'Hmm. So, what's to be done? You say your mother knows of your condition and wishes you to marry Signore Panesse?'

'Yes. It was she who brought the wedding forward. She believes, like him…' she shot Arlecchino another glare, 'it's the only solution.'

'What is your name? Who are your family?'

'My name is Giulia. I am the only daughter of Federico Olivieri and his wife, Isabella.'

Pantelone looked stunned. He turned and walked away. Arlecchino stubbornly refused to look at her. Pedrolino offered a sympathetic smile. 'I came here,' she told them, 'because I wanted *him*,' she pointed at Arlecchino, 'to accept his part in this. I had thought no further.'

'He cannot marry you,' said Pantelone.

'Thank Christ for that!' exclaimed Arlecchino.

Giulia looked round; Pantelone's attitude had changed. 'But you are right,' he said hastily, dabbing his neck as he returned to her side. 'My son must accept responsibility for his wanton behaviour. It's long overdue.' He flicked the cloth back over his shoulder. 'However, I can think of no way to help you other than offer to take you with us when we leave.'

'What?' gasped Arlecchino. 'No!'

Pantelone rounded on him. 'You have no say in this! And, since we will be leaving much sooner than expected, we had better work out how it is to be arranged.' He turned again to Giulia. 'If, my dear, that is what you want?'

Looking up into those warm brown eyes, she felt oddly secure. 'Yes,' she said. 'I… I think I would like that.'

'Very well.' Pantelone spoke through Arlecchino's stream of curses. 'Ignore his churlish behaviour. This time, Arlecchino will reap what he has sown. And, when the child is born, *you*…' he pointed an accusing finger at him, 'will pick up the tab. This one, my lad, will be supported out of *your* share of the takings!'

Arlecchino swore again and sat heavily on the bed, fist pressed against his cheek.

'Pedrolino, go and get Brighella. We're going to need his expertise.'

Giulia's gaze went to Arlecchino. He did not look at her but she could tell he was worried. And when Brighella entered the room, even with his face hidden behind its ugly mask, she sensed his alarm. She had no desire to increase her shame by telling Pantelone exactly what had happened to her in the barn; yet she guessed, if he knew, it would mean trouble for both guilty men.

16

'othing discussed here,' said Pantelone, casting a warning eye over all, 'is to be repeated outside this room.'

Brighella began. 'The arrival at the inn of a well-to-do woman wearing a veil is already the gossip of the street. And, when the girl disappears, it is bound to be linked to our leaving. They will send the guard after us, and search the caravan. Following her escape, therefore, I suggest she be taken to a secret place until it's safe to join us.'

'Can you arrange this?'

'I will need a closed carriage. That should present no problem. For now, she should go back home and wait for instructions.'

'Is there someone you can trust to pass on a message?' Pantelone asked Giulia.

'My servant, Silvia.'

'I know how to reach her.' Brighella left the room.

'Very well my dear,' said Pantelone, 'this is how it will be. The company will be ready to leave by tomorrow, noon. Some time before that you will be contacted. You must follow Brighella's instructions to the letter. If you fail to turn up at the appointed time and place, I will assume you have changed your mind.'

'I shall not change my mind.'

'One more thing… your inclusion in the Immortali will cost the company. Arlecchino will support the child.' Arlecchino glared at him. 'But you will have to do something to pay your way. In this condition, you are of little use to the Immortali so bring with you as much money and small valuables as you can, without arousing suspicion.'

Giulia stood. Before lowering her veil, she tried to catch Arlecchino's eye. He was determined not to oblige her.

'Shall I escort her?' asked Pedrolino, stepping forward.

'No,' said Pantelone sharply. 'None of us can risk being seen in her company.'

Giulia left the inn, her hopes of being spared the fate of becoming Signora Panesse resting with these men. They were risking a lot, she knew. Arlecchino had been given no choice. Pedrolino she believed to be a genuinely kind person who wanted to help. Brighella would do what his master ordered. But why, she wondered as she crossed the yard under the scrutiny of the old man with the shovel, had Pantelone offered her this chance when he could have sent her away, knowing that she would have had no choice but to marry Panesse? Either that, or throw herself off a high tower.

On her way home, she attracted even more attention. Brighella was right: her presence on the street was an open secret and folk made it clear they resented her, especially the women. Some spat on the ground as she passed. Relieved once she reached the gate, she noticed it was not Franco who opened it and the new guard looked anxious. Her mother was waiting in the loggia. She took Giulia's arm and accompanied her upstairs, chatting merrily as if nothing was amiss. On reaching the room, she shoved her in and slammed the door. 'What did you think you were doing? I told you, the gypsy's been paid off. If you think she'll have any more to do with you…'

'I just wanted to go out by myself. It will not be long before I am married, not longer after that confined. I desired to taste freedom for the first and very last time.'

Her mother eyed her with suspicion. 'From now on, my girl, you'll be closely watched. Be assured no guard will allow you past the gate unaccompanied.' Giulia hid her alarm. 'Oh. And the wedding takes place in a week.'

Giulia nodded calmly; even managed a smile as she removed her cloak. Her mother threw her one final narrow-eyed glance then swept out. Almost immediately, Silvia slipped in. 'I saw Signora Olivieri leaving. What happened at the inn?'

Giulia put a finger to her lips then checked to see no one was listening. She shut the door. 'He wasn't pleased,' she said, not knowing now whether to laugh or cry.

Silvia brought a scrap of paper from her skirts. 'A scruffy boy came to the gate and said he had a message for me from Vincenzo. He wouldn't give it to the guard. But it's not for me, Mistress. I can't even read.'

'He wasted no time,' muttered Giulia, snatching the note and reading. As the enormity of what she was doing hit her, she sat on the bed. 'I am to go with the actors when they leave town tomorrow.'

'Mistress!' Silvia was horrified.

'My mind is made up.' Giulia's tone was firm, despite growing anxiety. 'I had to wait for a message. This is it. Will you help me, Silvia?'

Silvia was shaking her head.

'What? Are you refusing, when you said yourself that you were to blame? If you won't help me, Silvia, in exactly one week I shall be forced to entice an old man who disgusts me into bed.'

Silvia came and sat next to her. 'Of course I'll help. But how will you get away? I thought I heard your mother say…'

'I know. And, short of scaling the courtyard wall, I have no idea. I must be ready to leave here one hour after Matins then make my way to the coachmaker's yard. Do you know where that is?'

'I can take you.'

'No. I asked you to help, not become involved. Just give me directions.' She looked back at the note. 'A closed coach will be waiting at the side of the building hitched to a pair: one chestnut, one black. I have to get in and wait.' Giulia decided not to say who was behind the arrangements.

Silvia had been thinking. 'There's one place Signora Olivieri would not object to you visiting. You could perhaps escape from there?'

The same idea had already occurred to Giulia and the girls exchanged glances. She got up. 'I'll give my mother time to calm down, then, at dinner, express a desire to visit Signore Panesse tomorrow morning. I'll ask father to escort me – say that now my wedding is imminent I want the two most important men in my life to spend a pleasant hour in each other's company…' She began to feel quite excited. 'I do believe it might work.'

'But how will you get away from there?'

'I don't know, but it's my only chance.' Giulia pushed the note down her bodice and took all the money she had from a drawer, together with the key to the casket in which she kept her jewels. She brought that from under the bed.

'What are you doing?'

'I have to take with me money and small valuables.' Sensing the maid's alarm, she unlocked the casket and tipped the contents onto the bed. 'Here!' she said, picking out a pearl and diamond bracelet. 'Yours.' She forced Silvia to take it, together with six gold coins. 'Even if my mother cannot connect my disappearance to you, at best you'll find yourself back in the kitchens. You can wear the bracelet when you and Vincenzo wed.'

'Mistress,' gasped Silvia, gazing at the precious things. 'I don't know what to say.'

Giulia found a drawstring bag for the money and jewels. 'Now,' she said briskly, 'tell me how to get to the coachmaker's yard – and then we must have a row. Not such a bad one as to make my mother worried you might not stay loyal, but loud enough for the house to believe you when you tell them I wish to spend the time before my wedding alone, in quiet contemplation.' So they faked a disagreement audible to any servants close by.

At dinner Giulia's timing was impeccable and, when she broached the subject of the visit, it emerged naturally out of the conversation. Her father was overjoyed. What her mother's reaction might have been was swept away in the tide of his enthusiasm.

'You seem more compliant, my dear.' Her mother caught her up at the foot of the stairs. 'More at ease with your situation.'

Giulia turned. 'I am. I realise now, this is my only path.'

Her father joined them. When he opened his arms, Giulia threw herself into them. He hugged her and a twinge of guilt swept through her; but it was only fleeting. He let her go and walked briskly towards his study, rubbing his hands and calling for a servant to take a message.

'I am beginning to discern something I'd given up hope of ever seeing,' said her mother.

'Oh? What is that?'

'Myself in my own daughter.' Isabella Olivieri placed a hand on her daughter's arm and whispered, 'You will not be doing anything hundreds of women in the same position have not done before you.'

17

hat night Giulia found it hard to get to sleep. When eventually she sank into an uneasy slumber, she dreamt she was in a cell. A thin bearded man was sitting at a table, writing furiously. Another man – a guard perhaps – snatched away his parchment and tore it to pieces.

She woke with a start and hardly slept again. By the time night had dragged its weary way through and grey forms took on mantles of colour, she was almost ready to give up on her plan. Almost.

She had not seen Silvia since their faked row but needed her help getting ready for what was likely to prove the most challenging day of her life. 'I'll bring out your dresses,' said Silvia. 'Help you decide which to take.'

'I cannot take any, Silvia. How can I? This is not a trip.' Giulia reached for the bag. 'Well, at least I have money. I can buy clothes once we reach a town. Come along.' She tried to sound positive as she seated herself before the mirror. 'Work your magic one last time. Turn me into a happy, compliant bride-to-be.'

So Silvia made a pretty girl beautiful with a pinch of the cheek and the twist of a strand of hair. They decided on a simple dress of dove-grey velvet with few trimmings, just black beaded ribbon running down the sleeves. It seemed most appropriate for a shy bride-to-be and a girl about to enter a world where, no doubt, ostentation was reserved for the stage. Giulia felt satisfied she was now the picture of chastity and modesty. Then suddenly she recalled a more joyous moment when an innocent girl arrayed in lavender silk, heart bursting with love and excitement, had gazed back at her from this mirror. 'I shall wear my green cloak with the fur-trimmed hood,' she said, pushing the memory firmly aside. 'It's quite plain but by far the warmest.'

Silvia nodded. 'Should you not also wear one item of jewellery?'

Giulia reached for the bag, took out a simple cross of silver set with amethyst and handed it to Silvia, who hung it around her neck. Tears filled the maid's eyes. It was Giulia who provided the strength to say goodbye to her friend, firm in forbidding any more tears. With a kiss, she sent her away.

Before leaving, Giulia paused to look round. Ever since she could remember she had slept in that bed. Still tied around the top of the bedpost was the shawl she had used to blindfold the imp. She smiled at her foolishness and turned to leave.

But that was her warmest shawl. And the fact that she had noticed it on the point of leaving... She put the bag down. Scrambling onto the bed, she untied the shawl but it remained where it was, snagged on the imp's pointed ear. She pulled and, to her horror, thought she saw his legs move. With a cry, she let go; then told herself not to be silly. She tugged again and the shawl came away so easily she staggered and almost fell.

At such a tense moment, it made her giggle; then she stopped, heart thumping. The imp had definitely moved this time, not brought to life by demonic forces but revealed for what it was – the front of a drawer, its unpolished wood bottom jutting out from the post.

For a moment she could only stare. Then curiosity overcame her. She was not tall enough to see inside so dropped the shawl and reached up. Again she hesitated. This *was* a secret drawer and, if someone had gone to the trouble of making it, it meant they had something to hide. Something unpleasant, perhaps.

There came a knock on the door. 'Who is it?' she called, stepping back unsteadily. It was only the housekeeper telling her that her father was waiting. 'I'll be down soon.' Giulia wrapped one arm around the bedpost and closed her eyes.

That terrifying moment when she plunged in her hand was over in an instant; now her fingers were tracing a hard rectangular object. A box, perhaps? No, not a box. A book! She brought out the small volume, which was bound in knobbly black leather and closed with a strap fixed to the front by a clasp worked in silver. Indented on the cover was the figure of her imp.

80

She had half a mind to put it back. It looked like a book of magic and she did not want to own such a thing. But this had lain hidden inside her bedpost for as many years as it had taken for her to grow to womanhood and had come to her at a moment of great significance. Perhaps she was meant to have it? She fumbled with the clasp but it would not come undone; so she pushed the drawer shut and stuffed the book inside her bag. Then she scrambled off the bed, forgetting all about the shawl.

By the time she got downstairs her father was looking anxious. There was no sign of her mother, thank goodness. 'Your mother is busy with wedding preparations,' he told her. She smiled and took his hand, bag tucked beneath her cloak. 'Giulia, I just want to say how delighted I am to see you happy. I have been aware that this marriage…' She smiled again and signalled for him to say no more.

The first thing she noticed on entering the palazzo of Signore Panesse was the statuette of the young man with wings on his heels, now sited in an alcove. The old man greeted them warmly and offered to take her cloak. She declined, saying she felt cold and wanted to protect against catching a chill so close to the wedding. He beamed and invited her to sit by a table laid out with silver bowls filled with peaches and walnuts. A tray of biscuits – made by his finest pastry cook, he told her – looked tempting. Nerves had killed her appetite but she forced herself to try one. It was delicious, tasting of almonds. Signore Panesse looked smarter than usual in black velvet. His hair was flattened with grease.

Well, thought Giulia. *Here I am. What now?* While the men chatted about business, the harvest and banking, she tried to think what to do. Forcing an interested smile soon induced a headache. She ate another biscuit and suddenly an idea came. At the next gap in the conversation she leant forward. 'The pair of you have so much in common, I find myself out of my depth.' Both men apologised for their lack of consideration.

'When I was here last,' she told her father, 'Signore Panesse was good enough to show me a wonderful suite of rooms he has set aside for my use. I should like to go there now, if neither of you mind.'

'Not at all. Not at all,' returned the old man, getting up. 'Would you like me to escort you?'

'No, thank you. I can find my own way.'

'Then I shall send a maid to inform you when your father is ready to leave.'

She thanked him again. 'Oh,' she said, turning, one finger pressed to her cheek. 'Might it not be possible for me to stay on for a while? I should very much enjoy another tour of the house.'

Signore Panesse looked as though he had been offered the elixir of youth. 'That would afford me great pleasure,' he breathed.

Giulia stole a glance at her father. 'Signore Panesse will, of course, arrange for me to be escorted home. Or perhaps he might accompany me himself?'

Her father pronounced it an excellent notion.

18

Giulia closed the doors of the suite and crossed to the windows. Pushing them wide open, she took several deep breaths, then, stepping back, looked up at the gods on the ceiling. If only she hadn't been with child, she could have embraced a life of luxury here with a kind old man who saw her as a daughter.

Her thoughts swung to her chosen path as she looked once again out of the window. What would it be like, living out there? Soon it would be autumn; then winter. Who would look after her when her time came? How could she bear such great pain amongst strangers? She told herself they would no longer be strangers. But Arlecchino did not love her, nor did he want the child. Then another emotion engulfed her. She had just said goodbye to her father, would probably never see him again. How would he feel once news reached him she was nowhere to be found? She swallowed the lump in her throat.

Perhaps, if she told him the truth, begged his forgiveness and threw herself on his mercy? She thought about it for a while. Suddenly all she wanted was to run downstairs and find him. However weak he was, however harsh her mother, they were still her family. Right now, even her mother's plan seemed acceptable. After all, she would only have to entice Panesse into bed just the once and that might not be so bad. Perhaps she would not have to endure his caresses at all? She could ply him with wine so that he would fall asleep and the next morning she could tell him what he had done. He would be so full of remorse he would never come near her again. Yes, it might work. It had to! She hurried from the suite.

Downstairs there was no sign of her father. Signore Panesse was asleep in a chair. He looked peaceful, almost endearing. She approached him cautiously. He was wheezing, chin wedged between the lapels of his

83

doublet. A strand of saliva made a sagging bridge between the corner of his mouth and the stiff collar. And what was that smell? It reminded her of the time a stray cat had got into her bedroom. It was then that she noticed the damp patch spreading on his hose. She put a hand to her mouth.

Escape took her past the bronze statuette. There it stood: arrogant, perfect. She hated it. She loved it! She snatched it off the plinth and pushed it underneath her cloak.

iulia hurried to the gate where Vincenzo was engaged in a game of dice with the guard. Catching sight of her, he made a great play of shaking the dice and joking to distract his opponent. Bless you, Silvia!

With a discreet nod of thanks to Vincenzo, she slipped through the gate unchallenged.

Silvia's directions had been clear and, on Giulia's part, well learned. To her enormous relief, the carriage was still waiting. The blinds were pulled down. She scrambled in and slammed the door behind her.

'Is my passenger aboard?'

The voice made her jump. 'Yes,' she returned and felt the coach dip. She hid the statuette in her bag.

They drove slowly at first and took several tight turnings. The sound of hammers striking wood told her they were nearing the square. Was Arlecchino amongst those dismantling the stage? Tempted to lift the blind, she refrained; most likely, he was still in bed. Soon all noise grew faint. Where was she being taken? *A secret place*, Brighella had said. She wondered who her driver was; she knew from the voice it was not him.

When the coach came to a halt another took over. She heard the crack of a whip and the carriage shot forward. Now she *knew* it was Brighella driving. As the coach gathered speed, it put her in mind of a previous journey, which had carried an unsuspecting virgin to a terrible tryst in a barn.

The coach stopped so abruptly she was forced to thrust out both arms to save herself. Angry now as well as queasy, she resumed her seat, making sure her bag was concealed. The door opened; light flooded in. 'My lady.' Brighella offered her his hand.

'You cannot call me that any more,' she said, allowing him to help her down.

'What should I call you?'

'Giulia.' She was shocked when she realised where she was. The vine leaves were withered now; grape juice stained the table. She felt suddenly dizzy. Brighella grasped her arm but she tried to push him away.

'Pride has its place,' he muttered, maintaining his grip.

She found his closeness repellent yet oddly reassuring; the scent of him was musky and exotic. She shrugged him off as soon as she could and he walked ahead of her, carrying a small sack. She kept her eyes fixed on his broad shoulders, long brown doublet, high knee boots. His straight black hair was drawn back in a knot and she could see the wide strap that kept his mask in place. She had good reason for not looking about her, knowing that if, for one moment, she allowed her gaze to stray, the joy she had felt on first treading this path would return to torment her.

It was cool inside the barn although a shaft of sunlight fell upon the spot where she had been raped. The straw there was flattened. 'How long must I remain here?'

He told her to make herself comfortable then let the sack drop to reveal a leather bottle and a hunk of bread. 'I'll be back within the hour.'

She picked up the sack and went and sat some way from the light. A noise made her look up. She smiled. Perhaps the grey mouse would like some bread? Pulling open the drawstring of her bag, she put a hand inside and was immediately filled with regret as her fingers closed over the head of the statuette. Was it not enough to have deceived poor Signore Panesse, without robbing him as well?

She brought out the book, intending to pass the time reading; that is, if she could get the clasp undone. An extraordinary thing happened. As she traced the imp motif, the clasp sprang open.

19

hen Giulia opened the book, disappointment made her frown. Its pages were nothing but a random assortment of scribbles and sketches. Riffling through, she almost dropped the thing. Illustrated in detail was the naked figure of a man. Parts of his body were covered with signs of the zodiac. On his head sat a ram. He was standing on two fishes. A cruel-looking arrow pierced his legs below the thighs and a nasty black creature with claws and a tail was attached to his member.

Not one page followed on from another. And the thickness and quality of the paper varied too. Some leaves had been cut, others torn. But a few in the middle did look as though they belonged together. These were filled with exquisite drawings, quite unlike the crude one of the naked man. There were birds and their skeletons, delicate flowers and grasses, rocks, running water, seed heads sliced in two. And then there were some less finished sketches. She could not make those out; although some looked like weapons and others had wheels. Some of the drawings had numbers scrawled over them and there were lines of meaningless sentences; meaningless until she realised it was mirror writing. She had practised that with Rosa. Even so, when she managed to work out the words, they made no sense to her.

After the fine drawings came more crude ones of men and women engaged in carnal acts. Giulia was intrigued. Did men really do that to each other? She began to feel hot and ashamed, as though someone was watching. Flicking through the remaining pages, she found something more to her liking; a love poem.

Sun rages against its own fire, moon weeps for lack of it.
My lady outshines the one, shames the other with her mysteries.

What gifts might I bring to win her heart and so bind her to me?
And so on.

Beneath the poem was a list of ingredients for a love potion. Nothing unpleasant, she was relieved to see; just crushed flowers and morning dew. She smiled. Perhaps she might make it and try it out on Arlecchino. Hoping for more poems, she carried on through; but the rest of the book was a jumbled assortment of letters in Latin and some unfamiliar languages – although she did come across an enchanting description of a pastoral scene in which nymphs and satyrs danced around a stone sepulchre. With a sigh, she put the book down, still open. Its leaves fanned out then fell apart at an intriguing illustration of a naked couple holding hands. The man had the head of the sun, the woman a crescent moon.

On the page opposite was a diagram made up of concentric circles. Realising it was meant to represent the heavens with a planet on each of the circles, she picked up the book to study the drawing more closely. But it was all wrong because the sun was at the centre.

Hearing the scraping of the latch, she hurriedly pushed the book under her skirts and hid her bag.

Brighella entered. 'I have to leave again soon. You'll be here for most of the night alone.' He came and looked down at her. 'Are you afraid?'

She shook her head.

He crouched and held out a hand. 'Give me that bag you've been at pains to conceal.'

'I shall give it to Pantelone.'

'Tiresome creature. He instructed *me* to collect your valuables and arrange for their safekeeping. Hand it over.'

She brought the bag from inside her cloak and dropped it onto his outstretched palm.

'My!' he said, grasping the string. 'Let's hope the value lives up to the weight.' When he brought out the statuette, he gave a low whistle. 'This is a fine piece! Where did you get it?'

'It's mine. I have always owned it.' She flushed at the lie.

He turned the figure this way and that. 'I can see why you're so attached to it.' He laughed at her failure to hide embarrassment, then, putting the statue aside, emptied the bag and pawed her jewels, holding some pieces up to the light.

'I'll need some of that money for clothes,' she told him.

'Take that up with Pantelone.' As he put everything back, she shifted a little. He looked at her sharply. 'What else have you got there?'

'Nothing.' She sat very still.

He made a move towards her.

'Don't you dare! If you lay one finger on me, I'll tell your master what really happened in this barn.'

He appeared taken aback and, picking up a length of straw, moved to a sitting position. 'I see there's more to you than I realised. You did well to say nothing of that.'

'I may do so yet.'

He chewed on the straw. 'Few get the better of Brighella. None have ever kept it!' Flicking away the straw, he lunged at her. 'Ha!' he said, yanking her over by the wrist and snatching the book.

'Give me that!'

She made a grab for it; but he held it up out of her reach, maintaining a painful grip on her wrist. It was then that she noticed a thin white scar running across the back of his left hand. He continued to tease her; then gave her a hefty shove, which sent her sprawling.

She quickly sat up, dusted her skirts and watched with indignation as he looked through the book. 'Please may I have that back?'

'This also belongs to you, I take it?'

'Of course.'

'Strange kind of reading, for a genteel young lady. Where are the others?'

'Others?' Sensing he was about to come at her again, she sprang to her feet. 'I swear, if you touch me again, Pantelone *will* know what part you played in my violation.'

He gave a sniff and turned his attention to the volume.

Looking down, Giulia noticed a folded piece of parchment lying close to her foot. She moved discreetly to cover it. 'Anyway,' she said, sitting down. 'I know of no others.'

Closing the book, he tapped the cover. 'This is one of three – at least.'

'Well I have only ever owned this one.' Perhaps there had been more in the drawer. It was quite possible. She had been in such a hurry, she had grabbed the first thing she came to. 'May I have it back?'

'If this belongs to you,' he thumbed through, 'tell me what is on page six.'

She shrugged. 'The pages are not numbered.'

'Well then. What lies between some mirror writing,' he flicked over the page, 'and a sketch of water running over rocks? Get it right and you can have it back.'

Of course she had no idea.

Prising open the pages, he held them open in front of her face, laughing as she averted her gaze from the sketch of a hideous devil raping a naked girl. Having had his fun, he pushed the volume inside his doublet. 'Give me your cloak and shoes.'

She stared at him, horrified. 'Why?'

'Just hand them over.' He stood. 'Or, if you'd prefer me to take them…'

'I don't understand,' she said, tugging off her cloak. 'Would you leave me with nothing, not even the clothes on my back?'

'You can keep the dress. Now hurry.'

She pulled off her shoes. 'I'm sure these can't be of any value.' She threw them at him and he wrapped them in the cloak.

Snatching up her bag of jewels, he turned to go.

'Why do you never remove that hideous mask?' she called after him. 'Is your face even uglier?' Instantly she regretted the childish outburst.

He looked back. 'Make no attempt to leave,' he said coldly. 'You'll be safe from discovery here. No peasant will come near the place. They believe it to be haunted.'

20

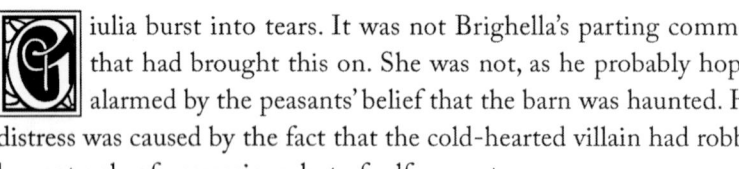iulia burst into tears. It was not Brighella's parting comment that had brought this on. She was not, as he probably hoped, alarmed by the peasants' belief that the barn was haunted. Her distress was caused by the fact that the cold-hearted villain had robbed her not only of possessions, but of self-respect.

She wiped her eyes. At least he had left her something to eat and drink. She took the bread from the sack, tore off a piece and put it into her mouth. Instantly she pulled a face – it was sour. Inspecting what remained, she saw that the crust was mouldy. She forced herself to swallow what was in her mouth then threw the rest away. Unstopping the leather bottle, she took a tentative sip – at least the wine was palatable. She drank some more. Soon the effects of it on her emotional state made her feel drowsy. She curled up in the straw and fell asleep.

She woke to find herself looking into a pair of tiny black eyes. She remained very still; the little grey mouse was nibbling the bread she had discarded. When she raised herself up, he scuttled off into the straw.

Light was still shining through the hole in the roof but it had mellowed. She guessed it was late afternoon. By now, her disappearance would be known to at least three people. She tried to block out that thought but images of a confused and panicky Signore Panesse, an irate, shrieking mother and, worst of all, a distressed and possibly heartbroken father played before her.

She reached again for the bottle, took another swig then pushed the stopper in. Feeling the need to stretch her legs, she stood up and disturbed the parchment on which she had been lying. She had forgotten all about it.

She picked it up. It was probably just a page of the book come loose – she hoped not one of those disgusting drawings.

It was not a page. It was a letter, written in a clear, bold hand. She walked as she read:

To the owner of the books.

So, Brighella was right. There were more than one.

You have discovered these volumes and are now their owner. I bequeath them to you and pray you come to no harm on account of them. That was alarming.

The three books... three then ... *you have in your possession contain certain papers which came into mine by way of settlement of an unpaid debt for work completed on behalf of a man known only to me as Little Devil, the said work being the panelling and ornamentation of his abode, together with the creation and carving of a fine four-poster.* That must be her bed! *Since none of the work was paid for, and, considering the straits in which this Little Devil found himself, I accepted his papers, albeit unwillingly, in the knowledge that his master, now deceased, had a reputation as a creator of fine and interesting things.*

Suffering as I am from a debilitating disorder for which I have been assured by my physician there is no cure, I have set about putting my house in order and caused these papers to be bound into three volumes. There is little amongst them of great value, I ascertain, although I have been told a number of the drawings are of some quality, having being executed by the said master of this Little Devil. However, none of these is of use to me now and the rest of the papers, some of which contain profane images and ideas contrary to Christian doctrine, and in more than one instance, I am sure, merit the title heretical (these I had a mind to destroy but, having now my mind fixed upon my own end, feel inclined to leave that to another) are at the very least unpalatable to me and I therefore choose not to hand them on to my descendants.

So you (perhaps one who has spent many restful hours in the bed I created) the finder of these volumes, are to become my beneficiary. I wish you joy of the fine things they contain and offer my continued prayers to ward off any evil those entries of a base nature might bring.

Jacopo Bruno

Master Carpenter

Giulia let her hand fall to her side. She frowned, deep in thought; then read the letter again.

Now she understood why the book was a jumble of pages. Presumably Jacopo Bruno had handed his papers over to be bound without bothering to sort them – the fact that he found some offensive would explain this. She decided Brighella was welcome to it and serve him right if evil did befall him. In the whole world, she could not think of anyone more deserving. But it gave her pleasure to know she possessed a secret he would be keen to discover.

She pushed the parchment down her bodice and glanced nervously towards the shaft of light, which was rapidly fading. Thoughts of the darkness to come filled her with flutterings of fear. Quickly she gathered armfuls of straw to heap around her and keep out the cold. For no reason she understood, she chose to sit in the very centre of the barn. Any hope of passing the lonely dark hours in sleep was gone. Having so recently rested, she felt not the least bit tired.

Seated in her nest of straw, clutching the leather bottle, she watched the shaft of light grow steadily weaker until the spot where she had lain with Arlecchino blended into gloom.

Then night swept in like a spectre clothed in velvet, swirling its cloak to fill every corner. This was a blackness much deeper, thicker, more palpable than any she had ever known. Now every scuffling, each creak of dry wood was alarming. There were still shadows, even within the darkness. Blacker than black, they could have been spawning grounds for the progeny of demons.

She tried to shake off such imaginings but a sickening thought occurred to her. Had she been duped? Was this just a trick to rob a gullible girl of money and jewels? The more she thought about it, the more she became convinced it was so. She started to panic. What was she to do? She could try to get back home, but apart from the shame she would have to endure, what would she have to face to get there? It was dark; she had no shoes or cloak. Besides, she had no idea where she was. She might wander for days, be attacked by wild animals or brigands. Or worse! She shuddered, yet not with cold. It was fear that turned her shudders into uncontrollable trembling.

Hot tears welled. She swallowed and clawed at her throat. There she found a reassuring form. Brighella had left her with her crucifix! Tears of despair became those of gratitude escaping to run down her cheeks. She clutched her cross and did the only thing she could. She began to pray.

❧

Flaming torches left in their wake bright trails of yellow fire. Shouts of men filled the air. The hunt was on. A girl had disappeared, a girl of good family. Snatched from under the very nose of her worthy husband-to-be. An affront to the town and civic pride. This was not to be countenanced!

During the hours of daylight the search had been of the town itself. Houses had been ransacked, citizens questioned. And the answers to those questions, jumbled and misinformed though most proved to be, had been steadily building a picture of where the girl was.

The innkeeper found himself the centre of unwelcome attention, hauled out by the guard and forced to repeat time and time again what he knew of the visit a young girl had made to his establishment. A rough sort who did jobs for him – shovelled horse shit, that kind of thing – had pointed a grimy finger in his direction.

'There was a young woman,' the innkeeper eventually told his interrogators. 'She came to see the Arlecchino.'

'Why? What business had she with the actor?'

'I have no idea. I don't pry into my guests' affairs.'

The chief interrogator smiled and gave a knowing nod to his companions. 'Well,' he said, drawing closer to the prisoner, 'I'm here to tell you that it's my job to pry. And pry I shall for as long as it takes to get to the truth. You have a choice. Tell me all you know and go home now. Tell me later and spend the intervening time in jail.'

The innkeeper gave a weary sigh. 'There were a number of women came to see him.' He waved a hand in a gesture signifying the number to be countless. 'The Arlecchino gave me instructions to send them all away and so I did, but she...' he paused.

'Yes?'

'Well this one was different. She insisted, pushed her way in. My wife told her no, she couldn't go upstairs, but she took no notice and stomped on up and when she burst in on him...'

The guards waited keenly.

'Need I say more?' He spread his hands.

'So. You got the impression there had been a liaison between this young woman and the Arlecchino?'

'I'm saying nothing on that because I don't know. How good would it be for my business if it got about that the innkeeper could not be counted on to be discreet? No, throw me in jail if you will, I'm saying no more.' He folded his mighty arms and remained tight-lipped.

But where he was unwilling to elaborate, certain women of the street were happy to fill in the details. 'Yes. A well-to-do female wearing a veil had come swanning through their streets as if she owned the place. Who did she think she was?'

'Do you know where she was headed?'

'Of course,' replied one keenly, a sharp-faced woman dressed in tangerine satin whose face was a mask of white powder and red-painted lips. 'Madam was on her way to the inn to a secret assignation with the Arlecchino. Everyone knows that!'

That was enough.

But when the news was broken to Giulia's parents, it was met with dismay; then, on her father's part, an abject refusal to believe it. He simply shook his head.

After a moment's frantic thought, Giulia's mother began her customary shrieking. 'How dare they suggest..? An outrage to imagine ..!'

Her husband tried to calm her.

'You're to blame for this!' she screeched at him.

He did not deny it, since he truly believed he was. After all, it was he who had been responsible for Giulia and made the decision to leave her with Signore Panesse.

The guard who had broken the news shifted uncomfortably and watched the scene with distaste. It was clear this father's anxiety was genuine, while all the mother was concerned with was her public face.

Meanwhile, across the street, poor Signore Panesse was also being supplied with the information. As Giulia had imagined, he could take little of it in. Within moments the shock had brought on an attack of the tremors and he was forced to retire to his bed.

There was, of course, one person (or rather two) who knew the truth.

'My mistress had absolutely no dealings with actors,' was all Silvia would say. They pressed her but she remained loyal. And Vincenzo also kept what he knew to himself.

The unfortunate man who had been guarding the Panesse gate at the time of Giulia's disappearance was at a loss to explain how she had slipped through without being seen. In an effort not to become at a loss for his job as well, he came up with the theory of abduction. Some conspiracy had clearly been afoot, a clever plan must have been in operation to smuggle the young woman out. And so, that is what Giulia's disappearance became – an abduction. It suited her mother to believe it and made her father feel a bit less guilty.

The news soon spread on the street and in the taverns. Once darkness fell a different mood reigned. Someone was to blame. People had to pay. The search moved out beyond the walls. Some went on foot, those who had mounts saddled up.

At a place where the road snaked back upon itself and the rock support-ing it was a sheer drop to a fast-flowing river, two weavers with their dog, a scrawny beast with an appetite for the chase, came to a sudden halt.

An hour or so before news of Giulia's contact with the actors had been broken to her parents, these men had had the temerity to approach Signore Olivieri, expressing their deep regret at the disappearance of his daughter and offering to find her if he would provide them with an article of her clothing. He had readily agreed and they had readily set about searching – for a rich man in distress is known to be worth helping. The dog had been given a shawl and shoe to maul and sniff and, within moments, was hot on the trail. From the palazzo of Signore Panesse to the coachmaker's yard and then… nothing. But the weavers reasoned that the coach must have carried her out of the town so they made for the gates. There the hound picked up on the scent once more. Yelping with excitement, it dragged its breathless handler onward down the road and now it had stopped and was sniffing around.

'Give me a torch,' cried one weaver to some followers who, seeing the likelihood of a positive outcome to the trio's venture, had come after the weavers and their dog.

A flaming brand was passed to the man. Cautiously he leaned over the precipice, grasping the trunk of a tree growing impossibly out of

95

its side and swearing as he slipped and almost lost his footing. Tension mounted. Curious individuals huddled forward, forming a crowd. The weaver tried again to get a footing and this time succeeded. He thrust the blazing head of the torch into the blackness of the ravine.

There below him on a narrow ledge, was a woman's shoe. He remained motionless, ignoring the shouts of those above for news of what he had found. No grieving father would pay handsomely for his daughter's empty shoe. And there was another one further down, close to the rushing water. The weaver drew back, ashen-faced, and was helped onto solid ground by his companion.

But the news was out! Another man, searching the roadside, had discovered caught up in bushes a cloak; green it looked to be by the light of his torch and it had a fur-trimmed hood. So the weaver was forced to share his findings and the crowd slipped away, flaming torches diminishing to mere sparks. Only the hound remained happy, wagging its skinny, threadbare tail in the hope of some reward.

Meanwhile, another band of searchers had ridden on at speed. For the most part young and wealthy, they were satisfied in their own minds as to the identity of the abductors. And some had scores to settle.

21

he Immortali were encamped for the night in a pleasant spot by the edge of wood close to a shallow stream. All was quiet. Children slept. Men and women busied themselves with the tasks life on the move brings with it. Most were content to be on the road. All but four were puzzled as to why they had left the town in such haste.

Everything seemed peaceful until the pounding of hooves brought the four men running. The raiding party rode into the camp, twenty or so men with a mission. They did not stop to ask questions but yelled abuse and started knocking things over.

Pantelone went forward to face them, backed by the other three. 'What is all this, gentlemen? Please! What have we done to incur your wrath?'

'You have a girl with you, abducted from our fair city. Give her up now and we'll spare you. Leave your punishment to the guard.'

'There he is!' shouted a gangly youth with a beard that looked hard pressed to flourish. He pointed at Arlecchino. 'That's the bastard I caught with my Dorabella. I'd recognise him even without his flashy suit and mask.' The youth swung down off his horse.

'And I,' growled a thickset man, dismounting. 'My sister will be spending the next few months in a nunnery on account of you.'

A third, who said nothing, but in whose eyes dark purpose burned, also got down.

Pantelone moved to protect his son. Arlecchino pushed him aside. 'Come on then,' he called, stepping back and beckoning. 'If the three of you think you can take me. Though from what I hear...' he addressed the gangly youth, 'should *your* punch prove as strong as your cock-thrust, I'll hardly feel a thing.'

The youth roared an oath and took a running jump at him. The other men piled in. Pedrolino came to Arlecchino's aid but three against two were not odds to be tolerated. More actors came running. Most of the townsmen dismounted and the fist-fight turned into a brawl.

Meanwhile Pantelone ushered frightened children woken by the fracas to the safety of his wagon, shouting to everyone else to stay inside theirs. The few townsmen who had remained on horseback began riding around the encampment, whooping and yelling. *Gypsies, mountebanks, scum* – and worse, they called the actors. It seemed they had forgotten entirely the purpose of their visit.

The fight became ferocious. Vicious blows were exchanged. Opponents lay flat out. Those still standing punched, thumped and kicked one another until they too were knocked down or fell over others. The youth with the beard hard-pressed to flourish was already out cold. Arlecchino was engaged in a furious slogging match with the thickset man whose sister he had impregnated. The man with dark purpose was seen creeping up behind him. A sudden flash of steel disappeared in an instant, as did the man with dark purpose.

In the midst of the mayhem came the thundering of hooves as the town guard swept in. 'Round up those hotheads!' bellowed their captain.

Some guards set about intercepting riders. The rest dismounted and tried to stop the brawl, only to get caught up in it.

It was a while before order was restored. In the wake of battle, there were plenty of bloodied noses, cracked jaws. Men lay doubled up and groaning. Yet it appeared there were no serious injuries. Those still unconscious, the youth being one, were doused with water from the stream. He sprang to his feet and rushed at Arlecchino but was caught by a guard and frogmarched away. Arlecchino whistled to attract his attention. 'Looks like the rumours were true,' he called, conspicuously dusting down his doublet. 'I hardly felt a thing.'

The youth had to be restrained and forced onto his horse.

The captain dismounted and hailed Pantelone. 'Sir, please accept my apologies on behalf of my fellow citizens. Feelings are running high. A young woman of good family has disappeared. Rumour had it she might be amongst your number.'

'Ah, rumour!' Pantelone cleared his throat.

'Just so. I have orders to search your encampment, and my men will do so with the minimum of upset to your people. But between you and me…' he drew Pantelone aside. 'I already know it will be without result. Certain items belonging to the young woman have been found. It's likely her disappearance is the result of a tragic accident. Or more probably, in my personal opinion, a determination on her part to put an end to own her life. Terrible business. Terrible.'

'Indeed. Indeed.'

The captain gave the order to search the camp then placed a hand on Pantelone's shoulder. 'Now, my friend, don't leave it too long before your next visit. This business will soon be forgotten. Whenever my duties allowed, I came to watch your performance. I swear I have never enjoyed anything half so much.'

The search was soon completed. Honouring Pantelone with a salute, the captain remounted and the guard rode from the camp, driving the hotheads before them.

While the rest of the actors began clearing up, Brighella approached his master.

'Your plan worked well,' Pantelone told him; then he passed on what the captain had said.

Brighella drew him behind a wagon. Close by a horse was tethered.

Arlecchino joined them, rubbing his chin. 'I lied about that young cuckold's punch,' he laughed; then he caught sight of the body Brighella was hauling from under the wagon. The man's doublet was soaked in blood which gushed from his gaping throat. 'He's one of those who first came at me!'

Brighella threw down a stiletto. 'He had this at your back.'

Arlecchino grasped his fellow actor's hand in gratitude.

'He'll be missed,' said Pantelone. 'And they will come looking.'

'He may be missed,' Brighella picked up the dagger then hoisted the body up onto his shoulders, 'but he'll never be found.' Untethering the horse, he strode into the woods.

Arlecchino and Pantelone went back inside the circle. There was still a great deal of mess. Children were crying. 'Is she worth it?' growled Arlecchino, delivering a hefty kick to a broken pail.

Pantelone turned away.

'Almost makes me think you want to fuck the girl yourself.'

The master spun round, grabbed his son by the doublet and shoved him up against a wagon.

~

In the barn a terrified girl sat huddled in a nest of straw, clutching her crucifix. Every prayer that Giulia knew she repeated over and over again, beseeching God to save her, imploring the saints – in particular the Blessed Virgin – to come to her aid. Now she understood why peasants laboured under the yoke of what she had considered ignorant superstition. Ghosts, demons, the curse of witches. These she had believed to be no more than the fanciful imaginings of uneducated minds. But she had never been in the dark before. Not this kind of dark.

As a child, she had sometimes cried in the night if she woke in an unlit room. But there had always been Rosa to rush to her side, a candle to be lit. No candle here. No devoted Rosa to kiss away bad dreams. Giulia was alone. Or was she?

For some time she had been plagued by the feeling she was not. An eerie presence was making itself known, not through sight nor sound nor even smell, but rising out of an instinct she had not known she possessed. A sense of evil assailed her and the cold was so acute it seemed to enter her chest with the air, making it hard to breathe.

How much longer? When would they come for her? She craved human company – even Brighella's. But the thought that had filled her with panic before returned to torment her. Perhaps no one was coming.

The air, though cold, felt heavy and laden with menace. Giulia tried not to look into corners but her eyes were inexorably drawn towards them. There the blackness was so complete it should have signified emptiness; yet it had substance. The harder she stared, the more convinced she became there was something moving within it. Her eyes began smarting with the effort of trying to see what she prayed she would not.

At last her efforts were cruelly rewarded as darkness crept out of the corners to reach like sinuous arms along the base of each wall. At the same time, dim light shone through the hole in the roof. At first she felt cheered, taking it to be cast by a moon no longer obscured by cloud. Then terror gripped her. The light appeared unnatural, more like thick liquid and it grew more intense, forming a translucent green tunnel.

Giulia's gaze flew back to the shadow, which was twisting round on itself like a skein of wool, or length of dough. Spiralling, it moved slowly to the left and, as it did, there came a faint sound; faint yet unmistakeable. The playing of Pan pipes.

She opened her mouth but no sound came out.

Round and round went the nebulous coil, gathering speed; spiralling still, faster and faster. It seemed to draw in the very air she was trying to breath.

Giulia threw herself on God's mercy. This must be her punishment for running away, deceiving her parents. Or a curse come with the book. Brighella had taken it, but it was still really hers. What had Jacopo Bruno said? *I offer my continued prayers to ward off any evil?* He was probably long dead by now but, if he was in heaven looking down, she begged him to intercede for her deliverance.

She squeezed her cross until her palm hurt, mesmerised now by lumps of black shadow, which flew off the coil and fell into the straw. The closest one split and transformed into two skinny waifs who stood hand in hand, hollow eyes fixing her. When they each held out one hand, she managed to scream, 'I have nothing to give you!' Stuffing their fingers into their mouths, they shrank back into shadow.

The second lump reared like a giant snake and coiled itself round a high beam. A man's head appeared within the noose. The rest of him grew, body twisting, legs kicking. Was Giulia screaming? She thought she was; but all she could hear were the Pan pipes and demonic shrieking. This foul cacophony issued from the spinning coil, which again had substance, filled now with diminutive pulsating bodies, engaged in a frenzied caper. The hanged man disappeared.

And now the third, and largest, lump of shadow stretched out to slither towards the viscous tunnel. In that unclean pool of light, on the very spot where Giulia had been raped, lay the girl in the book, naked, legs wide apart.

Giulia watched in horror as the shadow took on the form of an enormous phallus. Searching out the girl's vagina, it thrust itself inside

101

her. She cried out with pleasure, embracing her demonic lover whose hairy legs and scaly torso grew out of the same phallic shadow.

Now revulsion replaced terror as Giulia recognised the girl's face as her own. And, when the demon looked in her direction, she saw that *his* was the mask of Brighella.

She screamed and, this time, did hear herself.

The barn door flew open. Wholesome light poured in, cast by a lamp held by the one who came running. Giulia reached out, even in the midst of distress, praying it would be Arlecchino come to rescue her. 'You poor thing,' cried Pedrolino, wrapping a warm cloak around her shoulders. He carried her from the barn and set her on a horse.

Giulia blanched at the sight of Brighella, who followed on foot as Pedrolino led the way.

After a while, Brighella caught up. 'What did you see in the barn?' he whispered.

'Nothing,' she told him.

22

iulia entered the Immortali encampment at dawn. Fires were being lit and there was the smell of warm bread. Whatever kind of welcome she had been hoping for, her arrival was met with silent stares. Most eyes expressed surprise; a few flashed open hostility. Pedrolino brought the horse to a stop and Pantelone came to meet them.

Exposed to the scrutiny of those members of the company who had not already turned their backs on her, Giulia lowered her gaze. Only one person spoke, the boy who had directed her to Arlecchino's room at the inn. 'What's she doing 'ere?' he chirped and received a clip round the ear from a matronly woman.

Then suddenly Giulia saw *him*. Arlecchino was seated in the back of a covered wagon, stripped to the waist and shaving. He stopped what he was doing and, cut-throat poised in the air, threw her a withering glance.

She fought back the tears as Pantelone took her hand and helped her to dismount. 'You are welcome here, Giulia.'

Knowing he spoke only for himself and perhaps for Pedrolino, she stood in the midst of her new family, convinced she had just made the worst mistake of her life. Waving everyone away, Pantelone beckoned to the matronly woman. 'Now, Giulia, this is Spinetta. She will have charge of you until your child is born. Do as she says and you will have no cause for complaint.' He walked off.

Giulia smiled at the woman who, in response, sniffed then folded her arms under her ample bosom. 'Come along, then,' she said and, turning, marched off across the encampment.

Giulia hurried after her. As she passed Arlecchino's wagon, she could not help but glance in his direction. He cast her a look filled with hatred and yanked the canvas across between them.

Now she almost cried. But what had she been hoping for? That he would have experienced a change of heart? The backs of her eyes felt ready to burst with the effort of trying not to cry. Fist pressed to her mouth, she hurried on.

Pride alone held back the tears. She was deprived of that too when, clambering into the back of a covered wagon, she was ordered to take off her dress. In spite of pleading glances, Spinetta made no effort to let down the flap and Giulia was forced to undo, then step out of, her gown in plain view of anyone who passed. 'You'll have to toughen up, if you want to fit in here,' she was told.

Giulia handed over the dress and the woman's ruddy cheeks broadened at last into a smile. 'This'll do nicely for Franceschina, our leading lady. She needed a gown to play a countess and, with a bit more trimming and some fancy lace…' Spinetta stroked the velvet.

Giulia stood shivering in her chemise; then she heard giggling. Two girls were staring in at her. When she heard a boy whistle, she gave a cry and hid behind Spinetta's skirts. 'Shoo!' yelled Spinetta, waving the youngsters away. 'If you've no work to do, I can soon find you some.' She pulled down the flap then lifted the lid of a long wooden coffer. 'Here,' she said, passing Giulia a dowdy linen dress. She frowned at her stockinged feet. 'What happened to your shoes?'

'Brighella took them.'

Spinetta pulled a puzzled face.

Giulia hastened to put on the dress, which was similar to the one of Silvia's she had worn to meet Arlecchino. 'I reckon this'll see you through until your time.' Spinetta gave the laces one final tug before tying them.

Giulia burst into tears.

'Now, now. No point in that. Not now milk's been well and truly spilt.'

But Giulia could not stop. She sat on the coffer and sobbed.

'I don't know.' Spinetta sighed and sat down next to her. 'Told you he loved you, did he?' Giulia nodded. 'He's a wicked boy. I told him he should learn to tie a knot in it.'

Giulia wiped her eyes. In response to her frown, Spinetta laughed and slapped her hands down on her knees. 'Lord, you never thought I meant that?' She shook her head. 'No, my innocent, it's just a saying. I can see we're going to have to attend to your education, once all this…' she waved a weathered hand across Giulia's front, 'is over and done with.'

'Out of my way!' shrieked a woman's voice. 'Nobody tells me a damn thing.' The canvas flew open and a skinny dark-haired woman with a pale pockmarked face glared in at Giulia.

Spinetta stood up and held out the grey dress. 'Look, Franceschina. Just what you needed for the countess.'

The woman gave it a cursory glance; then her small glinting eyes settled on Giulia's. Thin lips curved into a mocking smile. Snatching the dress, she flounced off, laughing shrilly.

'You'll need to stay on the right side of her,' Spinetta said quietly. 'Now, girl. What can you do?'

'Do?'

'To earn your keep. I doubt you ever learned to cook?'

Giulia shook her head.

'Can you sew?'

'Oh yes.' Giulia nodded enthusiastically. 'Everyone says my needle-work is very neat and…'

'Good.' Spinetta plonked a basket of clothes on the coffer. 'There you are then. Start with that lot.' She left her to it.

Suppressing distaste, Giulia peered in at the pile of smelly garments. She took out and untied the pouch containing needles, selected a shirt, the sleeve of which had come away from the shoulder, and bit off a length of thread. *This might be his*, she thought as she began to sew the sleeve back in place.

By the time Spinetta returned with a bowl of warm milk and a thick slice of bread, she had almost finished. Giulia took the milk. Spinetta put the plate down on the coffer. 'Not bad,' she said, scrutinising her handiwork. But you'll have to speed up. This isn't a needlework class.'

The milk tasted good. Recalling Brighella's mouldy bread, Giulia pushed the plate aside. 'I'm not very hungry. Thank you.'

Spinetta pushed it back. 'Eat it and no argument. The master's given me care not just of you, but the little one you're carrying.'

The bread tasted delicious.

Just then, a head of blond curls popped up at the back of the wagon. Two rows of chubby fingers gripped the floor and a chin came to rest between them. The little girl grinned. 'This is Lella,' said Spinetta.

The child scuttled up the steps, followed by a small sandy-coloured dog. 'Hello,' she said and sat next to Giulia. The dog jumped onto the child's lap. 'This is Crespo. He's mine.'

'He's very nice,' said Giulia, stroking the dog's wiry back.

'Lella, this is Giulia. She'll be sharing our wagon from now on.'

'Lovely! Are you going to have a baby?' Lella shuffled back and forth along the coffer. 'My mummy was going to have a baby but she died. She screamed and screamed and then she died.'

'Lella, dear,' said Spinetta. 'Take Crespo out. He wants a pee.'

'No he doesn't.'

'Do as I say. Quickly now.'

'I'm never having any babies,' announced Lella as she scrambled out, followed by her dog.

'Take no notice of the child,' said Spinetta. 'Her mother was getting on in years. And she was always ailing. You're young and strong. You'll be all right.' She brought a sackcloth mattress stuffed with straw from under the front seat of the wagon, unrolled it and laid it on the floor. 'You do a bit more mending then have a lie down. Soon we'll be back on the road and, from tomorrow, you'll have to pull your weight like the rest of us.'

Giulia mended another shirt, did her best to darn a big hole in some red hose, then put the sewing away. When first she lay down on the mattress, it felt itchy. It took a while to get comfortable but the sackcloth did not smell unpleasant. In fact, the straw inside it was aromatic. She lay listening to voices, fingering her amethyst cross – the only thing of value she still possessed – and gradually drifted off.

Then suddenly she was wide awake. Men were shouting, a horse was neighing. She felt the wagon sway and Spinetta popped her head through the front flap. 'We're moving off.' The cart jerked into motion.

More gentle rocking lulled Giulia back to sleep and into a dream filled with people from her old and new home. She was trying to run away from Signore Panesse's palazzo. Silvia was crying, begging her not to go. But she ran through the gate, chased by the old man who seemed to be running on all fours. Behind him came her mother, shrieking at her to be grateful. Then Silvia turned into Spinetta, who was stern and tipped a basket of filthy clothes over her head.

Giulia woke up, turned over and sank into another dream. Cold fear overwhelmed her. The walls of the barn were closing in. Again she woke, this time through her own efforts. She tried to stay awake but sleep sucked her back. Curiously, this time, she was not afraid; even though Brighella was in the barn with her. He did not seem able to see her as she watched him search through the straw.

She awoke with a jolt. The letter! Her hand went to her bodice. It must have fallen out of her grey dress when she had taken it off. She sat up and searched frantically, lifting the mattress, scanning the boards. But there was no sign. Perhaps it was still inside the bodice? Then Franceschina would find it!

She told herself to stay calm. What did it matter if Franceschina did find Jacopo Bruno's letter? It would mean nothing to her. And she might return it, although that seemed unlikely. She would probably just throw it away. Anyway, why was it important? Brighella had the book. *Brighella had the book.*

Without understanding why, it suddenly became of the utmost importance to find that letter.

23

iulia was glad when the wagon came to a halt and Spinetta peered in at the back. 'You look rested.'

'Yes, but… I need…' Giulia glanced round. 'I need to relieve myself.'

A cheerful face appeared, framed by curls and blue sky.

'Lella, Giulia needs to go into the woods. You take her.' Spinetta told Giulia to take off her stockings. 'You never know, you might need them again one day.'

Giulia scrambled barefoot out of the wagon. Lella grabbed her hand. 'Over there!' she cried, pulling her towards some dense bushes. Crespo followed.

It was a strange but pleasant sensation, running barefoot over grass. Once behind the bushes and hidden from sight of the caravan, Giulia lifted her skirts. As she crouched, Lella turned her back. 'Here,' she said, still facing away while offering Giulia a bunch of leaves.

On the way back, Lella skipped ahead with her dog. As she came to a sudden stop, Crespo began to growl. Seeing Brighella step out from behind their wagon, Giulia caught her breath. The sight of his mask was alarming, even in bright sunlight. He towered over the child, his broad frame dwarfing her. 'Shush Crespo!' said Lella and picked up her pet.

Giulia hurried forward.

'I see you've made some friends,' Brighella remarked.

'Yes I have.' Her fingers found Lella's.

He nodded in the direction of the bushes. 'And you have also been learning the ways of a travelling people?'

Giulia tried not to blush; then thought about her missing letter. Did he have it? Had Franceschina found it and given it to him? She told herself not to be silly. This business with the letter was turning into an obsession. 'Please excuse us,' she said. Crespo gave another growl.

'Crespo doesn't like him,' whispered Lella once they were out of earshot.

Giulia found herself scanning the wagons, wondering which one was Franceschina's. She did not have long to wonder. The leading lady came flouncing down her steps, shrill voice complaining. Giulia experienced a stirring of anxiety because, in spite of what common sense dictated, she knew, in the end, she would be compelled to go looking for Jacopo Bruno's letter.

The caravan was ready to move. 'Walk with me?' begged Lella.

'I have no shoes.'

'Neither have I,' Lella laughed.

'Here's some that might fit Giulia.' A pair of old brown shoes came flying out of the back of the wagon.

Giulia put them on. They did fit, just about.

The sun was hot; yet the breeze brought with it the hint of summer's end. Giulia found its freshness exhilarating and she recalled the first time she had stood on Signore Panesse's balcony when she had caught the aroma of grapes ripe for harvest. Here, in this wilder terrain, there was the smell of something different. The intense light, the lush green woods, a splashing of hidden streams along the way; all inspired in her a thrill she suddenly recognised – the joy of freedom.

A brief twinge of guilt over those she had left behind was easy to ignore. She had made the right choice, even though Arlecchino did not want her and her left shoe was rubbing.

Suddenly she heard, then felt, the pounding of hooves. 'Get the girl out of sight!' yelled Pantelone.

'Quick! Quick!' Spinetta beckoned from the wagon and Giulia scrambled in. They sat very still.

As soon as they heard a man speak, it was clear there was nothing to worry about. The party had come to invite the actors to perform in their village. Pantelone accepted the invitation.

'I would have preferred to put more distance between us and the last place,' he told Spinetta once the riders had gone, 'but we're in no position to turn down offers. One performance, then on our way.' He gave the order to encamp.

Whilst happy to walk in the company of Lella, Giulia was reluctant to leave the wagon alone. Spinetta had other ideas. 'Don't think you can hide away in here all day and night. You'll have the others thinking you consider yourself a cut above.'

'But…'

'No argument. Out with you! Go and enjoy yourself.'

That was not how Giulia viewed the prospect of mixing with the actors. She hoped Lella would be close by but the child was nowhere to be seen. Ambling away from the wagon, she tried to appear relaxed, while wincing at the pain from the blister on her heel.

In the middle of the camp men were building a fire. Women were preparing food. Everybody ignored her; yet she thought she sensed a hostile gaze. Glancing round, she realised no one was paying her any attention. Perhaps it was just the heat of the flames she could feel, now the fire had been lit.

24

n the midst of so many people, Giulia felt alone. She wanted nothing more than to run back and hide in the wagon. It was Lella who saved her. The child came hurtling across the encampment and flung her arms around her skirts. 'Giulia!' she cried. 'Come and meet my daddy. I've told him I'm sharing my wagon with a lady and he wants to meet you.'

Giulia let herself be pulled towards a short stocky man who was standing next to an open cart full of tackle. 'This is my daddy,' said Lella. 'He looks after the animals. There isn't *anything* my daddy doesn't know about animals.'

Lella's father doffed his hat and bowed awkwardly.

Giulia curtsied, stepped forward, grasped his calloused hand and shook it soundly. 'I am very pleased to meet you,' she said.

He stared at her, dropped his gaze then mumbled something inaudible. Lella clapped her hands. 'Sit with me, Giulia.' The child skipped to a bench. 'There's going to be music and dancing.'

And so there was. But not before feasting. Well, it seemed like a feast to Giulia. Served from the spit, the pork was no less delicious than any presented at her father's table. Her father. What would he be doing? Searching for her? Enduring the wrath of her mother, who she could not believe would be missing her? Once the music started, she forgot all about them both.

A man playing a pipe, whilst beating out a rhythm on a tabor with his left hand, began the entertainment. He was joined by a woman with a leather bag with several pipes sticking out of it tucked under one arm. When she grasped one and blew hard, the bag filled with air, as did her wrinkled cheeks. A discordant whine issued from the instrument, followed by a rich nasal sound.

Several actors got up and danced. Giulia smiled and, reaching for the cup of wine at her side, discovered it had been filled to the brim. On the far side of the fire, she noticed Arlecchino come and sit next to Pedrolino.

Lella threaded an arm through hers. 'Do you like dancing?'

Giulia nodded.

'Will you join in?'

Giulia shook her head.

As the rhythm of pipes and tabor quickened, the dancing grew livelier. Music and laughter mingled. Dancers turned red-gold, bathed in firelight. Giulia tapped her foot whilst, in her imagination, she was stepping and bowing with the rest. Once or twice she caught Pedrolino's smile. She smiled back, trying not to let her eyes stray to his companion.

Seeing the musicians stand down, she felt disappointed – until she saw others take their place. One had a lute. The other was Brighella. And, although she disliked him thoroughly, she knew from bitter experience how enchanting his playing could be. This time his instrument was the guitar, an item she knew to be of great value. How could an actor come by such a thing? Probably the same way he came by everything else. She wondered just how much of her jewellery had reached Pantelone's hands.

The music of lute and guitar created an entirely different mood. Now it was romance directing the dancers' steps. Men and women not only touched, but held each other close. Giulia felt a bit shocked yet found herself sighing at the beauty of it all. Lella's blue eyes shone.

Such childlike joy was catching. The circle of warmth within which these people moved; partners in the dance, women serving food, men laughing and joking, excited children chasing, babes in arms sleeping – all seemed to be contained within a glowing cup of magic.

Giulia took another drink and her gaze came to rest on the heart of the fire where embers glowed before collapsing into ash. The alchemist hides away, she thought, hoping to discover mysteries within his crucible. Were he to become part of this, he would learn all life's secrets.

She looked up and, through the firelight, saw Arlecchino get to his feet. Hurriedly her gaze returned to the fire. Surely he could not be coming to..? No. She smothered the foolish notion, yet dared to steal another glance. And now it hurt to breathe for excitement. Yes! Arlecchino was coming to ask her to dance.

A slender apparition in grey drifted across her line of vision. Giulia frowned. Franceschina was wearing *her* grey velvet gown! Arlecchino held out his hand – but not to Giulia. Bringing his leading lady's fingers to his lips, he led her to join the dance.

As she covered her eyes, Giulia heard Franceschina's shrill laugh.

'What's the matter?' asked Lella, tugging at her sleeve.

Sensing another presence, Giulia looked up. In Pedrolino's eyes, she saw clear recognition of her pain. 'Would you do me the honour?'

'I regret…' she waved him away as she got to her feet. 'I'm afraid… I am suddenly unwell.' She ran to the wagon.

25

'iulia.' A small, worried voice found its way through her misery. 'Are you poorly?'

Giulia wiped her eyes and sat up. 'Not now.'

Lella undressed to her shift and snuggled up next to her. Crespo joined them.

'Where does Spinetta sleep?' asked Giulia.

'On the coffer. She's got another mattress.'

Spinetta entered, carrying a lamp. 'Crespo will have to sleep outside from now on, Lella. You've got Giulia for company.'

'Oh no!' cried the child.

'It's all right,' said Giulia. 'I don't mind.'

'Nonsense. I've been indulgent up until now but he belongs outside. Come on, Crespo. Out you go.'

'No!' wailed Lella, hugging her pet. 'It's not fair. He hasn't done anything wrong and he'll get eaten by wolves.'

'Rubbish. Now, give him to me.'

'No. I won't let you.' Lella shuffled out of Spinetta's reach.

'How about if Crespo sleeps at the end of our bed,' suggested Giulia. 'There's plenty of room. And, if there are wolves, he'd make a good guard dog.'

'Oh yes,' cried Lella. 'Please!' She shuffled to the foot of the mattress as Spinetta gave a sigh. 'There,' she said, plonking Crespo on the boards. 'You be a good boy and stay. From now on you're our guard dog.'

Spinetta laughed. 'Fine fierce guard dog he would make! He's no bigger than a rabbit!' She continued to shake her head but it was clear she had been won over. Taking two blankets from the coffer, she handed one to Giulia. Giulia spread it over the mattress she was to share with Lella.

Spinetta undressed to her shift and stepped out of her shoes. Giulia took off her dress. Lella snuggled under the blanket. They bid each other goodnight and Spinetta blew out the lamp. No sooner had she turned to face the canvas than she began to snore. Crespo, tail wagging, came and licked Lella's face. She patted the mattress and he nipped in under the blanket. 'Don't tell,' she whispered.

'I won't,' Giulia whispered back.

Giulia slept well in spite of the strangeness of it all and the pain of Arlecchino's rebuff. But she woke once during the night with the impression it was Crespo's growling that had roused her. She got up at dawn, feeling sick. Moving carefully so as not to disturb Lella, she left the wagon and ran to the bushes where she vomited. Shivering, she leant against the trunk of a tree, wondering whether her nausea had been caused by too much wine, or the sickness Silvia had told her about that pregnant women sometimes suffered from.

As soon as she felt better, she turned to go, then heard a noise coming from the direction of the woods. It sounded like an animal howling. Alarmed by Lella's talk of wolves, she was inclined to run back; but instead found herself drawn towards the sound. *Madness*, she thought as she stumbled into the woods, barefoot. Tripping over a great gnarled root, she managed to stop herself falling and there, directly ahead, saw something that made her want to vomit again. Her grey velvet dress lay in a crumpled heap and Franceschina, raven hair flowing, was pinned to a tree, thin white legs wrapped round Arlecchino's waist, ankles resting on his naked buttocks. With every thrust, she howled with pleasure.

Giulia covered her ears. Tears made her blind. Merciful blindness!

She hurtled back through the trees, numb to the roots and lashing branches as, behind her, the sound of lovers' mutual joy rose to a sickening pitch.

When she stopped at the edge of the woods, a diaphanous mist weaving between the wagons led her gaze to one in particular. The idea was insane. But right now she was insane, with anger and jealousy. And there could be no better opportunity.

Encircling the encampment, she sidled up to the back of Franceschina's wagon and scrambled in.

The place was a mess. Grubby cloths, discarded dresses, crude jewellery littered the floor. Piled high on a small table were jars of coloured paste. Bottles too were crammed on its surface, one of which had tipped to spill a sweet but sickly perfume. It looked as though someone had deliberately thrown things around. Giulia sighed. If Jacopo Bruno's letter was here, she would never find it.

Still, she did move a few items; picking them up then replacing them in the exact same spot. That seemed unnecessary. A woman who lived in such disorder was unlikely to notice if anything had been moved – but there was nothing resembling a letter; in fact no papers at all. Giulia turned to go and, as she did, knocked the table. Jars toppled off. Panicking, she picked them up, pushing them back on where she could and, in doing so, moved a hand-mirror. Beneath it lay a parchment. Giulia's heart leapt. It was her letter! She drew it out carefully, folded it into a tiny square, which she pushed into her palm, then backed out of the wagon.

'What have we here?' Brighella grabbed her by the arm and yanked her to him.

'Let me go or I'll scream!'

'Really? And what will Pantelone say once he finds out you've been stealing from our leading lady?'

'I wasn't stealing.'

'What were you doing?'

She could give him no answer and decided not to struggle in case he noticed she was concealing something in her hand. 'Let me go,' she hissed at him. 'Or I *shall* scream. And when you accuse *me* of thieving, I will ask Pantelone to show me the jewels and money I gave to you. I'll wager there will be items missing.'

He gave a harsh laugh and let her go.

Giulia ran back to her wagon where Lella was sitting up, rubbing her eyes. Crespo wagged his tail. 'Crespo was worried about you.' The dog came to Giulia and she ruffled his ears while stuffing her letter under the mattress.

Spinetta woke up. 'Heavens! I should have been up ages ago.' Swinging her thick legs off the coffer, she frowned at the dog. 'Did Crespo do as he was told and stay at the bottom of the bed?'

'Yes,' replied Lella and Giulia in unison.

The day began with a wash in a bucket of cold water drawn from the stream. Once dressed, Giulia tucked her letter down her bodice, determined not to lose it again. She started on some mending but Spinetta had to keep moving her to get at costumes in the coffer so she was glad when Lella asked if she would go with her to pick wild flowers for the dancers.

Giulia chose to go barefoot because of her blister and it proved a pleasant way to spend an hour, walking through fields and woodland. Lella did not know the real names of any flowers. Neither did Giulia, having been ignorant of the fact that flowers grew in the wild. But the child had given some names of her own. *Sun-face* and *Madonna's Bells* were two Giulia found particularly delightful.

On their return, Lella asked her father if he would bring them a bench so that they could sit together and separate the best of the flowers, which would be made into a bouquet for Franceschina to receive at the end of the performance. The rest would be laid in baskets for the dancers. Once they had finished, Lella put the baskets in the wagon and Spinetta brought out some mending. Giulia resumed her sewing and Lella sat beside her, swinging her legs to and fro whilst humming a tune. Crespo curled up in the shade beneath the bench.

Giulia was mending a torn shift but her attention was only half on her work. Arlecchino was on the opposite side of the campsite with Pedrolino. Arlecchino, bare-chested, goblet in one hand, was – as far as she could make out – attempting to do a backwards somersault without spilling wine. His first two attempts had ended in failure and a great deal of laughter.

'Hello,' came a boy's chirpy voice.

Giulia looked round. 'Hello,' she said.

He sat down next to her, clasped his hands and paid close attention to Arlecchino's third attempt. When the wine spilled again, he chuckled. 'He'll do it. In the end.'

'I have no doubt,' returned Giulia stiffly.

The boy grinned at her. 'I saw you – at the inn. I showed you where his room was. Remember? And you went and told him off. I expect you're in love with him, like all the others?'

She frowned, wondering how many others there were.

117

'I saw you too,' said Lella, threading an arm through Giulia's. 'I stroked your cape.'

Giulia looked down at her. 'So you did!' Only now did she realise this was the same little girl.

'I thought you were beautiful,' said Lella. 'I still do.'

Giulia laughed. 'So are you.' She hugged her.

'Can't you practise that with water?' Pantelone's voice boomed across the encampment.

'Wine concentrates the mind,' Arlecchino shouted back.

Pedrolino refilled the goblet.

'You let him fuck you then?'

Shocked, Giulia stared at the boy.

'Don't talk like that to Giulia,' said Lella. 'She's a lady.'

'Not any more, she's not. Not with Arlecchino's kid in her belly.' The boy wiped his nose on his sleeve.

Lella pulled a face and left.

'My name's Guido. And that...' he pointed at Giulia's abdomen, 'is my little brother or sister you've got in there.'

'What?'

'Arlecchino's my father.' He beamed.

Giulia's gaze quickly returned to Arlecchino, who was preparing to make his fourth attempt; then it swiftly took in every woman of child-bearing age, including one who was heavily pregnant. 'Is your mother travelling with us?'

'Gawd, no! I never knew 'er. She left me in a basket in the back of the master's wagon. Look!' Guido plunged a hand into his doublet and pulled out a tatty strip of linen. 'See!' He smoothed it out with pride and held it taut under her nose. On it was written in faded ink *Arlecchino's boy.*

'It was tied round my ankle. Don't expect she wrote it herself. She must have got it scribed.'

Just then, there came a loud *Yes!* Pedrolino cheered. Arlecchino had mastered his trick. He drained the goblet. Guido leapt to his feet, applauding. 'I told you he'd do it!'

Suddenly, with confusion, Giulia noticed that Arlecchino was walking in her direction. She paid close attention to her mending.

'Hurray,' shouted Guido, skipping off to meet his father. 'Hurray for Arlecchino!' He tried to slap him on the back but Arlecchino swerved and flicked his ear with a cloth.

'Get back to work, you lazy tyke.'

The boy ran off, laughing.

Arlecchino came and stood behind Giulia. Nervous fingers were forced to work hard, in order to maintain an even stitch. 'Very neat,' she heard him say.

'Did you have to speak to the boy like that?' she muttered. 'He's your son.'

'There's no proof of that.'

'Just like there's no proof this one's yours, I suppose?'

Arlecchino stalked off.

26

h why had she said it? Giulia could have bitten off her tongue. That was the first time Arlecchino had spoken to her since she had arrived and now…

'May I?' Pedrolino was in costume, carrying his big straw hat.

She invited him to sit.

'I hope you're feeling better today.'

'I am. Thank you. I'm sorry I ran off last night. It was kind of you to ask me to dance.'

'I wasn't being kind.'

They fell silent and watched the activity across the encampment. Lella's father was hitching mules to a wagon and the actors were assembling in full costume. Arlecchino was not amongst them. 'When will you leave?' asked Giulia.

'Anytime now.'

Franceschina's shimmering dress reflected the afternoon sun yet made the light appear cold. Her raven locks were plaited and pinned, revealing a slender neck. Her waist was unbelievably tiny.

'Pedrolino.'

'Yes?'

'May I ask you something?'

'Of course.'

Giulia braced herself. 'Is Arlecchino in love with Franceschina?'

He gave a soft laugh. 'Because he asked her to dance?'

'No,' she replied, burning at the memory of the scene in the copse. 'Not just that.'

Arlecchino's sudden appearance took her by surprise. It was almost as if he had stepped through a gap in the air. He was still unmasked but wearing his new suit, the one he had told her about. Such colours! His livery rivalled the rainbow. In contrast with his monochrome lady, his lithe but muscular form burst with living lights.

'I don't know the answer to your question,' said Pedrolino, running the brim of his hat between finger and thumb. 'He hasn't confided in me.'

Giulia watched Arlecchino take Franceschina's hand and guide her to the leading wagon.

'All I know is, Arlecchino's in love with his art. And Franceschina *is* his leading lady.'

Giulia frowned as a germ of hope unfurled inside her, inspiring her to ask, 'Are you saying he pretends to be in love with her?'

'No. Not pretends. But it helps, with the acting.'

Giulia could not help but smile.

Arlecchino took his seat on the wagon next to Franceschina. 'I have to go,' said Pedrolino and, getting up, limped towards them.

Pantelone's false beard waggled as he bellowed out orders. Guido gave a sharp rap on his drum. Lella, white ribbons in her turbulent hair, carried a basket of flowers. Her violet satin dress was too long for her and, as she ran to join the other dancers, she had to keep hitching it up. 'Go on! Go on!' Spinetta flapped a hand to hurry her.

Lella waved to Giulia. Giulia waved back. Suddenly she was filled with the longing to go with them. She had never experienced a feeling so powerful, except perhaps her love for Arlecchino.

'Let the acting begin!' commanded Pantelone.

hile the troupe was away, Spinetta introduced Giulia to some of the women, including the girl who was heavily pregnant. Her name was Carla. She was not much older than Giulia and already had one child: a chubby, gurgling boy of ten months. Dismayed at the thought of becoming pregnant so soon after giving birth, Giulia said nothing of that, but asked her new friend about looking after babies. Carla was happy to pass on what she knew. Just before sunset, the troupe was heard returning. The loudest voice was Franceschina's. 'You made a complete fool of me!'

Arlecchino brought the wagon to a stop, jumped down and offered her his hand.

'That was supposed to be a romantic scene,' she screamed at him, getting down clumsily and without assistance. 'And you! You played it for laughs.'

'They're peasants,' he replied with a shrug. 'What did you expect?'

'I expect a degree of consideration from my leading man. *Not* to be humiliated.'

'You're exaggerating. Come here and don't be silly.' He reached out but she pushed him away. 'Sod you then!' He walked off.

'Arghh!' Franceschina stamped her foot. 'Don't you dare turn your back on me!'

Giulia tried not to laugh; then she noticed Lella carrying the bouquet they had made for Franceschina. She ran to the leading lady but, when Franceschina was offered the flowers, she swiped them clean out of the child's hands and flounced off.

'Franceschina, I'm sorry.' Arlecchino strode after her. 'Surely you understand? That kind of audience doesn't appreciate sophistication. If I hadn't done something, they'd have booed us off stage.'

Lella ran to Giulia, carrying the rejected bouquet.

'What did he do?' whispered Giulia.

The child giggled.

'It'll be a different matter once we get to Florence,' Arlecchino called after Franceschina.

'We're not going to Florence.'

'What?' Arlecchino spun round and everyone's eyes fell on Pantelone. 'What did you say?'

'I have decided. We are not going to Florence.'

'But you said…' Arlecchino strode towards him. 'Florence next, you said. Then Rome.'

'Rome? Pah! The place is full of priests.'

'So, where are we going?' asked someone.

'To Venice.'

'But we've just come from there,' groaned Arlecchino amidst murmurs. 'We left with the city eating out of our hands.'

'Precisely! That means we are assured of a warm welcome.'

Arlecchino banged his hat against his thigh. 'How, in God's name, are we to become the most illustrious troupe in all Europe, if you keep taking us back to the same old place?'

'We are going to Venice and that is final! Anyone else with anything to say on the subject – speak now!'

Nobody did, apart from Arlecchino, who bellowed an oath then shook his fist at the sky.

Franceschina was, by now, inside her wagon, throwing things out of the back.

'Did you hear that, Franceschina? We're going back to bloody Venice!'

'I don't care,' she shrieked. 'At least *there* I'll get the audience I deserve and *not* a load of country bumpkins.'

'What are you doing?' Arlecchino watched her, hands on hips, as she added to the growing pile of items.

'Something's gone missing.'

27

ow can you tell?' laughed Arlecchino. As he turned to walk away, a hand mirror came flying out of the wagon and hit him on the back of the head. 'Ow!'

Spinetta laughed out loud; Giulia hid her amusement.

'Can I keep the flowers?' Lella asked Spinetta.

'If the leading lady doesn't want them. And it doesn't look to me like she does. Give them here. I'll hang them upside down in the wagon so they last longer.'

'Tell me about the performance,' said Giulia.

Lella told her how much the audience had liked their dance. 'They even asked us for an encore!'

'But what did Arlecchino do to make Franceschina so cross?' The leading lady was still hurling things out of her wagon.

'Something rude,' giggled Lella, behind her hand.

Guido came walking by and helped himself to some nuts Spinetta had been shelling. He tossed several into his mouth. 'Stop that!' she told him, winding twine around the stem of the bouquet. 'So, what's put our leading lady in such an almighty paddy?'

He grabbed another fistful. 'She was in the middle of her speech. You know, the sloppy one where she drivels on about love and stuff. And, when her back was turned, Arlecchino pulled his trousers down and shoved the bouquet up his arse. Course, he didn't stick the stalks right up his bum. Just held them in his crack. It was really clever though, how he waggled the flowers about so they looked like…'

'Yes thank you, Guido.' Spinetta held the bouquet by the twine.

Lella giggled. The boy sprang forward onto the ground and walked away on his hands.

Pedrolino was unloading baskets of vegetables; there was also a crate of hens. Spinetta spoke to Pantelone. 'Not much in the hat, I take it?'

He shook his head. 'They were poor folk.'

'Is that why we're going to Venice?'

He shrugged and pulled off his false beard.

Giulia led Lella away. 'Tell me more about the performance,' she said, but her attention was mainly on Franceschina, who had changed out of costume and was busy retrieving her things. Brighella went to help. Giulia noticed him pick up the hand mirror and, when he offered it to the leading lady, she flapped her hands and launched into an animated, yet uncharacteristically quiet, discourse.

'Did you, Giulia?' asked Lella, pulling on her arm.

'Sorry, Lella. What was that?'

'Did you make friends with Carla?'

'Oh, yes. She's very nice.'

Just then Arlecchino came striding across the encampment with Pedrolino in hot pursuit. They had both changed out of costume.

'Where are you going?' Pantelone called.

'Back to the village,' called Arlecchino, 'to get drunk. Where's Brighella? Oh, never mind! He knows where to find us.'

Giulia looked back towards Franceschina's wagon. There was no sign of her now, nor of Brighella.

After the evening meal, Giulia helped Spinetta and the other women clear away and wash the utensils. She found the work surprisingly enjoyable, mainly on account of the company. The women chatted, sang and joked. Giulia derived mischievous satisfaction from the fact that they all found the row between Arlecchino and Franceschina highly amusing.

When it was time to go to bed, Lella came to Spinetta, looking worried. 'I can't find Crespo.'

'He's around somewhere.' Spinetta unrolled her mattress and shook it.

'He was asleep in the wagon before supper but now he's gone.' Lella looked round, eyes glistening.

'He can't have gone far. Call him.'

Lella began calling her dog. 'Shall I help you look?' offered Giulia.

'Oh please.' Lella grabbed her hand. 'He sometimes visits my daddy and the animals,' she said hopefully. But, when they found her father, he had not set eyes on the dog.

'Don't worry,' said Giulia. 'He's probably just wandered off.'

'No he hasn't,' returned the child crossly. 'He never just wanders off.' She started to cry. 'Something's happened to him. Something bad.'

Giulia gave her a hug. 'Come along. We'll find him together.'

They searched the encampment, visited every wagon; but no one had seen Crespo. Everyone promised to keep an eye and ear open, everyone except for Franceschina. Her response was, 'How the devil should I know where your stupid dog's gone?'

'We'll have to look outside the camp,' pronounced Lella and made off towards the trees.

Giulia caught her. 'No, Lella. We cannot go into the woods. Not at night.'

'We've got to!' Lella stamped a foot and tried to squirm free. 'If you won't go with me, I'll look for him on my own.'

Giulia glanced anxiously towards their wagon. Light was shining through the canvas. She should call for Spinetta, but did not want to disturb the others. And Lella was just a child. She really ought to be able to deal with this herself. 'Lella. Lella. Listen to me. All right. We will go and look for Crespo. But not far. Not deep into the woods. And if we can't find him, promise you'll come back to the wagon. We'll look for him again in the morning, when it's light.'

The little girl stopped struggling, wiped her eyes and nodded.

They set off towards the woods. Fortunately, the moon was full and the sky cloudless. But, once beneath the trees, Giulia's misgivings grew and the further in they went, the stronger became the desire to be back in her old life, safe in her room with no one but herself to worry about. 'I can hear him,' cried Lella.

All Giulia could hear was the sound of rushing water and that was much too close. It sounded as if the stream plunged away not far to their left. But Lella was determined and hauled her in that direction. Giulia knew they should go back; but knew as well it would mean a battle with this determined little girl. She did not think she could face that. Besides, she was not even sure she could get her back safely, kicking

126

and screaming as she surely would be. Oh why had she let things come to this? Her first time in charge of a child and she had done something really stupid. It did not bode well for her future role as a mother.

Stepping out from under the trees, Giulia could make out a grassy ridge ahead with a bare rocky ledge jutting from it. The splashing of water confirmed there was indeed a fall beyond. She yanked Lella back. 'We must go no further.'

'Shush!' said Lella. 'Listen.'

Faint yet unmistakeable, came the pathetic yelping of a dog.

'He's down there!' Lella slipped free and ran to the rock. 'Crespo! Crespo! I'm coming to save you.'

Giulia dashed after her and managed to catch her by the skirts.

'He's down there!' screamed Lella, leaning over the ledge. 'We've got to go and get him.'

'No, Lella. We can't. Not alone.' Giulia hauled her back 'We must get help.'

'But…'

'No!' Giulia was determined. 'We're going back. We need men and torches. Now come along. Your daddy will know what to do. The sooner we tell him what's happened, the sooner we can rescue Crespo.'

The child gave a whimper, which mingled with the whining of the dog. Giulia hardened herself and, getting a grip on Lella's hand, pulled her away.

As soon as they appeared in the encampment, Spinetta came running. 'Where on earth have you been? Giulia, what could you be thinking of?' Lella's father strode towards them, carrying a torch. 'They're all right,' gasped Spinetta. 'Thank the Lord!' She tried to hug Lella but the child wriggled free and ran to her father.

'Crespo's in the ravine. You've got to come and save him.' She grabbed his hand and pulled him towards the trees.

'What in heaven's name possessed you?' Spinetta frowned at Giulia. 'I've been out of my mind with worry.'

'I'm so sorry. But Lella was insistent. And her poor little dog…'

'Is just a dog!'

Giulia hung her head. Several of the actors had come to see what was happening, Pantelone amongst them.

'Everything's fine,' Spinetta told him. 'Lella lost her dog and this young lady thought it a good idea to go off and look for him in the woods.'

'Where's the child now?' asked Pantelone.

'She's gone with her father to see what can be done.'

Lella's father was already on his way back, his daughter tucked under one arm. She was wriggling and yelling, a furious bundle of curls and flying fists. He put her down next to Spinetta, who caught hold of her and tried to calm her. 'I'll get you another dog,' he grunted.

'I don't want another dog!' she screamed at him. 'I want Crespo. He's mine!'

'The dog's too far down,' he told everyone impassively.

At that moment there came the sound of laughter; Arlecchino and Pedrolino had returned from the village. Arlecchino was leaning on his friend. Lella broke free of Spinetta and hurtled towards him. He crouched to catch her. 'Lella, Lella.' He lifted her up and swung her round.

'Put me down,' she cried.

'What's wrong, my angel?'

'Crespo's in the ravine. My daddy says he can't be saved. But you can save him, can't you, Arlecchino? Please! Go and get Crespo out of that horrible place.'

'Of course I will, sweetheart.' He put her down then held out his hand and she grasped it. 'Show me.' Staggering, he let himself be led into the wood.

Pantelone went after them. 'I forbid it! The dog is out of reach and you have been drinking.'

'Bring rope and torches,' Arlecchino called.

Guido came running. 'What's going on?'

'Lella's dog's fallen down the ravine,' another boy told him. 'Arlecchino's going to save it.'

'Great!'

This may have been just an adventure to the boys but as everyone, including Giulia, followed Arlecchino and Lella into the woods, a desperate Pantelone tried again to dissuade his son. According to Lella's father, the animal had to be sixty foot down. Nothing short of a miracle could save him.

'That's what I trade in,' came the slurred reply. But when they reached the jutting rock and Arlecchino, blazing torch in hand, looked down, even he appeared to have second thoughts. 'Whoa,' he gasped and staggered back.

Pedrolino took the torch. 'Where is the dog?' He thrust the head of flame into the chasm. 'Ah, I see him! Stuck in the bush on the far side.' Crespo started to yap.

'Hang on, Crespo,' called Lella. 'Arlecchino's coming to save you.'

'How are you going to get across?' asked Pedrolino.

'We could chop down a tree,' came one man's suggestion. 'Then he could walk across and climb down.'

'I shall jump,' declared Arlecchino.

'What?' bellowed Pantelone.

Arlecchino unbuttoned his doublet.

'This is madness! I absolutely forbid it.'

'My father is worried about the takings. Fear not, venerable parent. Before making any attempt, I shall put my affairs in order. To my good friend, Pedrolino, I bequeath my worldly goods,' he draped his doublet over Pedrolino's outstretched arm, 'paltry as they are, the old man being an inveterate skinflint.' He wrenched off his shirt and threw it aside. 'To Guido…'

'Yes?' piped the boy, stepping forward.

'To you, Guido, I pass on the role of Arlecchino, together with my leading lady. Where is she, by the way? Typical! Not to be here to witness my finest, and possibly final, performance. Guido here may prove a trifle small for the part to begin with. But, if his grandfather provides him with a box, I am sure he can rise to the occasion.'

'Did you hear that?' exclaimed Guido. 'That's the first time ever he's admitted I'm his!'

'He must really think he's going to die,' scoffed his friend.

'In God's name,' said Pantelone, 'do not attempt this. You are drunk!'

'Just as well.' Arlecchino eased his father aside. 'Right then.' He rubbed his hands. 'Stand back, everyone. I shall need a run-up.'

'I can't watch,' gasped Spinetta and covered her eyes.

Giulia was unable to believe hers. Apart from Pantelone and Spinetta, nobody else seemed worried that this man was about to leap to his death.

She looked hopefully to Pedrolino but he said nothing. Was she dreaming? Had she wandered into a world full of callous fools? Arlecchino must be insane. Gifted acrobat he undoubtedly was, but no man could jump that gap. She wanted to shout at him *No, don't do it*! But would he listen to her? Then she felt a small hand curl around hers and, looking down, saw Lella smiling up at her.

'Holy Mary, Mother of God' Arlecchino crossed himself, 'pray for us sinners,' he prepared to make his run, 'now,' he sprang forward, 'and at the hour,' he sped up until running full-tilt, 'of our deaaathhh…' He leapt from the rock, sailed through the air a considerable distance and disappeared into the ravine.

28

here was silence, the kind that comes with shock and disbelief. It lasted no longer than it takes to blink then the air exploded with gasps, cries and oaths. Giulia stood rigid, mouth completely dry. The leaden ache inside had rendered her speechless, immobile. Tears brimmed. She felt Lella let go of her hand and watched the child run to the edge with the rest. Sickened, Giulia turned from the scene the same moment a deep rich laugh came echoing out of the ravine.

'He's alive!' shouted Pedrolino.

Impossible! Giulia turned back.

'I'm standing on a ledge,' called Arlecchino. 'The dog's caught up in a bush a few feet away.'

Pantelone cursed his son in a voice that betrayed a father's love. Spinetta, who had not rushed forward with the rest, thanked God. Then Giulia understood. These folk had not been callous or uncaring. Celebration filled the air. They had been in possession of something she had lacked: faith. Faith in the ability of the Immortali's most cherished son.

She cried openly, gave silent thanks for a miracle. Then she almost laughed. The love she felt for this child of a man was ridiculous. She should not love him; she should hate him. And she had tried. But something within him demanded to be loved. How unjust. How completely contradictory.

He was calling for a rope and there was a scramble to fetch one. 'Wind it round a tree,' he called, 'with two strong men on the end. I'll get only one chance. Pedrolino, gammy leg or no gammy leg, I want you on that rope.'

Lella came and took Giulia's hand. 'I told you he could do it.'

131

'Not yet,' whispered Giulia. 'Not quite yet.'

The rope was secured. Pedrolino and two others took up their positions. Another threw the rope. By the second throw, Arlecchino had hold of it. 'I'm tying it around me. When I yell to *pull*, tug for all you're worth.'

Crespo could be heard, yapping loudly.

'Ready up there?' called Arlecchino.

'We are.'

'At the count of three, then.'

Giulia held her breath.

'One,' came the count. 'Two.' Momentarily the rope seemed to slacken. 'Three!... Pull!' There was a sickening jolt followed by an agonised cry and the rope cut into the side of the ravine. As Pedrolino and the others fought to take the strain, Pantelone leaned over the edge. 'Keep pulling, damn you!' Arlecchino roared. 'Pull. Pull harder!'

Giulia willed them on and, at last, glimpsed the desperate fingers of one hand grasp the turf. With his father's arms about him, Arlecchino was brought up safely.

Crespo leapt from his arms. Lella gave a cry, let go of Giulia and ran to her pet. 'He's broken his leg, I think,' said Arlecchino as the dog limped to meet her. Lella scooped him up and he licked her face.

'I'll make him a splint and bind his leg,' said her father, taking Crespo.

Amidst all the handshakes and slaps on the back, Giulia noticed the bloody graze across Arlecchino's chest. Lella ran to him and he crouched to receive her. She flung her arms about his neck, kissed his grimy cheek. 'Thank you! Thank you! I love you, Arlecchino.'

He laughed. 'Ask your daddy to make Crespo a collar and leash. Then he won't get into any more trouble.'

'I will. I will.' She kissed him again.

Excitement over, everyone made their way back to the encampment. Giulia walked at the rear, happy like the rest, yet pondering on the rescue. There was something odd about it. Exactly what eluded her. She was not sure but it was to do with a trick of the light.

～

he next morning Giulia helped Spinetta sweep out the wagon. Lella was sitting outside, singing to Crespo, who was lying in the willow basket she had lined with a baby's duck down pillow. His leg had been splinted and bound and he seemed to be enjoying the attention.

'I'd swear I left this coffer open last night,' said Spinetta; she gave the lid a final quick dust. 'You know, when you ran out of the wood with news of Crespo. 'I grabbed the lamp and came running. Then, when we got back here, the coffer was shut.'

'Perhaps the lid fell down,' suggested Giulia.

'Perhaps.' Spinetta shrugged. 'Well, we're finished in here. You go and get some fresh air.'

Across the encampment, next to the wagon he shared with Pedrolino, Arlecchino was basking, bare-chested, in the late summer sunshine. Giulia went and spoke to Lella, half her mind on something she felt inspired to do. She wavered, then decided, and, taking a deep breath, crossed to where he lay.

The burn from the rope was now dark red. His eyes remained closed.

'That was a wonderful thing you did, last night.'

He opened his eyes, then shielded them. 'I was drunk.'

'Even so.'

'Lella's a sweet child,' he said, stretching and wincing.

'She is,' agreed Giulia.

'And she's had a lot to put up with. I know what it means to lose someone when you're so young.' Giulia hoped he would elaborate; instead he waved a hand at her. 'Could you move please? You're blocking the sun.'

'Just like you once blocked out the stars,' she murmured and walked away.

Spinetta did not need her. There was mending to be done, but, since there always was and Lella appeared content to stay and nurse her dog, Giulia decided to go for a walk. It was not entirely aimless, nor was her chosen path without direction. And it was easy to follow, the grass having been flattened by so many feet the night before.

She was pleasantly surprised when she reached the ravine. Sunshine imbued the place with mellow calm and the sound of rushing water, no longer threatening, was musical. She sat for a while on the springy turf surrounding the flat rock from which Arlecchino had leapt; then she got up and walked to the edge. Spray kissed her face. It came from a fall decked in crystal that plunged over rocks below to become a clear ribbon descending into white foam and aquamarine.

Turning her attention towards the far cliff face, she noticed halfway down the bush from which Crespo had been rescued. That had to be it because it was the only vegetation, otherwise the rock was bare. But how had he got there? Crespo was a tiny dog; he could never have leapt so far. And why jump into a ravine? Common sense dictated he must have slipped but, if so, he would have fallen to his death below where she was standing. She looked down, then all around, trying to make sense of it. There was no way she could see that Crespo could have crossed the ravine then fallen. Perhaps something had been chasing him and he had leapt in fear? Even so, he could never have jumped so great a distance.

Then something else occurred to her. Arlecchino had called, 'I'm standing on a ledge. The dog's caught up in a bush a few feet away.' Again Giulia scanned the cliff face. Last night's events were still confused and the air had been charged with high emotion. Perhaps she had misheard him. She left the rock but paused. Compelled to return, she stood staring at the far cliff. Then it came to her with a jolt. There was *no* ledge!

Giulia was transfixed. A chill of unease rippled down her spine. The question of how the dog had got into the bush, the lack of a ledge – or anything else on which Arlecchino could have been standing – were puzzling enough; yet neither of these things were what had drawn her here.

Memories crept out of the dark. The flaming torches had not dazzled her, nor tears made her blind. Yet it *must* have been an illusion. Surely? Those streaks of light she had seen shoot from Arlecchino's heels the moment he leapt from the rock.

29

he rush of water turned into a roar. Birds were singing, the day was still bright; but the chill inside Giulia intensified. She hurried back to the encampment; then, reaching the limit of the trees, stepped back into shadow. Brighella was walking with Franceschina on the grass surrounding the wagons. The pair looked relaxed, familiar. Brighella bent to whisper in the leading lady's ear and she laughed – not in her usual shrill tone. Her laughter was coquettish.

Giulia waited until they had gone then stepped out from beneath the trees. With the sunlight came shocking insight. Last night, the one man conspicuous by his absence was Brighella!

She walked briskly to the wagon where Lella was still fussing over Crespo. Spinetta's comment about the lid of the coffer being down now meant something and Giulia thought she knew how Crespo had ended up in the ravine. That monster of a man must have thrown him in! She felt panicky as she scrambled up the steps. Brighella had been here! And it did not take much imagination to work out why. It must have been him who shut the coffer. Careless, yes. And out of character. No doubt, while he was searching, he had been disturbed by the return of the actors. But why try to kill the dog?

Giulia pondered only a moment. Of course! Who was it Crespo disliked enough to growl at? If Brighella had tried to enter the wagon before, perhaps during the time she and Spinetta had spent with the other women after the meal..? She sat on the coffer and tried to gather her thoughts. Franceschina must have told him she had found a letter in the dress. Giulia had suspected as much when he was helping the leading lady gather her things. And he had caught Giulia coming out

135

of her wagon. So now he would know she had recovered her letter and most probably kept it on her person.

She tried to stay calm and managed to do so until Spinetta rushed up the steps, carrying Carla's baby. 'Here!' she said, plonking him on Giulia's lap. 'Carla's gone into labour.' She left the wagon. The baby took one look at Giulia and screwed up his face.

'But I know nothing about looking after babies,' Giulia called after Spinetta.

'Learn!'

Giulia was left trying to comfort a baby who made his distress at being left with her all too plain. She tried rocking him as she had seen Carla do, but his body went rigid, his once pleasing features contorting into a puffy red mask of rage.

Lella appeared at the back of the wagon. 'Try holding him up, so that he's looking over your shoulder.'

Giulia did so but the baby continued to cry. 'This is hopeless!'

'Bring him outside. Sometimes, if you walk round with them, they stop.'

Giulia tried that too. If anything, he howled even louder.

'What's all this?' Pedrolino came over, smiling broadly.

'Carla's having her new baby,' Lella told him.

'Oh, right.' He glanced briefly in the direction of Carla's wagon.

'I can't stop this one crying,' said Giulia. 'Do you think he's hungry? Perhaps, if we get him some milk?'

'He's just not used to you. And he's missing his mother. Here, give him to me.'

'Gladly.' Giulia handed him over.

After a while being patted on the back and spoken to in a reassuring voice, the infant stopped crying. Lella went back to her dog.

'You're very good with babies.'

'I've had a lot of practice. Oh, I don't have any of my own, you understand. But the company's numbers increase from time to time. Shall we sit?' Pedrolino indicated the turf.

They sat side by side with the baby between them. The child seemed content and even let Giulia hold his chubby fingers.

'Do you have any family amongst the actors?' she asked Pedrolino.

'We're all family. But, if you mean blood relatives, no.'

Across the campsite Giulia noticed Brighella with Franceschina. 'Brighella's a strange man,' she remarked. 'Do you know where he comes from?'

The baby moved onto hands and knees and started crawling away. Pedrolino caught the hem of his garment. 'You ask a lot of questions.'

'Sorry. I didn't mean…'

'That's all right.' He gave her a smile. 'You're new here. But let me ask you something, Giulia. Since you arrived, has anyone asked you about your past life?'

'No,' she replied, feeling suitably chastised.

'Well, that's how it is with the Immortali. Once you join, you become part of the family. And the life you had… well…' he shrugged, 'it ceases to exist.'

There came a groan from Carla's wagon. Pedrolino scooped up the baby. 'Much as I'd like to stay and be nursemaid, I've got work to do.'

They stood and she brushed down her skirt. 'Will he be all right with me now?'

'I think so.' He placed the child in her arms. 'Although perhaps he would like some milk.'

'I'll get it,' chirped Lella.

Pedrolino held a hand up in front of the baby's face and, making a fan of his fingers, produced, as if by magic, a soft leather ball. He let the child take it, ruffled his hair then walked away. As Lella returned with the milk, there came another moan from Carla's wagon. Catching the little girl's expression, Giulia remembered what had happened to her mother. 'Come along,' she said brightly. 'It's up to us now to keep… what's his name?'

'Angelo.'

'It's up to us to keep little Angelo amused. Let's hope he lives up to his name.'

Lella laughed.

Angelo did live up to his name and seemed perfectly content. He was a heavy child but Giulia chose to carry him while holding Lella's hand as they took walks around the encampment. Eventually though, he began to rub his eyes so they returned to their wagon. Giulia rocked him and he soon fell asleep. Now all she had to worry about was Lella. Every time there came a groan from Carla's wagon, the child covered her ears. She had brought Crespo inside, still in his basket. But even his presence failed to distract her. Angelo, on the other hand, slept through all his mother's pain.

Now, with each mounting cry from Carla, Giulia found herself holding her breath. She felt she was going through her friend's ordeal with her. After about half an hour the groans became more frequent and heartrending. Then, at last, Carla gave one long protracted scream, which was followed by silence. Giulia held her breath. Lella's eyes were closed tight, her fingers stuffed in her ears. Suddenly the cries of a newborn rent the air. 'Lella. Lella.' Giulia gripped the child's shoulder. 'Everything is all right. Carla's had her baby.'

Lella opened her eyes and cautiously took her hands from her ears.

Within minutes, a beaming Spinetta appeared at the back of the wagon. 'Well,' she said, rolling down her sleeves. 'That's a good job done. Carla's had a fine strong girl.'

Lella gave a squeal and clapped her hands.

As she entered the wagon, Spinetta whispered to Giulia, 'See, sometimes it is that easy.'

Easy? thought Giulia.

'You've done well too,' said Spinetta, smiling down at the slumbering Angelo. She collected some bedding and linen then returned to Carla's wagon. Soon afterwards Angelo woke. When he looked up at Giulia, his face puckered. Much to Giulia's relief, Spinetta came back and told them they could take him to see his new sister.

Carla was sitting up, new baby at her breast. She looked tired, flushed, but completely happy. Seeing her like this, Giulia felt that perhaps it would not be so bad becoming a mother. When Angelo was brought near to his little sister, he showed no interest whatsoever, preferring instead his new ball.

That evening after the meal, most of the men, Arlecchino amongst them, were drinking in celebration of the safe arrival of a new Immortali member. Giulia lost count of the number of times they drank a toast to Carla's husband.

'Just look at them,' mocked Spinetta. 'Anyone would think it was Marco who'd done all the hard work.' Even so, she called, 'Well done,

Marco. You have a beautiful daughter. Have you and Carla decided on a name?'

'Serafina,' he called back. 'We're going to call her Serafina.'

'A beautiful name for a beautiful child.'

Marco raised his cup to Spinetta.

'He's a good man,' she said. 'Carla couldn't wish for a better husband.' Catching Giulia's expression, she patted her hand. 'Arlecchino may come round yet.'

Giulia wished with all her heart it might be so but only once this evening had his gaze met hers. Immediately afterwards, he had moved his stool to face the other way.

Early the following morning the caravan was ready to leave. Giulia was amazed to see Carla up and about outside her wagon, a baby on each arm. Spinetta smiled at her look of surprise. Her smile grew broader when Giulia showed her the gown she was making for the new baby out of a shirtsleeve and some lace she had unpicked from a shift beyond repair.

The company had been ready to leave the day before, but Serafina's arrival had put a stop to that. Now there was a feeling of anticipation in the sharp morning air as each wagon peeled off from the circle onto the track. 'How far is it to Venice?' Giulia asked Spinetta as they sat together in the back of the wagon.

'Lord, I haven't the faintest.'

'It will take about two weeks,' called Pantelone, who was driving. 'That is, if the weather and good fortune hold.'

'Well, at least there are no more babies to be born,' Spinetta shouted back. 'Not yet awhile, anyway,' she added, with a wink at Giulia.

30

iulia smiled. In spite of Arlecchino's lack of interest in her condition, she was beginning to warm to the idea of having a child. And Pedrolino had been right in describing the Immortali as a family. She had been amongst them such a short time yet felt a deeper sense of belonging than she had ever experienced at home.

Her old home. She had hardly given it a thought recently. She wondered about Rosa and Silvia. What would they say, if they could see her now? Rosa, no doubt, would disapprove of her new family but would be pleased she was happy. Silvia would be nothing less than delighted!

Whilst taking this brief excursion into her past, Giulia had tried not to think about her parents. But her conscience troubled her regarding her father and also Signore Panesse. She told herself it was best for him that she had run away. Theirs could never have been a happy marriage, in spite of his promises. And what if her mother had been right? *All men want one thing.*

Well, Arlecchino had certainly proved her right. But what about Pedrolino? No, he was kind and courteous. Not all men were the same.

❧

few days on the road and it began to rain. The rain became a downpour and it was not long before the track turned into a river of mud. One of the wagons shed a wheel and the caravan came to a standstill. They had only just set off again when Spinetta and Giulia's wagon got stuck.

'I'm sorry,' called Pantelone, after several attempts to get the mules to haul it free. 'You'll have to get out. We're going to need to lift this.'

140

'Come along,' said Spinetta. 'We'll shelter in Carla's wagon until ours has been freed. It'll be a squeeze but I know she won't mind.'

'And Crespo?' asked Lella.

'Oh no, dear. Not with a new baby.'

'Then I'm not going. I'm not leaving him on his own. Ever again!'

'The child can stay in the back,' yelled Pantelone above the sound of lashing rain. 'She's no weight.'

'Oh all right,' said Spinetta. 'Come along, Giulia.'

Giulia made to follow, then remembered the dress she had made for the baby. 'Just a minute,' she called. 'I'll follow on.'

Spinetta glanced back, shawl held over her head. She waved then hurried on up the line. Giulia folded Serafina's dress and tucked it beneath her shawl. As she stepped from the wagon mud splashed up over her ankles.

Carla and Marco's wagon was close to the front and, to reach it, she had to pass Franceschina's. She was surprised to see the leading lady standing by the open flap. 'Giulia,' she called. 'Shelter in here.'

Giulia paused, peering through the curtain of rain.

'Come on,' Franceschina beckoned and, unusually for her, she was smiling. 'You'll get soaked. What are you waiting for? Or isn't my wagon good enough for you?'

'I'm coming,' called Giulia, lifting her skirts to mount the steps.

Franceschina moved back out of sight.

Giulia's gasp of relief at being out of the wet was immediately smothered by a hand clamped over her mouth. It muffled her cry of shock and pain as her right arm was wrenched up her back. Even before she glimpsed his mask, she knew her attacker. Eyes wide, she stared at Franceschina, who came at her, hand poised to thrust down her bodice. Giulia kicked out and sent her reeling.

Taken by surprise, Brighella let his grip slacken. Giulia took her chance and, twisting to face him, tried to push up his mask. He grabbed hold of her wrist.

'Punch the bitch!' screamed Franceschina but he was more concerned with keeping his face concealed. Giulia clawed at his neck and he swore. He tried to restrain her but she managed to break free.

In her haste to get out, Giulia slipped. Her foot shot from under her. She bounced down the steps, the small of her back hitting each one in turn. Snatching up the dress, she burst into tears then scrambled up and hurried back to her wagon which had, by now, been freed. 'Giulia!' gasped Lella as she clambered inside.

'I'm all right.'

'Poor you! Just look at your dress. And the sweet little one you made for Serafina!'

'Never mind. It will wash.'

Crespo hobbled from his basket. 'That's the first time he's got up on his own,' said Lella, delighted.

Giulia stroked the dog. When he caught the scent on her fingers, his tail stopped wagging. She put Serafina's dress aside and unlaced her own soaked garment, being careful to keep hold of her letter. 'I think there might be another dress in here,' she said, lifting the lid of the coffer.

Just then Spinetta returned. 'Lord in heaven! What's happened?'

'I fell,' said Giulia. 'I'm fine. I just slipped in the mud. I was looking for something to…' she put a hand over her nose and gave a loud sneeze.

'Here, let me.' Spinetta found her a dress.

Giulia longed to tell her what had really happened but knew it would cause trouble. Awkward questions would also be asked of her as well as her attackers. Clutching the letter, she wondered if it was worth the struggle. She had reacted instinctively in fighting back. Now she was worried.

'A slip in the mud won't do any harm,' remarked Spinetta as if reading her mind.

The journey continued arduously and the caravan was frequently brought to a halt. Pantelone was determined to press on and was visibly frustrated by the lack of progress. By the following morning however the rain had ceased and the hazy yellow orb returned to the sky. Giulia felt relieved to see it again. The incident in Franceschina's wagon had left her shaken and the continuous rain and upsets with the wagons had made her realise that life on the road was not always pleasant. And something else was preying on her mind, a nagging ache in her back, which grew steadily worse throughout the day.

She had not left the wagon since she had been attacked, other than by necessity. But late that afternoon she decided to deliver Serafina's dress.

She had managed to wash out the mud, there being plenty of fresh water in the barrels. And the sun had shone all day so that the garment had dried on the line Spinetta had strung across the back of the cart. Reaching up to take the dress down, Giulia endured a searing pain. It felt like hot needles pushing up from deep inside her. She clutched herself, held her breath and prayed it would go away. It did, but returned within seconds, severe enough this time to make her cry out.

Spinetta was there in an instant. She said nothing but helped Giulia to the coffer then she hurriedly laid the mattress on the floor. 'Giulia,' she said quietly but firmly. 'You must lie down.'

The pain came back. Giulia could hardly bear it and cried out again.

'What's the matter?' asked Lella, peering into the wagon.

'Giulia needs a rest,' Spinetta told her. 'Pantelone!' she called at the top of her voice.

He appeared. 'Brighella's gone missing,' he grumbled. 'A fine time to...'

'That doesn't matter. Take Lella.'

'But I want to stay with Giulia.'

'Take her!'

Pantelone grabbed Lella and drew her away.

'I'm losing my baby,' wailed Giulia. 'Aren't I?' Spinetta helped her lie down. Gripped by another spasm, she cried out again then felt blood trickle from her.

'Shush. Shush.' Spinetta spread a blanket over her. 'It's all in God's hands.' She gathered up Giulia's skirts and laid some clean cloths on the mattress.

'I'm frightened,' said Giulia; her hand sought Spinetta's.

'I'm here, child.' Spinetta squeezed her fingers. 'There's nothing to fear. But you have to be brave.' She stroked her brow.

Another griping spasm wracked Giulia, followed by another. She gave a loud groan and clenched her fists. The urge to push overwhelmed her. She drew up her knees to bear down and expelled a warm rush. The raw smell of blood filled the air.

Free of pain now, she started to cry.

Spinetta let her sob then removed the miscarried child, wrapped it in cloths and took it away. When she returned, she washed Giulia clean and covered her. 'Rest now,' she whispered and left her alone.

Giulia did not rest. As she lay in a daze, a strange mood overtook her. She felt a cold kind of anger, and loss. Remorse overwhelmed her. This was her fault. She had fought to keep something that did not matter and lost something that did. Then guilt crept in. This was her punishment for wanting to rid herself of her unborn child. She had even been willing to pay. Now she had lost the life growing inside her and felt it as a judgement.

Some time later she began to shiver. Looking up, she saw the blurred face of Spinetta, who was spreading too many blankets over her. Immediately Giulia threw them off. Now Spinetta was kneeling beside her, supporting her head and trying to make her drink from a cup of cold water. But her throat was too sore. The wagon seemed to be swaying, the canvas billowing out then sucking back in. She felt she was suffocating.

She tossed and turned on a mattress hard as iron. She could hear voices.

'Well, we both know who should be here. Don't we?'

'There's nothing I can do.'

'Nothing you can do? He's your son. Speak to him!'

'I'll leave Pedrolino with you.'

'Good. He's worth ten of him.'

'Spinetta,' called Giulia.

'I'm coming.'

'What's happening? Why do I feel so ill?'

'You've caught a chill, my love. But you'll be fine. We've got to keep you warm.' She replaced the blankets Giulia had thrown off. 'The other wagons are going on without us.'

'No!' Giulia struggled to sit.

'It's all right.' Spinetta eased her back. 'We'll catch them up in a day or two but you've had a bad time and need to lie still. Pedrolino is staying behind to look after us.'

'And Lella? Where's Lella?'

'With her father.'

'And Crespo – the little dog. He's in great danger!'

'Lie still, Giulia.' Spinetta stroked her brow. 'What do you mean, Crespo's in danger?'

144

Then Giulia remembered, or thought she did. 'Has Brighella gone?'
'Yes.'

With a sigh, she lay back.

Time passed. Days perhaps, Giulia could not tell. Her body ached and burned. She dreamt she was on fire. Flames licked her feet, her legs, her thighs. She tried to scream but smoke rose to choke her and her screams went unheard. Then she woke suddenly, drenched in sweat. Her hair was lank, her shift soaking wet. Her shift! Her hand went to her breast. Someone had removed her dress. Where was the letter?

31

iulia felt a cool hand slide under her neck and heard a voice urging her to take a sip of weak wine. 'I have lost something,' she gasped and her gaze came to rest on the line where she had hung Serafina's dress. The tiny garment had gone.

'You lost your baby,' Spinetta told her softly. 'But you will have others. Sometimes these things are not meant to be.'

'I lost my baby. Yes.' Tears welled in Giulia's eyes and she turned her face away.

One morning, she woke from a very deep sleep. The sun was shining through the canvas. Her body no longer ached and she felt cool. Again she heard voices outside the wagon.

'How is she?'

'Much the same. If this fever doesn't break soon…'

'I'm sorry to hear it. Yet it's a blessing she lost the child.'

'May God forgive you, Pantelone! I never thought to hear you say such a thing. Would you defend a libertine son, at the cost of your own conscience?'

'Woman, you know nothing about it!'

Giulia lay still. She smiled at Spinetta when she entered the wagon.

'Lord be praised!' Spinetta clasped her hands.

That night Giulia slept soundly and woke the next morning feeling well but weak. On the coffer stood a small earthenware jug filled with flowers. 'From Lella?' she asked as Spinetta folded a blanket.

'Pedrolino. He's been with us these past three days, keeping watch. Not once closed his eyes.'

Giulia reached out to touch the delicate petals and sweet perfume filled the air.

'Do you feel well enough to get up today?'

'Oh yes.' Giulia sat up too quickly and felt dizzy.

'You must take it easy – and stay in the wagon. Your dress has been washed. It's there when you're ready.' As Spinetta turned to go Giulia noticed, lying on top of her folded dress, the letter. 'In case you're wondering, nobody's read it. The things we keep close to our hearts are meant to stay secret.'

'Thank you.'

Giulia touched the parchment. How wrong Spinetta was. This held no place in her affections. In fact, she felt inclined to screw it up and throw it away. It had brought her nothing but misery.

In the days that followed Giulia was surprised how exhausted she felt even after the least exertion. Their wagon soon caught up with the rest and the weather continued fine. But although her body grew strong, her spirits waned. Try as she might, she could not shake off sadness, or the feeling that she was to blame for the loss of her child. Kind words from Spinetta could only do so much and Giulia had to hide the pain of seeing Carla with her beautiful daughter, who continued to thrive.

'Giulia,' said Spinetta early one morning as they sat together sewing. 'I've been thinking. You can't spend the rest of your life mending holes in other people's clothing – although from my point of view it would be very welcome. This has certainly piled up while you were unwell. But, as I say, I've been thinking, and I've had a word with Pantelone…'

Giulia stopped sewing and paid close attention.

'How would you feel about teaching some of the children to read and write? Lella in particular. I should have been doing it but I'm not much cop at reading and I don't have the time. Guido too. He's of an age when he should know his letters but, as far as I know, nobody's bothered to teach him.'

'I should love to,' said Giulia, welcoming the opportunity to do something positive.

Spinetta patted her arm. 'I hoped you'd say that. I'll let Pantelone know and you can start when you like.'

Giulia looked across the encampment to where Pedrolino was helping Lella's father hitch up a wagon.

'Pedrolino's a good man, whispered Spinetta.

147

Giulia nodded.

'He loves you, you know.'

Giulia felt herself blush.

'Couldn't you try to love him back?'

'I do love him. But not in the right kind of way.'

'The right kind of way!' Spinetta threw up her hands. 'Look where that got you!'

Giulia blinked and looked down.

'Oh, I know what you think. I'm a silly old woman who's past it. How could I possibly understand? But I tell you, Giulia. I know what it is to love a man in your *right kind of way*. And believe me, when the years have passed and what you need most is someone to be there by your side, through thick and thin, good times and bad…' she shook her head. 'You're not hearing me, are you?'

'I am,' insisted Giulia; but, in truth, her thoughts were elsewhere. Arlecchino was across the campsite, stretching, yawning, covering his eyes against the morning sun.

'How about giving Pedrolino a hand?' came Pantelone's voice.

Arlecchino gave his father a wave but showed no sign of taking him up on the suggestion.

Spinetta got up and went into the wagon.

She wasted no time in getting Giulia started as teacher, bringing out a board and a stick of brown chalk she said she had bought off an artist for Lella. The child was delighted at the news of Giulia's classes. Not so, Guido, who flatly refused to be taught by a girl.

'You'll do as you're told,' said Spinetta but left Giulia to do the telling.

'He's just stupid,' said Lella. 'And he doesn't want you to find out.'

'Are you well?'

Giulia was startled by the sound of Arlecchino's voice, not having seen him approach. 'I… I am well enough, thank you.'

'I'm glad.' He turned his attention to Guido, who had been standing, sour-faced and arms folded, and was now walking away.

'Spinetta has asked me to teach Lella and Guido their letters. But Guido doesn't want to…'

'Guido!' bellowed Arlecchino. 'Get back here.'

148

The boy spun round, a scowl on his face. 'But she wants to teach me stuff that's not important.'

'I'll decide what's important. If you think juggling with balls and doing handstands is all Arlecchino needs to know, you've got a lot to learn.'

'But I've got nothing to write on. Lella's got the only board.'

'Then I'll find you something.' Arlecchino inclined his head in a bow to Giulia, then walked off in the direction of his wagon.

32

uring her hours on the road, Giulia reflected on things that had happened. She realised now sadness at the loss of her baby was something she would have to live with and guilt would always haunt her. But *life must go on* – Spinetta's phrase. And the luxury of pining for things lost or out of reach was denied to those Giulia now called her family.

She was extremely relieved that Brighella had disappeared. Various theories as to why he left so suddenly spread but it was generally believed he would return. He was, apparently, in the habit of coming and going without explanation. The reason Pantelone tolerated such behaviour was, Giulia managed to elicit from Spinetta, due to the fact that Brighella was useful. In what way she did not say but Giulia guessed it was as a provider of what the company was always in need of – money, or the means to come by it.

She, of course, knew his real reason for leaving; fear she would tell all. And although she hoped he would never return, she felt confident that, if he did, she could hold it over his head like a sword of Damocles and he would never touch her again.

Only once since being attacked had she come face to face with Franceschina and the leading lady had averted her gaze and hurried past. Giulia wondered what she had made of the contents of Jacopo Bruno's letter.

There was one pleasant thing to which her thoughts kept returning: the change in Arlecchino's attitude. He had been as good as his word in providing Guido with a board and something to write with and made sure the boy attended her classes. Guido remained quietly disgruntled but did as he was told, aware that his father was keeping an eye on him.

While pleasantly surprised by Arlecchino's new-found consideration towards her, she told herself not to read too much into it, other than the disagreeable fact that he was no doubt relieved she was no longer pregnant. The comment she had overheard Pantelone make – *it's a blessing she lost the child* – reinforced this. She found the words hurtful, but had not been surprised by them.

She enjoyed giving lessons, which took place in the early morning before the caravan set out and sometimes after they had encamped, weather and light permitting. On one such occasion, Giulia was complimenting Lella on her neat hand when Guido jumped up and brought her his board. 'That's very good,' she told him, even though his writing was barely legible.

Lella scrutinised it. 'He's missed out the *u* in Guido. He can't even spell his own name.'

'Now, Lella,' said Giulia. 'That's not fair. Guido has done very well.'

'No, I haven't!' He threw the board on the ground. 'I'm rubbish.'

'Guido!' came Arlecchino's stern voice.

'I don't care,' the boy shouted back. 'Why should I have to learn this crap?' He pointed to Franceschina, who was across the campsite, bending Pantelone's ear. 'She doesn't know 'er letters. And she's our blooming leading lady!'

'Guido!' came Arlecchino's voice again, this time much louder and sterner.

Guido plonked himself down on his stool, fist pressed against his cheek.

'That's all right, Guido,' said Giulia. 'We've finished for today. I'm pleased with what you've done.'

He scowled at her, clearly unconvinced.

So, Franceschina could not read! And that meant that no one, apart from Giulia, had read Jacopo Bruno's letter. No wonder Brighella had been so keen to get his hands on it.

Once the children had gone off to play, Spinetta joined Giulia, bringing with her the basket of mending. 'You don't mind, do you? I've still not caught up.'

'Of course not.' Giulia picked out an article. 'I like to keep busy.'

'You're doing well with the children.'

'I'm not sure. Guido resents me telling him what to do.'

'That's because he's been allowed to run wild. It's about time someone took him in hand.'

'Arlecchino seems to be taking an interest in his learning,' Giulia remarked, eyes fixed on her sewing.

'Mm.'

'Spinetta.' Giulia stole a glance at her companion. 'Pedrolino told me that it's not the done thing to ask members of the company about their past lives?'

Spinetta nodded but also gave Giulia a look that she took to be an invitation.

'The other day you told me you knew what it was to love someone in *the right kind of way*.'

'Oh, so you were listening?'

Giulia smiled. 'I just wondered if you had been married. Have any children?'

'I was married.' Spinetta let her sewing rest in her lap. 'Still am. He was handsome, charming. And no damn good!'

'But you loved him?'

'Oh yes, with all my heart. I made excuses for his drinking and gambling. I even turned a blind eye to the other women. He left me in the end, with two little boys to bring up. Then, when they were just about grown, he turned up again out of the blue, filled their silly young heads with stories of adventure and riches and took them off to fight in another man's war. I've not seen them since.'

'I'm so sorry,' whispered Giulia, reaching out to touch her hand.

Spinetta's eyes were shining and she smiled. 'I have all the family I need right here. The Immortali's long been the resting place for lost souls like me. Well,' she said, 'it's almost time for the meal. And it won't cook itself.'

Giulia put down her mending.

'No. You carry on. You're more help doing this.'

Giulia was content; she much preferred sewing to cooking.

In the middle of the encampment Arlecchino was teaching Guido how to balance a long wooden pole on his forehead. 'No,' he said patiently, catching the stick as it fell. 'Not like that. Like this.'

Watching them, Giulia was filled with a curious feeling. That unexplained image of light shooting from Arlecchino's heels still haunted and puzzled her. And just now, Spinetta's eyes had shone with a mysterious light. What was it that made these people so special?

The following day, twin girls joined her class. That meant Guido became even more disgruntled, until an older boy asked if he might also join and the enthusiasm with which the newcomer approached his learning soon brought about a noticeable improvement in Guido's attitude.

While the caravan was on the move, Giulia planned lessons and caught up with the mending. When she was walking, she took in the landscape. The weather was growing discernibly cooler but the sun shone most days. Leaving behind a hilly region, they entered much flatter, open terrain. One morning, in the distance, Giulia spotted the dome and high towers of a city rising proudly from the mist. 'Padua,' Pedrolino told her as he fell into step beside her.

She felt her heart quicken. By reputation, she knew the city to be a place of great learning.

'We'll be skirting it to the north,' called Pantelone.

'Naturally,' returned Arlecchino, who was driving the leading wagon.

Giulia and Pedrolino smiled at one another. Lella ran ahead of them with Crespo on his new lead. Pedrolino laughed. 'He limps just like me now.' Then he answered the question Giulia had felt unable to ask. 'My leg was broken when I was a child – by my drunken father.'

To the left a river meandered, snaking away to the north. 'Veer to the west, away from the city,' Pantelone called to Arlecchino. 'There's a bridge not far ahead.'

'Yes, Sir!' As Arlecchino swung the leading wagon in that direction, a party of riders emerged from the table of mist.

33

uick!' called Pantelone. 'Giulia, hide in the wagon.'

Listening from inside, she discerned a clear note of arrogance in the voice of the first man to speak. 'You are travelling to Venice?'

'That is our destination,' returned Pantelone.

'What business have you there? Are you traders?'

'We are actors.'

'Actors?' The man gave a laugh.

'Our company goes by the name of the Immortali.'

Giulia heard a murmur.

'It seems some of my companions have heard of you.'

'I am honoured.'

Another man spoke. 'You must come to Padua and entertain us at the university.'

'Venice is our destination.' Pantelone's tone was polite, yet firm.

'I have to inform you, Sir,' came the first rider's voice, 'the land across which you are presently travelling belongs to me.'

'Come, now, Master Actor,' coaxed the other, 'why not break your journey for our pleasure? What hardship can it cause you to enter Padua?'

'Gentlemen. I mean no disrespect. And I humbly beg leave, Sir, to cross your land. But we are guaranteed a favourable audience in Venice and have no wish to disappoint its citizens.'

'Yet you would disappoint those of Padua!'

'We will play for you,' came Arlecchino's voice.

'And who are you?'

'I am Arlecchino. And, while I am happy to accept your invitation, I bow to my father and master's will in declining to enter the fair city of

Padua. Yet, if you can recommend a sheltered place hereabouts where we might erect a stage…'

'I can do better than that,' replied the landowner. 'Over there lies my family home. Within its grounds are many barns. One large enough, I think, to accommodate your stage together with a good-sized audience. Master Actor, would you be content with that?'

'Sir,' came Pantelone's voice, 'the Immortali are at your disposal. Be so good as to show us the way.'

Giulia heard the sound of hooves growing fainter. Leaving the wagon, she saw the party of riders making for a wooded patch, dust rising in their wake.

The barn proved more than large enough to hold the Immortali stage and at least a hundred spectators. Having pronounced it satisfactory, Pantelone spent some time with the landowner, who ordered his peasants to supply the company with food and wine, together with anything that might be required for the performance.

'Until tomorrow night then!' The landowner and his companions were preparing to leave. 'Make sure you don't disappoint us. The students of Padua demand a high standard when it comes to their entertainment.'

'Not just the students,' laughed another. 'We will be bringing our professor to see your play. He could do with his eyes and thoughts being taken off the heavens for an evening.'

The others laughed.

'And the name of your professor?' enquired Arlecchino.

'What might that signify to you?' asked the rider, wheeling his horse to face him.

'His name, Sir.' Arlecchino bowed. 'With respect.'

'Galileo,' came the answer. 'He goes by the name of Galileo Galilei.'

he landowner and his companions were hardly out of earshot before Pantelone rounded on his son. 'What the devil were you thinking of?'

Arlecchino spread his hands. 'I simply offered to entertain them.'

'Yes.' Pantelone slapped one palm against the other. 'And these fine gentlemen will *have* their entertainment. But at whose expense? Surely you know? Such educated types care nothing for the actor's skill. Or the quality of a performance. They seek only to mock. And mock us they will!' He threw up his hands then wagged a finger at his son. 'Mark my words, they will bring with them a hundred more of their kind all set upon ridiculing our honest efforts.' Though it seemed he would say more, he whirled away and strode off.

Arlecchino called after him, 'Then we will make sure we give them no cause! Our play will be the best ever seen.'

Giulia watched him walk away in the opposite direction to his father. Arlecchino's words had been defiant and spoken with bravado but the slump of his shoulders betrayed an uncharacteristic lack of confidence. Pedrolino, who had also witnessed the altercation, gave Giulia a smile but she could tell he was also worried. 'Is it true?' she asked. 'Is that really what those gentlemen have in mind? To amuse themselves at the company's expense?'

Pedrolino sighed. 'It wouldn't be for the first time. We suffered badly once at the hands of the students of Bologna.'

Giulia's gaze went to Pantelone who, on reaching the doors of the barn, kicked them open with such force it sent hens fluttering and squawking.

During the evening meal she questioned Spinetta, hoping to discover more about the humiliation of the troupe at Bologna. Spinetta claimed to know nothing about it. Later, Giulia sat with Lella and Crespo. The camp-site was quiet, the atmosphere tense. Groups of actors sat huddled around fires. Arlecchino, clutching a fistful of papers, went from one to another.

Eventually, the groups dispersed. Pedrolino began to play his lute and the atmosphere improved. Arlecchino remained seated alone by a dying fire, flagon at his side.

'Time for bed,' Spinetta told Lella. 'Here.' She handed Giulia a plate of bread and cheese and nodded towards Arlecchino. 'Take him this. He's not had a bite all evening.' Spinetta and Lella retired.

With a deep breath, Giulia crossed to Arlecchino. On reaching him, she gave a light cough. 'Spinetta told me to bring you this.' She thrust the plate at him and a hunk of bread slid off. She bent to retrieve it but, at the same time, so did he and their fingers touched. 'I'm sorry,' she said. 'I'll get you another…'

'No.' He shook his head and dusted off the bread. 'Please. Sit down.'

Giulia put the plate beside him and drew a stool up to the fire.

He ate quickly and in silence; then picked up the flagon. He offered it first to her but she declined. He drank deeply, put the flagon down and leaned forward again to stare at the embers. Giulia smoothed her skirts. She felt inclined to excuse herself and leave, yet she wanted to stay. Most of all, she wished he would say something. At last he did. 'Sometimes I can see it, in the flames.'

'What?' She leaned forward eagerly.

He shook his head. 'Nothing. You wouldn't understand.'

'I should like to try.'

He glanced at her, his troubled features bathed in firelight. 'The play. How it should be. I see it in the flames sometimes. But not tonight.'

'I also like to look into the fire,' she said. 'Sometimes I imagine I see other worlds.' She felt suddenly embarrassed.

'My father was right,' he muttered. 'Tomorrow night the students of Padua will not be laughing with us, but at our expense. It will be a disaster.'

She could think of nothing to say.

'Brighella might have helped us out. His music has sophistication. And one of his cynical monologues on the fruitlessness of man's existence would have gone down well with such men.'

'I'm glad he's gone,' she muttered.

Their eyes met. 'I do have regrets,' he said, 'concerning my behaviour in the past.'

She frowned and looked away. Was this an apology? She dared hope so.

Across the campsite she noticed Franceschina. Arlecchino cast a cursory glance at his leading lady. 'Illusion is everything,' he murmured. 'Love. Magic. Fear. These are things real people understand. I can bring pleasure to them because we share the same source, drink from the same spring.' He grabbed the flagon and took another drink. 'All I have is my art. Those men of learning...' he put the vessel down carelessly and it almost toppled over, 'they have their minds set on higher things,' he said, righting it, 'things beyond the understanding of a man like me.'

'I don't believe that,' she replied. 'In my opinion all men, and women, are the same. The only real difference between rich and poor – between the gentleman and his servant – are the lengths to which each one goes to pretend.' Feeling awkward at having expressed herself so freely, she nevertheless continued. 'Once, when I was watching you walk hand in hand with your leading lady, I imagined the pair of you to be the sun and the moon. Franceschina, in her dress of silver, was the moon. You, resplendent in your suit of glowing colours, were the sun.'

Arlecchino sprang to his feet.

'Have I said something wrong?'

'Not at all. Thank you.' He bowed and walked away.

34

hroughout the morning the hectic pace of preparations filled Giulia with anticipation, yet left her feeling dissatisfied. She was keen to do what she could to help and worked hard mending costumes in need of last-minute alterations. But she longed to be more directly involved in the performance.

She had not spoken to Arlecchino since the previous night and was still puzzled by his reaction to her words. This morning he flew round like a whirlwind, issuing brisk orders.

With every costume ready by mid-afternoon, Giulia gained permission to visit the barn. Spinetta warned her not to get in the way. On a clear patch of ground outside the doors, the dancers were rehearsing. Giulia watched for a while, then, with a wave to Lella, entered the building.

The interior of the barn was vast. Dust motes swirled within a shaft of amber light that poured through an open hayloft. The beams were hung with fresh, green garlands and the floor had been swept so clean you could have held a banquet in the place. Actors and peasants busied themselves carrying benches, painting scenery. The stage was complete with two flights of steps, one either side. To the left, was a kind of booth with a curtain of sackcloth pulled across.

She approached the stage as Pantelone signalled for quiet and Franceschina mounted the right-hand steps. The leading lady was followed by a girl and a portly actor dressed in black frockcoat and breeches; he reminded Giulia of the lawyer her father had employed. Watching the three rehearse a short scene, she marvelled at their flawless mix of dialogue and movement.

Looking towards the back of the barn, she noticed Pedrolino leaning across a low table, deep in conversation with Renaldo. It was not until they moved apart that she saw Arlecchino, seated with his back to the wall, feet on the table, reading a book. Not far from them knelt Guido, surrounded by earthenware pots and juggling balls. Loading his brush from a pot, he picked up one ball and began painting it red.

Giulia looked back at the stage. The man dressed as a lawyer was now holding forth and she could not help but laugh at his words – a nonsensical jumble of philosophical terms, legal jargon and bizarre medical remedies. 'I see you're enjoying our Dottore's oration?'

At the sound of Pedrolino's voice, Giulia turned. 'Very much,' she replied. 'His speech is so clever, in spite of being completely ridiculous.'

'That's the point.' He joined her. 'In holding up a humorous mirror to the audience, the master hopes to steal a march on their intention to ridicule us.'

'The Dottore has a distinctive accent, yet I cannot place it.'

'Bolognese. Again, the intention is to play upon the rivalry between the two universities.'

Giulia became engrossed. She was particularly charmed by the quick lively movements of the servetta, whom she now recognised as Carla's younger sister, Suzanna.

'Would you like to act, Giulia?'

'More than anything,' she breathed.

elping Spinetta prepare the evening meal, Giulia chatted about the rehearsal. Spinetta listened indulgently, sometimes with a wry smile.

Once darkness fell and lamps and torches were lit, the mood turned magical. Music drifted from the barn and Giulia was thrilled to learn she would be accompanying Spinetta to help with change of costumes. She would, however, have happily forgone the honour of carrying Franceschina's silver gown, which the leading lady would not be requiring until the final act. There existed some mystery concerning that. Apparently, Arlecchino had something special in mind.

There were dozens of fine carriages arriving and well-dressed young people spilled out, all in jovial mood. Perhaps Pantelone had been worrying unnecessarily, Giulia thought; then she realised that most of the men had been drinking and some had brought flagons. She ignored their coarse remarks and hurried past.

Pantelone was at the doors to greet his audience. In full costume, he was already playing a convincing part, welcoming each one as a friend.

Inside the building, Giulia paused in wonder. It had been impressive in daylight; now it was breathtaking. Chairs, benches and stools had been placed in rows facing the stage. Behind the seating, there was space for at least a hundred to stand. Right at the back, hay stooks were piled, providing a vantage point for the most agile.

Light cast by candles on sconces imbued the rough walls with warmth. A pair of iron fire baskets framed the stage. Flickering flames sent tongues of ruby licking over skeins of glossy, green foliage looped across the front. Two screens, one depicting a house, the other a landscape and a fountain, made the scenery.

Giulia hurried on after Spinetta. Pushing through the sackcloth curtain, she caught the odour of face-paint and sweat. The top half of a stable door leading out to the side of the barn was wide open; still, the atmosphere was close. A few actors sat on a bench, the rest leaned against the walls. Franceschina was standing by the open door, looking radiant in pale pink, her hair gleaming blue in the moonlight. As Giulia stepped forward, Spinetta whispered, 'Not yet. Keep hold of it, for now.'

Giulia sat down next to Suzanna whose costume was much like her own simple dress, the only addition being the servetta's crisp white apron. Suzanna looked anxious; beads of sweat laced her brow and upper lip. 'Are you all right?' whispered Giulia.

'I will be,' Suzanna croaked back.

The noise of the crowd grew louder. There were shouts and peals of laughter. Pedrolino popped his head round the curtain. Giulia heard the tap-tapping of dancers' shoes on boards. Pedrolino waved. Then Arlecchino's masked face appeared briefly over his shoulder. 'He's here,' he whispered. The pair disappeared.

Giulia glanced round. With the exception of Suzanna's, all faces were calm. Nobody spoke. Music stopped. The dancers left the stage to warm applause. Then Giulia heard Pantelone's voice. It quelled the restless murmur of the crowd. Arlecchino's voice broke over his and the audience cheered.

There followed banter and acrobatics. Laughter filled the barn. Applause swelled to thunderous. Pedrolino ran down the steps and grasped Giulia's hand. 'We're winning,' he said, then disappeared as suddenly as he had arrived.

Pantelone came down the steps, took Franceschina's hand and the pair went on stage, followed by the Dottore and servetta. Giulia listened closely to the scene she had watched in rehearsal and was pleased to hear the Dottore's speech having the desired effect, his references to systems of learning and some derogatory remarks about how things were done in Bologna delighting the Paduan students. As his speech came to an end, Spinetta took charge of Franceschina's gown, much to Giulia's relief.

The leading lady came down the steps, followed by the servetta; and there followed a scene between Pantelone and the Dottore discussing a rebellious daughter. Franceschina returned to the stage in the company of Renaldo dressed as a soldier of fortune. For a while, romance took over from humour. When the pair came off to somewhat muted applause, Pedrolino beckoned from the top step to Suzanna.

She ran up to join him.

Within seconds, she came hurtling back down. Pushing past Franceschina, she barged through the stable door. 'Ugh!' shrieked the leading lady as the girl was violently sick outside.

Arlecchino appeared at the top of the steps. 'What the..? Shit!'

'You'll have to carry on without her,' Pantelone hissed as Suzanna continued to vomit.

'But this is a saucy scene with a pretty girl! This lot's had enough of knockabout.'

It was true, the atmosphere had changed and there was an ominous lack of laughter. Pantelone threw up his hands.

'How about the dancers?' suggested the Dottore.

'Fuck!' Arlecchino disappeared back on stage.

'Carla could take her place,' suggested Spinetta.

'No time,' snapped Pantelone. 'Arlecchino's right. We're losing them.'

Giulia shared the worry – jeers were audible and chilling. How could the mood of an audience change so suddenly? Pedrolino almost slid down the steps and fell to his knees before her. 'Giulia! You said you wanted to act.'

With a gasp, she shook her head.

'Now's your chance.'

She shook her head again as the rest of the actors gathered round – with the exception of Franceschina.

'Help us, Giulia! We're doomed if you don't.'

'But I can't... I have never...'

Pantelone bent to whisper in her ear. 'We need beauty, child. Only Aphrodite can save us now.'

'But surely the audience would notice a change in servetta?'

He laughed. 'Most, my dear, are too drunk to notice – or care.'

'You can do it, Giulia,' coaxed Pedrolino.

'I don't know,' she said, biting her lip.

Arlecchino appeared on the top step.

Pedrolino squeezed her fingers. 'All you have to do is go out there and tell those rich folk what it means to be poor and unloved.'

'This is turning into a riot,' growled Arlecchino as foot stamping joined with the booing and jeers. 'Stop wasting time, Pedrolino! Get back up here and die with me.'

'No,' Pedrolino called back. 'If you stay on any longer, there'll be no time for...'

'I'll do it,' said Giulia.

'Great!' An audible sigh swept through the actors. Pedrolino drew her to her feet. 'Don't worry. Words will come. Just speak from the heart.' He kissed her hand and someone thrust a broom into the other.

Giulia found herself pushed up the steps and, to mutterings from Arlecchino about this being a disaster in the making, was bundled on stage to face a hostile crowd.

35

rlecchino took hold of Giulia's trembling hand and drew her centre-stage. Buffeted by deafening noise, she forced herself to face the mob. All she could see was a broiling sea of discontent, humanity at its most ugly. Men – and women too – yelled, swore and even threw things. A wooden beaker just missed her head and bounced off the screen behind her.

Yet, within seconds of her appearance, the mood of the crowd seemed to change. Boos and jeers gave way to high-pitched whistles. Pedrolino appeared at her side. 'They love you already,' he whispered in her ear and took her hand from Arlecchino, who promptly left the stage.

Pedrolino presented Giulia to the audience with a flourish. Then, feeling his fingers slip free of hers, she had to fight the panic. As he left by the steps to the booth, it was all she could do not to run after him. But she remained, staring at the morass of blurred faces. Only one appeared defined. But why her eyes focussed on this unremarkable bearded man, seated calmly in the front row, she had no way of knowing.

The audience, now more restless than hostile, was waiting for her to do something. She must act. Now! Forcing herself to smile, she gripped the handle of her broom and began to sweep the floor. She swept the objects thrown on stage into a pile; then took a deep breath and faced the crowd once more. But her mouth refused to open, so she quickly resumed her rhythmic sweeping, which turned into a kind of dance that seemed to please the crowd. A few even clapped.

Glancing down the steps into the booth, she noticed Arlecchino standing at the bottom. He had pulled off his hat and mask and cast her a look that left her in no doubt of his lack of faith in her ability.

'Keep going, Giulia!' she heard Pedrolino hiss.

She carried on moving, more briskly now, sweeping, swaying, presenting a bright smile to the crowd. Again she tried to speak. The words that filled her heart should have poured forth in a torrent of emotion. Instead they threatened to choke her. *Just tell them Giulia*, she heard Pedrolino whisper, or imagined she did. *Tell them what it means to be poor and unloved.*

Faces were turning ugly again. How could she feel so desperately lonely in the presence of hundreds? She had been given her secret heart's desire, the chance to act. But all she wanted was to plunge down the steps. She stood rigid, fighting tears; and the booing began.

A small mean voice whined in her head, *'Give in to failure.'*

But a louder one told her, *'You have nothing to lose. And the whole world to gain!'*

She walked to the front of the stage and, at last, words came; but not in the way she had expected. She started to sing.

The tune came out of her childhood, a simple refrain she had learnt from Rosa. The words told of unrequited love. At first, the crowd seemed unaware she *was* singing. And she could hardly hear herself. But she persisted; thin, high voice trembling as she sang of bittersweet sorrow and the heartbreak of rejection. Gradually the audience fell silent.

Her song endured until the only sound in the barn was her voice; strong now, delivering to the rafters and a spellbound audience all her passion and pain. The soft sweet strains of the lute drifted in to accompany her.

When she came to the end of her song, she simply carried on as new words arrived like strangers, setting themselves to her music.

Sun rages against its own fire, moon weeps for lack of it.

My lady outshines the one, shames the other with her mysteries.

What gifts might I bring to win her heart and so bind her to me?

Then she remembered from whence the poem sprang.

At the same moment, men carrying buckets of earth doused the fire-baskets. Others snuffed out the candles, plunging the barn into darkness. The audience gasped. Giulia was too afraid to move but suddenly Pedrolino was beside her. 'Thank you,' he whispered. 'You saved us. You were wonderful!' He led her down the right-hand steps and they stood against the wall.

165

The playing of Pan pipes joined with the lute. The rustling of satin garments centre-stage sent a shiver down Giulia's spine. The crowd waited in silence, subdued by the dark, filled with expectation.

They were made to wait a few moments longer; then a tiny spot of light spread into a pool. Spectators shaded their eyes as they peered at the vision. Arlecchino stood hand in hand with Franceschina, he in glowing colour, she an apparition of silver. Her skin was pale as white marble, jet-black eyes the only discernable feature within an oval face. Her hair was drawn back, hidden behind a glittering crescent moon that framed her features in a sweeping arc. The light surrounding her matched her cool beauty.

Arlecchino meanwhile was bathed in gold. Masked, he wore a headdress. He was the sun and light shone from the rays of his sunburst corona.

The couple began a slow dance. Hands clasped, they moved together; then apart, as if skating over frozen water. Franceschina circled her leading man while he remained stationary, facing the crowd, guiding her with the tips of his fingers. As the people began to applaud he let go and, with a sharp clap, dismissed the light.

Once again, the stage was plunged into darkness. A roar of dismay burst from the crowd. Music stopped. Tension mounted. Robbed of a spectacle they had been enjoying, spectators expressed their annoyance with mutterings.

'What's happening?' whispered Giulia.

'Watch closely.'

Dim light filled the stage once again. At first, it was hard to see anything. Then the light focussed on a solitary figure. Arlecchino was juggling. Within his moving arc, Giulia recognised the red ball she had seen Guido painting. There was also a white one and another of fiery orange. A grey metallic orb followed after a blue and green one. The final ball was many-hued and fuzzy.

The vision was enchanting and, with the eerie sound of Pan pipes weaving a mystical thread throughout the tableau, the excitement in the barn increased. Gradually, the juggling balls began to glow. Stranger still, they rearranged themselves. A troubled murmur rippled through the audience.

166

As the orbs continued to circle Arlecchino, some moved closer to his sunburst. Closest of all came the grey metallic ball, the shining white one beyond it. Next came the blue and green sphere. Giulia strained her eyes. Was that a tiny silver orb rotating it, in turn?

Guido's red ball was the next to find a home; then came the one of fiery orange. Last of all, the misty orb, which seemed now to be ringed, took up its position on the outer limits. Against the sable void beyond Arlecchino's circle of magic, a myriad stars twinkled.

Giulia watched, spellbound.

The crowd gasped in wonder and fear. One spectator rose to his feet – the bearded man on whom her gaze had previously settled.

'The children of heaven salute you.' Arlecchino's voice rang out. 'I urge you, Sir, look to Jupiter! But do not neglect sweet Venus, the goddess of love. For, it is she who will, in the fullness of time, show you the way.'

'Who are you?' called the man, voice trembling.

'Phoebus Arlecchino. Your starry messenger. I salute you, Galileo Galilei. God guide you in your quest!'

There came an ear-splitting clap of thunder and the stage was plunged into blackness. Women screamed. Men's voices erupted.

Giulia's hand found Pedrolino's then light filled the barn and music transformed the perilous atmosphere.

Arlecchino, centre-stage, stood hand in hand with his leading lady. There was no sign of juggling balls; and the pair took bow after bow to cheers and rapturous applause.

36

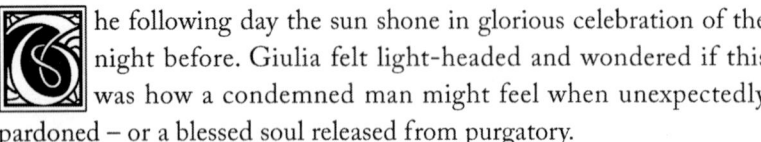he following day the sun shone in glorious celebration of the night before. Giulia felt light-headed and wondered if this was how a condemned man might feel when unexpectedly pardoned – or a blessed soul released from purgatory.

That afternoon she carried a basket of washing to a nearby river. Kneeling on the grassy bank amongst smooth rocks, she unwrapped the tiny piece of soap Spinetta had given her and took a shirt from the basket. It crossed her mind that she might have felt a bit put out, having been assigned so humble a task following her acting debut. But this was just what she needed. Some kinds of happiness were not for sharing; and, in this place with nothing but the sound of the river to break the silence, she could relive and savour last night's success.

She plunged the shirt into the water then held it down, allowing her mind to become immersed in remembered pleasure. Lifting out the soaked garment, she spread it over a rock then rubbed the grimy collar with the soap. The chattering of women's voices made her look up and she saw, on the far side of the river, two elegantly-dressed young women emerging from a wood. They were carrying a basket. Not of washing; such well-to-do ladies were not the sort to have chores. The basket they swung between them was covered in a white cloth – they had come here for a picnic.

Giulia turned her attention back to her work, immersing the shirt once again so that the soap rinsed away downstream. Out of the corner of her eye she continued to watch the girls as they selected a suitable spot; then suddenly she heard familiar laughter. Three more people stepped from under the trees. Heart thudding, she wrung out the shirt as Arlecchino, a girl on either arm, flagon in each hand, strode to the picnic area.

Composure shattered, Giulia spread the wet garment out on a rock then hurriedly took another from the basket. She worked industriously, trying to avoid looking across the river. Soon all her washing was spread out to dry.

Meanwhile, the party was enjoying the al fresco feast. The girls shrieked and giggled at everything Arlecchino said and did. Try as she might, Giulia could not suppress a growing resentment. Not only had she been robbed of her dreaming time, she was experiencing envy. Here she was scrubbing other people's dirty clothes, whilst those privileged young ladies were enjoying a carefree afternoon in the company of the most desirable and, right now, the most irritating man she knew. Last night he had appeared to her something close to a god. Now he was flirting and using his masculine charms in the most obvious way. Which of his unsuspecting victims would he select, she wondered – it was clear he could have his pick. Perhaps he had it in mind to make love to them all!

She began to feel ashamed of her own bitter thoughts and longed for the washing to dry so that she could leave.

Once the picnic was over, there began a silly game across the river. One of the girls hid her eyes while the others ran with Arlecchino to hide. There was much hilarity once the seeker tracked down her quarries. This nonsense carried on until it was Arlecchino's turn to seek. The girls scurried off into the trees and he covered his eyes. He did not count for long and, taking his hands from his eyes, made no attempt to look for his companions. To Giulia's dismay, he began to undress. First he pulled off his boots, then he cast aside his doublet and shirt. Finally, he removed his breeches and stood on the grass completely naked. Giulia watched, dry-mouthed, as he ran to the riverbank and dived in. As he swam across, she felt herself turning to stone, fixed like the rocks surrounding her.

Arlecchino rose up from the water like a youthful Neptune. With a shake of the head, he sent shimmering streams of crystal flying from his hair. She scrambled away as he stepped onto the rock right beside her and snatched up one of her cloths. 'You have a beautiful singing voice,' he told her, using the cloth to rub moisture from his hair.

She managed a *thank you*.

He continued drying himself, concentrating now on another area of glistening dark hairs. 'What are you looking at?' he asked, smiling and lifting his member. 'You've seen this before.'

As Giulia hurriedly gathered her washing, a muscular arm encircled her waist like a bullwhip. She squealed, being lifted clean off her feet. Half-dragged, half-carried to nearby trees, she breathed in the musky scent of him. Once her feet touched the ground, she fought. 'No!' was the word which flew from her mouth. But *no* meant nothing to him and he forced her to face him. She managed to push him away but only because he let her. With a laugh, he yanked her back to settle the fullness of his mouth upon hers.

In spite of herself, Giulia shared in the kiss – until he lifted her skirts, then her hand went to stop him. Spinning her round to face the trunk of a tree, he forced her up against it. Serpentine coils of wet hair draped her neck. Seductive murmurings, only half-heard, dripped into her ear. 'I said, *no!*' she insisted as, once again, he lifted her skirts. But he pressed himself into the small of her back and his fingertips found her rosette of pleasure to slide within her moisture. Such was the thrill, she recalled with shame, she had experienced at Silvia's hands.

A kiss to the nape of her neck felt more like a bite then he eased her legs apart. She jabbed back at him with her elbows. His body set hard and she cried out as he tried to penetrate her. 'You hurt me before,' she gasped.

His lips brushed her ear. 'Not this time.' Fingers played to persuade her. 'You're ready for me, this time.'

'Dear God! I've just lost our child. Would you put me through such agony again?'

'Trust me.'

Hardness drove down between her buttocks and the touch of his smooth tip on eager flesh felt like a honeyed sting. She braced herself for pain. Instead, a pillar of marble wreathed in silk slid deep inside her. She gasped, then sighed as rhythmic thrusts induced a pliable plain, suffused with pleasure. Inner flesh dissolved, her need matching his and vanquishing caution. Nothing short of a thunderbolt hurled by an envious god could put a stop to their lovemaking.

The girls were calling *Arlecchino, Arlecchino.* He was approaching climax. Delirium reigned. For Giulia, the spectre of disaster brought a frisson. A deep groan began, was expelled as the roar of a giant. He withdrew just in time, spilling his warmth down the backs of her thighs.

Passion quenched, he stepped away and left her with a lingering incandescence, achingly precious. Giulia watched through a lattice of yellow leaves as he dived into the river, broke through the surface and swam to the other side.

The girls were still calling his name. Their shrieks in response to seeing him naked were followed by screams and they ran into the woods. He picked up his clothes and followed.

Giulia covered her ears as girlish screams turned to laughter. It was some time before she felt able to emerge. When she did, all was quiet. The remains of the picnic had been abandoned.

Lifting her skirts, she waded into the stream. When the shock of cold water washed her free of desire, she felt truly ashamed. Arlecchino had used her. Again. He was nothing more than a lecher. Their union had been bestial. But she had not been forced; not if she was honest. She left the stream, quickly dried herself then draped the damp cloths over the side of the basket.

On her way back to camp, her mind was in turmoil. How could she hide what had just happened? Entering the circle, she was relieved to see few people about, although she heard excited voices. Spinetta was standing outside their wagon and nodded towards the crowd – Brighella had returned! Not only returned; was being fêted.

Giulia steadied herself as she handed over the basket. 'I dropped these by accident,' she said, removing the damp cloths. 'I'll hang them up to dry.'

'You've made a good job of the washing,' remarked Spinetta, inspecting a collar. She frowned when she studied Giulia's face. 'You look a bit flushed?'

'I'm fine.' Giulia tucked in a strand of hair, forced now to summon all her composure. Arlecchino, fully dressed, apart from doublet slung over one shoulder, came striding into the encampment.

Catching sight of Brighella, he gave a shout and broke into a run. The two men clasped hands when they met.

Giulia slipped out of sight behind the wagon. It was hard pegging cloths to the line with trembling fingers.

37

ny worries Giulia had concerning the transparency of her state of mind were dispelled in a whirlwind of activity. Pantelone gave the order to strike camp immediately and leave for the Venetian lagoon.

The buzz which filled the caravan told of a deal made by Brighella with a rich nobleman who had offered to provide, not only free board and lodging for the actors, but also a theatre in which to perform. There was a heady mood within the company as the Immortali prepared for the journey. Only Giulia, it seemed, was unable to share in the euphoria. Still unsettled by what had happened at the river, she could not shake off doubts that good fortune could drop quite so easily from the heavens.

The Immortali's departure was accompanied by shouts of '*Come back soon!*' which issued from a merry band of students, peasants and assorted admirers who had drifted in to watch last night's performance and failed to go home. Several travelled with the caravan for some distance, singing, laughing and carrying torches, which provided a welcome haven of moving light. Even the landowner sat up for a while on the leading wagon with Pantelone, his mount tethered to the back.

At last it came time to say goodbye to those not belonging to the company, although a few young men continued on to the lagoon to help load heavy items. In return they were to be supplied with meals and some wine.

For most of the night Giulia travelled in the back of her wagon. Spinetta rode up front with Pedrolino driving.

When Giulia woke, dawn was breaking and the caravan was stationary. Lella still lay curled up in slumber and Spinetta was fast asleep. Giulia left the wagon. She stretched, yawned and gazed round at a vast, flat plain. In the distance she saw water glistening. Above it, grey sky was streaked with yellow. She took several deep breaths of moist air, which smelt of something new to her: the sea.

The caravan was soon on the move again and, within the hour, had reached the lagoon. There the wagons were unloaded. Only the essentials were to be carried across and an agitated Pantelone paced up and down issuing orders as to exactly what must go. The carts were being left behind; so too the livestock, some of which would be sold. Brighella had arranged it all and a deal had been struck with a local farmer. Lella was up and about and hugged her father goodbye. He would be staying behind to look after the company's belongings.

It took two barges and a trade galley to accommodate all that was needed. Most of the actors boarded the galley. The deck was packed but Giulia managed to find a place overlooking the side. Not far away stood Pedrolino and Pantelone.

Ropes were untied, the sail unfurled, and a sudden, cold breeze swept the craft away from the quay. Almost immediately, Suzanna leant over the side to be sick. 'That girl is quite hopeless,' Giulia heard the master say.

Although she tried not to, Giulia found herself looking for Arlecchino. She had hardly set eyes on him since their encounter. Now she saw him, standing on the prow with Franceschina, his arm about her slender waist.

Suppressing hurt, Giulia looked back in the direction of the quay where two riders were dismounting. Both were dressed in long, black, hooded robes. One beckoned to the boat-master.

What happened next was intriguing, particularly when Giulia noticed Pantelone step back out of sight of the quay.

As the hooded men pressed in on the boat-master, he became agitated, waving his arms about. Breaking free, he strode away and jabbed a finger firmly in the direction of the galley.

The boat swung round towards open water and Giulia caught one final glimpse of the quay. The men were standing side by side now, hoods thrown back revealing their tonsures.

She eased her way through to Pedrolino, who had also been watching. 'Who were those men?'

'Priests.'

'I know that. Why were they watching the ship?'

'Who knows?' He faced the lagoon. 'Behold! The Serenissima.'

Giulia refused to be diverted. 'The master was in a great hurry to get here.'

Pedrolino shrugged then slid the lute strap from his shoulder. 'Venice is his home. Wherever Pantelone roams, his heart remains in the Republic.' He began to play and sing of a fortress ruled by reason, set in a sea of plenty.

Giulia leaned over the side and gazed out across the water. Thick mist covered the lagoon and that morning the sun seemed reluctant to reveal its splendour. Ahead, dark islands seemed to float on the sombre grey waters.

A soft breeze carried the galley forward. Behind came the barges, the creaking of their oars marking time with Pedrolino's playing. When the boat passed between two islands, Giulia noticed they looked very wild. Yet others seemed inhabited, crested with untidy shacks built on stilts. The largest island was still some way ahead and boasted a handsome, domed building.

The boat swung away from the shore as they approached. The wind cut across the bows, making Giulia shiver. Pedrolino had stopped playing and the pair stood side by side now, watching a moving backcloth of unbelievable beauty. Never had she seen such splendour. Could it be real? In answer, sun burst through the mist.

'Venice!' announced Pantelone. The actors cheered.

'How long will we be staying?' Giulia asked Pedrolino.

'For as long as they want us.'

Fronting the water was an impressive façade. The magnificent palazzo gleamed in the sunlight. It was greater in length than any Giulia had ever seen and might have appeared austere, had it not been for the patterning on its upper levels and a miracle of carving adorning the lower floors. The building looked as though it had been cut from a single immense slab of white marble, then etched with delicate archways and columns.

Slender boats with upturned prows and bows were tied to long poles and bobbed in the water fronting it. Men in colourful garments propelled similar craft back and forth. Now, as the galley sailed past a wide paved opening, the gleam of gold flashed from somewhere beyond and an elegant campanile, topped by a spire, soared towards heaven.

The sails of the galley were taken down and oarsmen took over. The deeper the craft went into the canal, the more congested the water became. There were angry shouts from sailors trying to manoeuvre. Elegant buildings, ornate like the grand palazzo, lined both sides of the canal.

As they rounded a bend, a fine-looking bridge of stone came into view. But already the craft was being brought about and slid between tall iron gates to dock in the shade of a building. Once the gangplank was in place, excitement erupted.

Brighella was the first to disembark. Pantelone followed, carrying Lella. He was followed by Spinetta. Guido sprinted down the plank, Crespo tucked under one arm.

To Giulia's consternation, she found herself queuing behind Arlecchino. He scooped up Franceschina and carried her down the gangplank. 'Here at last!' he cried, letting her down. 'I know I complained. But it's good to be back.'

'Only just in time,' grunted his father, 'with *God's dogs* on our heels.'

Arlecchino laughed. 'You worry too much, old man.'

The stones underfoot were green and, as Giulia stepped off the gangplank, she slipped. She grabbed the hand that shot out to save her.

'Welcome to Venice.' Brighella tightened his grip and raised her up safely.

38

Giulia got away from Brighella as soon as she possibly could.
Servants came rushing to assist with trunks and baggage.
Wine was brought, the delicious smell of roasting meat drifted
out of an enormous kitchen. 'Giulia, come with me.' Spinetta pushed
through the throng of actors to the foot of a great marble staircase.

Giulia followed, overtaken by Lella, who ran, skirts hitched, all
the way up to the next floor with Crespo. 'Where's ours?' she shouted.
'Which is our room?'

A smiling maid appeared on the landing. 'Mistress of the Immortali?'
she asked with a curtsy to Spinetta.

'Lord!' laughed Spinetta. 'I've never been called that before. No, dear.
That would be Franceschina, our leading lady.'

The servant curtsied again. 'Begging your pardon, Madam, but this *is*
your room. I was given instructions to prepare it for the venerable mistress
of the company, her young friend and a sweet child with her pet dog.'

Spinetta's jaw dropped.

The maid led the way. Lella rushed in and clapped her hands.

Giulia entered the large, airy room. Its faded elegance was no less
appealing for the crumbling patch of plaster on the ceiling. She crossed
to the tall, open window and breathed in the scent of the sea. The sun
shed its brilliance over the scene below. Boatmen were shouting; some
were singing. The maid came to close the window. 'No,' said Giulia, 'leave
it – that is, if you don't mind.'

The woman smiled and turned to Spinetta. 'If there's anything
you need, Madam. Anything at all. At any time of the day or night.'
She crossed to a high mantelshelf and, lifting the bell, gave it a tinkle. 'I,
or a member of my household, will attend.'

'Thank you,' said Spinetta.

Giulia remained at the window.

Lella jumped up and down on the bed Spinetta told her was hers. The child pulled back the covers and, inviting Crespo in, dived beneath them.

Two men arrived, carrying the coffer. Spinetta told them to put it by the foot of her bed, then they left. 'You have the one next to the window,' she told Giulia.

'What can I do to help?'

'Nothing. Seems everything's provided here, even before it's needed.'

Suzanna and Carla, baby Serafina in her arms, appeared in the doorway. Lella stopped pretending to be asleep. 'Look at our lovely room!' she cried.

The sisters entered. 'This is very grand,' said Carla. 'Ours is nice too. Seems Brighella has worked one of his miracles.'

Giulia asked Carla if she could hold Serafina. She carried the baby to the window.

'Marco and Pedrolino are going to the market,' Carla told them. 'Pantelone says we can go with them.'

Spinetta gave a wry smile. 'If I will look after the children.'

Carla smiled back.

'Of course I will.'

'Can I go?' cried Lella.

'No dear.'

'Oh!' The child folded her arms and pouted.

'You have to stay and look after Crespo. You can't take *him* to the market. He'd get stolen.'

'Oh well then, I don't want to go.' Lella hugged her dog.

'You can go, Giulia.'

Giulia looked round. 'But the children?' She glanced at the babe in her arms.

'Good heavens. Don't you think me capable of looking after a couple of little ones by myself? Besides, if I need any help…' Spinetta crossed to the bell and touched the handle, 'all I have to do is ring.'

Giulia found the prospect of going to the market thrilling. One of the narrow boats, gondolas they were called, carried the party of five to the bridge. So busy was the canal, in places the water was invisible. It appeared there were no rules as to who had the right to dock, or where. It was simply a matter of nipping in when you could and persisting. As soon as the gondola docked, Pedrolino and Marco scrambled onto the quay and helped the girls disembark.

A babel of voices assaulted Giulia's ears. Men in floppy red hats gabbled and gesticulated. If they were trading, it was hard to guess in what. The smell pervading the quay was a mixture of foul and exotic. Crates were stacked high. Liquor was being decanted from barrels into flagons; and the stones were awash with wine, fish heads and slime.

Giulia lifted her skirts above the mire and followed the other girls up the steps to the bridge. Lining both sides were small shops and stalls, which seemed to sell everything. There were fruits, spices, fine boots and shoes in colours she had never seen worked in leather. One pale-blue pair with gold piping caught her eye. 'Very pretty,' called the seller, snatching them up. 'Exquisite shoes for a ravishing beauty. Made for you, lady.'

'But how do you know they would fit?'

'They will.' He thrust them under her nose. 'I had your dainty feet in mind when I made them. Buy these shoes, pretty lady. How can you live without them?'

She laughed. 'But I have no money.'

'The gentleman will pay.'

She shook her head. 'Oh no.'

'How much?' asked Pedrolino.

When the vendor told him, he laughed. 'Not today. Thank you.'

The man threw up one hand in a gesture then hailed his next prospective customer.

Marco and Carla went to look for items Pantelone needed. Pedrolino stayed with the girls. Suzanna bought a skein of thread from a woman selling cloth. Giulia was attracted to a shop selling masks. She had noticed several people wearing them, here in the market. It seemed it was not only Brighella who chose to keep his face hidden.

On reaching the end of the bridge, she caught sight of a couple in an alleyway. The woman's breasts were bare, the man had his hand up her skirt. Looking away quickly, she noticed a sign that said *Shop of Miracles*. But it was really only a stall. Laid out on the table were trinkets, toys and coloured bottles. Pedrolino had bought something and was paying the elderly vendor, who had a full white beard, was dressed in a fur-trimmed hat and wore a long purple gown covered in silver stars and crescent moons. The man gave Giulia a broad wink. She smiled at him briefly then hurried on after Pedrolino.

Marco and Carla were waiting on the quay, Marco loaded up with goods. 'We've got it all,' called Carla. Suzanna ran down to join them.

A wild-looking man dressed in nothing but a loincloth came hurtling up the steps. 'Repent!' he cried, brandishing a crude wooden cross. 'You servants of Mammon, throw yourselves on God's mercy while there's still time!'

Angry shouts followed his progress, until he was brought down by a booted foot. Two vendors seized a skinny arm apiece, dragged him down the steps then threw him into the canal. Giulia gave a cry. Pedrolino ran to the quay.

But already the man had been hooked on a pole. 'Repent!' he spluttered as he was pulled out. 'God's mercy is infinite.' A gondolier gave him a kick up the backside and he stumbled off, leaving his wooden cross floating in the canal.

'I'm sorry I couldn't buy you those shoes,' whispered Pedrolino on the way back.

'Don't be silly.' Giulia squeezed his hand then noticed, in the other, a small wooden box. 'What's that?'

'A present, for Lella.'

ack at the palazzo, Giulia was told by a servant that Spinetta was waiting for her in an upper room. She thought it a little strange but followed him through the kitchen to the bottom of a wooden staircase. 'Top floor,' he told her and scuttled off.

Giulia climbed the steps. On reaching the top landing, she saw the door slightly ajar. 'Spinetta?' she called.

Nobody answered, so she pushed open the door and stepped in. On a table, beneath a small round window, lay a book. The door slammed shut behind her.

'I was looking for Spinetta,' she gasped, whirling round. 'A servant told me she was here.'

'On my orders,' said Brighella. 'Your book.' He indicated the volume.

'Why have you brought me here? Not to give it back, I imagine.'

'Oblige me. Look through the pages.' He took a step towards her so she hurriedly picked up the book. When she opened it, a parchment fell out.

'You may find the contents of that letter interesting, although part of it is missing.'

She frowned. 'Do you mind if I sit?'

'Not at all.'

She drew up a stool and read in silence.

Concerning the painting I have in my possession and which your client has offered to buy, I am willing to part with it – at a price. I shall not give it away since the work has personal value, although I expect you will tell me I am in no position to make demands.

You know, of course, that my master painted this over a number of years during our travels. Others offered to buy the portrait but he would never part with it, working on it obsessively, repainting, refining. I do not think he was ever entirely satisfied with the end result. I told him he would work the thing to death but he was driven by his search for perfection.

And we both know why. I think you are the only man to whom I can speak of such things. Yet, in committing them to paper, I am inviting the devil to sup at my table. I beg you, then, burn this letter once you have memorised its contents.

Recently there has been speculation as to the inspiration behind my master's masterpiece. Ha! There's a neat slip of the tongue. And yes, that was another!

My master's piece. We both know to whom that belonged. You may think me unnecessarily crude, but I tell you he never made me feel less than divine.

Only persons not acquainted with my loving benefactor would give credence to the rumour that a certain lady who, I admit, did sit for her portrait at the very start, ended up being its subject. And only those who understand nothing of an artist's mind could believe that he would, so doggedly, persist with trying to catch a likeness of someone he did not love. The great artist paints but two faces during his lifetime – his own and that of the creature he adores. Sometimes the two become one.

Decide for yourself, my friend. The St. John the Baptist, which caused such a fuss (I told him it was risky). Whose face is that?

And, if still you have doubts as to the truth of what I have written, look to the lady's smile. I will present you with it when we meet.

One last thing. When the deal is done and you admire your extremely expensive purchase, allow your gaze to wander beyond the sitter to the landscape. You are looking. But are you seeing?

God bless! The painting will cost you ten thousand ducats.

Yours, Salai

PS I expect you are wondering why I have chosen to tell all since the knowledge, should it become widespread, would do my late master's reputation great harm. The answer is vanity. I am ruined and in poor health. Is it too much to ask that I, the passive partner of a genius, claim a small share in his immortality?

'You have an interest in this painting?' Giulia asked, folding the letter and slipping it back between the pages.

'Not especially. Although I am curious. My interest lies in the book's other contents. As well as another letter, which, I believe, once lay hidden between the leaves.'

'I should like to go now.' Getting up, she returned the book to the table.

He crossed the floor in one stride and she backed away, hand raised. 'I swear, if you touch me, I'll tell the master what you and Franceschina did to me in her wagon. And the part you played in my violation.'

'Ha! And what about Arlecchino? Would you betray him also? Don't imagine I haven't noticed the lovelorn glances. You still have feelings for the man.'

'That doesn't mean I wouldn't tell the truth and shame him.'

He regarded her a moment then sneered, 'he's had you again. Arlecchino has plucked you a second time. And this time you enjoyed it!'

She made a dash for the door but he reached it first and pressed his hand against it. 'I could take the letter from you now. I know you carry it on you. But you'll give it to me of your own free will – in time.' He let go of the door.

As Giulia fled down the stairs, she could hear him laughing.

39

he mood within the palazzo during the evening meal was one of merriment and optimism. There was food fit for nobility. Wine flowed. Pantelone sat at the head of the table with Brighella on his left, Arlecchino and Franceschina to his right. The master was ebullient and appeared more relaxed than Giulia, seated halfway down on the left-hand side, had ever seen him. The many toasts he proposed to his beloved Venice revered the Star of the Sea as *Queen of Earthly Reason.*

In common with everyone else, Giulia was lulled into a feeling of ease and began to forget about her unpleasant encounter with Brighella. She had already decided that, like it or not, she would have to put up with his presence. He had far too much influence within the company for anything she might say to discredit him.

The only thing marring her enjoyment was the difficulty she was having ignoring Arlecchino. Throughout the meal, he paid Franceschina close attention and the sight of them touching and whispering and the sound of their shared laughter grated on her nerves. Worst of all, on one occasion, he caught her watching them and had the effrontery to smile. She looked away quickly but her cheeks continued to burn.

As soon as the meal was over, there was the call for music. Giulia left the table, using a headache as her excuse for retiring. As she made for the staircase, Pantelone called her name and, looking round, she saw him leave the table, followed by Suzanna. Visibly flushed with drink, his expression became oddly stern as he approached. 'I'll come straight to the point, Giulia. Suzanna has proved unsatisfactory in the role of servetta. I want you to take over. You'll need training, of course. Carla will oblige. She can fill in until you become proficient.'

Giulia wanted to protest, but, catching his stern expression, managed only a breathless, 'thank you, Sir,' then curtsied.

He went back to the table and music began.

'Suzanna,' breathed Giulia.

Suzanna grasped her hand. 'Before you say anything, I don't mind. I always knew I wasn't any good. I hated going on stage and only kept going for Carla's sake.'

'Is that true?'

Suzanna nodded. 'Really. I'm glad. I'll be much happier looking after the children and helping Spinetta with costumes.'

Giulia's relief at not bringing pain to a friend proved fleeting. Now excitement fought fear, making her stomach churn. She had been given the role of servetta!

'I'm going back to tell Carla,' she heard Suzanna say. 'Will you come?'

'If you don't mind, Suzanna, I was on my way to lie down. I have a bad headache.'

'See you tomorrow then.'

Giulia's headache was no longer an excuse. She tried to get to sleep but, instead, kept going over in her mind what had happened. Gazing up at the ceiling, she watched dancing lights cast by the reflections of lanterns. The singing of a gondolier mingled with music from below.

She was the Immortali's new servetta! Her dream had come true. So why did the thought of going on stage terrify her? Because the one and only time she had tried to act, she had been dumbstruck. Her singing had saved her; but she could not always sing her way out of trouble. Her heart began to pound. Palpitations forced her out of bed. She went to the window and thrust it wide open.

Immediately below, a tall figure was skulking on the quay. A gondola was being propelled across the canal towards him. When the vessel docked, the skulking figure and the gondolier unloaded a large wooden crate and moved into shadow.

Next morning Giulia had to be woken by Spinetta. She dressed hurriedly and picked up some mending.

'What do you think you're doing?' asked Spinetta.

There came a knock on the door and Carla popped her head round. 'I've come to fetch Giulia.'

'Well yes,' laughed Spinetta. 'That is, if she's not too busy. Go on then! No more mending for you.'

Giulia dropped her work and followed her friend down the staircase. Carla called, 'We'll have to be quick.'

Through the kitchens and up one flight of the steps Giulia had taken the day before, they scurried along an unlit passageway which twisted and turned so many times they might have been going round in circles. The floorboards creaked and were so uneven that, at one point, Giulia grasped Carla's skirts to stop herself tripping. At last, they came to an open door with bright light flooding through. The room beyond echoed with hammering. Pantelone's voice boomed.

Giulia followed Carla in.

Arlecchino was sitting on the floor on the far side of a large ballroom. Resting against the wall, he looked to be asleep.

'Well then!' was all Pantelone said as the girls rushed in and curtsied.

'I'm really sorry,' gasped Giulia.

Franceschina whizzed round. 'What's she doing here?'

Arlecchino stretched and yawned.

Franceschina marched up to Pantelone. 'I said, what is she doing here?'

He put a hand on her shoulder. 'Suzanna was never a worthy servetta to you, my sweet. You deserve better.'

'I know but…'

'And for matchless talent like yours to shine, we need a girl who can provide sufficient shade.'

Giulia felt a bit crushed until she noticed Franceschina, who had been about to further object, close her mouth abruptly.

'Now!' he said and, with a clap of the hands, dismissed the carpenters. 'Let's begin. Giulia, stand over there.' He waved her towards the wall.

Arlecchino sprang to his feet.

Giulia watched a scene in which he and Franceschina exchanged romantic pleasantries. Carla moved around the pair, pretending to sweep and eavesdrop. She was brilliant, her actions so expressive that Giulia felt she not only understood what was happening, but could also read her mind. Such an inspirational performance was also a little depressing.

184

How could Giulia ever become so proficient? 'Your turn now, Giulia,' Pantelone beckoned.

'Don't try too hard,' whispered Carla.

Giulia found the experience overwhelming and working in close proximity with Arlecchino did not make things any easier. She had no idea what she was doing and whirled around in what felt to her an ungainly frenzy until Pantelone clapped his hands. 'A bit clumsy,' he called. 'But not bad, for a start. Now do it again, but this time acknowledge the audience. No actor exists without them.'

Giulia tried again and, this time, felt confidence flow. *Acknowledge the audience.* Those words made the difference. Before long, she was enjoying herself and felt quite disappointed once the rehearsal came to an end. She and Carla were told to get something to eat then come straight back.

When they returned to the ballroom, the rest of the actors were assembled. 'Gather round,' called Pantelone, taking the stage. 'You will all, with the exception of our newest member,' he twirled a hand in Giulia's direction and the rest of the actors smiled her a welcome, 'be familiar with this one. An old favourite, yet guaranteed to please. Three acts, of course.

'Two girls then.' He held up two fingers. 'One,' his index finger remained in the air, 'the daughter of a rich merchant, a girl of sweet disposition. The other,' two fingers again, 'an impoverished cousin employed as her companion, lively of wit and sharp-tongued.'

'Guess whose part that is,' whispered Renaldo to Carla. She giggled and Franceschina shot them a glare.

'Two suitors next. A young gentleman returned from the Turkish wars and his companion, a trusty servant who fought *bravely*,' Pantelone thrust a fist into his palm, 'at his side.'

'That can't be me then!' called Arlecchino.

Pantelone carried on through laughter. 'The gentleman gains the merchant's consent to marry his daughter and the happy pair, wishing to share their good fortune with their friends, plot to unite them. Meanwhile, the merchant's estranged brother pays him a visit. A cold-hearted villain.' Brighella raised a hand and the master gave him a nod. 'This scheming man is set on ruining the forthcoming nuptials. Meanwhile, the reluctant lovers are tricked into overhearing conversations – secret arbour device. Audience loves it.'

'Reportedly praised to the skies by the other, the pair of lovers' antagonism develops into mutual admiration. But the wicked brother bribes a young rogue to dress up in the bride-to-be's clothes and speak words of love from her balcony to a second rascal below.

Pantelone began to pace the stage. 'The evil man tells the young gentleman of his intended's infidelity. On the day of the wedding, he accuses the innocent girl, who promptly falls into a faint and is taken for dead. This brings the other pair closer. The girl urges her suitor to challenge his master to a duel. He embarks upon a different plan. Both rogues are caught and forced to confess.'

Now he rattled on even faster, acting out the play as he spoke. 'The young gentleman, mortified that he falsely accused his bride-to-be and caused her death, agrees to the old merchant's request that he marry her cousin, who is, reportedly, so ugly she must wear a mask. The moment the marriage is solemnised, the innocent girl removes her mask to great rejoicing. The young gentleman begs her forgiveness. The second pair of lovers ask to be united in marriage and the play ends with a double wedding. Any questions?' He whirled round to face the actors. 'No? Good! Scenario pinned in the wings.'

Pedrolino came to Giulia. 'All right?' he asked.

'I think so,' she gasped. 'It seems very complicated.'

'Not really. I'll help.'

'The plot,' she said, wrinkling her nose. 'It does sound rather silly.'

Pedrolino laughed. 'Of course!'

From the far side of the ballroom there came a grating sound. Brighella was dragging a large wooden crate to the centre of the room. Giulia recognised it as the one she had seen unloaded from the gondola.

All the actors, including Pedrolino, hurried to see what it contained and, when the lid was prised off, there were shouts of excitement. The fine handbills were passed round. Guido and another lad were dispatched with a sackful each to nail up in the Rialto and distribute around prosperous neighbourhoods.

'These must have cost a fortune,' said Pedrolino, passing a handbill to Giulia. Flanked by angels blowing cornets, the printed words announced the forthcoming play to be performed by the most illustrious company, the Immortali. *Much Ado About Nothing* was its title. But the date! How on earth could they be ready to open in three days?

Brighella was being congratulated and, as Giulia watched, something unexpected crept into her mind. Why not give him Jacopo Bruno's letter? Perhaps the time had come to put aside personal feelings. There was no denying he did a great deal of good for the company and, if she gave him the letter, he might leave her alone.

The actors were dispersing. Pantelone stayed on. Giulia went to speak to him. 'Master, I should like to ask…'

'The answer is *yes*.'

'Yes?'

'You demonstrated in rehearsal that you're capable of playing second servetta. Learn as much as you can from Carla. She is very gifted.'

'Thank you,' she said, feeling quite overcome. 'But really I came to ask your advice. Is there anything you can tell me which might help…'

'Never upstage Franceschina.'

40

pening night came around all too soon for Giulia. Assembled with the rest of the cast in the anteroom behind the stage, she asked herself what she was doing there. Giulia Olivieri, an actress? Ridiculous!

Spinetta had found a smart grey dress for her role as second servetta. It was plain; it had to be. But the crisp white apron had been neatly trimmed with lace by Suzanna and gave it, in Giulia's eyes, that something extra.

The sound of an excited audience filling the ballroom fed her fears. Now she understood what poor Suzanna had gone through. She took several deep breaths and told herself: *You have nothing to fear. You are only here to make up the numbers. No one in the audience is even going to notice you.*

Carla appeared completely calm. Giulia's admiration for her had increased beyond bounds. She told herself that all she had to do was conquer her nerves and follow her mentor's example.

The music of lute and guitar struck up to mingle with expectant murmurings. Giulia recognised Brighella's playing; cultured, alluring. How could such a man produce so sweet a sound?

Pedrolino came and stood beside her. 'You look very pretty,' he whispered.

She flushed and felt butterflies grow into trapped birds.

'No need to be nervous.' His fingers brushed hers. 'Let your spirit blend with ours. The body will follow.'

She did not understand but his tone was reassuring.

At last it began. Pantelone took the stage. The instant he appeared, the theatre filled with applause. From the brief glimpse Giulia had managed to sneak of the audience, she knew most were well to do; so the unrestrained clapping, whistling and cheers came as a surprise. It took a while to silence them. The master thanked them for their gracious welcome and sang the praises of their fair city, from which he claimed to spring in body and soul. Then he introduced the play.

The action began with a scene between Pantelone as the merchant, Renaldo playing the part of the young gentleman and Arlecchino as his manservant. The suitors met their prospective partners, the first pair falling in love straight away and quitting the stage arm in arm. Franceschina was left listening to Arlecchino recounting his exploits in the Turkish wars.

Franceschina yawned; then, cupping an ear, asked the audience, 'What's that noise?'

They laughed.

'Oh, it's only you,' she said, turning to face her leading man. 'Still prattling on? Even though no one is listening.'

'Not even you?' He strutted towards her.

'I'm told you consider yourself a wit? A charmer!'

'Most certainly!'

'And even – a lady's man?' She observed him coyly over a fluttering fan.

'Indeed!' As she whirled away with a rustle of satin, he leapt to intercept her. She gave him a shove and he faked a backwards stagger. 'Perhaps you are no lady, then?' He pushed his hat down over his mask and inspected his knuckles.

'And you, Sir! Are definitely no gentleman!'

'If you say so. I don't recollect ever claiming to be one.'

There was more laughter as the pair walked briskly back and forth, pretending to ignore one another. Franceschina came to a sudden stop. 'Sir?'

'Yes?'

'Not only are you no gentleman. Neither are you a lady's man.'

'What?' Spinning round to face her, he straightened his hat with the tip of his baton. 'How so?'

'Because, if you were, you would understand a lady's need to dissemble.'

'I understand that well enough.'

'Well then.'

189

'Well then?'

'Might you not try harder to win my good opinion?' She fluttered the fan with a furious motion.

'I might. But if I did, I fear you might scratch my face.'

'I might!' Snapping the fan shut, she stood, hands on hips. 'But, if I did, I would most certainly make an improvement!'

Amidst laughter and applause, the couple met head to head. Then they spun round and stood back to back, arms folded.

Giulia felt a tap on her shoulder. 'We're on,' whispered Carla.

The moment Giulia stepped on stage, Pedrolino's words made sense. Giulia Olivieri – no, second servetta – was part of the Immortali.

Action flowed. Trickery fizzed. Romantic scenes weaved through knockabout. There was much flying in and out of scenery doors and some eavesdropping behind a leafy arbour. For Giulia, the instinct to act came naturally. But she never forgot that, to survive within this craziness, she had to make use of what Carla had taught her.

Neither did she neglect the audience; yet, when she peered out into the sea of faces, it was they who seemed less than real. The stage, this world of the imagination, was true reality.

In the third and final act, Pedrolino sang to the servettas:

Sigh no more, ladies, sigh no more,
Men were deceivers ever;
One foot in sea, and one on shore;
To one thing constant never:
Then sigh not so,
But let them go,
And let your loving hearts fly free
Converting all your songs of woe
Into one of love – for ME!

The audience adored it and called for an encore. Pedrolino whispered to Giulia, 'Sing with me.'

So Giulia sang with Pedrolino and the audience showed their appreciation with thunderous applause and some high-pitched whistling. Pedrolino swept his hat before him in a bow. Light-headed with joy, Giulia curtsied.

In the penultimate scene, Arlecchino and Franceschina returned. Now very much in love, they moved around the stage exchanging romantic pleasantries. The servettas had their parts to play, fussing and gossiping in the background.

'You girl! Why are you skulking back there? Are you spying on me?'

Giulia looked towards Franceschina, who was standing at the front of the stage. But where was Carla? Her mentor was nowhere to be seen. And neither was Arlecchino!

How could this have happened? A moment ago there had been four people acting. Now Giulia was alone on stage with the leading lady.

'Answer me then!'

Giulia curtsied; it was all she could think of to do.

'I will not tell you again!' Franceschina beckoned frantically. 'Come over here and tell me what you're up to!'

Giulia gulped. She had not expected to be required to speak. She felt tempted to sidle away and scuttle off down the steps; but something prevented her. Not just the desire to avoid humiliation. Within her, rose the urge to turn this crisis to her advantage. 'I beg your pardon, Mistress,' she said, with another curtsy. 'I am here to *serve* you.'

'Well come down here and do just that!' Franceschina looked fit to explode.

Still Giulia hesitated. Surely joining the leading lady at the front of the stage would be gross impertinence?

'I will not tell you again!' shrieked Franceschina.

Suddenly Arlecchino sprang on stage. 'Fret not, my sweet. The girl is a trifle simple.'

'Indeed she is!' laughed Franceschina as he whirled her round and round to great applause.

Giulia fled the stage.

At the end of the performance, the cast took their bows. Giulia lost count of the encores. But her elation was muted by the mistake she had made in not leaving the stage the same time as Carla. Once the theatre was empty, she spoke to her. 'I really am sorry. I didn't see you go.'

Carla laughed. 'You don't always have to follow me. Do what comes naturally.'

'No, but...'

Carla squeezed her arm. 'Don't worry. You did well. Go and get something to eat. I'll see you later. I have to check on the children.'

Giulia felt reassured but unsettled. Having no appetite, she remained in the ballroom alone. The sight of the stage filled her with excitement and she began again to experience the joy she had felt while performing.

Then suddenly she was slammed against the wall. 'Don't you ever, EVER do that to me again!' Blazing eyes bore through her. 'You might have been a lady once, but you're nothing now. NOTHING! Do you hear? You're lucky he gave you paltry servetta. That won't last. And you will never, NEVER be as good as me!'

'I'm sorry,' gasped Giulia. 'I didn't mean…'

The leading lady let her go but yanked her hair. With a howl of pain, Giulia put up a hand to defend herself. Franceschina tore her apron. Then she was gone, the furious whirlwind disappearing as suddenly as it had arrived.

Shocked and trembling, Giulia tried to tuck in a loose strand of hair as she burst into tears.

41

irm, gentle hands came to rest on Giulia's shoulders.

'I'm all right,' she said, wiping her eyes. She turned, expecting to see Pedrolino. Confusion, embarrassment and a multitude of other emotions bowled her over as surely as Franceschina's attack.

'No need for tears.' Arlecchino stroked her hair. 'She'll get over it.'

'I know I should have left the stage but she kept insisting I join her. I didn't know what to do. Why did she get so angry?'

'Because you upstaged her.'

Giulia frowned. 'But... I tried not to be noticed. It was Franceschina who kept telling me to come to the front.'

Arlecchino laughed. 'Come with me. I'll explain.'

'Your father told me never to upstage Franceschina,' she told him as they mounted the steps and he drew her centre-stage.

'I'm not surprised.' He waved an arm from front to back. 'What do you notice?'

Suddenly it dawned on Giulia the floor was sloping, ever so slightly, but unmistakably, towards the front.

'We're standing centre-stage. There's down.' He pointed towards the pit then jerked his thumb back. 'That's up. Understand?' She nodded and he walked to the backcloth. 'You go and stand at the front. Face the audience, just like Franceschina was doing when the pair of you were on together. Now, talk to them. Get them to notice you.'

She felt a bit foolish but made up a few lines.

'Are they listening?'

'I don't know.'

'I doubt it. Turn round.'

When she did so, she burst out laughing. Arlecchino was standing on his head. He righted himself then came to her, dusting his hands. 'I just upstaged you. A little extreme, I admit. But that's what you did to Franceschina. And, in your case, standing upstage of my leading lady, looking pretty, was enough to throw her into a paddy.'

Now it all made sense. No matter what Giulia had done or said, by standing upstage of Franceschina she would be noticed and, making the leading lady turn away from the audience to address her, had ensured all eyes would be drawn towards *her*.

'I should apologise.'

'I wouldn't bother. Like I said, she'll get over it. I'm hungry and in desperate need of a drink. Coming?'

'In a minute. Thank you,' she called as he ran off down the steps.

He paused at the door. 'Oh, Giulia. You may have upstaged Franceschina but I must say you did it rather well.'

Giulia hid her delight.

When she entered the dining hall, Pedrolino beckoned. 'The audience loved you,' he whispered. She smiled and sat down, stealing a glance at Arlecchino, who was seated a little way down on the opposite side, next to Franceschina. Throughout the meal, he paid close attention to his leading lady, who cast Giulia several dark looks.

Suzanna mended Giulia's apron in time for the next performance and the following night the play went without a hitch. Giulia made sure she never upstaged Franceschina again and each performance went better than the one before. Report after report came in singing the praises of the gifted Immortali and their excellent play. Within days, it was proving impossible to accommodate all who wanted a seat. There were some angry exchanges outside the theatre and a few scuffles. One man was so enraged he drew his sword but the men employed to deal with such situations disarmed him and sent him on his way.

Giulia felt she was living in a dream.

One fine morning, some of the actors decided to visit St. Mark's Square. The outing was purely for pleasure. Giulia waited on the quayside with Suzanna while Pedrolino organised gondoliers. 'Do you know if Franceschina's coming?' she whispered.

'She's not,' Suzanna whispered back.

That was a relief. Now the only thing spoiling her perceived enjoyment of the forthcoming outing was the fact that Arlecchino was too busy to accompany them. She had seen him moments ago in the ballroom, deep in conversation with Pantelone. They were apparently planning improvements to the set.

It took five gondolas to accommodate the party. Giulia was seated in the first, next to Suzanna. As it left the quay, she caught sight of Brighella half-concealed behind a column. She had not made a decision yet as to whether to give him Jacopo Bruno's letter.

'Hold up!' Arlecchino came running out of the palazzo and leapt into the final gondola. The craft rocked perilously and there were some anxious shouts. But the gondolier averted disaster and, amongst laughter and expressions of delight that Arlecchino had joined them after all, the small fleet sped away.

Giulia tried not to show how pleased she was but was immediately forced to suppress a quite different emotion. Brighella was not alone. Something about the way he and Franceschina were standing – the tilt of their heads, her urgent hand movements – filled her with unease. The pair's demeanour was one of conspirators.

St. Mark's Square was magnificent. The sun-kissed campanile pierced a sapphire sky, wet paving glittered as though shot with silver.

The actors received a warm welcome from the proprietor of a smart establishment tucked beneath an elegant colonnade. He shooed some customers out of seats by the windows to accommodate them; yet those ousted were not disgruntled since they were invited to join the party. Wine was brought without being ordered, as were delicious baked titbits. Arlecchino was in good spirits and, as ever, became the centre of attention.

Giulia was determined not to look at him but found it hard, especially as she felt his gaze fall on her several times. The heat induced by the delicious game she was playing blended with the effects of an excellent wine and soon her spirits were soaring higher than the campanile. Glancing out of the window, she noticed a group of tumblers entertaining a small crowd.

Suddenly the door opened and a young man with reddish blond hair stepped in. His hose was spattered with paint.

195

'Peter!' called Arlecchino and sprang to his feet. He grasped the young man's hand and drew him into the group. 'This is my good friend, Peter the painter. A gifted artist. A man of enormous talent. And, I can confirm, of equally enormous appetites!'

The artist gave a laugh.

'Now, Peter. I need you.' Arlecchino sat him down and poured him a drink. 'The Immortali must have a magnificent backcloth for the new play.'

The man shook his head.

'Don't shake your head! I know you don't like doing scenery. Peter's more of a – how shall I say?' he made a curving outline with his hands. 'A figures man. But, Peter, listen. We need to bring an air of sophistication into our theatre. So, what do you say? You could always dot in a few cherubs, here and there – and the odd nubile nymph.'

'I will think about it.' The painter had a foreign accent.

'Good!' It was clear that, as far Arlecchino was concerned, the matter was settled. 'Come back with us and I'll show you what's needed.'

The party spent an enjoyable hour in the place, then strolled across the square where the tumblers had been joined by jugglers. 'Go and show them how it's done,' Renaldo told Arlecchino.

'I'm off duty,' came the response.

Then Giulia noticed another group of men on the steps of the cathedral. They were monks and seeing them reminded her of those she had seen watching the galley set sail for Venice.

Back at the palazzo, hers was the last gondola to dock. As she disembarked, she grasped the hand offered and was finally forced to meet Arlecchino's gaze – not without blushing.

Returning to her room, she found Lella kneeling on a chair by the window.

'I saw you coming!' laughed the child, holding up the spyglass Pedrolino had bought her from the *Shop of Miracles* in the Rialto.

A servant came to the door and told Giulia the master wished to see her in the ballroom. When she entered, she saw Pantelone and Arlecchino on stage with the artist. 'Ah, Giulia.' Pantelone came down the steps.

'Is anything wrong?' she asked, worried by his expression.

'I'm afraid so. From my point of view, I have no complaints. But...' he rubbed his chin. 'Well, I *have* received some comments from our leading lady.'

'I am so sorry,' she gasped. 'I know I made a mistake on opening night. But I've tried really hard...'

'What's going on?' Arlecchino came and stood behind her.

Pantelone waved a hand. 'Franceschina.'

'Exactly! And we both know what this is really about.'

'Still, I have to consider what's best for the company.' He gave a sniff. 'Run along, Giulia. Try not to make any more mistakes.'

42

iulia was determined not to be driven from the stage by Franceschina.

But Arlecchino was wrong in thinking his leading lady would get over the slight inflicted on her by Giulia and avoiding trouble by staying out of her way on stage proved impossible. Franceschina did her best to put her in difficult situations. On one occasion she tried to draw her into an exchange between herself and Brighella on the subject of ignorant servants. Made the butt of their repeated jokes, Giulia was forced into playing the part. For the second servetta to retaliate with wisecracks of her own would have been unpardonable and disastrous for the play. Yet she came close to doing so. The following day she confided in Pedrolino.

He smiled. 'Franceschina's treatment of you must seem unforgivable. And there is no denying, it springs from a selfish spirit. But… well, generous-natured as you are, Giulia, there must have been occasions when you felt the same kind of fear?'

'Fear?'

'Franceschina is afraid you'll take her place.'

'But that's ridiculous. I'm second servetta. Besides, that's not what I want.'

He smiled. 'Are you sure?'

She took his words to heart, but it did her no good; and there entered into the leading lady's verbal attacks something of the mad dog. Even the audience picked up on it. Laughter became awkward and spasmodic. One accusation over a lost ribbon turned into a tirade in which Franceschina accused the second servetta of stealing. With repeated curtsies, Giulia succeeded in getting off stage, hands trembling.

Immediately Arlecchino came hurtling down the steps. 'That woman's becoming impossible!'

Somehow Giulia managed to get through the performance. Afterwards, she resigned herself to the inevitable. Since Pantelone would have to dismiss her, would it not be better to approach him with her resignation? Dream shattered, trampled by an unstable woman filled with irrational hatred, she made her way to the dining hall.

On reaching the end of the passageway, she heard whispering and, peering round the corner, saw Franceschina standing with Brighella at the top of the steps. Giulia moved back, out of sight. Were they waiting for her? She would never forget the last time they had joined forces to attack her. But, if Brighella's intention had been to take her letter by force, he could have done so in the attic room. He had no need of Franceschina.

The whispering continued, on Franceschina's part becoming more agitated. Giulia risked another look and saw her wagging a finger into the mask. Her words were inaudible but delivered as a threat. Brighella reacted calmly, towering over the small, irate woman. This exchange continued until someone was heard coming up the steps.

Giulia retreated back down the passage and waited until she was sure it was safe to emerge.

During the evening meal, she told Pedrolino and Carla she was going to resign. They tried to dissuade her and, in the end, she agreed to sleep on it, fully expecting Pantelone to summon her after the meal and dismiss her as he had done with Suzanna. But nothing happened and, not in the mood for conversation, she excused herself and went to her room.

She found Lella at the table, writing by the light of a candle. The child was copying one of the handbills. 'Do you like it?'

'I like it very much.' Her script was neat and Lella had made an excellent attempt at copying the angels blowing cornets.

'I love writing.'

'You're very good at it.'

'Just like you're good at acting!' The child beamed.

Giulia sat down and Lella resumed her writing.

Giulia's thoughts fell to her decision. Perhaps it was for the best. She still helped Lella with reading and writing; but the other children no longer had lessons. If she had to give up acting, then she could return to something else she enjoyed. The thought helped lift her spirits.

There came a knock on the door.

'I'll get it.' Lella ran to open it. The caller spoke quietly. 'It's for you.' The child ran back, giggling.

Giulia took a deep breath in preparation for the bad news but, reaching the door, stood amazed.

'Can we talk?'

Stepping out, she pulled the door to.

'Pedro tells me you're thinking of resigning.' Arlecchino placed a hand on the wall above her.

'Yes, I am.'

'Why?'

'Why do you think?'

'That's not a good enough reason.' He took his hand from the wall. 'But, if you really are prepared to let Franceschina drive you from the stage, you never belonged there in the first place.' He turned.

'Wait!'

'The stage is a cauldron, Giulia.' He faced her. 'We make magic there. We try. Sometimes it blows up in our faces but, when it works… well…' he shook his head and smiled, 'then there's nothing to compare.'

'Do you want me to stay?'

He had no time to answer as Spinetta appeared on the landing. She frowned at them both.

'I bid you both a good evening,' he said and left.

❧

rlecchino had succeeded in persuading Peter the artist to paint a new backcloth. In return, Peter was to have free entry to every performance for himself and his assistant, together with a night out at Arlecchino's expense. The work would take a week. That meant the theatre had to close temporarily and, when the board went up announcing it, the burly men had their work cut out dealing with disgruntled folk.

The break was good news for Giulia though, since it meant she could put off the decision to resign. She kept Arlecchino's interest in her future close to her heart. He never mentioned it again.

200

Pantelone took the opportunity to prepare the play, something more ambitious according to Pedrolino, who also told Giulia the master was intending to include a more significant role for Franceschina. The leading lady had complained that her part in *Much Ado About Nothing* had relegated her to little more than servetta and he was hoping to mollify her.

More musicians were employed. In addition to lutes, mandolins, guitars, shawms and viols, there was a large harp. No expense had been spared in engaging the very best players.

The new backcloth was to be complemented by exciting props such as a working fountain. Spinetta and Suzanna were kept busy creating exotic costumes for satyrs, water sprites, and even Turkish slaves.

The title of the new play was *Misrule in Arcadia* and the dramatic business was a result of collaboration between the master and Brighella. Since the plot was unfamiliar to the actors, rehearsals were held. To everyone's relief, Franceschina appeared happy with her role, that of daughter to an elderly nobleman with magical powers who lived on a deserted island.

For Giulia and Carla, the servetta's garb was exchanged for that of shepherdess. Giulia took delight in the fittings and thoughts of quitting slipped to the back of her mind, especially as Franceschina seemed content. There was no repetition of the ugly scenes played out in the previous play.

The day before opening night, the cast was assembled in the ballroom. This was to be the only dress rehearsal. There were expressions of wonder at the new backcloth. Peter had created an enchanting pastoral scene against which the creatures of Pantelone and Brighella's imaginations could play. At its centre was a stone temple, the entrance to which was flanked by elegant pillars over which vines tumbled. The portico featured a painted relief depicting the youthful messenger of the gods, bearing his staff wreathed in serpents. He wore a winged hat; tiny wings sprouted from his heels.

The only part of the backcloth Giulia did not like was the entrance to a cavern, half-hidden by thorn bush and gorse. Sitting cross-legged on the roof of the cave was a small, grotesque, shadowy figure.

The musicians took their seats. Arlecchino sprang up the steps. 'Where's her ladyship, then?'

'No doubt putting the final touches to her big effect,' laughed Renaldo.

'We'll give her a little longer,' muttered Pantelone.

But Franceschina did not appear, so the master sent Carla to fetch her.

Carla returned within minutes, looking anxious. She went straight to Pantelone and whispered in his ear. Giulia noticed his expression change. He beckoned Arlecchino from the stage. Together they hurried from the ballroom.

The actors gathered round Carla.

Giulia hung back; but the news still reached her. Franceschina had been taken ill.

43

here was consternation at the news of Franceschina's illness and, when neither Pantelone nor Arlecchino had come back within the half-hour, Pedrolino went to find out what was happening. He returned with Pantelone, who made light of Franceschina's indisposition, putting it down to a mild attack of stomach cramps. There were expressions of sympathy and relief it was nothing serious, although Giulia thought the master was trying a little too hard to sound relaxed. When Arlecchino walked back into the room, he looked worried.

Pantelone soon whisked the company into action. Carla was given the part of leading lady until Franceschina was fit to return.

By the following day it was clear she would not be returning; at least not in time for first night and, since new handbills had been distributed announcing the starting date of *Misrule in Arcadia*, it was decided not to postpone. Dozens of people had been calling at the theatre enquiring as to when it would re-open. Not to do so at the appointed time could, Pantelone feared, lead to a riot.

So the new play began with Carla playing opposite Arlecchino. She took it in her stride and the audience appeared well satisfied. There were some enquiries as to the previous actress and, when it was discovered she was suffering from a slight malaise, good wishes for her recovery flooded in, together with gifts.

After five days Pantelone called a meeting. There was silence as he mounted the stage. 'Franceschina is making a steady recovery. However, she is still rather weak and in need of rest, so I've asked Carla to continue for the meantime. I trust you all agree she has proved more than equal to the task and I ask, on her behalf, for your continued support.' There was clapping and some cheers for Carla, who smiled. 'I ask, also, that you pray for the speedy recovery of our leading lady. Thank you for your attention.' He quit the stage.

Giulia felt unsettled. One thing concerning her was her own lack of sympathy for Franceschina, whose current absence from the stage was making life easier; she knew she ought to be more charitable towards this woman in her time of trouble. In addition to harbouring selfish thoughts, Giulia was worried about Carla, who, in spite of being popular with her fellow actors and the audience, did not seem happy.

The task of nursing Franceschina had fallen to Spinetta, who remained tight-lipped as to the leading lady's true condition. Giulia chose not to ask probing questions but some details were forthcoming by way of Lella's casual chatter. Being a child, she was largely ignored by servants discussing the state of Franceschina's health, which was, apparently, worsening. The stomach cramps had not abated. All through the day and night sick bowls were carried from the leading lady's room just along the corridor. Soon Spinetta took to sleeping in the same room as her patient.

One night Giulia was awoken by screaming. She glanced anxiously at Lella, who, mercifully, remained fast asleep. The pounding of footsteps hurrying past their room forced Giulia out of bed. Now she felt genuinely sorry for Franceschina. There was probably nothing she could do. Even so, she went to see if she could help.

The door to Franceschina's room was ajar. For the moment, the screaming had ceased. Giulia approached. Then suddenly there erupted the most dreadful din. More terrible than a scream, it assaulted her senses. She moved back against the wall listening to the protracted wail which was followed by a loud crash and anxious shouts. The door flew open. Franceschina ran out of the room.

Giulia stood aghast. The once neat woman looked like a wild thing. Her bony white legs stuck out beneath a stained shift. Her raven hair was tangled, lank and streaked with grey. Her pockmarked face looked paler than ever and might have been a death mask, had it not been for the crazed expression in the fierce dark eyes, which were rimmed with red.

Spinetta dashed from the room, followed by a maid. Together, they tried to coax Franceschina back in but she shook her head and wailed

204

again, then, wrenching free, came hurtling towards Giulia, hands drawn up like claws. Giulia backed away.

Spinetta caught hold of the desperate woman. 'Go to bed, Giulia!' she hissed.

'But…'

'Do as I say!'

Franceschina struggled and spat. As the women dragged her away, she shot out an arm and pointed at Giulia. 'You're next!' she screamed. 'He's taking me now. But he's coming for you!' Hysterical laughter burst from her lips. She fell to her knees and vomited down the doorframe. The women hauled her to her feet, bundled her into the room and slammed the door shut.

Giulia returned to her room, shaken by the pitiable sight. And those words! Most probably, they were no more than the delirious rantings of a woman driven mad by pain. Yet they had been spoken with such clarity – terrifying clarity.

Not long afterwards, Giulia heard more footsteps together with muffled voices. She tried to ignore them; but it was no good. She opened the door a fraction and peered out. Pantelone was standing outside Franceschina's room in the company of a cloaked figure. When the stranger turned his head, Giulia gasped then hurriedly shut the door. The sight of that smooth white mask with its sinister eyeholes and long beaked nose induced in her a fit of trembling. Snatching a shawl, she wrapped it round her and scrambled into bed.

The screaming began again. Giulia pulled the quilt up over her head and tried not to imagine what the poor wretch was going through.

When she woke the following morning, she was surprised to see Spinetta back in her own bed, fast asleep. Lella yawned and sat up. Giulia put a finger to her lips. The pair of them rose and dressed quietly.

At the foot of the stairs they met Pedrolino. Giulia sent Lella on ahead. 'Last night,' she whispered. 'I saw a man… he was wearing a mask.'

'The plague doctor.'

'Plague?'

'Shush.' He drew her aside. 'It's all right. She doesn't have it. Still, it has to be reported. Any case which might…'

Giulia shook her head. 'Poor thing.'

Giulia ate a small breakfast then went back upstairs. An elderly man was on his way down. His full white beard shone like snow on a mountain and, when he smiled, his wrinkles grew deep. 'Good morning.' He doffed his fur-trimmed hat.

Now she recognised him. But today, in place of his cloak decked with crescent moons and stars, he wore a plain one of indigo velvet. 'Good morning,' she replied.

'It is for you, my dear, and may the radiant sun shed blessings upon your pretty face for many more to come. However...' he came so close, Giulia was forced against the wall, 'it does well to be watchful.' He put a finger to his lips and glanced about. 'There are those who wish us harm.' A smile creased his face once again. 'Yet never let go of hope. Love until your heart bursts! And always put your trust in a greater power than the demons of envy and fear.' Lightly pressing his thumb to her brow, he whirled off down the stairs.

Puzzled by this encounter yet curiously not alarmed, Giulia carried on up. Meeting Spinetta on the landing, she enquired after Franceschina.

Spinetta crossed herself. 'The poor soul is sleeping. There's no more to be done, apart from pray.'

Franceschina had one more visitor. In the dead of night the priest came.

Giulia left Lella asleep and went into the corridor. The door to Franceschina's room was open. Candlelight cast flickering shadows across her far wall, making silhouettes of the actors gathered around the door. The only sound was that of the priest's rhythmic murmurings. Soon that ceased. The light in the room flickered one last time then failed. The actors turned away. Giulia went back to her own room.

From what source sprang the genuine tears she could not tell.

'Don't cry, Giulia.' Lella's touch was as light as a petal and Crespo's cold wet nose nuzzled Giulia's fingers. 'Would you like to look through my magic spyglass? It cheers me up when I'm sad.'

Giulia wiped her eyes. 'No, thank you,' she said, taking Lella's hand and squeezing it. 'Franceschina is at peace now.'

'I know.' The little girl pulled free and, seating herself on the stool by the window, trained her spyglass on the night sky. 'She's gone to join the stars.'

44

he morning of the funeral dawned damp and grey. Mist obscured a world of water and stone. Ashen faces watched the gondola slide from the quay and begin its journey to a lonely island. Laid on the polished surface of the coffin was a green garland crowned with a single white flower.

Giulia's final glimpse of the scene remained in her mind long after the vessel had slid away. Pantelone had been seated one side of the casket, Arlecchino on the other, hand resting upon it. The gondolier had been only too well known to Giulia. Dressed from head to foot in black silk, Brighella had stood like a sentinel at the stern, ploughing the leaden waters.

The remainder of the day passed quietly, a sombre mood pervading the palazzo. During the morning, Spinetta supervised the clearing of Franceschina's room. Giulia offered to help but her offer was declined so she spent the time reading with Lella.

The evening meal was eaten in silence. Only Pantelone and Arlecchino engaged in hushed conversation. Not wishing to stare, Giulia could not help but wonder what they were discussing. The future of the company was not in doubt; but changes would have to be made. No announcement came after the meal. Only Carla, who had said very little since Franceschina's death, was summoned to the master's table.

Giulia had been back in her room a short time when there came a knock on the door. The servant informed her that the master required her presence in the ballroom. She took a candle to light the way and found Pantelone in the anteroom with Arlecchino. Carla was also there, seated on a bench. Giulia expressed her regret at the passing of Franceschina. 'There were difficulties between us,' she said. 'But I admired her greatly.'

'Good of you to say so.' Pantelone waved her towards the bench.

She put the candle down and sat next to Carla.

'Now.' Pantelone cleared his throat. 'I have offered Carla the position of leading lady.'

Giulia smiled at her friend but Carla's gaze remained lowered.

'She has agreed to continue in the role, for now, but feels the needs of her family come first. And I respect her decision.'

The silence grew strained. Giulia frowned, then she glanced up at Arlecchino.

'We are all in agreement,' said Pantelone.

Then it hit her, the same moment he put it in words. 'I would like you to become our leading lady.'

Giulia stared at him, speechless.

'What do you say then?'

'But… I have only just… surely there must be another? Isabella, for instance?'

He shook his head. 'She is soon to marry Renaldo. And likely, in the fullness of time, to have the same concerns as Carla.'

'Maria then?'

'Too young.'

'Constanza.'

'Too old.' Pantelone frowned deeply. 'No one can force you, Giulia, yet…'

'I should be honoured,' she gasped.

His face lit up. 'Good.'

Still stunned, Giulia felt her friend squeeze her hand; then Carla got up and left the room. Pantelone lifted something from an open chest. He carried it reverently, draped over both arms. 'My son and I have discussed this and we are of the same mind. I believe the garment will fit.' When he removed the linen cover, Giulia caught her breath. The exquisite gown he laid across her lap shimmered in the light of candles. Its stiff, satin bodice was fashioned from diamond shapes, just like Arlecchino's – yet the colours were muted: pastel pink, green and silver. Its voluminous skirt was a haze of white silk overlaid with lace. The billowing sleeves were trimmed with black velvet. 'This…' she breathed, fingertips hardly daring to touch the bodice, 'is the most beautiful thing I have ever seen.'

'The dress was my mother's,' said Arlecchino.

She looked at him, amazed. 'And you want me to wear it?'

'Yes,' replied Pantelone.

'You pay me a great compliment.'

'Now, Giulia, you have a great deal to learn. We will begin tomorrow. For now, I leave you with Arlecchino. The pair of you have things to discuss. But never forget,' his stern gaze swept over them both, 'the partnership formed between you tonight is, and must remain, one of the spirit. Your first and only loyalty is to the Immortali.'

Once he was gone, she stole a glance at Arlecchino. 'Are you and your father really of the same mind? I hope so. I feel deeply honoured to be given the role of leading lady – but more so to be considered worthy to wear this beautiful dress. It looks almost new.'

'Soon after it was made, my mother fell pregnant. She gave birth to a daughter. Both died.'

'I... I'm sorry.'

'I was five years old.' He stooped to stroke one of the black velvet bows that graced a cuff. 'I have few memories of her, but I know she was beautiful. I expect you think that's no more than a son's idolisation of a dead mother. Yet I do have proof.' He went to the chest and brought out a small oval frame, which he handed her.

Giulia gazed at the portrait of a dark-haired girl, cradling a basket in which nestled a pair of white doves. 'You're right. She was very beautiful.'

'And now to another matter – your name. You must take a new one, now that you're my leading lady.'

'Really?'

'Of course. It's tradition. And Giulia was a runaway, remember. From now on you'll be in the public eye. Do you have any preference?'

Giulia shook her head.

'Well, if I might make a suggestion? What would you say to being known by the name Colombina?'

Glancing back at the portrait, she smiled. 'Two doves! That was your mother's name. Again, you do me a great honour. But what about your father? How would he feel..?'

'It was his idea.'

he world of Colombina dawned with a pale winter sunrise over Venice. Giulia was no more; that name had been shed with the darkness.

Colombina had not spoken of this, not even to Spinetta and Lella. They still slept as she stood looking out of the window. She had hardly shut her eyes all night. Yet she had treasured those seconds, minutes, hours spent in blissful contemplation. Pedrolino had been right; this had always been her dream. Now it had come true and, as light transformed the Serenissima, her heart swelled to bursting.

As soon as Spinetta and Lella were up, Colombina broke her news. Lella leapt onto the bed, then into her arms. Spinetta cried and hugged them both.

On her way to rehearsals, Colombina harboured one niggling concern. How would the others react?

Her anxieties proved groundless. The moment she entered the ballroom, everyone applauded. Pedrolino's smile was the broadest. Carla waved and blew her a kiss. The loudest applause came from an unexpected source; Brighella's clapping was audible above the rest. After rehearsal, he caught up with her. 'Congratulations, Colombina.' For once, she was happy to face him.

'You'll make a fine leading lady.'

'Thank you,' she replied.

'Glad to be of service.' He gave an odd laugh and walked away.

45

righella's parting comment seemed at first merely strange, yet it burrowed into Colombina's mind. She told herself it was, most likely, just another attempt to make mischief.

Pantelone set no time limit for her to take over from Carla and, for the moment, she remained in the role of shepherdess. Now she paid even closer attention to her friend's skills. Carla was unendingly patient when demonstrating the best way to do things; but sometimes Colombina despaired of ever attaining her high standard. Although Arlecchino had welcomed her promotion, she found him harsh when she failed to grasp what was required. It was on those occasions the ghost of Franceschina seemed to stalk the stage.

One complicated dance routine was particularly difficult to master and, when he stomped off in exasperation, Colombina shared her miseries with Pedrolino. He reminded her that Arlecchino's first concern was his art; and his criticism, however harsh, sprang only from a desire for perfection. Understanding that would be her key to success. She felt encouraged; even more so when he added that Arlecchino had told him she was coming on rather well.

Misrule in Arcadia continued to play to a full house, its humour and romance charming every audience. Pantelone, as master magician, directed his world of mythical creatures, steering them through an elegant plot filled with tricks and devices. His main purpose was to take revenge on his treacherous half-brother, who had robbed him of his birthright. In addition, he struggled to guard his innocent daughter from the attentions of Arlecchino, a shipwrecked mariner in pursuit of a pretty girl. He had tricks of his own. Yet he had a rival, a shape-changing monster who wooed the magician's daughter by casting spells that made him appear handsome in her eyes. That was Brighella's part. Unbeknownst to her, the heroine had a third would-be suitor. Pedrolino, faithful servant to the magician, never spoke of his feelings but expressed them by means of gestures and song. One haunting refrain never failed to reduce the audience to tears.

Every moment not performing, Colombina practised her routines with Arlecchino but sometimes his closeness brought back their unspoken history, shattering her concentration. Carla's advice continued to be of immeasurable value. She told Colombina not to mimic her, or try to force things. 'It will come,' she said. 'Relax and enjoy your acting, then true Colombina will appear.'

On fine mornings Colombina took walks with Pedrolino. Heads bent, they walked by canals, over bridges, around squares, running through dialogues she shared with Arlecchino. Words came easily with Pedrolino, and, she was happy to find, sprang to mind later in the heat of Arlecchino's close proximity.

Christmas was barely a week away when Pantelone summoned her. She did her best to compose herself. She knew he had been monitoring her progress and, as he rubbed his chin and began to pace the floor, the suspense became unbearable. Suddenly he whirled round to face her. 'Take over as leading lady. Tonight.'

'Yes, Master,' she managed.

'Any questions?'

She shook her head.

Afterwards she cursed herself. She had a million questions. Top of the list was how could she possibly take over so soon? Self-doubt and fear of failure flapped round her like harpies. 'I can't do it,' she gasped.

'Yes you can.'

She felt Arlecchino's hand on her shoulder. 'But he's given me no time to prepare.'

'That was deliberate. It would be worse, if you'd had time to worry.'

'But I'm not ready. I know it. You know it! If I go on tonight…'

He turned her to face him. 'This is not about you.'

'But what if I fail?'

'You won't fail! I won't let you. Listen. You are my leading lady. Tonight you will not be acting *or* playing a part. Everything Colombina does is *real*.'

Dressing for the play, she kept those words in mind. The beautiful gown had needed no alterations and the sight of herself in the long mirror filled her with pride and excitement. 'There,' said Spinetta, tucking in the final lace at the back of the bodice. 'It might have been made for you.'

'I pray I do it justice.'

'No need for prayers. The master knows what's what. He wouldn't have made you leading lady if he didn't think you were ready.' Spinetta turned her attention to Colombina's coiffure.

'I still feel nervous.'

'That's as it should be. Sometimes Franceschina was sick with nerves.'

'Really?'

Spinetta fixed a white silk flower in place. 'She even took stuff, potions and the like. Too much, I reckon.'

'I didn't realise.'

'Who knows what those charlatans put in their bottles.'

Colombina frowned. 'Do you think that might have caused her death?'

'It's possible. So you take heed. Nerves are nature's way of telling us we're alive. Now, my sweet,' Spinetta stood back and smiled, 'you're ready. And Colombina is ready to steal the show.'

Colombina hugged her. 'Thank you – for everything.'

❧

The mood in the anteroom was tense yet optimistic. All eyes spoke encouragement.

Carla's last week would be spent playing shepherdess and helping young Maria learn the part. As Pantelone introduced the play then announced the debut of a new leading lady, Colombina felt her friend squeeze her hand. Arlecchino was facing the steps. Pedrolino gave her a smile. She smiled back, recalling their walks. What had he once told her? *The stage is reality, a glimpse of the eternal.* Or had those words been Arlecchino's?

The play began with a loud clap of thunder then the lights went out. Under cover of darkness, Arlecchino took his place on stage.

Pantelone's voice boomed out an incantation. 'Swift to come and sure to obey, I have need of powers dark. Winds must blow to drive a stately ship upon my jagged rocks. For I will have vengeance!' There came another clap of thunder, lights flickered then grew bright, revealing Arlecchino lying facedown near the front.

Colombina's moment had arrived. She ran up the steps. Catching sight of Arlecchino, she put a hand to her mouth then backed away. Driven forward by curiosity, she approached him again with halting steps. She knelt, stroked his hair. He groaned and rolled onto his back. She sprang away and ran to hide behind the fountain.

Someone threw water from a jug to rouse Arlecchino. He leapt up and staggered about, to laughter. When a chain of nymphs and satyrs ran up the steps and encircled him in a merry dance, he collapsed once again. There was a burst of applause.

The play went well and there were numerous encores.

Colombina's confidence increased with every performance. On three consecutive evenings she received a magnificent bouquet, sent by an anonymous admirer. She was flattered; but something far more wonderful happened the night before the theatre closed for Christmas.

The dance she had found hard to master, which brought each performance to a close, proved so popular, encore after encore was demanded. One by one, people rose to their feet. Mesmerised by music and the appreciation of the crowd, Colombina moved involuntarily as though in a trance, her only contact with the world of flesh the firm warm grasp of the man who led her.

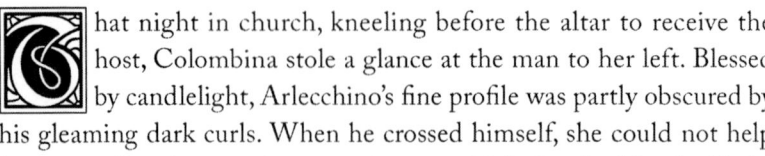

That night in church, kneeling before the altar to receive the host, Colombina stole a glance at the man to her left. Blessed by candlelight, Arlecchino's fine profile was partly obscured by his gleaming dark curls. When he crossed himself, she could not help but remember that previous occasion on which they had knelt side by side in church. Was that in a different life?

Back at the palazzo, supper was laid out in readiness. Pantelone strode to the blazing fire and spread his hands before it. The first goblet of wine was brought to him by the housekeeper, together with a letter. He broke open the seal, then, with a laugh, slapped the parchment. 'Children,' he called. 'This is an invitation. We are to be the guests of honour at Venice's first and most prestigious masked ball.'

46

Excitement clung to the foggy night air the evening of the masked ball. Gondolas festooned with lanterns converged on the magnificent palazzo, its balconies wreathed in thick green garlands. The first of the actors' boats slid through the iron gates to dock and, once secured, was immediately attended by servants. Pantelone stepped out, followed by Colombina and Pedrolino.

To Pantelone's annoyance, Arlecchino had insisted on arriving late. He refused to say why. It was the master who escorted Colombina beneath an ornate portico. As they entered the ballroom, more servants rushed forward to whisk away cloaks and, once the actors were announced, guests not engaged in the dance turned to applaud. Pantelone made a great show of expressing his appreciation. Colombina smiled as she took in the breathtaking scene.

At the end of the ballroom was a sweeping double staircase leading up to a gallery. White marble gleamed beneath light cast through droplets of glass that made up the lanterns. Most stunning of all was the living mosaic, which rippled across the dance floor. Such monochrome brilliance dazzled the eye; this was a black and white ball. White diaphanous silk brushed Stygian satin. Ermine-trimmed velvet flowed.

Every guest wore a mask, some of which were elegant, others grotesque. Many were studded with diamonds. Extravagant coiffures sprouted feathers and flowers. Rows of milky pearls graced necks; teardrops dangled from ears. The dancers moved within a mesmeric tableau, a swirling, undulating sea of contrasting splendour. 'Have you ever seen anything like it?' whispered Pantelone.

'Never,' breathed Colombina, glancing down at her own white dress. She had made it herself with Spinetta's help and had, until now, been delighted with its classic simplicity. The muslin skirt was overlaid with silk, the cool satin bodice embroidered with columbines around a low neckline. The only piece of jewellery she possessed was her amethyst crucifix and she had been reluctant to take it off. But the occasion demanded, so she had replaced it with a black velvet ribbon graced with a single white silk flower. She wore a mask of black velvet. Her hair was unadorned.

As soon as word spread of the actors' arrival, they were swamped by excited guests. Music stopped. Dancing came to a standstill. A portly man with a neat grey beard elbowed his way to Pantelone.

The master bowed.

'None of that, my friend.' The host grasped his hand and shook it soundly. 'Carnival is here. Chaos is king and misrule rules. Tonight the Immortali are the aristocracy, we your humble servants. Everything of mine is yours.' He bowed with a flourish and Pantelone laughed.

The man turned to Colombina. 'And here is your new leading lady. Enchanting! A vision of loveliness.' He took in her appearance as he kissed her hand. 'My dear, you put the rest of us to shame. But where is your leading man?'

Pantelone cleared his throat. 'He will be here. Shortly.'

'I should hope so, indeed! Or a hundred ladies will be baying for my blood. Sons, eh?' He shook his head. 'They squander our money and give us grey hairs. And, speaking of sons, here comes mine. Alfredo, let me introduce you to Pantelone, master of the actors. And the lady Colombina, Queen of the Immortali.'

A gaunt young man with a receding chin rushed forward and grasped Colombina by the hand. 'Would you do me the honour?'

'For goodness sake, Fredo. Let the girl catch her breath. There are refreshments to be had and...'

'I should be pleased to dance with you,' Colombina told Alfredo.

'Thank you, my dear,' said the host, 'for rescuing me and putting him out of his misery. I have not had a moment's peace since he knew you were coming.'

So Colombina danced with Alfredo whilst keeping an eye on the entrance. Her partner did not appear offended, or even to notice. He talked non-stop. He had, he assured her, not missed one single performance

217

since she had become leading lady. Two dances with him was as much as she could take and she was relieved when another cut in. Until she realised who it was.

Brighella, dressed in the suit of black silk he had worn for Franceschina's funeral, whisked her away before she could protest. 'You don't mind, do you? How does it feel?'

'What?'

'Being Queen of the Immortali.'

She made no reply and sneaked another glance towards the entrance.

'Perhaps he won't come.'

She stiffened and he laughed.

She escaped him after one dance and found Pedrolino. He filled her a silver goblet. She sipped the fine wine, unable to keep her gaze from straying. 'He'll be here,' whispered Pedrolino. 'In the meantime will you dance with me? Poor substitute, I know.'

'Don't be silly. I should love to.'

Being partnered by Pedrolino was a pleasure. He danced well in spite of his damaged leg. As the dance came to an end, there were sounds of a disturbance; shrieks of outrage filled the air. They hurried to join Pantelone, who was standing near the host, eyes fixed upon the entrance.

'Why, the impudent pup!' gasped the Count.

Pantelone groaned, watching a rogue shock of peacock force its way through a black and white crowd. 'Sir, I cannot apologise enough for...'

The Count placed a hand on his shoulder. 'Like I said, tonight is carnival. And chaos is king.' He strode to meet the man in blue. 'Arlecchino, you dog! I should have you escorted from my house and thrown into the canal.'

'Sir,' Arlecchino bowed. 'I have to agree.'

There was laughter and continued exclamations at his shining blue suit.

'May I beg one favour first?'

'What might that be?'

Arlecchino took Colombina's hand and brought it to his lips. 'A dance, with my leading lady.'

The Count laughed and signalled to the musicians. 'Let the dancing continue!'

'You are outrageous,' whispered Colombina as Arlecchino led her to the floor.

He slid an arm round her waist and gave it a squeeze. He had exchanged his actor's mask for a black velvet one that hid less of his face. The intense colour of his satin suit set off his dark olive skin. In a world stripped of colour, he appeared the only man truly alive; the rest pallid ghosts.

Had Colombina dreamt of such happiness? Surely she must? For was this not every girl's dream, to be Queen for a night, to be whirled around the floor of a magnificent ballroom by the man she adored with no thought of tomorrow?

Their dancing caused a stir. Taking no heed of convention, he held her close and spun her round. When the music stopped, he kissed her briefly then left to meet the eager demands of other ladies keen to be partnered in the same way.

Neither had Colombina any shortage of would-be partners. She was relieved when Pedrolino nipped in, especially since Alfredo was hovering. They left the dance floor and went up to the gallery. There were rooms leading off, some filled with tables laden with food. They sampled a little then returned to watch the dance. Pedrolino suggested they go back down. Colombina persuaded him to go, promising to find him later.

She continued to watch the dancers. One in particular shone out like a jewel and appeared to be enjoying himself quite as much as he had with her. She sighed and moved back from the balustrade.

Ambling along the gallery, she peered into a room filled with gamblers. Men, and women too, were seated at tables, heads bent in concentration over cards and backgammon. A noisy group was gathered in one corner throwing dice. In the next room guests sat around, chatting and whispering. Some had removed their masks. It looked inviting, so she stepped in. Gentlemen got to their feet; others bowed. Women smiled.

One handsome man with flame-red hair brought her a chair and poured her a glass of wine. She sipped the sweet strong liquid while he stood looking down at her. Feeling awkward, she looked round at the paintings and tapestries. Most of the characters depicted were naked. She drank more of the wine, watching a couple engage in a long drawn-out kiss.

The red-haired man bent to whisper in her ear; she failed to catch what he said. Relieving her of her glass, he raised her up by the elbow and directed her towards another door, above which hung a painting depicting the back view of a naked woman looking out at the viewer through a mirror held by a slave.

When her escort knocked, Colombina glanced back. The door though which she had entered was closed now. The one in front of her opened and eerie music drifted out. She felt herself urged through; the door clicked shut behind her.

A single fat candle on a sconce cast flickering light across writhing bodies in various states of undress. She could hear gasps and moaning. A plump young man in a tunic was leaning against the far wall, plucking a lyre. His dark curly hair was wreathed in vine leaves. In a corner, on a pedestal, squatted a curious creature. No bigger than a three-year-old child, he was playing the Pan pipes. He reminded Colombina of one of the satyrs in the Immortali play. She rubbed her eyes. Surely he must be in costume? Yet his budding horns, crossed hairy legs and tiny hooves looked real. Below the waist the boy had all the appearance of a living goat.

The abandoned behaviour of the people around her was shocking; yet Colombina felt more confused than affronted and even suppressed the urge to laugh. Then hot breath brushed her neck, wet lips pressed against it. She recoiled and pushed the red-haired man away.

'Now now!' He yanked her to him. 'For a girl who's content to dance with a cripple, you are uncommonly proud.'

'Let me go,' she said, struggling.

'You don't mean that.'

'Yes I do. Get off!' She fought harder, all soporific languor banished.

A few of the guests looked up. Some laughed.

Suddenly the door burst open. Women shrieked and covered their nakedness. Men swore and hid their unmasked faces as a figure in shimmering blue appeared in the doorway. 'Apologies, ladies. Gentlemen, please!' Arlecchino stepped in. 'Forgive the intrusion. I come in search of a lady who, I fear, has lost her way.'

220

47

'And here she is!' Arlecchino held out his hand to Colombina.

She tried to reach him but her escort yanked her back. 'You, Sir, are mistaken. This lady is here at my invitation. And happy to be so.'

'Indeed? Then perhaps she might tell me so herself?'

Colombina swung her free hand round and struck the man across the face.

Arlecchino laughed. 'Seems she's spoken.' He took a step forward. 'Now, let her go.' The man pulled a blade from his doublet. 'Whoa!' Arlecchino backed off, hands raised.

There were screams and a scramble to get out of the way. The boy with the lyre began blubbering. The satyr was nowhere to be seen.

'This is some breach of etiquette,' said Arlecchino. 'Our host has rules about toting weapons.'

'Fine words, from a man who wears blue to a black and white ball.'

Again Arlecchino laughed. 'You have a point, Sir – in both respects. Well, Colombina, it appears that your hot-headed suitor has me at a disadvantage.' He sighed and turned away.

'Arlecchino!' she cried.

With a movement too quick to be seen, he was back. As the lyre he had snatched from the blubbering boy came crashing down, Colombina ducked and pulled free of her captor. Strings twanged, wood splintered. With an agonised groan, the man sank to his knees, wearing the lyre about his neck.

Arlecchino grabbed Colombina's hand and ran. But where, she wondered – they were heading for a wall. He thrust out one hand, pushed and a panel flew open. It swung shut behind them, muffling the noise of the furore erupting in their wake. They were in a dark passage. Arlecchino tried the first door they came to, which was locked. Opening the next elicited a stream of curses. 'Sorry!' he called. They ran to the next. This time, when he knocked, no voice warned them off.

They stepped into a bedroom lit by a smouldering fire; the air was filled with the smell of burning logs. Arlecchino locked the door, then leant against it, laughing. In response to some shouting in the corridor, they huddled together listening to the pounding of footsteps. Locks were rattled. Doors slammed. More oaths were bellowed and what sounded like a fight broke out.

Once things had quietened down, Arlecchino crossed to the fire. He removed his mask and proceeded to light some candles. Colombina was about to join him when she heard another sound; the light tap-tapping of hooves. It stopped right outside the door. She held her breath, straining to hear and the sound began again, growing fainter and fainter until there was silence. Arlecchino showed no sign of having heard a thing.

The room had a four-poster bed with drapes of crimson velvet. Colombina crossed to it, ran her fingertips over the silky black coverlet and ruffled a luxuriant sable. 'Thank you for rescuing me.'

'You're welcome.' He carried on lighting candles.

She sat in a damask chair and looked round. Dark wood panelled the walls, oriental rugs covered the floor. On either side of the bed hung tapestries, the one to the left depicting a lady embracing a unicorn, the other a naked Venus standing in an upturned shell. A long gilded mirror faced the stone fireplace. Reflected within it were the half-dozen candles Arlecchino had placed on the mantelpiece.

She got up and went to the window. Outside was a small balcony. Light cast from gondoliers' lanterns was strung out like molten gold along black ripples. Music drifted up from the ballroom. 'I feel very foolish.'

He gave a soft laugh. 'I have to admit, you do have a talent for wandering into perilous situations. 'Well,' he said, joining her, 'for the moment, we're imprisoned here. Not so bad, is it?'

'Not at all.'

'Of course, we can't leave before the ball ends.'

'And when will that be?'

'Dawn, I imagine. So,' he took hold of her hand. 'What shall we do to pass the time?'

'We could talk,' she said, pretending not to notice that his gaze had settled on the bed.

'We could.' He leant forward to kiss her.

She stepped smartly away and went to the fire. 'That secret panel – you knew it was there. I take it you've been here before?' When no answer came, she looked at him. 'And the creature playing Pan pipes. What on earth was he? I thought he must be in costume, until…'

'Let's go to bed.'

She experienced a rush of anger. Was that all there was to this man? 'I think I should remind you,' she said stiffly, 'the master said…'

'I know what he said. All he cares about is the company's reputation.'

'And you? What do you care about? Not me, I think.'

He frowned and looked genuinely hurt.

'I'm sorry. That was unforgivable. I don't know what would have happened if…'

'I do.' He sat on the bed.

She regarded him warily. 'I find you so hard to understand. You're never the same man from one moment to the next.' She decided to risk sitting next to him. 'But you're wrong about your father. He cares about more than you think. I witnessed his despair when you jumped into the ravine.'

He failed to react.

'I saw something else that night – something I didn't understand. I went back to the spot the very next day. That ledge you were standing on, it didn't exist.'

He got up.

'I know what I saw,' she persisted. 'Or rather, what I didn't see.'

'What do you want me to say?' He pulled off his doublet.

'Help me to understand.'

'Understand what?' He threw the garment on the bed.

'This world I am part of – the Immortali.'

'There's nothing to understand. You're Queen now. Enjoy it.'

'Did you love Franceschina?' She shocked even herself with the question.

223

'Great stars of heaven! You're worse than the Inquisition. If this is how it's going to be all night, I'll take my chances out there.' Grabbing his doublet, he made for the door.

'No!' She sprang after him. 'Don't go! I promise I won't ask any more questions.'

He turned. 'It was magic, Colombina. Sleight of hand, tricks of the trade. Whatever you want to call it. What difference does it make?' He came and took her in his arms. 'This is real.' He led her to the fire and she watched him pile fresh logs on dying embers; then he drew her to the mirror. Catching sight of her reflection, she smiled. She had forgotten she was still wearing her mask. 'No,' he said, 'leave it.' He stood behind her and kissed her neck. 'I'm a simple man. I love life and beautiful women. Tonight, even masked, you, Colombina, are the most beautiful woman in the world.'

'Tonight?'

'Every night. But especially tonight. Not one of those decorated ladies, be they Venice's finest and dripping with diamonds, comes close.'

'Is it only beauty you value?'

Again his lips brushed her neck. 'You promised not to ask questions.'

His white silk shirt had slipped from his shoulder and the scent of him stirred sensual memories. He untied the velvet ribbon from around her neck and let it fall. 'I want to see you naked.'

She chose not to resist as he unlaced her, tried not to think and not to watch her reflection as the dress slid from her shoulders to her waist, then into a shimmering heap around her ankles.

The fire was going out and she shivered.

When he clicked his fingers, the green logs burst into flame. 'Magic,' he whispered.

48

he room filled with firelight and warmth.

Colombina gazed in the mirror, focussing not on her own nakedness but the face of the man who had undressed her. Bathed in radiance of his own making, he was Arlecchino the mercurial. Immortal perhaps, yet flawed.

Once again he had manipulated her. But all that mattered was, he was here – with her. His fingertips travelled over her shoulders. 'No words,' he whispered. 'No words can describe such beauty.' He took the pins from her hair, unplaited and set free her locks. He left her mask in place.

Pressing his lips to her neck, he cupped her breasts. The thrill was all too brief as he caught her up and carried her to the bed. She felt cool sable caressing her back. He removed her shoes but left her white stockings in place.

A ceiling painted with stars was momentarily blocked by his face. He kissed her throat, forcing a sigh from her lips, which he trapped in his mouth. She held his head; but he broke away to undress and she watched him cast off white silk and blue satin then welcomed his weight as he returned to spread himself across her. Tracing the contour of his shoulders, she felt his muscles tense. He moaned in response to her fingertips exploring the small of his back, the rise of his neat firm buttocks. The part of him she had tried not to see rested hard between them.

He raised himself up on taut arms, gazed down at her with a compelling mix of pleading and threat. He peeled off her mask and threw it aside then spread her locks like the rays of a sunburst. 'I never loved Franceschina,' he murmured, lowering his body into glorious contact with hers.

She wrapped her arms around him. Hearing those words was reason enough for celebration and carnival took on meaning. Yet she dared to hope the words meant something more.

He pinned her by the wrists, ran the tip of his tongue from her throat to her nipples, circling each one in turn. When he moved further down, she tried to stop him; but he slipped free to spread her legs. Open to the night, revealed to the delight of voyeuristic demons but, best of all, exposed to his close scrutiny, she experienced illicit pleasure. Fingertips stroked silky hairs then parted her mound like the skin of a fresh ripe fig. She caught her breath as he licked, tasted, devoured her.

The moment he stopped was hard to endure. As he moved up to face her, she took hold of his member – once he had forced her to do this, crushed her fingers to slide his skin back and forth. Now she derived almost cruel satisfaction from watching his features contort with too much pleasure. When she guided him into place, he kissed her fiercely then stabbed a sharp entry.

She gasped and gripped him with her thighs, contained and control-led him. One move, one touch; perhaps one single word might tip him into a vortex from whence he would rush to spill dangerous liquid. But he moved slowly to take back control, subjecting her not to grinding lust, but sweet fluid rhythm.

He had kept his promise not to impregnate her once before. Now it hardly signified. In response to flesh meeting and parting, she would have begged him not to stop. Her fingernails clawed his back; her head rubbed the fur.

Such exquisite brimming could not be sustained for long. She succumbed with a cry to suns bursting, oil pouring. Her sweet release endured as his muscles locked and she became his willing victim. One final thrust and his own paroxysm melted, flowing into synergy with hers.

She stroked his hair as they lay bathed in sweat and passion's issue.

'Our first time was brutal,' he murmured. 'I'm sorry.'

She kissed his face. There was nothing to forgive. Only the odious presence of another cast darkness over the memory. He withdrew from her and they lay between the sheets, silently entwined like growing forms, unnaturally fused.

During the night, they made love twice more. The first time he took her from behind, arousing her in persistent gentle manner so that she floated like the Venus in the tapestry. When her climax came, she believed her soul had soared to perfection. Later, he roused her from slumber and carried her to the mirror. He raised her up and she wrapped her legs around him. Head resting on his shoulder, she watched their every movement. Then they slept, night cradling them like children.

Colombina woke at dawn. Arlecchino was already up and dressed and she was astonished to see him yank a drape from the rail then rip it down the middle. 'What are you doing?'

'It's time to go.' He tied the lengths of velvet together.

She sat up and he nodded towards the window. 'It's best we leave by an alternative exit. I happen to know that lyre I crowned your ad-mirer with was worth a king's ransom.' As he tore down more drapes, Colombina dressed quickly. She crossed to the window. The new sun was failing to penetrate thick fog.

Arlecchino took his makeshift rope out onto the balcony.

Colombina hung back. 'I don't think…'

'Don't worry.' He leant over the balustrade and gave a whistle. Securing the end, he threw the rope over. She joined him and looked down. Directly below them bobbed a gondola.

He nipped over the balustrade. 'Cling to me. Just like you did last night.' He held out his hand.

With his help, she managed to clamber over the ironwork then clung to him, much like she had seen a little monkey do around the arm of its keeper in the Rialto. Arlecchino descended with the agility of such a creature, dropping effortlessly onto the deck. As the gondolier steadied his craft, they scrambled under the felze.

Arlecchino took off his doublet and laid it across her bare arms. He slid a hand up her skirt. 'No,' she whispered. 'The gondolier will see.'

'He's paid not to.'

'There's no time.'

'Time enough.' He kissed away objections.

The gondola glided through cloud. Nothing existed beyond it. Her flicker intensified, breathing grew deep. Gloom descended, then fled. They had passed beneath the bridge.

Light bathed her face, and, through half-closed eyes, she glimpsed the Rialto's saintly guardians. Sun triumphed to burst through the haze, drenching the world in incandescent yellow. On the edge of the sublime, Colombina gave in to lingering satisfaction.

As the boat sped forth she glimpsed a figure on the bridge, a man in purple moving across it. In his wake, he shed stars and crescent moons.

49

olombina remained in a blissful haze all morning. She was glad there would be no performance until the following evening. She and Arlecchino had shared a night of intimacy but she remained unclear as to his true feelings. Uncertainty verging on regret grew stronger, even though regret was futile. She was hopelessly in love.

At midday, filled with trepidation, she entered the dining hall. Her heartbeat faltered when she saw his place unoccupied. Everyone else was present, with the exception of Pedrolino. As she sat in the place she had inherited from Franceschina, she sensed a presence behind her; warm breath brushed her ear. 'Good day, my lady. I trust you are well?'

Suppressing a start of surprise and delight, she caught Arlecchino's smiling profile as he sat down beside her. 'I am, thank you,' she replied, risking a glance round the table.

Only Pantelone was watching and he immediately engaged his son in hushed conversation. Colombina could not hear what was said.

She forced herself to eat. Eventually, Arlecchino turned to her and spoke about a new dance they might try at the next rehearsal. His manner was easy, hers controlled. Reassured, she was nevertheless glad once the meal was over. On her way up the stairs, she met Pedrolino. 'Colombina.' He bowed and she smiled.

'I missed you at the meal,' she said.

'I have no appetite.'

'You're not unwell?'

He shook his head and there followed an awkward silence. 'Last night...' she began.

He raised a hand and a sad smile crossed his lips. 'I understand,' he said.

They went their separate ways.

Back in her room, Colombina helped Lella with her reading, wondering all the time if she should confide in Spinetta. When the child went downstairs to walk her dog, she broached the subject. Spinetta continued sewing, listening to her description of the beautiful gowns and fine jewellery and the reaction of the guests to Arlecchino's arrival in blue. She put down the mending. 'Anything else you want to tell me?'

Colombina swallowed hard. 'We spent the night together.'

Spinetta nodded.

'Does everybody know?'

Spinetta's stern glance gave the answer.

'Oh.' Colombina stood.

'No one will question what takes place between the leading man and his lady.'

Colombina faced her. 'Tell me what you think, Spinetta.'

'He broke your heart once before, remember?'

There came a knock on the door. Colombina went to open it and found herself facing the man in question. He bowed. 'It being carnival, some of us are proposing to visit the squares. If you would like to come, Colombina, I would be honoured to escort you.'

'I should like that,' she told him, glancing back at Spinetta, who was tactfully busying herself with the mending.

'Good. We will be leaving from the lobby in half an hour.'

Colombina closed the door, struggling to contain her excitement. She sat next to Spinetta and touched the back of her brown wrinkled hand. 'I owe you so much.' Spinetta waved the comment aside. 'It's true. You've been like a mother... no, better than a mother, to me. You took in a girl whose life was in ruins, guided her, looked after her. Though I admit, I found you stern at first.'

Spinetta laughed. 'I did no more than I would have for any poor creature. And you worked hard to fit in, proved yourself a worker – in spite of your fancy background. You're a good girl, Colombina. You deserve success. My dearest wish is for it to continue. But never forget, there was a time I became your nurse. And being leading lady won't shield you from hurt, nor shame.'

'I know.'

'And I'm not the only one who's been a good friend. Pedrolino's always done his best to bring a smile to your lips. Is there really no hope that his good and constant heart can fill the gap left by one who treats women in the same way workers of Murano deal with rejects?'

'No hope at all.'

'Very well. I'll say no more. Yes – I shall. Two words. *Be careful!*'

Colombina kissed Spinetta on the cheek, happy they were still on good terms. 'We are visiting the city squares,' she said; then added, 'several of us are going.'

'You'll need to wrap up warm then.'

'Yes.' Colombina got up. 'Oh!'

'What?'

'I left my cape, at the ball.'

Spinetta sighed. 'Well, well. We'll find you another.'

There was a lot of noise rising from the lobby. Halfway down the stairs Colombina paused to watch Arlecchino entertaining Lella. The little girl was laughing to see Crespo dance around him on hind legs. When Arlecchino clapped his hands, the dog leapt into his arms. Colombina smiled, recalling the night she had seen him risk his life to save the animal. Or had she? When Arlecchino caught sight of her, he handed the dog to Lella.

Renaldo led the group out. Colombina and Arlecchino walked at the back. Guido came running. 'Can I come with you?'

'Certainly not,' said Arlecchino.

The boy pulled a face.

'Come with me, Guido,' Pedrolino called from the kitchen. 'I've a trick I want to teach you.'

'Great!' The boy ran off.

St. Mark's Square being flooded, the party took gondolas to the Rialto where they disembarked. The first square they visited was filled with stalls and entertainers. There were jugglers and acrobats, street traders selling masks, cheap jewellery and medicines. A man led a bear on a chain. The little monkey was there too, dressed in red waistcoat and green breeches.

From the Rialto they made their way through narrow streets and over a bridge to a space where some men were kicking a ball about. To

231

Colombina's amusement, Arlecchino joined in, intercepting the ball and bouncing it up and down on his knees. Letting it drop, he kicked it with such force it knocked one of the men clean over. He ran and pulled him to his feet and they shook hands.

Stopping at an inn, they sat by a window and watched a procession. At its head walked men in long black gowns wearing masks painted as skulls. Behind them came others dressed in sackcloth, dragging chains. At the rear pranced red demons, carrying pitchforks. At first, Colombina took this to be a carnival attraction; but Arlecchino's expression suggested otherwise. Right at the back walked the man in the loincloth she had seen thrown into the canal. The cross he was hauling today was large enough for a crucifixion. 'Who are they?' she asked.

'Those who would have us fear the future.' Arlecchino took a drink. 'The year is about to turn and, with it, a century. For some, the number has special significance.'

The year 1600. Of course!

'And what are they telling us?'

'That the world will end soon,' muttered Renaldo.

She frowned and looked at Arlecchino.

'A generation ago,' he told her, 'plague decimated Venice. Many believe it will return. Some of those men would welcome pestilence, fire and war.'

'I see they make you angry.'

The innkeeper brought a fresh jug of wine. 'He's not the only one,' he grunted. 'Those freaks are upsetting my customers.' He moved to fill Arlecchino's flask but he covered it.

'Time to move on.' He paid the man and the party left.

The moment the actors stepped out, men dressed as demons rushed to accost them. 'Repent!' shouted one. 'Deny the fleshpots. Be shriven while there's time.'

Renaldo pushed past them but one demon continued to follow the party, directing his words at Colombina. 'Beauty will not save you. The reaper is nigh. Death withers flesh!' He brandished his pitchfork. 'Exchange your finery for sackcloth. The day of judgement is at hand!'

Arlecchino grabbed the man's fork and snapped it in two. When he threw it on the ground, the demon danced up and down, pointing a quivering finger at him. 'The fires of hell are stoked and ready for you, ungodly one!'

Arlecchino grabbed him by the smock front. 'First look into your own soul, fake demon, before pronouncing on the state of mine.' He thrust him away and sent him sprawling into the mud.

The actors laughed. The innkeeper stood on his threshold applauding.

'Where to next?' asked Arlecchino.

'To the Campo San Stefano,' said Renaldo, 'for bull fighting.'

'That's not for us,' said Arlecchino, taking Colombina by the hand. 'We'll see you back at the theatre.' He pulled her close. 'You're trembling.'

'Those men.' She glanced back at the procession.

'Don't let them upset you. Evil feeds on fear.'

'Evil? Surely they are men of God?'

'Not my God.'

When they came to a small wooden shrine to the Virgin, he lit a candle and crossed himself.

'What did you pray for?'

'For her continued help.'

'In doing what?'

'Standing against those who would frighten us, men who take pleasure in pain. Their masters are worse, they elevate suffering to an art. You and I, Colombina, have a duty to celebrate life.'

They walked on. Pale sunlight lit humble dwellings; washing hung between their balconies. 'Are we lost?' she asked.

He smiled. 'I think we are.'

'I spoke to Pedrolino this morning. 'He knows about…' she looked away. 'Last night, when he told you I was missing…'

He stopped and made her face him. 'Pedrolino didn't tell me. I came looking for you myself.'

She smiled. 'I'm glad you found me.'

'So am I. Otherwise, they might have been adding murder to my list of crimes.'

From somewhere close by came the sound of music. It led them to a tiny square. Fire burned in a brazier. Children chased each other round.

Women dressed in work clothes laid tables with basic fare. A fiddler and a player of bagpipes provided the tune for dancing. 'Come on,' said Arlecchino, drawing Colombina forward.

As they danced, Colombina remembered her first night in the Immortali camp. How different things were now. She felt close to heaven in this tiny square filled with ordinary people delighting in simple pleasures. The residents were delighted to have strangers in their midst; then suddenly someone shouted, 'It's Arlecchino and his lady!'

They were surrounded, everyone wanting to shake them by the hand, some trying to press on them food and drink. They did their best to satisfy the demand but escaped at the first opportunity. Across a pretty iron bridge, along the path bordering a canal, they paused for breath beneath an arch. 'I love Venice,' Arlecchino shouted at the top of his voice and his words echoed back. He drew her close. 'But not as much as I love you.'

50

hat did Colombina care if fanatics preached the world was about to end, when hers had been transformed by three beautiful words?

The next morning she woke from a sweet unremembered dream and allowed her thoughts to drift deliciously over the events of the previous two days. Not a moment passed when she could not hear Arlecchino's voice telling her that he loved her. Her happiness was further increased by the morning's rehearsal when his mood matched hers and his ebullience infected the rest of the company. There was, however, one notable exception. Pantelone was subdued and, when she and Arlecchino demonstrated the steps of their new dance, he dismissed it with a shrug.

The play reopened on New Year's Eve.

New Year's Day dawned with the world still in place but Venice was on fire with talk of *Misrule in Arcadia*. Colombina began receiving bouquets again. Gifts of jewellery and fans were also left. These became property of the company. Her flowers were used to decorate the lobby and dining hall, the sweet exotic scent of them filling the air. From where such magnificent blooms originated was a source of gossip and wonder. Each evening they were delivered by the same servant who professed to be dumb. The sender remained anonymous. Whoever he was, it was clear he must be very rich since nothing could grow here in the midst of winter.

Not content with the many accolades showered upon the play, Arlecchino devised new tricks. Ideas poured from his imagination and, in putting them into practice, he worked closely with Pedrolino, who, Colombina was relieved to find, appeared to have put aside sadness. One of their tricks involved the use of a high wire stretching from the back of the theatre to the stage. Guido had painted the entire length of rope black so that the first time Arlecchino appeared above the audience, there was panic. Disaster was narrowly averted by Pantelone dashing on stage and shouting to reassure the spectators. Arlecchino completed his walk through the air and the resultant applause lasted several minutes. Nothing, it seemed, could halt the rise of the Immortali in their bid to capture the hearts of Venice.

Colombina and Arlecchino spent as much time as they could together. Within the confines of the palazzo that was difficult, so they took walks whenever the weather permitted. One cold but dry afternoon they were strolling by the Rialto. 'I want to buy you something,' said Arlecchino, stopping at a goldsmith's.

Colombina shook her head. 'I don't need anything.' She squeezed his arm. 'I have everything I need.'

He took out some ducats as he scanned the display.

She touched his hand. 'Whatever you buy, I cannot wear openly.'

He looked at her and sighed.

Not far away sat a beggar. A bandage covered his eyes and a crutch lay at his side, although Colombina felt sure she had seen the man walking about unaided. 'Take pity on a poor blind cripple,' whined the man, thrusting out a skinny arm as they passed.

Arlecchino dropped the ducats into the outstretched hand.

'God bless you, Sir. God bless you indeed! The cripple touched the coins with his lips. 'You are a prince among thieves!'

'I don't think that man is blind or crippled,' whispered Colombina.

'I know,' returned Arlecchino.

'Your father,' she ventured. 'His mood today…'

'Ignore him.'

'Perhaps you should say something?'

'I shouldn't have to justify being in love.'

She kissed him on the cheek. 'I love you so much.'

He laughed. 'I'm glad to hear it. At last!'

She frowned. 'What do you mean?'

'That's the first time you've told me.'

She stared at him. But he was right. She had been so obsessed with hearing him say the words, she had failed to tell him. 'I've loved you from the first moment I set eyes on you,' she said, 'even before I saw your face. Do you remember, when you came to the gate and kissed my hand?'

'I remember.' They stopped and shared a passionate kiss. 'This is madness,' he said, 'skulking around as though we have something to be ashamed of.'

Before they entered the palazzo he grasped both her hands. 'I *will* find a way for us to be together.'

As soon as they entered, they were told that their presence was required in the theatre. The moment they appeared, Pantelone scolded them for not being available for an impromptu rehearsal.

'How the hell were we supposed to know?' Arlecchino shouted back. 'Besides, the action's fine. Routines are fine. Everything's fine. What the devil are you getting your beard in such a knot about?'

Throughout the evening's performance Pantelone's mood did not improve. Arlecchino showed no sign of being affected by it but the persistent dark glances cast by the master at Colombina disturbed her. The next day's rehearsal went no better. Pantelone criticised and carped and the session ended up in a full-scale row between father and son over nothing in particular.

'I've had enough of this,' Arlecchino told Colombina immediately afterwards. 'I'm going to tell him.'

'No.' She held him back. 'Wait until you've both calmed down.'

Once she was sure he was out of the way, she hurried back to the theatre. 'I should like to speak to you concerning a personal matter,' she told Pantelone.

He directed her to his office. Closing the door, he swept some parchments off a stool and indicated for her to sit. She smoothed her skirts and stole a glance at his face as he sat in his heavy oak chair. He said nothing to help her broach the subject. Colombina plunged in. 'It has become apparent I've done something to displease you. I should like to know what.'

'I think you know.'

She shifted uncomfortably. 'Not really.'

'I took you for a sensible girl, Colombina. Gullible yes, but capable of learning a harsh and painful lesson.'

She flushed. 'Arlecchino and I are in love.'

'Ha!' His laugh was cruel. 'I have no wish to be unkind but, on average, my son falls in love once a month. You have already fallen victim to his shallow charms. I would have thought it abundantly clear he is not to be trusted.'

'I don't believe that.'

'Then you are a lot simpler than I took you for.'

Colombina wanted to shout at him, make him see how wrong he was.

He spoke a little more kindly. 'When you became leading lady, do you remember what I told you?'

She lowered her gaze. 'You said that the partnership between Arlecchino and myself should remain one of the spirit.'

'Exactly. And I took my meaning to be plain. Yet the pair of you have deliberately disobeyed me. You even flaunt your affair.'

'Flaunt?' She was aghast.

He stood, it seemed, to dissipate anger. 'Do you imagine your disappearance from the ball went unnoticed? The Immortali were the guests of honour! The Count, being a gentile man of noble disposition, tried to spare my shame by not drawing attention to the fact that my leading man and lady had seen fit to absent themselves. He even made excuses for you. Yet, in truth, there was no excuse. You put me in the most humiliating situation once gossip spread like wildfire through the ballroom.'

'I hadn't realised. I am so very sorry.'

He shook his head. 'You are indeed an innocent, Colombina. And for that reason I do not hold you responsible. I could box his ears!'

'But this is different!' She leaned towards him. 'Arlecchino really does love me.'

He threw up his hand. 'When will you get it through your silly romantic head? Arlecchino is not capable of love – not the kind you crave. He will tire of the affair within weeks. Then what will happen?' He began to pace the floor, then stopped suddenly. 'How do you imagine you can carry on as leading lady, knowing his affections have transferred to another?'

'I don't believe that will happen. Besides, Franceschina managed and I know for a fact...'

238

'Franceschina was an entirely different creature. She may have appeared driven by her emotions, but she had a heart of granite. Just like Arlecchino! If... no, *when* he discards you, it will destroy not just you but all your dreams – as well as my company. You have it in your power to end this, Colombina. I beg of you, do so. Now.'

'I can't.' She shook her head. 'I would sooner cut out my own heart.'

It was getting dark; the air in the room felt cold yet suffocating.

'What would you do, if I ordered you to choose between this affair and continuing as the Immortali's leading lady?'

She stared at him. 'You would do that?'

'I would, if I thought it would spare you more pain. And save my company.'

She sprang up. 'Arlecchino said you care for nothing but the company's reputation.'

'Did he?'

'Yes. And I have given you my answer. Do what you will. I am not capable of denying my true feelings for any reward, however great.'

'And that is your final answer?'

'It is. I love Arlecchino more than anything. And he loves me.' Her blood was up. 'Arlecchino was right. A man like you can never understand the depth of our love.'

He sighed and shook his head.

'I see now that you *are* cold-hearted. Once I thought differently. I believed I saw warmth and kindness in your eyes when you offered me the chance to join the Immortali. But I still have another memory, one I shall never forget. Emerging from a fever, yet not so far out of my mind as to have imagined it, I heard you say '*it was a blessing she lost the child*'. I should have realised then you had it in mind never to sanction love between myself and your son.'

He frowned and turned away.

'Yet I would have thought you would be pleased to see him happy – relieved he's found true love at last.'

Pantelone drew audible breath. In his continued silence, she read something disturbing.

'It's me, isn't it? You think me unsuitable. If you thought me unworthy, why on earth did you make me leading lady?'

'Arlecchino can never find happiness with you, Colombina.'

'Why not? What have I done? Why do you hate me so?'

'Hate you?' He looked round at her.

She was close to tears.

'I don't hate you, Colombina. How could I? I love you.'

Her hand went to her mouth. Consumed by horror and disgust, she made for the door. Pantelone intercepted her. 'Let me go!' she screamed.

'You don't understand.' She struggled but he forced her to face him. 'I love you, Colombina, because – you are my daughter.'

51

olombina stopped struggling.

'I am your father.'

'No.' She shook her head at the monstrous lie.

'It's true.'

'No!' She wrenched free of him then staggered back. Pantelone must have taken leave of his senses!

'Have you never felt it? Or looked into a mirror and wondered?'

'Never!'

'You are disgusted.' He shook his head. 'I don't blame you.'

'Why are you saying this?'

'What can I say?' He spread his hands. 'It's true. I should have told you long ago. I made a decision not to. I know now that was wrong. But you were with child when you joined us. How would you have felt, knowing…?'

Again her hand flew to her mouth.

'Then, afterwards, I hoped it would not matter. Arlecchino showed no interest in you – you, none in him. I took a risk.' He shook his head again and turned away.

'Prove it! Tell me why you think you are… who you say you are.'

He regarded her mournfully then sighed. 'The company visited your town in the autumn of 1581. We remained there for some weeks. The Immortali was in its early days, hardly able to support half a dozen impoverished actors and their dependants. I played Arlecchino. Your name, Giulia…'

'Yes, I was born in that month. But that means nothing!'

'No, indeed.' He sighed again and went on. 'Isabella Olivieri, raven-haired and slender, skin pale as moonlight, wife to Federico.' Colombina stifled a groan. 'The couple had been married some years, yet were childless. Isabella was a passionate young woman, demanding, full of fire. She came every night to watch the play, then afterwards…'

Colombina struggled to take it in. Her mother passionate, full of fire? 'But you were married too!'

'Yes, to my shame. And with a young son. Worse, my beloved wife was expecting our second child. The affair should never have taken place. The night before the Immortali left town, Isabella told me she was with child and begged me to take her with me.'

'She would have left my father for you? I don't believe it. And what about your wife and child?'

'Isabella knew nothing about them, not until that night. She pleaded, clung to me. But I sent her away, told her I had all the family I needed. I told her to go home, pretend the unborn child was her husband's.' He raised a hand. 'I know. It was heartless, cruel, unforgivable.'

Words spoken by Colombina's mother came flooding back to her: '…you will not be doing anything hundreds of women have not done before you.' In arranging a hasty marriage to Signore Panesse, Isabella Olivieri had sought to complete the cruel cycle. But Colombina had escaped that fate, only to be brought to this. She clutched at one small hope. 'But it is still possible I am Federico's daughter?'

'Yes, it is. Yet your mother insisted the child was mine. And more than three years wed to your father without issue, then the few weeks she and I spent together..?' he shrugged. 'You told me, Colombina, you were an only child. So, what do you reckon? What are the chances of you *not* being my daughter?'

She could only shake her head, but without conviction.

'Then, when you came to the inn and told me what Arlecchino had done, I knew events had come round to punish me. I saw an opportunity to try to put things right.'

'Arlecchino doesn't know?' The thought horrified her.

'No. He may be a libertine but… well, if he knew about this…'

'You have destroyed my life,' she sobbed, and the irony struck her cruelly. 'What can I do?' When Pantelone tried to put an arm about her, she shrugged him off. 'How can I possibly tell Arlecchino?'

'You may not have to. You have it in your power to shield him, if you can make him believe that you no longer love him. You are a gifted actress. Play the part.' She shook her head. 'Play it well enough and, in time, he will find love elsewhere.

'I can't. He would never believe me.'

'If you do this, you will spare him your pain.

'But it would break his heart.'

'Think how much worse it would be, if he knew the truth.'

'Worse for whom?' She glared at Pantelone.

'I have no defence.' He held up his hands. 'The damage is all mine. But the decision is yours and, for my part, I believe it to be the best solution.'

There was no light in the room yet a deeper darkness engulfed Colombina. She hated this man. Part of her still refused to accept what he told her. Oh, that this could be just a nightmare! The gulf between the happiness she had felt so recently and her present despair became a yawning pit into which her spirits plunged.

'What will you do?' he asked.

'*I* should not have to do anything!'

'You're right. And I doubt you will ever forgive me.'

Her eyes shot him the answer. 'I will try to do what you have suggested,' she said stiffly, 'for Arlecchino's sake. You, Sir, have broken my heart. All I have left is the hope I might spare your son's.'

Out in the passageway, she leant against the wall. She wanted to slump to the floor and die, now there was nothing to live for. Even so, she found herself praying, to whom she had no idea – she no longer believed in a merciful God. Her prayer was that Arlecchino would be nowhere to be seen when she emerged.

She was crossing the lobby when he called out her name. 'Colombina, where have you been? I've been looking all over.'

She turned to face him, forcing a smile.

'You've been crying.'

'I'm fine.'

'Come with me.' He grabbed her hand and took her outside. It was raining. 'I wish there was somewhere – anywhere, better than this. But we don't have the luxury of time, or space.' He fell to his knees in the wet. 'I told you I'd find a way for us to be together. And I have. This way, neither my father nor the whole wide world can come between us. Marry, me, Colombina. Do me the honour of becoming my wife.'

52

hat greater torment could there be than seeing the hope in Arlecchino's deep brown eyes? He smiled up at Colombina in clear anticipation of her answer.

Gathering all her pain, compressing it into something small and hard as iron, she buried it deep within her and smiled. 'I love you,' she whispered.

'Well?' he urged.

Truth. How noble. How cruel! To do what Pantelone said would require all her strength of will. She had prayed for time to prepare and not even that had been granted.

'Will you not give me an answer?'

Her heart spilled over in pity. 'I had never thought to hear you speak those words,' she whispered, stroking his wet hair.

'Nor I.'

Did he appear different, now that she knew of their blood link? The answer overtook the thought. No, she still loved and desired him, in a way that would be condemned as profane. 'May I consider a while before giving my answer?'

A frown clouded his face.

'It's just... this is so unexpected. And so important.'

'Of course.' He smiled and stood up; then kissed her hand, reassured, no doubt, that, in time, she would accept him.

Their meeting was, mercifully, cut short by the arrival of gondolas filled with early spectators. Yet back in her room, Colombina was still denied respite. All she wanted to do was hide in her bed, pull the covers up over her head and cry. But in front of Spinetta and Lella she had to continue the charade.

The performance was torture. She could think of nothing other than how to extricate herself from this unforeseen and unwelcome situation with as little hurt as possible to Arlecchino. Before he had proposed, her task had been to let him down gently, withdraw from the affair over time. Now she must put a stop to things quickly. But playing opposite him that evening, she could not find it in her heart to say, or do, anything to dent his conspicuous happiness. He performed brilliantly, the crowd rising to his witty dialogue and inspired acrobatics. She, in contrast, felt controlled, a mindless puppet with no will of her own. Curiously though, the applause she received was also loud and long and everyone congratulated her on a magnificent performance. If they only knew.

All she remembered of her time on stage was the small painted figure squatting on top of the cave in the backcloth. It seemed to be mocking her, just as the grinning imp on her bedpost had done to a girl named Giulia.

By the time she got to bed, she was exhausted. She had a crippling headache and a damn of hot tears burst forth. She sobbed into her pillow, stifling the sound so that Spinetta would not hear. In the end, she cried herself to sleep.

She woke, petrified by the dream from which she had escaped. She had been standing alone centre-stage, dressed only in her shift. The theatre was empty and the sound of sniggering had made her look round at the backcloth. The eyes of the figure squatting on the cave were glowing. The glowing orbs met, spreading swiftly into a circle of fire that devoured the canvas. The heat was so intense she felt her skin burning, could smell her shift scorching. Her hair singed and crackled. She tried to run down the steps but the stage was surrounded by tall hooded figures with skulls instead of faces. She tried to scream and it was the effort of trying to make herself heard that roused her from the nightmare.

Drenched in sweat, Colombina stared up at the ceiling. The air in the room was freezing; yet her face burned. She had fled the dream, only to enter a more terrible reality. Nowhere was there refuge. She threw back her covers, wondering if she had a fever. The thought brought grim comfort, now there was nothing to live for.

She woke in the morning, shivering, but only with cold. Otherwise, she felt well. She got up and her misery hardened to resignation. Now it must begin, the task of making Arlecchino fall out of love with her.

Seated in front of the mirror, she dressed her hair and put her mind to the challenge. She tried not to look too closely at her features. *Have you never looked into a mirror and wondered?* She quickly got up.

No strategy presented itself so she resorted to avoiding Arlecchino, staying in her room, not even going down to eat. All day she remained on edge, expecting a knock on the door. But Arlecchino never came to press her for an answer and she met him for the first time at the performance. He displayed no concern that she had not yet spoken; but he did use one love scene to remind her subtly that he was waiting for an answer.

Then, when the play was over, he drew her aside. 'I am counting the minutes, hours and days. May I beg a favour? I have a number in mind. Today, day one, you have played the recluse. Tomorrow you may shun me again. I know how it is and why you need time. You doubt my intentions. I deserve your mistrust and have given you no cause to think me capable of devotion. But, believe me, Colombina, if you say yes, I will spend the rest of my life as your slave.'

'Slave?'

'Slave. Lover. Friend. Creature. Whatever you want me to be. Three days, Colombina, I cannot wait longer. The day after tomorrow must be my day of judgement, for good – or ill.'

Recalling a previous occasion on which she had gazed into those seductive lambent eyes, she thought about the lies he had told. Then an innocent girl's need to hear the words *I love you* had lured her into ruin. Perhaps, if she could summon back the pain and outrage she had suffered, she might find it easier to do what she had to. 'Three days,' she whispered. 'The day after tomorrow I will give you my answer.'

His face lit up.

'If you will, in return, grant *me* a favour.'

'Anything.'

'Not to speak of it again until then.'

'I promise. Though, Colombina, you are killing me with time.' He brushed his lips across her fingers, bowed and walked away.

Delaying the inevitable did nothing to improve her situation. The anger, bitterness and hatred she had once felt for Arlecchino proved as impossible to recapture as the physical pain of miscarriage. Yet she was determined. Tomorrow she would refuse him and destroy their love.

Tomorrow turned into today. She rose and dressed in much the same way as she currently approached her acting, driven only by the duty to perform. Once dressed, she went to the window. The rain that had fallen relentlessly all night had not abated. Grey sky, buildings and canal were indistinguishable. Soon she hoped to be free to add tears to a world drenched in water.

She was glad to be left alone. Spinetta had laundry to do and Lella was helping Guido in the theatre. Halfway through the morning there came a knock on the door. Panic surged. She took a deep breath, opened the door, then sighed with relief at the sight of Suzanna. She was dressed to go out and appeared agitated. 'Oh, Colombina. Carla's sent me to fetch you.'

'Is something wrong?'

'No. Everything's fine. Can I come in?'

'Of course.'

'Carla and Marco want you to come.'

'Where?'

'To church? For Serafina's baptism.'

'But she's already been baptised.'

'No.' Suzanna shook her head. 'They found out the man who christened her wasn't a proper priest.'

'Oh.'

'Will you come then?'

'I… I'm sorry, Suzanna. I have something important to do.'

'Oh please! They'll be ever so upset if I don't bring you.'

Colombina gave a sigh. 'Very well,' she said. 'But I'll have to come straight back.' She went to get her cloak.

'Could you wear a different dress?' Suzanna crossed to the rail. 'The one you're wearing is really pretty but… this one,' she cried excitedly, snatching down Colombina's newest and most expensive gown.

'But I've never worn that. And… well, don't you think it's a bit showy for a baptism?'

'It's perfect!' exclaimed Suzanna. 'I'll wait for you in the lobby.'

Keen to get this over and done with, Colombina took off her dress. Jacopo Bruno's letter fell out of the bodice. She picked it up. She had still not decided whether or not to give it to Brighella; but she had begun to think of it as a kind of charm, protection against his machinations. She changed into her dress of carmine velvet and rose brocade, considering it most unsuitable. At least it would be hidden beneath her plain black cloak. She pushed the letter down her bodice.

On her way down she fancied she saw Suzanna secrete something beneath her cape.

It was still raining; a bitter wind blew. Hoods held up against the squalls, skirts hitched clear of the mud, the pair hurried on. Colombina paid no attention to the route. It was only when they reached the church that she realised it was not the one in which the actors attended mass. Suzanna ran up the steps. Colombina followed.

Suzanna pushed the door open; hinges creaked. When the girls slipped in, candles smoked and blew flat. Once the door was shut, flames burned upright again in homage to a serene white marble Virgin. Both nave and altar were hidden from view by a painted screen and the air was heavy with incense. In the body of the church, all was quiet.

Suzanna went on ahead but Colombina hung back, her sense of unease increasing with a distant rumble of thunder. Suzanna beckoned. Reassured by the sound of a gurgling baby, Colombina hurried forward. When they met, Suzanna thrust a small bunch of flowers into her hand.

Colombina frowned at the bouquet. Was it a gift for the child? Peering round the screen, she saw Carla and Marco with their children; not gathered around the font, but in front of the altar. Pedrolino was there too. And so was…

Arlecchino, smartly dressed in dark-blue velvet, came striding down the aisle towards her. Now she understood and it was all she could do not to faint.

53

loying incense caught at the back of Colombina's throat.

'The third day,' whispered Arlecchino, taking hold of her hand. 'I claim my right to an answer. Be it good. Or ill.'

'You should not have done this.'

'I know.'

She glanced towards the altar where the priest and server were waiting; then down at her bouquet – pink and white lilies, taken from the lobby.

'You must tell me the truth,' said Arlecchino. 'I didn't trick you here to force you into saying yes. I did it so that, if – and only if – you agree to us being married, no more time will be wasted. Please Colombina, I cannot live a moment longer without knowing. Will you be my wife?'

She had just sustained another deep wounding of her soul. The first had come with Pantelone's shocking news, the second when Arlecchino had proposed. This must surely be the last and mortal blow? All hope of happiness drained away, until nothing was left but shards of love tumbling into oblivion. How could she speak, when her mouth felt parched, her lips completely numb?

'Do you love me?' he whispered. She managed a nod. 'Then allow me to plead my case one last time. The night of the ball you asked me questions, questions I chose not to answer. But you have a right to know the truth, at least as much as I know myself. There are things I can do. I do them without knowing how. Such things, I believe, are within the power of us all. Yet some mortals seem blessed, or cursed perhaps, with skin through which magic flows. Some put their gift to the service of good, others to evil. All I do is entertain. Magic brings me fame, affords me the best life has to offer and – as you know to your cost – helps me charm women. Now fate has turned the tables on me. I am the one who is charmed – by you, Colombina. I have never felt like this and would gladly become a herder of pigs, if it meant I could have you for my wife.'

She smiled and found words. 'I would not have you become a herder of pigs.'

'Nevertheless, if you let me take my marriage vows, I shall not only forsake all others but, if you ask it of me, throw away Hermes's hat, pluck the wings from his heels and live without magic. All I want is you, Colombina. I love you more than I love life.'

What could she say? She was finding it hard to breathe. Beyond the high windows the sky was leaden, although it was not yet midday. She looked towards the altar where the server was lighting a candle. The priest was ready, prayer book in hand.

'Colombina.'

She met Arlecchino's gaze and knew what she must do. At last she found the strength. But, when she opened her mouth, a voice that sounded like hers spoke words she had not intended. 'I will marry you.'

She saw the joy explode in his eyes. Perhaps it was lightning but stars shone all around him. The vision transformed her. It might have been someone else who had given her answer but she had no wish to retract it.

'You have just made me the happiest man alive.' He led her to the altar.

She kept her head bowed, eyes cast down. Suzanna removed her cloak and draped a lace mantle over her hair.

The couple stood side by side. Happiness radiated from Arlecchino. For Colombina, in place of bridal joy, there existed grim determination. Perhaps he mistook it for nervousness since he gave her hand a squeeze.

Facing the priest, she thought to herself, *Once this is over, Pantelone can do nothing. He will have to stay silent because the scandal would ruin the Immortali.* Colombina and the father foisted upon her by fate would take their shared secret to the grave.

The priest began intoning. His words, spoken in the ancient language, meant nothing to Colombina; yet she might have made an effort to understand, had this marriage not been a sham, a godless device to keep hold of her lover. The cost would be high. But what price damnation? Arlecchino would be hers until death.

Not even when the candle on the altar flickered, throwing sickly light across a fresco of the Day of Judgement, did she waver. Those crudely painted demons with their lolling red tongues and eyes of fire did not frighten her.

There came another flash, which lit up the damned. Naked and tormented, they tumbled into the pit. A clap of thunder alarmed the fresh-faced server who almost dropped the burner, sending out a cloud of incense engulfing the altar. Meanwhile the priest continued his monotonous recitation.

Colombina was getting impatient. She had made her choice and her sin was grave; but something told her there was a need for haste. She offered up one final prayer before passing beyond redemption. *Please, God. Let this be over quickly.*

From the back of the church came the creak of hinges, followed by the sound of wood hitting stone. Candles fluttered in a strong gust of wind and a voice bellowed, 'Stop! Stop the service!'

54

ith the exception of Colombina, everyone looked round. The priest fell silent. Baby Serafina started to cry.

'What the..?' gasped Arlecchino. He muttered a curse before leaving Colombina's side to march down the aisle to confront his father.

Colombina kept her eyes fixed on the priest. Her soul had teetered on the brink. It may have been saved – but now *she* was lost. Forcing herself to look round, she saw Pantelone push past Arlecchino and come striding to the altar. 'Clear the church,' he bellowed, condemning her with a glance.

The guests left hurriedly. Arlecchino shouted at his father.

'Sir,' said the priest, above his remonstrations. 'I trust you have a good and valid reason for interrupting the blessed sacrament of marriage?'

'I have,' returned Pantelone, with another dark look at Colombina.

'No,' she wailed.

'What the devil's going on?' demanded Arlecchino.

Pantelone took the priest aside. As he whispered in his ear, Colombina saw the cleric's face cloud. Regarding her as he would the Whore of Babylon, he crossed himself then ushered his baffled server away.

Only one of the three left at the altar had words. He addressed them to his father. 'I will give you one chance to justify this outrage.'

'Will you tell him?' asked Pantelone.

She shook her head; words were beyond her.

'What is this?' A puzzled Arlecchino looked almost on the verge of laughter. 'My father bursts in on my wedding with no good reason – other than, as far as I can see, a prejudice against me marrying. But you know more, it seems?'

'I'm so sorry.'

'Sorry? Sorry for what? Will someone tell me what the devil's going on? The priest quits the church as though pursued by demons. My bride-to-be is struck dumb.'

Pantelone went to him and placed a hand on his shoulder. 'There is no easy way to say this. I could try to find better words but…' he shook his head. As he spoke into his son's ear, thunder rolled.

Colombina tried not to watch Arlecchino's face.

'No.' He pulled away from his father, his smouldering gaze fixed on her.

She felt herself burning as surely as if she had toppled into the pit.

Again he shook his head. 'It cannot be!'

Pantelone reached out to Arlecchino as there came another loud clap of thunder. He swung round and sent a fist crashing into his father's face. Pantelone fell backward, nose gushing blood.

Colombina gave a cry. Arlecchino came and looked deep into her eyes. Fear rose in her breast; then, when he did nothing, mingled with a modicum of hope.

A streak of blue sheared the dark and, in that split second, the eyes she adored became as cold as death. He turned and strode off down the aisle. Colombina ran after him, clutching at his doublet.

Arlecchino shook free; then he whirled round to face her. His voice was icy. 'I took you to be heaven-sent, Colombina. Now I know you were sent to take *me* to hell.'

55

eaf to her pleas, Arlecchino was gone from the church before she reached the screen. There was no sign of him when she hurtled through the door. It was Pedrolino who caught her. 'What have I done?' she cried.

'I don't know. I don't want to know.'

She peered frantically through the driving rain. 'I think Pantelone's hurt,' she gasped.

Pedrolino left her and ran into the church. Still clutching her bouquet, Colombina fell to her knees. Within seconds, Pedrolino had returned and he raised her up as Pantelone appeared, holding a bloodstained cloth to his nose.

'I have to find Arlecchino,' Colombina sobbed.

'I'll help you,' said Pedrolino.

'Leave him,' ordered Pantelone, voice thick and nasal.

'But I have to go after him,' she cried.

Pantelone cast her the blackest of looks then walked off down the steps.

'Where would he go?' she gasped.

'I don't know, Colombina. But if you'll tell me what's wrong…'

'I can't.' She turned away and tried to decide which direction to take. 'Which way? Which way did he go? Back to the palazzo?'

Pedrolino shook his head. 'Whatever all this is about, Arlecchino was extremely angry, so…'

'So?'

'He will probably be found at an inn.'

She made off down the steps.

'Colombina, wait!' He came after her. 'You can't go to such places. I'll find him for you.'

She paused. 'I have to tell him. Try to explain.'

'Yes, I understand. Now, go back home and wait.'

She shook her head. 'I'll stay here.'

'All right. But go into the church, out of this rain. I'll find Arlecchino. I know where to look.' She regarded him miserably. 'Go on.' He waved her on up the steps.

She watched him hurry away then she entered the church. But she did not remain there. Donning her cloak, she hurled her bouquet at the feet of the marble Virgin and scurried back out into the pouring rain.

She went the same way as Pedrolino but was lost within minutes. She came across no inns. Venice appeared deserted. Thunder growled, lightning flickered. The beautiful city turned into a sinister labyrinth as she hurried along narrow streets, through dingy passageways, over bridges. Perhaps she had already been damned and this was her punishment; to wander until the end of time in search of something she could never have.

And what would she say if she did find Arlecchino? There was no excuse for what she had done. Her actions made her no better than Pantelone. Worse, in fact!

Still, she refused to give up. Mud-spattered and drenched to the skin, she stumbled on, slipping on the stones, alarmed by flashes of lightning. Dank alleyways pressed in like the walls of dungeons; the stench of foul water pervaded the air. The only signs of life were bargemen and rats.

As the dim light of day gave way to a premature twilight, the storm retreated. Rain fell less heavily. At last, on the far side of a canal, she noticed a building with lights shining out. The door was open, noise came from within; a man staggered out.

She crossed by the nearest bridge. Screwing up all her courage, she peered inside. Straw covered the floor. The air felt warm on her face and stank of fish, sweat and wine. As she stepped in, the place fell silent; but only for a moment. Then laughter and whistles erupted from the workmen at the tables. She saw at a glance Arlecchino was not amongst them, so marched up to a ruddy-faced man in an apron whom she took to be the landlord. He regarded her with a mixture of scorn and amusement. 'Sir,' she said, 'I wonder if you can help me? I'm looking for a man.'

'Will I do?' called a voice.

Others laughed.

The landlord picked up a jug and began filling it from a barrel.

'He's a well-dressed young man in a blue velvet suit.' She spoke through continued derision. 'Has he been here?'

A blond serving girl came and took the jug of wine. 'You looking for Arlecchino?'

'Yes,' she gasped. 'Have you seen him?'

'He was in about an hour ago.'

'Do you know where he went?'

'Keep your trap shut,' the landlord muttered.

'I'll say what I like,' the girl retorted. 'And you show respect. This is his leading lady.'

'Bloody 'ell!' came a voice.'

'How do you know who she is?' the landlord asked.

'Cos I've seen her perform at the theatre.'

'Since when has a daughter of mine had money to chuck away on the theatre? I'll have to dock your wages.'

His customers laughed.

Colombina tried again. 'Please,' she urged, 'this is very important. If you know where he went…'

The girl put down the jug. 'Saracen's Head, most like.'

'Thank you,' said Colombina. She made for the door, then turned back. 'How do I get there?'

'She can't go in there!' called a man. 'Tell 'er, Rosina.'

The girl joined Colombina. 'He's right, Miss. The Saracen's Head is a really bad place. Makes this dump seem like the Doge's boudoir. You'd best go home.'

'I can't. I have to find Arlecchino.'

'What is it you've done to him, pretty lady?' called the landlord. 'He left here cursing all womankind.'

'Ignore him,' muttered his daughter. 'But do as I say and stay clear of the Saracen's Head. It's no fit place for a lady. Bravi drink there.'

Colombina did not know what she meant but was impressed by the gravity of the warning. 'I really am grateful,' she whispered. 'But it's vital I find Arlecchino.'

The girl gave a shrug. 'You go careful then. It's over the bridge. Turn left, then right under the second arch. You'll hear it before you see it.'

Colombina grasped her hand. 'Thank you,' she said. 'Thank you so much. I wish there was some way I could repay you.'

The girl's eyes lit up. 'Free entry to a performance?'

'Of course.' Colombina doubted there would be any more in which she played leading lady.

She followed the directions, and, as the girl had said, well before reaching the tavern, heard a raucous din. A dim lamp hung over the doorway lighting up a painted sign depicting the head of a grinning man in a turban. His severed neck dripped with blood. Colombina felt courage desert her. It sounded as if a fight was going on inside. Suddenly a man tumbled out, followed by another. The second jumped on the first and began pounding him with his fists. A third appeared and joined in, kicking the man on the ground in the ribs. Colombina moved back out of sight.

Rosina was right. This was no place to be. She thought about going back to the palazzo but had no idea how to find it. Perhaps, if she returned to the other inn, Rosina would give her directions. But she felt sick at the thought of going home. How could she bear all those looks? Or live with the knowledge of what she had done?

By the sound of things, the fight was over. She risked another look and saw the man on the ground drag himself down a slipway and thrust his head in the water. To her surprise, he got up and lurched off. Colombina remained where she was, listening to the alarming sounds coming from the tavern. Resigned to failure, she decided to go back to the inn and ask for directions home.

She was crossing the bridge when she heard a noise to her left. Peering through the blackness, she made out a shape slumped on a flight of stone steps leading into the water. Now, for the first time since leaving the church, she felt cold. Any fear of what might be lying there, partly immersed in the water, was swept away by the need to know for sure.

She hurried back over the bridge. Once she stepped off, she could no longer see the steps but she clearly heard a groan. It could be a beggar, or a drunk; anyone in the world in fact except…

She was a few steps away when her worst fears were realised. With a cry, she ran on, scrambled down the steps and almost slid into the canal. Brushing aside a squeaking rat, she cradled Arlecchino's head. His features were bloodied and swollen. His hair was soaked; so were his clothes. When she placed a hand on his chest, the moisture felt odd. She stared in horror at the smear on her palm. His doublet was cut to shreds and his life's blood was oozing.

56

olombina gave another cry. 'Dear God, have pity,' she sobbed. Afraid Arlecchino's attackers might still be close, she decided not to call for help but tried instead to drag him from the water. His weight proved too much for her and she burst into tears and held him. It was all she could do.

Then she noticed a light on the bridge. The lamp swayed across, carried by a tall figure. 'Sir, please help me!' she called in desperation.

The man left the bridge and came walking towards her. 'Brighella!' she gasped.

He stood over Arlecchino.

'He's badly injured. Stabbed, I think. Who would do this?'

'I could write you a list.'

'There's an inn close by. Between us, we could carry him.'

Brighella said nothing and an alarming thought entered her head. Looking up, she heard him laugh.

'You think I murdered my meal ticket? No,' he shook his head, 'if I'd set out to kill him, he'd be dead.' He crouched to hold the lamp over Arlecchino. 'This is Bravi handiwork.'

'Bravi?'

'Hired thugs. And they knew their victim. See?' He indicated bruises on Arlecchino's face. 'His face has been beaten, not sliced – because he wears the mask. Normally, with a pretty boy, Bravi would scar him. They like to hit a man where it hurts.'

'But he's bleeding to death.'

'Which tells me that murder was not their intent.' He stood. 'If it had been, his throat would be slit.'

'What difference does it make?' she cried in exasperation. 'He'll die if you don't help him.'

'In exchange for what?'

'You want payment? You truly are a monster!'

'Maybe. But I am the only monster available.'

'You said yourself you depend on Arlecchino for a living. How will you survive if he dies?'

Brighella shrugged. 'I'll manage.'

'I've nothing to give you,' she said, getting up. 'Not on me. But you can have all the money I possess, once we get back to the palazzo. And this,' she fumbled with the clasp of her amethyst cross. 'It's the only thing you left me with…'

'I don't want your money, nor trinkets. There is something I will take, however – something you carry on your person.'

She knew immediately what he meant and pulled Jacopo Bruno's letter from her bodice. 'Here,' she said, thrusting it at him. 'May it bring you the same ill-fortune it has brought me.'

Brighella stuffed the letter in his doublet, then handed her the lamp. Scooping Arlecchino up like a pile of old sacks, he strode off in the opposite direction to the inn. Colombina hurried after him; it was difficult keeping pace with his lengthy strides. 'Where are you taking him?'

He said nothing but turned down an alleyway that ended at a stout wooden door. Standing aside, he told her to knock. She did so and, from inside, came the scraping of bolts. As soon as the door began to open, Brighella kicked it wide. 'A customer for you, Master Barber,' he said, pushing past a short, stocky man and setting Arlecchino down on a long trestle table.

Arlecchino groaned. Colombina hurried to his side. She took hold of his hand, which felt deathly cold. The man closed and bolted the door. 'This one's a mess,' he said, tying on a leather apron. 'Bravi mischief?'

Brighella nodded.

'I'll have to cut away his clothing.' The barber glanced at Colombina.

'She's his mistress,' Brighella grunted.

'Hold the lamp high then,' the barber told her. When he cut away the blood-soaked velvet and Arlecchino's wounds were exposed, she was forced to suppress the horror she felt. 'Well, at least we know the motive,' said the man, waving a hand over Arlecchino's genitals. 'Bravi delivered their message with the deepest cut.'

'Will he live?' she gasped.

'He might. But to what purpose?'

'Please,' she said. 'Do what you can.'

'It will cost.'

Brighella set down on the table a full pouch of coin.

The man picked it up. 'Right, but no guarantees. If this man dies…'

'You can keep your money,' said Colombina. 'I'll pay you back,' she told Brighella, 'whatever it costs.'

'Seems this lover's worth a great deal. Like I say, I might be able to save him but, more than that…' he shook his head. 'Are you sure this young man will thank you, once he knows the score?'

'Just do your work,' Brighella told him.

Colombina continued to hold the lamp while the barber made close inspection of the wounds. The slashes across Arlecchino's chest and stomach were not deep; the most serious ran across his lower abdomen. Flesh gaped above his member and a line oozing red curved beneath it… 'Jesus!' gasped the barber, 'this is worse than I thought. Bring towels – from the chest. Over there!' He flapped a hand.

Thrusting the lamp at Brighella, Colombina rushed to get the towels. As the barber tried to staunch the blood, she kept the dressings coming, but each time he pressed a fresh one to the wound, Arlecchino cried out. When he started to struggle, more blood soaked through. 'Hold him down!' the barber yelled at Brighella.

Setting down the lamp, Brighella pinned Arlecchino by the shoulders.

'More cloths,' the barber snapped until a thick wad covered the wound. With no more blood seeping through, he stood back and wiped his brow with his forearm. 'Well,' he gasped. 'He's in God's hand now.'

'There must be something more you can do?' urged Colombina.

'Not without butchering him more than he has been. I'm a barber surgeon, lady. Not a miracle worker.'

Arlecchino's face was the colour of alabaster; he no longer seemed to be in pain. The barber shook his head. 'Time to call a priest.'

'You can't let him die!' She gripped his arm.

261

'There's no more I can do.' He shook free, then muttered, 'there is one man, but the hour is late.'

'Who?' asked Colombina. 'If there's anyone at all…'

'His name is Ishmael.'

'A Jew?' scoffed Brighella.

'He's the only one I know who might be able to save him, but it's already after curfew. He'll be locked in with the rest of his clan.'

Colombina glanced at Brighella. 'The Jews are confined to the ghetto after dark,' he explained.

The barber wiped his hands. 'You'll just have to pray your man makes it through until dawn.' He brought her a stool and, on his advice, she tried to get Arlecchino to take wine from a leather bottle. All she succeeded in doing was wetting his lips. Occasionally he groaned. Once he opened his eyes. She smiled at him but he cursed her and turned his face away. Eventually, he fell into an uneasy sleep. She also dozed, head resting on the table. When she woke, she found a blanket had been spread over Arlecchino. His features were swollen and very flushed. She glanced at Brighella who was seated on a bench, boots resting on a table. 'Where's the barber?'

'Gone to get the Jew.'

'Is it dawn yet?'

'No.'

As the door opened, she sprang to her feet. Hope soared when she saw that the barber was not alone. 'This is Ishmael, the physician,' he told her, indicating the slight, bearded man carrying a leather bag.

The physician pulled off his floppy red hat and came to Arlecchino. Colombina thanked him for coming. He regarded her with dark solemn eyes; he looked to be no older than his patient. When he touched Arlecchino's brow, she was struck by the slimness of his fingers.

'He's burning up,' the barber told him.

'The guard was amenable then?' said Brighella.

The barber gave a laugh. 'Once I told him he'd have the Doge to answer to, if his servant died. Your ducats helped too.'

'Where did you find this man?' Ishmael asked Colombina.

'By the canal.'

'Was he in the water?'

'He was lying on some steps, half submerged.'

He opened his bag and took from it a phial of gold-coloured liquid. 'We must get him to drink this.'

'I've been trying to get him to take wine,' she explained, 'but...'

'He *must* drink it.'

She nodded then spoke into Arlecchino's ear. 'The physician is here, Arlecchino. He has medicine you must take.'

He groaned and, when the phial was put to his lips, kept his mouth tight shut.

'Pinch and hold his nose.'

She did so.

Once Arlecchino opened his mouth, Ishmael tipped the liquid down his throat. Arlecchino gagged but Ishmael held him tight until he was forced to gulp. When released, Arlecchino spat and muttered something about being poisoned.

The barber removed the blanket, revealing dressings now soaked in blood. As the thickest pad was peeled away, Colombina fought her worst fears. Ishmael examined the wound, and, when he said nothing, she became convinced he was preparing to offer no hope. 'Very deep,' he muttered and asked for a bowl of water and more light.

A table was brought, another lamp placed upon it, together with a large bowl. The barber spread a cloth over the table and filled the bowl with water from a ewer. Ishmael took from his bag a roll of linen, which he unwound and laid close to the light. Colombina hid her alarm at the sight of the knives and instruments it contained. Three more items were placed on the table: two phials of colourless liquid and a jar of grey powder. When the contents of one phial were tipped into the bowl, the water turned milky white and a pungent but not unpleasant smell filled the room. 'What are you going to do?' she dared to ask.

'This wound,' Ishmael passed a hand above the most serious gash, 'it will not heal – not unless the flesh is sewn.' She swallowed hard.

Brighella stepped forward. 'You're going to need me then.'

'Not yet.' He turned to Colombina. 'This man, Arlecchino. Is he a believer in your Christian God?'

'Yes.'

'Then, would you be so kind?' He indicated her crucifix and she hurriedly removed it. He took it and whispered in the patient's ear.

Arlecchino opened his eyes and they became fixed on the cross held before him. Ishmael spoke softly, in a foreign language. Within seconds, the patient's eyelids flickered, then they closed. Returning Colombina's crucifix, Ishmael trickled clear liquid from the second phial over the wound. Then he washed his hands in the bowl, and, picking up a small metal hook and a length of what looked to be thin silver wire, told her, 'you may wish to look away now.'

'I have to see this,' said Brighella and took his place at the foot of the table.

The speed with which the physician worked was amazing. Colombina held Arlecchino's hand throughout the procedure; not once did he flinch. The barber mopped the blood, and, by the time Ishmael had finished, there was a pile of red linen under the table knee-deep. Finally, each cut was washed again in colourless liquid then covered with muslin sprinkled with powder from the jar. Ishmael washed his hands. 'I will wake him in a moment,' he told Brighella. 'Then you will be needed.'

The barber pulled off Arlecchino's boots and cut away the rest of his clothing. Then he strapped him to the table by the ankles. Ishmael indicated to Brighella to be ready. Holding Arlecchino down, he spoke into his ear. Arlecchino's eyes sprang open. Pain contorted his face. An agonized groan burst from his lips as he tried to draw up his knees. Brighella forced them down; the straps held his ankles. The barber poured wine down his throat.

57

ear that Arlecchino would die, the grim nature of his wound – neither had been permitted to weaken Colombina's resolve. Yet, confronted now by such raw agony, watching helpless as he struggled, she was overwhelmed by the desire to stop her ears, turn from the sight and run out of the room.

Somehow she managed to remain. There was nothing she could do to alleviate his suffering – so she did the next best thing. She stood firm in the face of it. At last, Arlecchino stopped struggling, his groans became less harrowing and Colombina gave thanks to a God she had almost abandoned. Ishmael lit the way upstairs as Brighella and the barber carried the patient, still strapped to the top of the table. Colombina followed.

The small room was basic with a bed, table and two stools. Ishmael hung up the lamp then spread a clean sheet over the mattress. The straps were unbuckled and Arlecchino was transferred. The barber lit a fire in the grate.

Once the others had left, Ishmael told Colombina, 'Arlecchino should rest now. The barber's wine contains a strong sleeping draught. Will you be nursing him?'

'Yes,' she answered eagerly.

'I ask only because…' he took in her appearance.

She glanced down at her bloodstained dress. 'Oh. This was supposed to be for a special occasion. I shall send for something more practical.'

'You are an actress, I believe?'

'Yes, I mean… I was.' She hid her confusion. 'Arlecchino and I belong to a company known as the Immortali. Perhaps you have seen our play?'

For the first time he smiled. 'You perform after dark, I believe?'

'Oh. Yes.'

'Can you read, Colombina?'

'Yes.'

'Then I shall write down some instructions and a list of items you will need which can be purchased in the Rialto.'

'Thank you. I have heard of a remarkable powder, a remedy for all kinds of injury and ailments, yet the cost, I believe…'

'You are referring to Teriaca.' He dismissed it with a shake of the head. 'What money you have will be better spent on nourishment. Give the patient broth to begin with. And fruit – dried will suffice, if no fresh can be found. I will leave you my own sleeping powder.' He handed her a packet. 'Give Arlecchino no more than would cover your little fingernail in half a cup of wine. But only when the pain is so severe it prevents him from sleeping. Rest, good food, boiled water and clean surroundings. These things cost little, yet they are priceless and all a strong young man needs to recover.'

She felt encouraged. 'You are sure he will recover?'

'I am sure of nothing. I do not work the miracle of healing, no more than the womb creates the child. I provide the conditions in which a miracle can occur.' She was surprised when he turned to Arlecchino and began to pray in his own language.

Dawn was almost upon them and he promised to return at midday. 'If you need me before then, the barber knows where to find me.'

'Thank you,' she said. 'Concerning payment…'

'I have already been paid.'

She was puzzled but did not enquire who had settled. 'The prayers you said for Arlecchino,' she ventured. 'I am not familiar with your language and am not of your faith, yet I should like to offer up prayers of my own, if…'

'Prayer is prayer, Colombina.' He left the room.

Making sure Arlecchino was sound asleep, she went down to speak to Brighella. But there was no sign of him and the barber told her he had left some time ago. When there came a knock on the door, he went to answer it and she was overjoyed to see Pedrolino. He came in and grasped her hands. 'Brighella told me what happened.'

She took him upstairs, pausing on the landing. 'His wounds, Pedrolino…' She broke down and he held her.

'What does the physician say?'

'He believes he will recover.'

'Well then?' He lifted her chin. 'Ishmael is, by reputation, the most skilful physician in Venice.'

'I was going to ask Brighella to bring some money. There are things I have to buy.'

'I've brought money. Pantelone instructed me to settle all accounts. He would like to see his son.'

'I don't think that's a good idea,' she said softly. 'Arlecchino blames us both.'

'Are you going to tell me what happened?'

She shook her head.

'Very well. Let's go in.'

He blanched when he saw his friend, and, when he crouched by the bedside, Arlecchino did not wake. 'Brighella believes he knows who did this. Or rather, who paid Bravi to do it. Apparently, there was an incident the night of the masked ball.' Colombina caught her breath and turned away. 'A red-haired man, of influence it turns out, considered himself insulted by Arlecchino. Perhaps you know more?'

She bit her lip, trying to come to terms with the devastating news that she was doubly to blame for Arlecchino's wounds.

Pedrolino got up. 'If you give me your list, I'll get the items.'

When Ishmael returned at noon, he changed the dressing on the most serious wound. Arlecchino became restless. Instructing Colombina to give him the sleeping draft once he was fully awake, Ishmael left with the promise to visit again before curfew.

Pedrolino came back with every item on the list. As Colombina unpacked them, she asked about the play. 'Cancelled until further notice,' he told her.

Arlecchino stirred and opened his eyes. Pedrolino hurried to his side.

'Good to see you,' whispered Arlecchino hoarsely and they clasped hands. His face contorted and Colombina brought the sleeping draught. Supporting Arlecchino's head, Pedrolino held the vessel to his lips. Arlecchino drank, then settled back. 'Do something for me, Pedro?'

'Anything.'

'When next you come, bring my picture.'

Pedrolino frowned then glanced at Colombina.

'He means the miniature of his mother,' she said quietly.

Colombina had rushed to take on the task of caring for Arlecchino but, though she remained committed, life had not prepared her for it. She soon came to realise that Spinetta had spared her the very worst domestic duties. Pedrolino came every day and brought the things she needed, including clean clothing and linen. She looked forward to his visits.

At night she slept on a small palliasse, close enough to Arlecchino to hear his slightest murmur. Since he woke often, lack of sleep took its toll on her and a comment from Pedrolino confirmed that fatigue showed in her face. Arlecchino was still the man she loved; she would have done anything for him. But his needs were those of a child and met only with her assistance.

She did not have to cook; the barber's housekeeper prepared meals. But Colombina fed her patient, washed him, emptied and cleaned out the piss pot. She also held the bowl or mopped up his vomit on the numerous occasions severe pain made him sick. Yet, during these intimate times, he barely acknowledged her existence. Not once did he thank her. She was not surprised. Nor did she blame him. It was herself she blamed.

The day came when Ishmael saw fit to remove the stitches. She wondered if he would use magic again. He reassured her it would not be necessary and Arlecchino suffered little discomfort. Thanking his physician, he praised his skill. In turn, Ishmael expressed satisfaction at the rapidity of healing. He said Arlecchino could, within a few days and with Colombina's help, take a turn about the room.

Seeing Ishmael out, she joined him on the landing; then braced herself to put to him the question she felt sure Arlecchino would have asked, had she not been there to hear it. 'This is somewhat delicate…'

Ishmael spared her blushes. 'He should make a complete recovery. The damage done was all to one side and that is healing. I cannot see any reason why he should not be able to father a child.' She thanked him and went back inside, allowing herself a bitter smile at the irony of the good news.

Arlecchino was keen to get up and walk. It proved difficult persuading him to wait a few more days. When he made his first attempt, his unsteady weight and undisguised resentment at having to lean on Colombina made it hard for them both.

On one occasion when Ishmael arrived, his patient was fast asleep. He told Colombina not to wake him. They discussed his progress then she said, 'I hope you won't be offended, but I have often thought how young you look to be so great a physician.'

Ishmael thanked her for the compliment. 'I learned my craft at my father's elbow, just as he learned his at the elbow of my grandfather.'

'Does your father still practise?'

'He does, but only amongst our people. He rarely leaves the ghetto.'

'I don't understand why you are imprisoned after dark.'

'Neither do I. But it has been so for as long as I can remember.'

'It seems very unjust.'

'We are used to injustice, and hypocrisy. Men spit on us in public, then pay us in private to save their lives or livelihoods. Yet life is better here than my race have known elsewhere. My great-grandfather was driven out of Spain.'

'Well, I cannot thank you enough for what you have done,' she said, touching his hand.

As the patient grew stronger and needed less care, Colombina paid more visits to the market in search of fruit, milk and anything else that would help build his strength. Soon the Arlecchino of old came back into his eyes. But she was not allowed a share in him; the best she could hope for was pleasure derived from sitting and listening to him laughing and joking with Pedrolino. Sometimes she wondered if he would ever forgive her. She dreaded the day, which was fast approaching, when he would no longer need her.

One morning she returned from the market and found him sleeping peacefully. She was surprised to see, seated at his bedside, the bearded man in fur-trimmed hat, dressed in his purple cloak covered with stars and crescent moons. Ishmael was also there. He stood as she entered. 'Colombina, may I introduce a colleague?'

269

The bearded man got up. He came and grasped her by the hand. 'I have long wished to meet you,' he said, dark eyes twinkling.

'But we have already met, I believe.'

'We have, yet only fleetingly. I have followed your career. You are a fine actress.'

'Thank you,' she said, glancing towards Arlecchino. 'Sir,' she said quietly, 'I doubt I shall be returning to the stage.'

'Arlecchino will soon be fit enough,' said Ishmael.

'Even so.'

The bearded man covered her hand. 'Humanity is flawed, Colombina. That is its charm. You are in a cold place now, alone and feeling beyond forgiveness. But you will not always be there. Learn to forgive your own human weakness. Time will do the rest.'

'May I know your name, Sir?'

'I am known by many names. But you may call me Hermes.'

'Like the Greek messenger to the gods?'

'The very same.' He went back to the bedside. As he stood looking down at Arlecchino, the pair seemed suddenly contained within a sphere of golden light. 'Our favourite child is almost restored, thanks to my good friend here.' Hermes held his hand out to Ishmael. 'And thanks to you, too, Colombina.'

'I have done very little,' she said, crossing to the fire.

'You did what I told you, loved until your heart burst. What more could he ask?'

'I sinned against God,' she found herself saying, 'and hurt Arlecchino.'

'My dear, who has not sinned? And Arlecchino's hurt will heal. Thanks to you, my son is destined to shine for years to come.'

'Your son?' She faced the bearded man. 'Do you mean the sun that lights up the sky?'

'Of course.' His smile was enigmatic.

58

olombina saw the men out then watched them go downstairs. Still puzzled by the words of the curious man Hermes, she was about to enter the room when she caught sight of something leaning against the wall. It was a scroll. Convinced it had not been there when she returned from the market, she picked it up, unrolled it and was surprised to find, wrapped inside, a single white rose.

She smiled. On the parchment was written: *For Colombina*. Most likely, the rose had come from the lobby of the palazzo and been placed there by Pedrolino. She took it inside and put it in a jug of water.

The following morning she went to the market with the intention of looking for Hermes. He was not on his stall and his place was occupied by a man selling cloth. Come to think of it, she had not seen him in the Rialto since her very first visit when Pedrolino had bought the spyglass for Lella.

The next time she met Ishmael, she asked him about his mysterious colleague. He was evasive and all she managed to find out was that he obtained medicines from Hermes.

More than a month had passed since the attack on Arlecchino. His minor cuts had healed; the most serious one still pained him a little. He maintained his coolness towards Colombina; in all the time they had spent together in this room, he had only ever spoken to her directly to tell her what he wanted. He kept the miniature of his mother face-up on his bedside table, a constant reminder of their father's betrayal and of her unworthiness to bear the same name as the pretty young woman with her basket of doves.

He still refused to see Pantelone. Pedrolino kept him in touch with news of the company, which was not good. The theatre had remained

271

closed and money was running out. Fortunately, for the moment, the Immortali's patron was allowing the troupe to stay in the palazzo.

Brighella had, apparently, disappeared again.

A few days after the rose wrapped in parchment appeared outside the door, another was left; and then another. They began arriving, on average, three times a week. By now, Colombina knew Pedrolino was not responsible because one day he commented on the half-dozen standing in the jug. When she admitted she had thought they might be from him, he laughed and said he wished they were, but his pockets were empty and times far too lean for such a gesture. He also told her the flowers displayed in the lobby of the palazzo had died weeks ago. He suggested it was, most likely, the same admirer who had sent bouquets to the theatre.

Arlecchino ignored the roses but, for Colombina, their arrival brightened her days and she began to experience a tingle of expectation every time she opened the door. A tentative enquiry put to the barber's housekeeper brought her no closer to discovering the identity of the sender; the woman claimed she knew nothing about any flowers.

One morning Colombina was shopping in the Rialto for thread when she heard someone call out her name. The voice was female and sounded familiar. Her first thought was of Carla or Suzanna; but, looking round, she noticed a well-dressed young woman pushing her way through the crowd. Shiny curls framed a pretty face and rosebud lips spread into a smile. 'Silvia!' gasped Colombina.

Silvia rushed forward and hugged her.

For a moment Colombina stiffened, embarrassed that Silvia looked so elegant whilst she was dressed like a servant. Yet the genuine warmth of Silvia's embrace soon overcame that. 'How did you know I'd changed my name?'

Silvia laughed. 'Silly. We've seen you at the theatre. Loads of times.'

'We?'

Silvia thrust out her left wrist around which she wore the bracelet Colombina had given her the day they parted. 'You told me to wear this on my wedding day. I did and I haven't taken it off since!'

'You're married?' asked Colombina, delighted.

'Yes! To Vincenzo. Just before Christmas. And that's not all! I think…' she grabbed Colombina's hand and placed it, palm down, on her belly.

'You're with child?'

Silvia nodded; then she looked troubled.

'It's all right,' Colombina said softly. 'I did lose my baby, but I believe it was meant to be. Yet I'm delighted for you and Vincenzo. Where is he, by the way?'

'Talking to some merchants. Oh Colombina, I've so much to tell you. But…' Silvia frowned, 'there are things you might not know. Have you had any news from home?'

Colombina shook her head and sudden fear struck her. 'My father?'

'He's well.' Silvia's hand touched hers. 'Very well.'

'Thank God.'

'Come with me,' said Silvia, linking arms. 'We'll go and find Vincenzo. Then the three of us can dine.'

'I'm sorry, Silvia. I can't. I have to get back to Arlecchino.'

'Oh yes, I heard. How is he?'

'Almost recovered. But…'

'Well then. Let's find somewhere quiet, where we can talk.'

Silvia's news shocked Colombina. But perhaps not so much as her own reaction to it. Colombina's mother was dead. Isabella Olivieri had taken her own life. 'Why?' was all Colombina could think of to say; yet the question was really addressed to herself and she recognised the sensation in the pit of her stomach as guilt. Could it be that her mother had killed herself because of what she had done?

'I'm sorry to bring such bad news,' she heard Silvia say. 'I have reasons for not liking your mother. But it must be terrible for you.'

'When did it happen?'

Silvia's brow furrowed. 'At the end of October, I think. After you disappeared, your father carried on looking for you, even though some men had brought him your cloak and a shoe they found in the ravine. He refused to believe you were dead. But something really odd happened to your mother.' They carried on walking. 'When you couldn't be found, she immediately dismissed me from her service. And she had Vincenzo sacked too! Signore Panesse took to his bed and she persuaded him that Vincenzo was involved. Which, of course, he was.'

'Poor Signore Panesse. I never meant to hurt him.'

Silvia came to a halt. 'He died, Colombina.'

'No!'

'You mustn't blame yourself. He *was* very old. And your mother should never have done what she did.'

'Even so. He was a kind man.'

'He was. And when he knew he was dying, he sent for Vincenzo. He forgave him and, in his will, left him three trading vessels, together with all the cargo they carried at the time of his departing this earth.'

Colombina was amazed. 'So you're..?'

'Rich! Yes. Well, richer than I ever imagined I'd be. And Vincenzo is so clever. Already he's made a profit on the bequest.'

'I am so very glad for you,' said Colombina. 'But please, tell me more about my mother.'

'Yes. Sorry. Well, like I say, it was odd. I heard she refused to speak about your disappearance. It was as if you had never existed. I'm sorry if that hurts. Your father sent out search parties and sometimes went with them. But nothing was heard and everyone else was convinced you were dead. Apparently your mother spent more and more time in her room. The maid had to leave her meals outside the door. Then, one night, a stranger turned up at the palazzo. Rumour had it he was an astrologer. He wore a cloak with a hood and always kept his head bowed, so no one ever saw his face. He was the only person allowed in. He visited your mother for about a week, then, one night, he didn't come. All the next day, none of the food was taken but she ate little so the maid didn't get worried until later that night. Then she told your father. He had the door broken down and found her. Dead!'

Colombina tried to take it in. 'How did she die?'

'She took poison. They found a phial by her bedside.'

'Did she leave a letter?'

Silvia shook her head. 'I can guess what you're thinking. But, for what it's worth, I don't believe she killed herself because you ran away. From what I was told, her mind became possessed.'

'Thank you for telling me, Silvia. My poor father.' Silvia appeared ill at ease. 'What's the matter?'

'There's something else you should know. But I'm not sure how you're going to take it.'

'Silvia, please.'

'Well, it's about your father. And... and Rosa.'

'Rosa?'

'It's only servants' gossip. And you know I wouldn't say anything, unless...' Silvia bit her lip. 'This is difficult but... well... since your mother's death, I hear they've become close.'

'Close?' Again Colombina struggled to take in something extraordinary.

'I expect it was loneliness. And the pain of losing your mother.'

Suddenly it all became clear. 'No,' breathed Colombina, smiling. 'He loved her before. I see it now!' She laughed at Silvia's shocked expression. 'How stupid and childish I was then, wrapped up in my own selfish dreams.'

'You knew?'

'No. But I should have. So you see, Silvia, there's nothing to worry about. I'm happy for them both. In fact, nothing could have made me happier.'

'Oh good. That's all right then.'

Colombina squeezed her hand. 'Thank you for being such a good friend. I've missed you.'

'And I you. I wish you would come and meet Vincenzo. I know he'd love to see you.' Colombina shook her head. 'Well then.' Silvia fumbled in her purse and brought out a crumpled piece of paper. 'This is where we live in Venice. Vincenzo drew this little map because he was afraid I might get lost. But I know my way around now. Come and see us as soon as you can. And, if there's anything you need...'

Again the pair hugged, then went their separate ways.

When she got back to the barber's house, Colombina met Ishmael coming downstairs. He told her this would be his final visit, and, when she expressed surprise, said that he had examined Arlecchino and considered him no longer in need of a physician's care. She did her best to thank him, knowing that words were inadequate.

On entering the room, she saw Arlecchino up and dressed. 'I'm leaving,' he told her.

'Leaving?' She hurried towards him. 'Where are you going?'

'Back to the theatre.'

'But...'

'According to Ishmael, I'm well enough to act. And the company needs me.'

She fought the inner churning. 'But what about your father?'

'He can go to hell. The company's what matters.'

'Arlecchino…' She reached out but he stepped back. 'What shall I do?'

'Do what you like.'

'Do you still want me to be your leading lady?'

'Frankly? No.'

She had not meant to tell him but the words came spilling out. 'I've just heard that my mother is dead.'

He regarded her coldly. 'So is mine.' He snatched up the miniature and, pushing it inside his doublet, made for the door. 'Tell Pantelone your news. He might be interested.'

'Arlecchino, I'm sorry.' She ran after him. 'If I could only…'

He was out of the room and halfway down the stairs before she reached the landing. Again she called out his name. He did not look back.

Emotion broke free. All that care. All her love! Dismissed within seconds. It seemed his capacity for cruelty knew no bounds and the hope she had harboured that he might soften washed away with hot tears.

Turning to go back inside, she noticed, propped against the wall by the doorframe, a folded parchment.

59

olombina picked up the parchment, which was sealed. On it was written her name. She went back inside and tore the letter open. No rose. Instead an invitation to dine this very evening, 16th February 1600.

She threw the letter on the table and sat down, feeling wretched. What had she ever done to merit such cruel fortune? To fall in love with her own half-brother; to be raped and made pregnant by him. To be forced to leave home to escape being married to an old man; then, swept from the depths of despair on losing a child into the euphoria of becoming the Immortali's leading lady, to gain the love at last of the man she adored – only to lose it. What had it all been for?

She felt helpless and full of rage at her seeming inability to make a difference to her own life. It was as if some evil force had been given her fate for a plaything. With a sigh, she tried to rise above this mood of self-pity and her gaze settled on the letter. She averted it, but not for long. Picking up the invitation, she read:

To Colombina,

Her company at dinner tonight is most respectfully requested by an ardent admirer of her acting. Should she decide to bestow upon his house the favour of her gifted presence, he would be most humbly grateful. In the hope that his request will be granted, the writer of this letter has employed the black gondolier to remain at the Rialto from sunset until the stroke of midnight.

If the gondolier's wait proves in vain, be assured of my disappointed yet undaunted admiration.

It was the next few lines that touched her and held her attention.

Whether or not you accept my invitation, Colombina, as an admirer of your beauty and talent, I call upon every celestial influence and universal power to shower upon your future life the blessings you so richly deserve.

The words fell like rain on parched ground.

Colombina poured herself some wine, then, picking up her broken scrap of mirror, she peered at her reflection. Her hair was untidy, eyes pink from crying. She got up and poured water into a bowl, washed her face then dabbed it dry. Her carmine and rose dress still hung from the beam where she had put it after removing the bloodstains.

What could she be thinking? She shook herself free of the notion and spent a few brisk minutes tidying the room. The letter still lay open on the table.

Suddenly defiance sprang up like a demon. What had she to lose? She owed Arlecchino no loyalty; shared blood denied their love. Her acting career was at an end. She was alone, with no one to support her. But she was free. And that felt exciting. She was at liberty to do what she wanted – or at least, what she had to – to survive. She felt suddenly infused with a curious power.

She snatched up the letter and read it again. It would soon be sunset but she had time to lose the pink eyes, to dress her hair, put on her gown. The tingle of nerves was exhilarating.

Dressed in her carmine gown, she could not help but think back to a time when she had stood before the altar and been driven by similar recklessness. She set out for the Rialto.

The cold night air worked on her senses, testing her resolve; but she carried on and soon reached the bridge. As she scanned the row of gondoliers for one dressed in black, a deep voice made her jump. 'My lady?'

She swung round to find herself facing a man in red velvet. 'I... I am looking for...'

'The black gondolier?' His smile lit up the night.

She nodded dumbly.

He offered her his hand and she took it. He was tall, stately and very dark-skinned. He wore a gold earring and a red satin bandeau. As he led her to the gondola, she sensed his amusement. His craft was upholstered in sumptuous red velvet and furnished with cushions trimmed with gold braid. He helped her board, steadying the craft as she took her seat beneath the felze; then, excusing himself, draped a black sable over her lap. As the boat left the quay, Colombina gazed across the water. A chill wind stung her face.

The gondolier turned his craft in the direction of the lagoon. 'Sir,' she called.

'My lady?'

'Are you acquainted with my host?'

'I have, on occasion, had the honour to serve him.'

'Could you tell me his name?'

'I know him by the name of Signore Menander.'

'Is there anything else you can tell me about him?'

'Only that he is reputed to be the richest man in Venice.'

She asked no more questions and he steered the craft towards the far side of the canal. It was not hard to guess which palazzo he was making for. Its magnificent façade spoke of incalculable wealth; yet no lights shone out and, as the boat slid between iron gates, she shivered. The gondolier helped her disembark. 'Enjoy your evening, my lady,' he said, bowed and left her on the quay.

Within seconds, a servant appeared. He also bowed then asked Colombina to follow him. Once inside the building, her anxieties dissolved. The place was brightly lit, the air as warm as a summer's day. The servant took her cloak then led her to the bottom of a sweeping marble staircase. 'If you would be so kind, my master awaits you.'

She began to climb the steps, admiring the glass lanterns and some fine statues in alcoves. This was another world, the like of which she had only entered on the night of the masked ball. She put that memory aside and continued on up two flights to a patterned floor of pietre dura. The walls and high ceiling of a spacious landing were decorated with frescoes depicting scenes of a classical nature. Facing her was a large double doorway. One of the doors was open. Music drifted out of the room; the strains of a lute, faint yet delightful. Colombina approached, paused a moment then entered. The music stopped.

The room was sparsely furnished, a huge white marble fireplace being its most impressive feature. On either side of the hearth in which blazed a great fire, stood a gilded chair. A hand was resting on the arm of one. The hand was withdrawn and a man dressed in grey stood in haste to greet her. 'Colombina! Please forgive me. I should have been downstairs

279

to meet you, but I hardly dared hope…' As he held out his right hand, she noticed he wore a brown leather glove on the left.

He was nothing like she had expected, and, when she allowed him to take her hand, he seemed overawed. In fact, his demeanour was that of a gauche young man; yet she took him to be well into his thirties. His dark shoulder-length hair was a little unkempt, but clean with no sign of grey. He was tall but he slouched, adding to the impression of a man somewhat out of his depth.

'Thank you for inviting me.'

His grey eyes lit up. His skin was quite pale, his nose narrow yet straight. His lips were not full but sensitive and quick to smile. She decided she liked him. Perhaps because he was so different from her perceived image of the richest man in Venice. 'Would you care to introduce yourself?' she said with a wry smile.

'Oh. Yes.' Again he apologised. 'I am Niccolo Menander. I am so very honoured to welcome you to my home.'

'It was kind of you to ask me.'

He smiled again and there followed an awkward silence. 'Right,' he said, rubbing his hands. 'Dinner.' He glanced towards the door, muttered something then went out onto the landing.

Colombina crossed to the fire. A finely crafted lute was propped against the chair in which he had been sitting.

'Dinner is served,' announced Niccolo Menander. He indicated a door at the far end of the room. As she moved forward, he hovered behind her then rushed to open it.

The dining room had an intimate feel. Another large fire blazed in a hearth of black marble. There were paintings and frescoes, astrological in subject. A silver plaque depicting phases of the moon hung above a doorway at the far end. When the door through which they had entered was closed, she noticed mounted above it a golden sunburst. 'I take it you have an interest in astrology?'

'Oh yes. Ever since the star of 1570. I was six years old when I saw it, a dazzling sight. Magnificent!' His features became animated. 'And you?'

'I confess I know little about the subject.'

He smiled and drew a chair out from the table. She took her place and he sat facing her. 'I cannot believe you are here.'

She smiled. 'May I ask if you are a merchant?'

'You've heard about my wealth.'

'Oh.' She was covered in confusion.

He waved a hand. 'Please. You were bound to be curious.' He reached for a napkin. 'My antecedents were successful merchants. It was they who made the family fortune. I take no credit, having no head for business – nor much talent for anything, it seems.'

'I doubt that.'

'It's true. Fortunately, enough money was made by my illustrious forbears to leave me in the position of not having to concern myself with things I don't understand.'

'So, how do you spend your time?'

'I enjoy music and astrology. And spending money on people who do possess talent.'

'Was it you who sent me the roses?'

'Yes.'

'And bouquets, to the theatre?'

He nodded. 'Watching you on stage, Colombina, was an inspiration. You became my new bright star. I was devastated when I heard the theatre had closed. Will it re-open soon?'

'I believe so.' She averted her gaze but stole a glance at him. 'Did you come to many performances? Some of our regulars I know by sight, but I don't recollect ever seeing you in the audience.'

'No, well...' It was his turn to look embarrassed. 'I have to confess that, like so many of my fellow Venetians, I sometimes resort to hiding behind the mask.'

The food arrived and was served discreetly. It tasted delicious, as did the wine; full-bodied, infused with the scent of wild berries. She complimented him on his table.

'Thank you,' he said. 'Again I take no credit. I depend entirely upon my excellent household to handle everything. Especially Alberto, here.' He smiled up at the elderly manservant who acknowledged the compliment. 'This rare man has been in my service since I was a boy. Without him I would be lost.'

The servant inclined his head again and, having filled Colombina's glass but not his master's, retreated. 'I drink very little,' her host explained.

281

'I have to admit to having no head for strong drink.'

'Signore Menander...'

'Nicco, please.'

She nodded. 'Nicco. There's something I should tell you.' He looked concerned. 'It's very likely I shall no longer be the Immortali's leading lady.'

'No!' His gloved hand reached for hers.

'I'm afraid so. But, if you don't mind, I would rather not talk about it.'

'Of course.'

'May I ask you something personal?' She caught herself looking at the glove.

'You would like to know why I wear this.' Withdrawing his hand, he rubbed the back of it.

'Only if you want to tell me.'

'It covers an unsightly burn I sustained as a child.'

'I see.' She glanced around the room. 'Do you live here alone?'

'Quite alone.' He offered her fruit from a silver bowl. She declined and he picked out an apple. 'I had always hoped to marry but...' he sighed, 'life does not always turn out the way we hope.'

'Indeed, it does not,' she agreed. 'Is that why you have an interest in astrology?'

'Perhaps.' He took up a knife and sliced the apple in half.

'Please, tell me more about the subject. Do you really believe the stars control our destiny?'

'Undoubtedly.'

'But, if our futures are fixed according to the heavens, that means we have no choice in life. I find that quite upsetting.'

'Not necessarily.' His tone was optimistic. 'By understanding how the heavens move we may direct their influence in our favour.'

'How?'

'Well...' He put down the knife. 'For example, the cross you wear around your neck.'

Her fingers went to touch it.

'Do you bear the amethyst by choice?'

'It was a gift, from my father.'

'And that makes it precious. Of course. But, in what month were you born?'

'In July.'

'I thought as much. Your true gem is one of fire. The ruby. It is rubies you should be wearing, if you wish to draw down upon your future life the very best of fortune.'

She laughed. 'I would love to wear rubies but I fear they will always be beyond the means of an unemployed actress.'

'Not necessarily. There is one who would delight in showering you with rubies, or any other gemstone you may choose to enhance your beauty.'

She smiled and looked away. 'I noticed your lute in the other room and heard you playing as I came up the stairs. Would you play for me now?'

'I should be honoured, if you are finished at the table.'

She nodded and he came to assist her. 'If you are serious about learning more of astrology,' he said, 'I could always devise a birth chart for you.'

'Really?'

'It's the one thing I flatter myself I have a talent for. And, since the gift of rubies would, I agree, be a bit much between friends, it would please me to do this small thing for you. I keep all my books and charts in my study.' He indicated the door over which hung the phases of the moon. 'Yet...' he looked suddenly awkward, 'that is also the room in which I sleep. So, you may not wish...'

'I am happy to enter,' she reassured him.

He smiled and made for the door. 'Your lute,' she reminded him.

'Oh yes.' He went to fetch it.

His study was panelled and appeared to be a mixture of bedchamber, library and gallery. One wall was covered from floor to ceiling in leather-bound volumes. There was a large window with a balcony, no doubt ideal for stargazing, framed by two tall tables. The one to the left was piled high with parchments; the one on the right supported a curious object, which appeared to be a model of the world suspended within bands of brass engraved with symbols. Close to the fire stood an expansive desk. His simple bed was tucked in one corner like an afterthought.

On the other walls hung an odd assortment of pictures. One depicted a man in a tunic holding a flaming sword above a giant egg. Colombina found herself drawn to another, which was bordered by arcane symbols. At the top was a single large eye with lines radiating out to some other strange images. There was a naked man supporting a sphere; and a woman in white who appeared to be trying to conceal the fact she only had one leg. This, together with something Colombina caught sight of in the bottom right-hand corner made her laugh.

'What is it?' asked Nicco.

'The man in this picture.' She pointed to the image in the corner, a likeness of the man she knew as Hermes. 'I know him.'

'That's not possible,' he said, joining her.

'No, really. I've met him on more than one occasion.'

'But, Colombina. This is Hermes Trismegisto. And he lived more than two thousand years ago.'

60

olombina stared at Nicco then looked back at the picture. 'But it's just like him.'

He smiled at her, somewhat condescendingly she thought. 'Hermes Trismegistos was an Egyptian sage who lived and walked with the ancients such as Moses.'

'But...'

Indicating a chair by the fire, he invited her to sit and brought her a glass of the delicious wine; then he settled himself at his desk. Taking up his pen, he asked for the date and time of her birth. She told him the day but had no idea of the time. 'That will make the prediction less accurate,' he said, eyes fixed on a chart. 'But it will still be useful.'

He soon became engrossed and eventually she put down her glass and went to look over his shoulder. He wrote swiftly with enthusiasm; words, numbers, odd strokes of the pen, all the time lifting papers and referring to charts. She placed a hand on his shoulder. 'You said you would play for me.'

He looked up. 'I am so sorry. I get carried away.' He left the desk and picked up his lute. 'I'm afraid I'm not much of a host.' She went back to her chair and he brought his to the fire.

His playing was entrancing. Only once before had she heard such exquisite music, made by a man who had no right to produce so heavenly a sound. She experienced a sense of peace as she gazed into the flames, disappointment when he stopped. But he only paused to refill her glass and, when he continued, she found herself drifting into a dreamlike state. She had not felt this happy since... Allowing herself to think back to happier times with Arlecchino, she reflected on how different this was.

Being with Arlecchino had always been exciting, stimulating yet also unnerving. With Nicco she felt safe.

'I fell in love with you the first time I heard you sing,' she heard him say. She looked at him. 'Do you remember the words of the song? Something about the sun raging.'

Perhaps it was the effects of the wine. Without hesitation, she began to sing:

Sun rages against its own fire, moon weeps for lack of it.
My lady outshines the one, shames the other with her mysteries.
What gifts might I bring to win her heart..?

She broke off and started to cry.

Immediately he stopped playing, put down the lute and came and knelt before her. 'Please don't cry, Colombina. I never meant to make you sad. I would do anything rather than hurt you.'

'It's not you,' she said. 'Or your playing. It's beautiful.' She looked into his concerned grey eyes and their intensely sad expression drew from her an overwhelming need to reassure him. Reaching out, she stroked his soft hair.

He took hold of her hand and kissed her fingers. 'All that I own I would give to make you happy.'

'I am happy,' she whispered, and, without pausing to think what she was doing, leant forward and kissed him on the cheek.

Before she realised what was happening, he was drawing her to her feet. Within his embrace she found something she had lacked these past long weeks. Here was someone who needed her, but also wanted to make her happy. The warmth and comfort of his magnificent home, delicious food, hypnotic wine, sublime lute playing; all had combined and worked on a spirit starved of affection. And now his kiss was tender and she responded.

He broke off. 'I'm sorry.'

'Don't be,' she told him.

'I have no wish to take advantage.'

'You wouldn't be.'

He wiped a tear from her cheek. 'Are you sure?'

She nodded.

He drew her close again and, when they kissed a second time, she was filled with longing. There was a pleasant scent about him, exotic yet strangely familiar. The room around her seemed to melt, then rush away. She allowed herself to be swept up into his arms and carried to the bed. When he laid her down, she felt she was floating.

His face appeared blurred above hers.

⌁

t was light when Colombina woke. She was naked and so was Nicco. She tried to remember what had happened. They had made love, she knew. The signs and pleasure lingered. But the details were elusive, like a dream that hides behind sleep's curtain. She was facing away from him, the front of his body pressing into her back. His muscular arm rested on her pillow, forming an arc above her head as if to shield her. She was gazing at his left hand. But now it was uncovered and there was no sign of an unsightly burn, just a long white scar running across the back of it.

He withdrew his hand and she felt him move away then leave the bed. She rolled over and watched him walk to the window. Naked, he stood looking out, silhouetted against a pale yellow dawn. He looked different. He no longer slouched and his shoulders appeared broader. 'Nicco?'

'Yes.' His voice sounded deeper.

'Is everything all right?'

'Yes,' he said again. 'Everything is perfect.'

Something unsettling stirred within her. She sat up too quickly and the room spun around. She touched her temple, closed her eyes briefly. 'You seem different,' she said.

He laughed.

The sound of it sent fear rippling through her. 'Who are you?'

Reaching out to the table on his left, he swept off the parchments and picked up an object they had been concealing. Turning, he raised the mask of Brighella in front of his face. With a scream, she covered her eyes but there was no blocking out the horrible image. The night of terror she had endured in a barn rushed out of her past and she witnessed again a hideous demon raping a girl who responded to its caresses.

Nicco, Brighella, whoever he was, began to laugh. His laughter grew loud as she scrambled out of bed and rushed to dress. She wanted to cry with shame and humiliation, but was determined not to. He threw down the mask and came and grabbed hold of her. She fought but he restrained her, laughing still.

She burst into tears. 'I hate you. What kind of devil are you?'

'Your kind, obviously.' He forced a kiss on her lips.

She continued to struggle, hit him as hard as she could across the face. That only served to amuse him. 'You and I are two of a kind.'

'I am nothing like you.'

'Oh yes you are! I know your secret. Sweet Colombina, the girl who set out to wed her own brother. Spat in the face of God for the sake of raw passion.'

'I love Arlecchino.'

'The man who raped you? I was there, remember. I witnessed it. And do you recall what he said once he'd finished? Brighella, the lady is all yours.' He let her go and she staggered back. 'I could have had you then, but instead I tried to help you. You rejected my help and, if you hadn't been a lady, I daresay you would have spat in my face too. That was when I began to desire you. Broken and humiliated, your eyes still burned and your belly was full of fire. But he'd filled it with something more. And still you continued to harbour an irrational fondness for the man! Even now, when he's thrown your love back in your face for the sake of his immortal soul, you cling to a silly romantic dream.'

She rounded on him. 'You cannot help loving someone.'

'Love?' He laughed with derision as he pulled on a black silk robe. 'Don't you know? Love doesn't exist. It's better to be feared than loved.'

'I'm not afraid of you.'

'I know,' he said, tying the cord. 'That's why I find you so appealing.' He came to her. 'Join me, Colombina and I'll give you everything you ever wanted.'

'Don't be ridiculous. Passing yourself off as the richest man in Venice!'

'Oh, but I am! Really. I am the richest man in Venice.' He flung out both arms. 'I own all this. I own a fleet of ships. I own lands that stretch further than your imagination. And… what's best of all, I own the Immortali!'

She was shaking her head.

'It's true. I am the true master. You and the rest of the puppets dance to *my* tune. And what a fine tune it is!' He smiled as he snatched up his lute and strummed it harshly. 'Did you not even recognise my playing? It was the one thing I made no effort to disguise. Oh, and I did make one slip. Your song, about the sun raging. You sang it at only one performance – your first. In Padua.'

'Padua?' she gasped.

'I was there, in the audience.'

She shook her head and sat down. This could not be happening. How could she have been drawn in and duped so easily?

Brighella sat next to her. Taking hold of her hand, he slid it under his robe.

'No!' She pushed him away.

'Last night you were not so unobliging.'

She felt sick at the thought but could remember nothing.

'Did you enjoy my wine?'

She frowned briefly then glared at him fiercely. So, that was how it was done? 'What you did was no better than rape. You are despicable!'

'I know. So, what do you say, Colombina? Are you ready to become rich and despicable with me?'

'Never.' She got up and, hurriedly fastening her dress, made for the door. It was locked.

He took a key from his pocket.

'Let me out!' she demanded.

'Not yet.' He grabbed her by the wrist. 'There are things you must see.'

61

righella yanked Colombina to the bottom of his bed then wrenched back a drape, revealing a door set in the panelling. This he unlocked and opened. Forcing her through into a gallery, he locked the door behind them.

Light filtering through high leaded windows all along one side fell on paintings lining the opposite wall. There were classical statues and urns on plinths. Books were piled high on tables. Some lay open and, as he dragged Colombina onward, she glimpsed their coloured pages glittering with gold.

Stopping at a marble table on which stood a silver casket, he flipped open the lid. 'In case you needed convincing.' He thrust in his hand and brought out a fistful of jewels. Allowing most to fall back, he retained one heavy gold necklace, which he held in front of her face. 'Your birthstone. *Who can find a virtuous woman for her price is beyond rubies?*'

'Go to hell!' she muttered, and he laughed.

'What need have I of a virtuous woman?' Yanking her close, he forced his lips on hers.

Colombina struggled and, at last, he let her go.

Running to the end of the room, she was brought to a sudden stop by the sight of two exquisite portraits: one of a woman with a mysterious smile, the other of a young man with a mop of curly hair. Beneath them, on a table, lay two small black volumes.

'Recognise those?' She turned and glared at him. 'Go ahead. Take a look.'

There was no mistaking the knobbly black leather and silver clasp, and, when she pressed the imp motif on the front, the book sprang open. Yellow leaves fanned out, some filled with exquisite drawings.

'Beautiful, aren't they?'

Taking out the folded parchment he had shown her in the upper room of the palazzo, she suddenly had a feeling she was being watched, and, glancing up, found herself looking into the eyes of the smiling woman. 'I take it this is the painting referred to in this letter?'

'That's right. I always get what I want.'

'You told me you had no interest in it.'

He shrugged.

The portrait was so skilfully painted the viewer might have believed the flesh was real; but there was something odd about the background. The face of the young man in the painting next to it looked familiar. He was clasping a slender cross and pointing upward into the heavens. 'John the Baptist,' said Brighella. 'Do you notice anything?'

'The faces. They look the same.'

'They do indeed.'

A memory was stirring – a dream in which an elderly man stood at an easel painting a fresh-faced young man with curly hair who had turned and smiled at her. She said nothing of this. 'So, this woman is really a young man. Is that what you're saying? And he is the one who wrote this letter.'

'Exactly.' Standing beside her now, he gazed at the portrait. 'A masterpiece! Beyond price. I've been told the King of France owns one just like it. His, of course, is a fake.'

She slipped the letter back between the pages, closed the clasp and returned the book to the table. 'Well, that's all very interesting but, if it's the only reason…'

'It isn't.' He grabbed her again and pushed her through the door into darkness. As he forced her down some steep wooden steps, she lost her footing and cried out. He yanked her back up as she pleaded with him to release her but he continued on down with scant consideration for her safety. The deeper they went, the warmer it became and there was an unpleasant smell. Was it sulphur? Below them red fire glowed.

At last her foot touched solid earth and Brighella let her go. The floor felt uneven. Not daring to move, she stared at the fiery mouth of a small cylindrical furnace.

Brighella lit a lamp. Now she saw that the room was vast, more like a cave. A few paces from her, the floor evened out into polished black stone. Painted on its surface were arcane symbols, the largest of which was a five-pointed star set in a perfect circle. There were two long tables covered in wooden structures, glass vessels, clay crucibles. There were also rows of sharp metal instruments. A cabinet filled with drawers stood against one wall. On top of that were some large glass jars containing things she was glad she could not see clearly. On the floor in one corner lay a heap of white bones.

Brighella stood close to the furnace and beckoned her over. She took a step towards him then screamed.

He laughed. 'It's stuffed,' he told her. The creature of nightmares lurking in the shadows had the body of a wolf, teeth bared. An eagle's head stuck out of its shaggy neck and a grey human face was embedded in the chest. 'He was only a convict.' Brighella waved a hand in the direction of the jars. 'His brain's up there.'

'This place is disgusting.'

He appeared affronted. 'This is a place of wonders. Here I come close.'

'To what?'

'To the truth, to essence. To understanding and control.'

'I believe you are mad.'

'Perhaps.'

She shivered in spite of the heat. 'Why have you brought me here?'

'I told you. I have things to show you.'

'And if I don't want to see them?'

'You must.' He came towards her. 'And you must understand. Knowledge is nothing, if not shared.'

'But what if I can't understand? I am only a stupid girl. I beg of you, please let me go.'

'You underestimate yourself, Colombina.' He narrowed his eyes. 'Or perhaps it's my intelligence you underestimate. Naive you may be. Stupid you never were. And, once you have shared the experience, you will be neither.'

'What experience?' Panic was rising. 'If you intend to conjure demons, like you did in the barn…'

His face lit up. 'Ah! So, my spell did work after all. And you told me you saw nothing. No, my dear, no demons this time. I've brought you here to watch a man die.'

62

'ear God!' Colombina looked round frantically for some poor wretch bound and gagged in the shadows.

Brighella laughed and slid an arm about her waist. 'Don't worry. I'm not going to murder anyone. I never engage in *mindless* violence. Everything I do is for a purpose. And, since this man's death is largely of your making...'

'What do you mean?' She pulled free.

'Today, in Rome, a heretic will burn, condemned by his own writings with which you have so obligingly provided the Inquisition.'

'But I know nothing of the Inquisition.'

'No, but they know about you. And, I might say, are very grateful. Seven long years he languished in their prisons while they searched for evidence. Now they have it, courtesy of your good self. Surely you noticed there were only two books on the table upstairs?' She frowned. 'The third went to Rome.'

'I don't understand. Where did you find my books?'

'Where you left them.'

'You went to my home?' He smiled. 'When?'

'I paid two visits. The first proved unsuccessful, in one respect. Although it turned out beneficial. But, until I had Jacopo Bruno's letter in my possession, I had no idea of where to look for the books. Then, when you gave me the letter in exchange for helping Arlecchino, I was able to go straight to their hiding place. One of the two you left behind in the drawer contained just what I needed – letters from the heretic to his relative, Jacopo, together with others sent by learned men from all over Europe. There was even one from Doctor John Dee, magician to the English Queen. Imagine that! And some documents verifying the heretic's support for the Copernican view of a sun-centred universe have also helped to condemn him. To confess that alone is anathema. Yet the reckless man went further, expounding belief in other worlds, multiple universes and even man's potential to move from one to another. It is those secret writings filled with thrilling yet dangerous thoughts which I sent to Rome, but not before I made copies.'

Colombina had heard only snatches of what he had been saying; she was preoccupied with something more personal. 'When was the first time you visited my home?'

'During the month of October.'

She steeled herself and took a deep breath. 'Did you murder my mother?'

'How very astute! I prefer to regard it as putting her out of her misery. I did the poor woman a favour. Not only her, since she told me all about her indiscretion with Pantelone – Arlecchino as he was then. Her state of mind was already precarious. It was only a matter of time before she confessed her guilty secret. So I became her confessor, then her secret – your secret, Colombina – was given over into my safekeeping.'

'You imagined by murdering my mother you were helping me?'

'I would do anything for you, Colombina. I said so in the invitation. Nicco told you, too, when his playing reduced you to tears. You liked Nicco, didn't you? Again he put his arm around her waist and gave it a squeeze. 'Well, I can be Nicco any time you like.'

Filled with revulsion, she longed to push him away. By now, though, she knew him to be insane. Horror at what she had heard, the repellent surroundings, her deep loathing of the man must not be allowed to get in the way of her need to escape. She feared his dark powers. His physical strength was undeniable. Creating a fuss, trying to fight might lead to him turning on her. She had one weapon to use against him: his fondness for her. She almost laughed – obsession was closer. But whatever it was, it seemed genuine. So she tolerated his embrace, endured the foul touch of his lips on her neck as her eyes scanned the walls for a way out.

The door at the top of the steps was not locked but to escape by that route would leave her trapped in the gallery. And there appeared to be no other way out of this dreadful place. Yet perhaps there might be. Some of the things in this room were too large and heavy to have been brought down a rickety staircase. He nuzzled her ear. 'If you're looking for a way out, you're wasting your time.'

Despair almost buckled her knees. Could he even read her mind?

Apart from his interest in her, she knew he had another weakness – pride. 'Well then,' she said, extricating herself from his embrace. 'This man you say is about to die in Rome. Tell me about him and how you propose to witness his death.'

She had surprised him. That boosted her confidence and, since she could not believe that even he could do what he claimed he was about to, she saw nothing to lose by playing along with his delusions.

'The heretic's name is Giordano Bruno,' he told her keenly. 'He was a Dominican who, from his youth, put forward ideas which brought him unwelcome attention. He ended up roaming the world, preaching, lecturing. He would stay in one place until his outspoken views forced him to flee. Seven years ago he came here to Venice and I became his most brilliant pupil. We were close, like spiritual father and son.' His expression clouded. 'Or so I thought. He turned against me simply because I pointed out the inherent weakness of his world view, the same weakness which plagues all good men.'

'And what is that?'

'Giordano seeks to turn all knowledge to the good, refuses to consider other possibilities.'

'What other possibilities?'

He ignored the question. 'The man I idolised, loved almost – if love had been part of my nature – excluded me from his circle. And that was enough to close the doors of learning.'

'Surely not to you? You said yourself, you always get what you want.'

He threw her a look of desperation. 'Not this time. Giordano possessed what I wanted more than anything, the secret wisdom of a man so close to God as to be a living immortal.'

'He's that special?'

His expression hardened. 'He's a fool. A blind and arrogant fool. Whilst seeing merit in the meanest of men, he makes enemies of the most powerful.'

'Yourself included.'

He flashed her a glare. 'I had to do something. My chance came and I took it.'

'You betrayed him to the Inquisition.'

'I did what was necessary.'

'You must hate him very much to want to see him die.'

'Hate is not something I indulge in. I told you, knowledge is what matters. It's knowledge gained from his writings contained in your books that have enabled me to create the miracle you are about to see. This has taken me weeks to prepare. Now everything's ready. How ironic that, through the application of Giordano's own theories, I will be the first to witness what no man has ever seen: a man's soul – *Giordano's soul* – departing the body. If, as I fully expect, he refuses to recant and dies in the flames, then his soul, more than any other, will be fit to transcend this base world.'

Some instinct within Colombina reached out unexpectedly. 'Brighella... Nicco... whichever man you truly are, it seems to me you harbour a longing for goodness.'

He glared at her briefly then his eyes narrowed. 'It's nearly time.' Gripping her by the arm, he drew her to the mouth of the furnace. 'Look deep into the flames.'

63

olombina had no choice but to obey. She watched as Brighella went to the cabinet and opened a drawer. From it he took a crucible, which he carried with care to the table.

Coming back to the furnace, he used thick cloths to remove its domed top. Bright yellow light from the fire lit the room, sending shadows fleeing to remote corners. Colombina shielded her eyes from the heat and the glare.

Brighella picked up the crucible and, muttering words incomprehensible to her, used iron tongs to place it like a nest amongst the flames. As he did so, she saw it contained powder the colour of dried blood. He continued his incantation as pungent black smoke began curling upward; then, selecting a bone from the pile on the floor, he pushed that into the front of the furnace.

'What should I be looking for?' she asked.

'Be quiet!'

He took a phial from the drawer and, swilling round the thick silver liquid it contained, raised the glass to the level of his eye. He spoke more arcane words, kissed the glass then broke the neck. When he poured the contents into the crucible it hissed and spat out metallic globules, which shot in all directions. Colombina stepped back.

'Stay where you are!' Taking a handful of what looked like salt from a vessel on the table, he sprinkled it over the flames. To Colombina's amazement the fire died instantly. He quickly replaced the dome. 'Keep looking into the alambic,' he told her.

At first nothing happened and she sensed his frustration.

After a while, the mouth of the furnace turned red. Bathed in ruddy light, Brighella's face appeared demonic. The glow intensified, changing from red to orange to yellow. When it faded to white, light began pouring out of the opening.

Colombina gasped in wonder to see the floating stream rise then hover above the furnace. Brighella stood behind her and she shuddered as he whispered in her ear, 'It's happening.'

Light continued to pour forth until the inside of the furnace turned pitch-black. Before her eyes hung a magical dawn and she stared in disbelief at the shimmering apparition, astonishment increasing as images appeared within it. At first they were indistinct but she could hear voices; then, as the scene came into focus, she saw a crowd. People were jostling, trying to break through a cordon, only to be beaten back by guards in striped uniforms. The image faded; then another appeared. 'He's there,' gasped Brighella.

Colombina focussed on a slow procession. In its midst walked a small thin man with a scanty beard. The harder she concentrated, the better view she had of him and she saw that he was barefoot, led by a chain around the neck. He was dressed in a sheet splashed with crosses, black devils and red flames. Either side of him walked monks. Some made the sign of the cross. Others muttered solemn prayers. All kept their heads bowed low.

One monk carried a tall slender crucifix, which he presented to the prisoner's lips. The heretic turned his face away. Men spat on the ground as he passed. Some cursed and damned him to hell. He walked on with head erect and his face became clearer; too clear for Colombina. This was the prisoner she had seen in her dream. 'That man is innocent,' she breathed.

'Silence,' hissed Brighella. The image shivered then disappeared.

Terrified, she felt him grip her arm. If she had broken the spell... but the light began rippling, like the surface of a pool into which a stone is cast; and the image returned.

The prisoner was stripped and tied to an iron stake. Bundles of wood were stacked around his feet. Once again, the cross was put to his lips; but he refused to kiss it. Monks gagged him then piled on more wood mixed with straw, heaping it high, right up to his chin. Colombina tried to extricate herself. 'I don't want to see this.'

Brighella tightened his grip.

The monks began chanting and singing litanies. Once again the crucifix was held up before the heretic. Again, he averted his gaze. The pile of wood and straw was lit and the monks scurried back. Flames quickly consumed the straw; wisps of blue smoke rose.

The crowd went wild, their savage joy building to a frenzy as the wood caught light. Fire crackled and licked greedily over the bundles, up towards the pale anguished face. Soon it was singeing the heretic's beard; he choked on black smoke.

Then came the moment Colombina saw his terrified eyes fill with pain. She heard a bestial grunt, saw his head thrash. His eyes grew round and bulged, as though being forced from his head. Neck muscles strained in a futile effort to lift his face above the column of fire. Wreathed in furious flame, his hair caught alight and the gag was consumed, freeing him to give vent to true agony.

A sound more terrible than anything Colombina had ever heard filled the room, echoing through the cavernous space, assaulting her senses. 'Stop this!' she screamed at Brighella.

He glanced down at her with a satisfied smile. 'I can't. This is happening.'

'I refuse to witness any more of this abomination.'

'You will watch until the end.'

'No!' She fought and lashed out at him. 'Do what you will. Nothing would induce me to watch any more!'

He roared out a curse and, pulling her to him, raised his fist.

She cowered and shut her eyes. The blow never came. Instead he hurled her across the room. She fell heavily and slid over the polished floor. Scrambling onto her knees, she clasped her amethyst cross and began to pray for the man whose pitiful cries filled her ears.

Brighella cursed her again and threatened to silence her. But she would not stop. She begged God to show mercy, called on the blessed Virgin to intercede. 'Please, God,' she prayed, 'hasten the end of this innocent man.'

Brighella was beside himself with rage. Out of the corner of her eye, Colombina could see that he was torn between continuing to watch the obscene spectacle and crossing the floor to beat her into submission. But then, when she looked at him fully, she noticed something else, something other than rage in his eyes. Was it fear? She shut her eyes tight and prayed harder for the soul of the man who was surely now only moments from death. But his screams persisted so she shouted her words in an effort to drown out the sound.

The ordeal seemed to go on forever. Colombina was almost screaming with Giordano when, at last, he stopped. She gasped with relief, thanked God and hung her head. The silence felt like a shroud; yet welcome. She began to cry.

Thinking she heard the beating of wings, she looked up. The shimmering light was blank and had taken on the shape of a bird that resembled a dove. It came and hovered over her, wings flapping gently. It remained on the spot growing steadily smaller as though it was she who was moving away. In the end, all she could see was a small spot of light, a shining white star which suddenly burst then disappeared.

'What did you see?' demanded Brighella.

'Nothing.' She got to her feet. It was then that she realised she had been kneeling within the five-pointed star.

Once she stepped from it, he seized her by the shoulders. 'Tell me!' He shook her. 'Tell me! What did you see?'

She faced him defiantly.

His features were twisted; his voice became a snarl. 'I was mistaken. You've proved yourself unworthy. Just like Franceschina.'

'Franceschina?'

'Her heart was good and hard. But she was vain and stupid. I thought your mind superior. Perhaps it is. But you, Colombina… you…' his expression spoke of utter contempt, 'are too human!'

'Did you poison Franceschina?'

'Of course.' He dragged her to the wall. 'She stood in your way. You have me to thank for becoming leading lady and this is how you repay me.'

Now courage deserted Colombina. Convinced he was going to kill her, she begged him not to. His right fist was clenched as he raised it but, to her amazement, instead of punching her, he sent it crashing against a raised brick. A door of stone swung open before her. 'Get out,' he spat and thrust her away. She stared at him. 'Get out! Before I change my mind.'

She ran through the opening and up a spiral stone stairway. Within a few turns she came to a wooden door. It was padlocked. She continued on up, round and round, until her chest hurt. Not daring to believe he had really let her go, she expected any second to hear footsteps behind her.

The higher she climbed, the lighter it became, yet there was no telling where the light was coming from. Blood pounded in her head, blackness swam before her eyes. At last, she came to a small arched window. Gasping for breath, she gazed at the bronze statuette on the sill; a young man with wings on his hat and heels. Hermes, messenger of the gods. This was the very one she had stolen from Signore Panesse! Now, for the first time, she noticed the figure was pointing upward, like the young St. John the Baptist in the painting.

It gave her hope and she ran on, cried out for joy when she caught sight of another door. She prayed it would not be locked, turned the ring and pushed hard. The door swung open.

Relief swept through her; she took great gulps of air. As she had expected, she had come out far above the Grand Canal. She hurried down a flight of iron steps, becoming suddenly aware of her bare feet as they trod the cold metal. But, on reaching the bottom, there was nowhere to run. She was standing on a narrow quay hemmed in by high spiked railings and, to get away, she had to cross the canal. Drenched in sweat yet shivering, she felt hope drain away. This was why Brighella had let her go. There was no escape! Either he would come and drag her back down to torment her, or leave her to die of cold and starvation.

She went to the edge and looked at the canal. Suddenly, it seemed to provide the answer. After all, what was she running to? She had no life. She had just spent a night of shame in the arms of a man she detested. His evil had penetrated not only her body, but her soul. The green water made a lapping sound, rather like the wings of the magical dove. Perhaps this was how it was meant to be. End it here!

She no longer felt afraid. A stiff breeze was blowing from the east. Within it, she seemed to catch the scent of worlds she would never visit; but she did not care. All she wanted now was to be at peace.

64

ust one more step. Colombina told herself that fear would not last long, not once she sank beneath the green waters. Then she would be fighting for breath, trying to stay alive. And yet she *did* want to die. No, that was untrue. She wanted to be dead. Dying, that was the hard part. How could she doubt it, after what she had just witnessed?

And after death. What then? To the bitter end, Giordano had refused to kiss the cross. Why, when he was so clearly a good man? The vision she had seen confirmed this in her mind. But, by refusing to be shriven, surely he was condemning his soul to hell? Perhaps the shining dove existed only in her imagination? Brighella had not seen it.

She began to cry in a strange kind of way: silently, without sobbing. Tears flowed, their salty taste combining with the sea breeze. She did not know if she was crying for Giordano or herself; but, in place of sorrow, swelled the ache of injustice. What kind of world was this, where the good were tortured to death and evil prospered?

She sank to her knees, gazed out across the canal; she could hardly see for tears. Then she heard someone calling. 'Signorina!' A man was waving from a barge. Another turned the craft towards her. Colombina scrambled to her feet.

'Please help me,' she called.

The barge came alongside and the man who had hailed her helped her board. She felt overjoyed yet embarrassed by her dishevelled appearance. 'I take it you'd like to cross the canal?'

'Yes,' she replied. 'Oh yes. Thank you.'

'The bargemen of Venice are always ready to help a lady.' He unfurled the sail while his companion pushed off with an oar. The craft swung round on a stiffening breeze and sped off in the direction of St. Mark's.

So, there was still goodness in the world; and kindness too. Giordano Bruno had died for his beliefs. He could have recanted, kissed the cross and been spared but had remained true to his vision. Suddenly Colombina understood that to have thrown her own life away through lack of courage would have been a betrayal of his.

The sun shone. Water glittered. In spite of not knowing what the future held, she felt happy. In a way, she ought to be grateful to Brighella; through him she had gained an insight. Then, when she looked back towards his palazzo, fear pierced her like a knife. He was standing on the quay.

His sudden appearance was an affront to the pure light of day. She held her breath as he reached out towards her, fearing he might have the power to sink the boat. Regretting deeply she had drawn others into danger, she glanced nervously at her rescuers. But when she looked back, to her enormous relief, Brighella had disappeared.

Setting foot on dry land, Colombina thanked the men and apologised for having no money to pay them. They dismissed the suggestion. 'If it ever got back to Rosina that we hadn't come to the aid of Venice's leading lady, we'd never hear the end of it.'

The other laughed. 'She'd be serving us rancid wine for weeks.'

Colombina smiled and thanked them again; then she hurried through the piazzetta, noticing as she did a long rope stretching down from the top of the Campanile to the Doge's palace. She wondered briefly what it was for but was more concerned with reaching somewhere less public. Her mood of optimism fled as well-dressed women sniggered, men laughed and made lewd comments. She was not surprised; she could easily have been taken for a street-walker. On entering St. Mark's Square, she glanced up at the horologium with its signs of the zodiac around the face and it reminded her of things she would rather forget.

Plunging down a side street, she came to a sudden stop. A corpse was lying next to a canal and a woman in black was standing over it, crying bitterly. Colombina's heart went out to her; but she had to turn from the sight and stench of the bloated body. When, at last, she reached the barber's house, it was the housekeeper who let her in. The woman frowned disapprovingly but made no comment. Colombina ran upstairs with nothing in mind other than to strip and scrub herself clean of the taint of Brighella. She burst through the door then stopped.

Pedrolino sprang to his feet. 'I've been so worried.'

She let him take her in his arms, suppressing her shame. 'I found this,' he said and held up the invitation. 'I went to the Rialto to question the black gondolier but he wasn't there. The others wouldn't tell me anything. I decided to wait for you here. What happened to you, Colombina? You look dreadful.'

She could not bring herself to tell him. 'Pedrolino. Would you mind leaving the room while I change?'

'Of course. I'll wait outside.'

As soon as the door was closed, Colombina wrenched off her gown. If there had been a stove in the room she would have burned it. But there was not even a fire, just ashes, so she rolled up the dress and pushed it down into a basket of dirty linen. Then she washed thoroughly. Afterwards, only her skin felt clean. She put on a plain dress then invited Pedrolino in. 'Arlecchino has returned to the theatre,' he told her.

'I know.'

'He's planning a comeback. Tonight. I'm worried, Colombina. There's something wrong. Something different about him…'

'What can I do?' She shrugged. 'Arlecchino has made it very clear I no longer play a part in his life.'

'Perhaps. But I know he still needs you. For his sake… for the sake of the company, please come back.'

She shook her head briefly then looked away.

'Well then, if not for the sake of anyone or anything else, will you do it for me? I foresee a disaster. I don't know what happened between you and Arlecchino – and, like I said, I don't want to. But I'd like to repair the damage done to the two people I love best in all the world.'

'I doubt anyone can do that.'

'Nevertheless. I'm begging you, Colombina. You're still one of us. The Immortali can't survive without you.'

She frowned, thought a moment then sighed. 'Very well.'

'Thank you. But first you need rest. I'll wake you when it's time.'

She had not expected to fall asleep. The next thing she knew she was being gently shaken. 'We must go, Colombina. The performance begins in an hour.'

Walking back into the theatre was the most difficult thing she had ever done. The actors were assembled and her arrival was greeted with embarrassed smiles, polite nods and silence. She held her breath as Pantelone strode towards her. 'I am not here to act,' she told him. 'Pedrolino asked me to come.'

'I'm glad he did.'

There was no sign of Arlecchino. 'Where is he?' she whispered when Pedrolino returned in full costume.

'On stage.'

She glanced at the stage, empty apart from a long wooden crate, which resembled a coffin. 'He's not..?

'No one knows what he has planned,' said Pantelone. 'He refuses to speak to me. He hasn't even confided in Pedrolino, other than to say, when the performance begins, he wants us all in full costume out here, watching with the audience. His mood is sour, Colombina. You and I can expect nothing more. But to try to make a comeback in this frame of mind is courting disaster.'

'Can't you stop him?'

Both men looked at her. 'We hoped,' said Pedrolino, 'that you might...'

She shook her head bitterly. 'He would not listen to me.'

The theatre began to fill. This being the first performance in weeks, it was soon packed. Many were standing. The atmosphere felt tense yet the customary tingle of excitement was missing. 'He's given the musicians instructions,' whispered Pedrolino as a dirge-like air began.

The actors filed into the theatre.

Expectation grew but nothing happened. A man shouted for Arlecchino. Others joined in. The demand turned into a chorus. Still nothing happened. Pantelone wrung his hands. Just when it seemed the house would erupt, the music stopped.

The lid of the crate began to move. Spectators gasped, some hushed each other. When the lid tipped then toppled over with a loud bang, several jumped and cried out. There were gasps. Women screamed as a grey ghostly figure rose up out of the coffin.

65

'ood God!' gasped Pantelone. 'He's not wearing the mask.

Arlecchino stepped out of the crate. Not only was he dressed in grey, he had covered his face and hair in ashes. 'I heard someone calling. Whom do you seek?'

'Arlecchino,' came the reply.

'Who is he?'

There were confused mutterings then a man shouted, 'You are. Aren't you?'

Others laughed.

Arlecchino shook his head as he came to the front of the stage. 'I might have been. Once. But have you not heard? Arlecchino is dead.'

There was a roar of disapproval.

'He was cut to pieces. Surely you've noticed your canals are running with blood?'

Disapproval grew to outrage. 'Well, if you're not Arlecchino,' came an angry voice, 'then who the devil are you?'

'I am his ghost.'

There was a loud gasp. Women whimpered. A few fled their seats.

'I am a wandering shade stripped of colour. I am all that is left of a brilliant tradition.'

'I can't let him do this,' muttered Pedrolino.

'I am a living corpse doomed to wander through countless ages. Unrecognised, no longer celebrated. Once I was splendid in livery and character. I brought laughter into grey lives. Now I am dull.'

'You most certainly are!' The comment was followed by raucous laughter.

'My costume lies discarded and empty. But it's still for hire. You, Sir,' he beckoned to the man who had shouted. 'You can play Arlecchino for a night, then send his skin back in the morning to be dusted off and given to another.'

'We want Arlecchino,' several called.

'I told you, he's dead.'

'We want Arlecchino.' It grew into a chant.

'He's dead. He's dead. Dead, you fools! Why do you keep shouting for a dead man?'

In her distress, Colombina had not noticed Pedrolino leave her side; but now she saw him step on stage, followed by Renaldo. They grabbed Arlecchino, an arm a piece, and dragged him back. 'Excuse us, dear people,' Pedrolino shouted above his curses, 'but we have to remove a madman from the stage.' They bundled him off stage.

Peals of laughter broke the tension and there was loud applause.

It had been heartrending for Colombina to watch but the audience were happy to accept that this aberration on the part of Arlecchino had merely been a piece of nonsense. Pantelone took the stage. Colombina hurried to the anteroom.

She found Arlecchino sitting, head in hands, on the bench, Pedrolino standing over him. 'I'll leave you two alone,' he said and closed the door behind him. Colombina sat next to Arlecchino, spoke his name softly.

He took his hands from his eyes. 'I am dead.'

'No. But you're hurt. Your body has healed but your spirit needs time.'

'I tried to tell them. But they wouldn't listen.'

'They didn't want to hear it. To them, you are immortal.'

He shook his head. 'I used to think so. Now I know different. I wanted to make them understand. Tell them what I've learned about darkness.'

'But that's not why they come. They know about the dark. They come here seeking light. And want to leave touched by magic.'

'My magic's gone.'

'I don't believe that.'

He glared at her. 'When I lay bleeding like a butchered pig, you should have left me to die. Why did you save me?'

'Because I love you.'

'Love!' His laugh was bitter. 'I never wanted it. Never felt it, until I met you. Then I let myself fall in love and… what did you think you were doing?'

'I didn't think.' She looked away. 'And yes, I sinned. But I was ready to go to hell if it meant I could spend my mortal life with you.' She faced him again. 'But you would have married me in ignorance, Arlecchino. You weren't to blame. I don't believe a loving God would have condemned your soul along with mine.'

'You would have sacrificed your soul, for me?'

'Yes. And I would still. On stage you spoke of death. Today I witnessed death of the most horrible kind. It has no place in the hearts of the living. You told me yourself we have a duty to celebrate life.'

'Did I?'

'Yes. And nothing is more true. In the blinking of an eye, each one of us reaches the moment when flesh fails. Wasted by disease, blackened by fire or putrefied in water, it will happen to us, sooner or later. Death is certain, out of our control. What is within our control is *how* we live.' She grasped his hand.

He looked at her mournfully. 'Now I've ruined the company.'

She smiled and shook her head. 'No, Pedrolino saved the performance. But the people are confused. It's you they want.'

'I've nothing to offer them.' He frowned up at his costume hanging from a nail. 'Not any more.'

'You have yourself.'

'An empty shell.' He leaned back against the wall and sighed. 'You don't understand, Colombina, I was telling the truth. Arlecchino *is* dead, or might as well be.'

Then suddenly she did understand as the barber's words came back: *Will this young man thank you, once he knows the score?* 'You're wrong,' she said, bringing her hand to rest upon his knee. 'What you fear exists only in your mind.'

He caught hold of her hand as she slid it inside his thigh. 'What are you doing?'

Kneeling in front of him, she removed his hand from hers then parted his knees. 'Your physical wounds are healed,' she whispered.

Easing the waist of his breeches down to reveal the scar above his member, she traced it with the tip of her tongue.

He shut his eyes and groaned. Sharing his thrill, she cupped his swelling mound. He soon outgrew her grasp and leant forward to grab her.

But she sprang away, and, snatching his costume from the nail, flung it at him. 'They're calling for you, Arlecchino.'

He stared at her; then frowned at his suit. 'Later then,' he said and exchanged grey for motley.

66

olombina had not lied; the crowd *was* calling for Arlecchino. Seconds after he left the room, she heard deafening cheers and went to watch.

'Reports of my death have been exaggerated,' he told the audience. 'I'm here to confirm that the dreary impostor has been dumped in the canal. Be gracious enough to accept true Arlecchino, courtesy of my good self.' He bowed, but straightened with difficulty. 'Please forgive me if I refrain from doing back-flips for a while.'

With laughter ringing in her ears, Colombina ran along the passage-way, down the steps, through the kitchen and on up the marble staircase until she reached her room. Breathless yet deliriously happy, she changed into her costume. Whatever happened now, she had restored the man she loved and returned Arlecchino to the people.

On her way back she could still hear laughter. And, when she joined Arlecchino on stage, the reaction of the crowd was overwhelming. He presented his leading lady with pride and their dance was accompanied by glorious music, cheers and applause. Yet, within this celebratory mood, Colombina noticed something troubling – a tall, hooded figure standing at the back of the theatre.

Throughout the dance, she could not keep her gaze from straying to the monk and, when he was joined by others, she began to feel afraid. Some of the audience noticed them too. Several got up and left. But Arlecchino appeared oblivious and whirled her round in a state of in-nocent joy.

As the theatre began to empty, one of the monks pushed his way to the stage. Colombina tried to warn Arlecchino. When the monk whispered in the chief musician's ear the music faltered then failed.

310

Arlecchino brought their dance to a halt. At the same time, armed men poured into the back of the theatre.

Women screamed and, in the rush to get out, there was panic. Pantelone mounted the stage. 'Good Sirs,' he bellowed over the din. 'Why do you interrupt our performance?'

A guard ran up the steps. He thrust a parchment into his hands then laid hands on Colombina. She cried out for him to let her go. Arlecchino came to her aid. His punch sent the man toppling into the pit. More guards ran up and the actors tried to stop them. Pantelone's pleas for order fell on deaf ears and, with Arlecchino embroiled in the fight, Colombina was bundled off stage.

'I demand to know the reason for this outrage,' thundered Pantelone.

'Read the bill,' the guard called back. 'It's clear enough. Your leading lady is accused of witchcraft.'

67

'Let me go!' screamed Colombina, struggling. 'I know nothing of witchcraft.' She called to Arlecchino for help but caught only a brief glimpse of him, before he was buried beneath armed guards. Dragged, protesting, from the theatre, she was marched across the quay to where a black barge was moored.

On board, the guards shackled and chained her. 'Please,' she begged. 'You're making a dreadful mistake. I am no witch.' Her captors ignored her. 'Who has accused me?' Still no one answered.

'I have never practised witchcraft in my life!' In desperation, she blurted out, 'There is a man who kept me captive, forced me to witness terrible things. He practises the black arts. It's him that you want. His name is Niccolo Menander.'

The guards burst out laughing.

'It's true,' she cried. 'I can show you where he lives.'

As the boat left the quay, she noticed the tall hooded figure standing close to the edge. His head was bowed but there was something about him suggesting authority. Perhaps, if she addressed her pleas to him? He pushed back his hood and all hope deserted her.

Brighella's cruel smile brought home the full horror of what she was facing. Panic wracked her. Only pride prevented her screaming. Mind racing, she took nothing in of the journey. Once the barge docked, she found herself looking up at the imposing façade of the Doge's palace. Hands still chained, she was dragged ashore and pushed up some steps. She felt sick with misery, betrayed by life, abandoned by God. Her trembling fingers touched her amethyst cross but it brought little comfort.

Led down one dark corridor after another, she was eventually pushed into a musty room. One of the guards removed her chains; another hung up a lamp. When they left her alone, she gave way to sobbing; then, after a while, dried her eyes. The room was panelled and had a gallery. There were steps at one end.

She jumped when the door flew open, gave a cry and backed away from a man dressed in black who wore a hood for a mask. He threw down a heap of shackles and cruel metal instruments then stood with his back to the door, thick arms folded. Never had Colombina felt so afraid, not even in the company of Brighella. Again she was overwhelmed by the urge to start screaming. She felt like a bird caught in a net, wings beating but taking her nowhere. 'Sir,' she sobbed, 'if you intend to torture me, may I first see a priest?'

The man said nothing. Colombina tried to pray.

The door opened and the man stood aside. A bearded cleric entered. Colombina could not help herself. She rushed forward, fell to her knees and clutched his black cloak; beneath it she caught a glimpse of scarlet. 'Father, I beg you. Don't let him torture me. I am innocent of any crime.'

The man reached out and patted her on the head. 'Stand up, child.' His voice sounded kind. 'No one here wants to make you suffer.'

She scrambled to her feet, trying not to look at the torturer's pile of iron.

'We find it helps to concentrate a prisoner's mind on the seriousness of their crime.'

'But I have committed no crime.'

'So you say. And I, for one, will be happy to have that confirmed. But you must realise you have been accused of something most grievous by a man of high regard.'

She opened her mouth to speak of Brighella, then thought better of it.

'I believe you have accused him in turn. That is unfortunate. It will not help your case. Signore Menander is not only well respected by the Inquisition, but has spoken up on your behalf. Whilst fulfilling his spiritual obligation in reporting your misdeeds, he has put forward a plea for mercy.'

'I am most obliged.'

'Your tone does you no credit.' When she looked into the cleric's eyes, she saw they were not kind.

Another man came hurrying in, carrying an enormous ledger.

'We shall adjourn to a place more conducive to reasoned thought,' said the inquisitor and left the room. The other followed and the hooded man grabbed Colombina by the arm and forced her after them.

There were no instruments of torture in the room they took her to but two paintings on a wall depicted in graphic detail the suffering of the damned. 'Sit,' said the bearded cleric. He took his seat at a long table and she sat facing him, and the paintings.

'I am Cardinal Bellarmino. You will listen to the following report of your crimes. Keep it short,' he told his clerk who remained standing.

Peering closely at his ledger, the clerk read: 'The actress known as Colombina is accused of collaboration with the heretic Giordano Bruno who was burned today in Rome for heinous crimes against God. She is, in addition, accused of engaging in witchcraft in her own right.' He glanced at Cardinal Bellarmino who responded with a nod.

'So, Colombina?' prompted the cardinal. 'What do you have to say?'

Colombina shook her head. 'It's not true. Today is the first time...' she paused when she realised how dangerous her situation was. If she told him what had really happened, she would surely be condemned. Pointing the finger at Niccolo Menander would only make things worse. 'Today is the first occasion on which I have heard the heretic's name. Yet I believe he has been imprisoned for many years, making me hardly more than a child at the time of our supposed collaboration.'

'That may be so, yet children have been known to consort with the devil. However, if that were the case, I would be of a mind to offer clemency. The evil one has many tricks at his disposal in his determination to ensnare the innocent and unwary. As to the other charge. It says here that you are an adept, skilled in black arts.'

'That's ridiculous.'

He glared at her.

'I mean, I know nothing of such things.' She lowered her gaze. 'What more can I say? I am innocent of the crimes.'

'Very well.' He stood up. 'For now, I will leave you to consider your position. We will speak of this again, once you have had time to reflect.' He beckoned to the hooded man who, once again, grabbed Colombina and escorted her from the room.

Relieved she was taken not to the torture chamber, nor to a dungeon, but to a room overlooking the piazzetta, she was further cheered to find it had a bed, table and chair. She went to the window. Far below, people went about their business. They might have inhabited a different world. She tried to gather her thoughts. She was innocent. Surely God would not let her suffer? Then she thought of Giordano and panic strangled faith. She threw herself on the bed.

Though she slept, she also dreamt and woke in a cold sweat.

Fear remained with her all night, and the following day. She was brought meals and a pail in which to relieve herself but saw no one other than the guard who refused to answer questions.

A second night passed. She began to hope.

Then, the next morning, after she had forced herself to eat, the guard took her to the room in which she had been read the accusation. Determined to give good account of herself, yet desperate enough to throw herself on whatever mercy Cardinal Bellarmino had to offer, she sat rigid until the door opened.

But it was not the cardinal who entered. Brighella dismissed the guard and sat in the cleric's place.

Colombina choked back her anger. 'I'm surprised you can face me.'

'Have you come to your senses?'

'And confess to crimes I did not commit?' She shook her head.

'You know the punishment.'

Her throat constricted.

'I can save you.'

So, this was how it was! Brighella had accused her. Now he was offering to save her.

'What must I do?'

He shrugged. 'Very little. Confess to being misled by the teachings of Giordano. Embrace the true faith; throw yourself on the mercy of Holy Mother Church. And give yourself over into my spiritual care.'

So, that was her choice! To join with Brighella or die. How she wished she had the courage to throw it back in his face; yet the memory of the heretic's death was too raw. His smile made her nauseous. How could she endure it? But, if life with this man was the only alternative to no life at all...

315

'It's your decision. Me or the fire.' He stood up. 'Oh, and there's one more thing. You'll have to denounce Arlecchino.'

'What?' She leapt to her feet and her chair toppled backwards.

'The Inquisition got to hear about his juggling in Padua. And who was present at the time.'

'I don't understand.'

'Stars and planets, my dear. The earth moving round the sun. He gave a sparkling performance and Venice was full of it. He was out of his depth. He should have stuck to juggling with hats. Galileo Galilei is a marked man in Rome. It's only a matter of time before he occupies your seat.' Brighella picked up the chair she had knocked over.

'You know I can't do what you ask.'

'That's a pity. For us both.' He gripped her by the arm and escorted her back to the room above the piazzetta. 'Take a look out of the window.'

When she did, she stifled a cry. A stake had been erected and bundles of wood were being stacked around it. 'No!' she wailed. 'I've not yet been condemned. Cardinal Bellarmino…'

'Has left it to me to offer your last chance of clemency. Look, people are gathering. How they enjoy a spectacle. There's your precious humanity, Colombina. Yesterday they hailed you Queen of Venice. Now they're jostling for position to watch you burn.'

'When?' she asked.

'Tonight.'

The room began to sway.

He kept her on her feet. 'Well then. It's time to say goodbye, Colombina. Who will be praying for your soul, I wonder, when flames lick your flesh. They say the monks smashed Giordano's charred body to pieces to make sure he never returned. If you do change your mind…'

'Never.'

'Then burn!' He threw her on the bed.

'Brighella.'

'Yes?'

'I hope you rot in hell.'

He laughed and closed the door behind him.

Colombina got up and went to the window. With a whimper, she tugged at her hair and backed away. Fear became a yawning cavern, hands clawed at her insides. It was all she could do not to call for the guard, scream at him to fetch Brighella back. She could not face it, not death by fire! But to betray Arlecchino?

She remained in a state of terror until it grew dark and she could hear the noise of the crowd. Soon guards would come. How would she stop herself screaming and struggling? And when they tied her to the stake, how could she not beg for mercy, offer anything, *anyone* up in return for her life? 'No,' she gasped, hearing footsteps approaching. 'Please God. No!' She rushed to the pail and vomited.

Wiping her mouth, she scrambled to her feet the same moment the door opened. A solitary guard stood back, allowing a hooded priest to enter. 'He's come to listen to your last confession,' he grunted and left them alone.

Here was her chance! Ask for Brighella – Niccolo Menander. Throw herself on the mercy of the church, give herself up to the monster. Do anything to save herself but… to betray Arlecchino? She said not a word.

Neither did the priest. He stood completely still, head bowed. When the guard's footsteps faded to nothing, he threw back his hood.

68

olombina sank to her knees as a rushing sound filled her ears. All she was aware of was someone lifting, then lowering her onto the bed. When she opened her eyes and saw who it was, she knew she must be dreaming.

'Dear God,' she heard him say. 'What have they done to you?'

Reaching up, she touched Arlecchino's face. 'You're real.'

He kissed her brow.

'But how?' As she sat up, he stood to throw off the priest's garb. 'And you're in costume.'

'They've been watching the theatre ever since they took you. Soon they will realise I've gone, so we have to hurry.'

'But…'

'I'm taking you out of here, my love. But not before…' He bent over her and kissed her. '*Later,* I said.' He eased her back.

'This is madness.'

'Yes.'

Colombina found it hard to understand how she and Arlecchino could be making love while outside the good citizens of Venice were preparing to watch her burn. Neither would she have believed it possible to relinquish fear for passion, not until she felt his hardness within her. For a brief time they entered a world where nothing mattered, only the mutual gratification of their flesh. When it was over she said to him, 'Before we did this you were innocent. Now you share my guilt.'

'Then we'll *both* go to hell. Together.' He pulled her to her feet and, draping the priest's robe over his shoulders, crossed to the door. He opened it cautiously. With no sign of a guard, they went into the corridor. 'This way,' he whispered.

She had no idea where he was taking her, yet no longer felt afraid for herself. Her heart felt light simply being with him. As he led her down a flight of steps, they heard shouts from the floor below. 'They must have found the real priest,' he muttered.

'You didn't..?'

'No. I bound and gagged him. Not well enough, it seems. Quick. In here.' He opened a door and pulled her through into a large unlit space. By the light of the moon, she could see that it was grand enough to be a room of state. He closed the door and they ran to the window. A wide balcony was covered by an awning. Arlecchino went outside and looked down over the balustrade. She heard him laugh. 'The Flight of the Dove!'

Puzzled, Colombina joined him. The piazzetta below was teeming. Torches blazed and the pyre was complete. She stepped back quickly, noticing Arlecchino's attention was focussed, not on the crowd, but on the Campanile. 'We're trapped,' she whispered.

'No.' He slipped off the robe and grasped her hand. 'Like I said, *the Flight of the Dove*. It will carry us to safety.'

'I don't understand.'

'The rope.'

She stared at the length of rope stretching down from the bell tower. 'You're not thinking of..?'

'It's the only way.' He drew her to the balustrade.

When she looked over, she saw that the rope disappeared into the loggia not far below them. 'It's impossible!'

He laughed.

'But not for you,' she added quietly.

He frowned. 'You don't think I would leave you?'

'You have no choice. You can't carry me.'

He drew her close. 'Colombina, do you still have no faith in me?'

'I have faith but...'

'And if not in me, in those who protect me? The gods have thrown us a lifeline. Not to grasp it would be ungrateful, not to mention cowardly.'

'But...'

He put a finger to her lips. 'To attempt this is foolish. But who is Arlecchino, if not King of Fools?' Without another word, he clambered

319

over the balustrade and offered her his hand. 'Come on, cling to me like you did when we escaped the masked ball.'

She did as he said, put her arms about his neck and wrapped her legs around his waist. He climbed down the ornate façade to above the spot where the rope went into the loggia. 'Arlecchino,' she whispered as he stretched out his foot, 'I love you.'

'And I love you. Don't be afraid, Colombina. If we die, we die together. I'd rather spend eternity in hell with you than find myself in heaven alone. Just promise me one thing. Whatever happens, you won't let go.'

'I promise.'

Holding on to the top of the archway with one hand, he got his footing. Back pressed against the wall, he manoeuvred her so that she was cradled in his arms; then, making sure of his balance, closed his eyes. She guessed he was praying. 'Here goes,' he whispered and took his first step.

Now it was her turn to shut her eyes. He had told her not to be afraid. So she imagined herself being carried through the landscape she had pictured in her young and innocent mind on their walk together to the barn when she had seen them as characters set within a living painting for all eternity.

'Talk to me,' he whispered. 'Take my mind off the task.'

She opened her eyes and, suppressing alarm, marvelled at the sensation of being carried through the air. 'Why do they call it the *Flight of the Dove?*'

'Every year before Lent, by means of ropes and pullies, a man flies down from the Campanile, sprinkling petals. When he reaches the loggia, he reads a poem to the Doge and receives, in exchange, a purse of money. But they say that a Turk once made this journey the same way I am doing now.'

'I imagine he was not carrying his lady?'

'I imagine not. Yet you weigh so little, Colombina. Hardly more than petals.'

She knew he was lying. Sweat was pouring down his face.

'Just think what a show we're giving! This is the biggest audience we've ever had. The flawed children of the Immortali are risking their lives to entertain the people of Venice. Do they know yet?'

320

She glanced down and saw people pointing. 'Yes. They've seen us.'

'Let's liven things up.' He paused and, steadying himself, snapped the fingers of his left hand. Sparks flew from them. A second later, a great burst of light came from below. There were cries and, when Colombina looked down, she saw that the pyre meant for her had burst into flames. People were trying to flee and there were anguished screams from monks who had been close to the stake, their habits now on fire.

Arlecchino resumed his walk.

They were halfway across but the strain showed in his face. Every muscle was taut. It was as if his very life was being drained out of him.

The Flight of the Dove, thought Colombina. Their perilous path to uncertain freedom bore a name uncannily reminiscent of the apparition she had seen following the death of Giordano. 'This magic,' she said in a further attempt to take her lover's mind off his ordeal. 'Is it the same as you used to rescue Lella's dog?'

'I suppose so,' he gasped. 'But I don't use magic. It uses me. Comes and goes at will. From the time I was a child I could feel it, the power of wings sprouting from my heels, carrying me out of danger in my greatest need.'

'You have it now?'

'No, Colombina. I don't.' His tone was desperate and her heart went out to him. He was doing this alone. 'I cannot go much further.'

'There isn't much further to go.'

'But it's so steep.'

'Then let me fall.'

'Pray for me, Colombina. I'm going to run.'

She fought back the instinct to shout at him *no*, closed her eyes and prayed they would be together always. A rushing wind filled her ears. She felt its cool fingers through her hair. He was running. But this was impossible. No mortal man could do this. When she opened her eyes she saw they had almost reached the top of the rope. Just a few paces more.

Then the noise from below turned into a din. People were yelling and waving a warning. She felt the rope jerk. Glancing back, she saw a guard hack at the base. 'Arlecchino!' she screamed, the same moment the rope gave way.

Together they fell.

She clung to him, as she had promised. On her way down to hell, she prayed they would not be separated. Then came a sickening jolt and sudden pain as they hit the side of the Campanile. They were still in this world, she clinging to him, him grasping the hand of another. A strong arm was drawing him upward into the bell-tower.

Arlecchino's left arm was still about her as the pair were gathered to safety.

Colombina cried with relief as the two men embraced.

'My son,' gasped Hermes. Looking over Arlecchino's shoulder, he held out his hand. 'God bless you, Colombina.'

The men moved apart. Arlecchino appeared relaxed, as if his walk had been no more than a stroll in the countryside. 'We're not out of trouble yet,' he murmured, glancing over the wall.

Fighting had broken out below and the crowd were obstructing guards who were trying to enter the Campanile. Then Colombina noticed that Arlecchino's gaze had settled on a second rope sweeping down towards the water. He sighed. 'I don't believe I have the strength...'

Hermes laughed and held him by the shoulders. 'You and your lady are dressed in our colours. Black, white, red, green and gold. Join hands the pair of you. Come along.'

They did so and he completed the circle. High in the air above the city of Venice the man in the cloak decked with stars and crescent moons began his incantation.

❧

Listening to Hermes, Colombina felt afraid as she was reminded of the time she had spent held captive by Brighella.

The old man smiled to reassure her. 'The Golden Treatise of Hermes,' he said, addressing them both in the tone of an indulgent tutor. 'Black, white, green, red and gold. This is the beginning of the sacred sequence. Your bodies, my children, are the prima materia. Human and base, they are destined to decay. Yet from you is released my namesake, Mercury. See, here comes his symbol.

To Colombina's astonishment, there appeared within their circle a tiny green creature. She had once seen a picture of this mythical beast, a dragon it was called. The diminutive dragon flew round and round then

322

disappeared in a puff of green smoke.

'King Sol,' Hermes nodded to Arlecchino. Then he addressed Colombina. 'Queen Luna. This is the occasion of your sacred marriage. Your colours are gold and silver. Your messenger is the raven.' A large black bird came flapping out of nowhere and perched on the balustrade. 'See, transformation is taking place. The peacock's tail adorns your union.' All around them shimmered iridescent colours.

'And finally. The son is invested with the red garment.'

Alarmed, Colombina saw Arlecchino wreathed in red flame. Yet where fire trickled from his fingers onto hers, it felt cool.

'I don't understand this,' she whispered to Hermes.

He whispered back, 'The more we understand, the less we know. Knowing will carry you further. Gnosis is insight, has wings on which a soul receptive to light can travel. You have such a soul, Colombina. You are sweet and vital. And Arlecchino?' he said in a loud happy voice. 'He is the child who knows his true father!' The old man gave her a wink.

'And now, finally, the purple garment is put on.'

Suddenly Hermes broke the circle and, wrenching off his cloak of crescent moons and stars, threw it over them both.

'Gold is your colour now, Arlecchino. Fly as you were born to!'

No longer a man of flame, Arlecchino shone like the sun. He was pure gold from head to toe. There were wings on his heels. Enfolding Colombina in his arms, he leapt from the Campanile and ran, feet barely touching, along the rope which was fixed to a barge far below.

As they drew close to the water, Colombina noticed a second boat moored alongside. Standing within it were Pedrolino and Pantelone. Spinetta was there too, seated next to Lella. When Guido caught sight of them, he leapt to his feet. The little dog Crespo barked and barked.

By the time Arlecchino alighted on deck, he was no longer gold. Dressed in his familiar livery he was congratulated by all. Everyone behaved as though nothing remarkable had happened.

'Vincenzo's vessel is moored in the lagoon,' Pedrolino told them. 'Silvia offered help as soon as she heard of our trouble. The rest of the company has already boarded.'

'So where are we headed?' asked Arlecchino looking out to sea.

323

'To France,' said Pantelone with pride. 'Our new patron, the King, has requested a performance at our earliest convenience.'

'Yes!' cried Arlecchino and snapped his fingers in the air.

'What happened to us?' whispered Colombina, as he slid an arm about her waist.

He smiled and drew her down to sit beside him.

Pedrolino and Pantelone took up the oars. Spinetta draped a warm shawl over Colombina's shoulders. Lella snuggled up next to her. 'Would you like to look through my spyglass now?'

'Yes, please,' said Colombina.

Lella passed her the toy.

Putting the glass to her eye, Colombina looked up at the sky. Deep blue and dotted with stars, it began to spin; slowly at first, then, against the blue, some pinpricks of light grew larger as they came rushing towards her. She recognised them as the juggling balls Arlecchino had used to entertain the students of Padua.

When they passed out of sight, her eye was assaulted by hot bright light emanating from a surface spewing out liquid fire. The blazing orb came frighteningly close before it also sped past.

As the spinning grew faster, Colombina felt herself sucked into a vortex. Drifting through oceans filled with exploding stars, swirling showers and blazing trails, she was carried past landscapes of intense floating colour. On her way, she glimpsed holes of blackness more dense than the inside of Brighella's alambic when drained of its magical light.

At last, she could take no more spinning and removed the spyglass from her eye. She gave it back to Lella.

The child laughed.

Looking up, Colombina saw that the stars were reassuringly back in place. Arlecchino's lips brushed her brow. 'I love you,' he whispered. As Venice retreated into the distance, she believed she must be the happiest person alive.

A figure clad in purple, surrounded by stars and crescent moons, was waving from the top of the Campanile. 'Goodbye Colombina,' he called and his words rang out clearly in spite of him being so far away.

He pointed up into the sky. 'Always remember – as above, so below.'

ermes Trismegisto probably never existed. The writings ac-credited to him, however, had a profound effect on the sixteenth century, inspiring much of what we think of as Renaissance thought. At the time, Hermes was believed to be an Egyptian magus or wise man, a contemporary with Moses, descended from the Greek god of the same name. He was and still is, regarded as the father of alchemy.

Hermetic thought influenced revolutionary thinkers such as Giordano Bruno who sought to combine the gnostic approach to Christianity with Catholic dogma. His efforts met with spectacular failure and he was burned at the stake in 1600.

In a world disillusioned with religion and the conflict it can bring, perhaps the time has come to re-examine a philosophy which teaches: as above, so below.

Lightning Source UK Ltd.
Milton Keynes UK
UKOW03n2137170414

230209UK00002B/11/P